Elizabeth Haynes worked for many years as a police analyst. Her debut novel, *Into the Darkest Corner*, won Amazon's Book of the Year in 2011 and Amazon's Rising Star Award for debut novels.

Elizabeth grew up in Sussex and studied English, German and Art History at Leicester University. She is currently taking a career break having worked for the past seven years as a police intelligence analyst. Elizabeth now lives in Kent with her husband and son, and writes in coffee shops and a shed-office which takes up most of the garden. She is a regular participant in, and a Municipal Liaison for National Novel Writing Month – an annual challenge to write 50,000 words in the month of November.

UNDER A SILENT MOON

ELIZABETH HAYNES

sphere

SPHERE

First published in 2013 by Sphere
This paperback edition published by Sphere in 2014

A CIP catalogue record for this book
is available from the British Library.

ISBN 978-0-7515-4959-1

Typeset in Times by M Rules
Printed and bound in Great Britain by
Clays Ltd, St Ives plc

Papers used by Sphere are from well-managed forests
and other responsible sources.

MIX
Paper from
responsible sources
FSC® C104740
www.fsc.org

Sphere
An imprint of
Little, Brown Book Group
100 Victoria Embankment
London EC4Y 0DY

An Hachette UK Company
www.hachette.co.uk

www.littlebrown.co.uk

For Samantha Bowles, who made
this book so much better

Author Note

In addition to the case documents contained in the text, additional material, including charts produced by the Major Crime analyst for the Op Nettle investigation, is available in an appendix at the end of this book. Further documents can also be viewed online at www.op-nettle.info.

Although intended to appear to be an authentic murder investigation, all characters, locations and situations in this book are fictional.

Day One – Thursday 1 November 2012

09:41

Dispatch Log 1101-0132

**CALLER STATES SHE HAS FOUND HER FRIEND
COVERED IN BLOOD NOT MOVING NOT BREATHING

**AMBULANCE ALREADY DISPATCHED – REF 01-914

**CALLER IS FELICITY MAITLAND, HERMITAGE
FARM, CEMETERY LANE MORDEN – OCCUPATION
FARM OWNER

**INJURED PARTY IDENTIFIED AS POLLY LUCAS,
FAMILY FRIEND OF CALLER

**CALLER HYSTERICAL, TRYING TO GET LOCATION
FROM HER

**ADDRESS YONDER COTTAGE CEMETERY LANE
MORDEN VILLAGE

**LOCATION GIVEN AS OUTSIDE VILLAGE ON ROAD
TO BRIARSTONE, PAST THE LEMON TREE PUB ON
THE RIGHT HAND SIDE

**SP CORRECTION POLLY LEUCHARS DOB 28/12/1984
AGED 27

**PATROLS AL23 AL11 AVAILABLE DISPATCHED

**DUTY INSPECTOR NOTED, WILL ATTEND

10:52

In years to come, Flora would remember this as the day of Before and After.

Before, she had been working on the canvas that had troubled her for nearly three months. She had reworked it so many times, had stared at it, loved it and hated it, often at the same time. On that Thursday it had gone well. The blue was right, finally, and while she had the sun slanting in even strips from the skylight overhead she traced the lines with her brush delicately as though she was touching the softest human skin and not canvas.

The phone rang and at first she ignored it. When the answering machine kicked in the caller rang off and then her mobile buzzed on the windowsill behind her. The caller display showed her father's mobile. She ignored it as she usually did. He was not some-one she really wanted to talk to, after all.

Seconds later, the phone rang again. He wasn't going to give up.

'Dad? What is it? I'm working—'

That was the moment. And then it was the After, and nothing was ever the same again.

11:08

Thursday had barely started and it was already proving to be a chal-lenge for Lou Smith. Just after ten the call had come in from the boss, Detective Superintendent Buchanan. Area had called in a suspicious death and requested Major Crime's attendance. A month after her pro-motion and the DCI on duty, it was her turn to lead the investigation.

'Probably nothing,' Buchanan had said. 'You can hand it back to Area if it looks like the boyfriend's done it, OK? Keep me updated.'

Her heart was thudding as she'd disconnected the call. *Please God, don't let me balls it up.*

Lou reached for the grubby *A–Z* on the shelf in the main office; it'd be a darn sight quicker than logging on to the mapping software. She couldn't remember ever having to go to Morden, which meant it was probably posh. The paramedics had turned up first and declared life well and truly extinct, waited for the patrols, and then buggered off on another call.

The patrols had done what they were supposed to do – look for the offender (no sign), manage the witnesses (only one, so far, the woman who'd called it in) and preserve the scene (shut the door and stand outside). The Area DI had turned up shortly afterwards and it hadn't been more than ten minutes before he'd called the Major Crime Superintendent. Which meant that this was clearly a murder, probably not domestic.

'Nasty,' the DI said cheerfully when Lou got to Yonder Cottage. 'Your first one, isn't it, ma'am? Good luck.'

'Cheers.'

Lou recognised him. He'd been one of the trainers when she'd been a probationer, which made the 'ma'am' feel rather awkward.

'Where have you got to?' she asked.

'They've started the house-to-house,' he responded. 'Nothing so far. The woman who found her is in the kitchen up at the farmhouse with PC Gregson, the family liaison. Mrs Felicity Maitland. She owns the farm with her husband Nigel – Nigel Maitland?'

The last two words were phrased as a question, implying that Lou should recognise the name. She did.

Maitland had associates who were known to be involved in organised crime in Briarstone and London. He'd been brought in for questioning on several occasions for different reasons; each time he'd given a 'no comment' interview, or one where he stuck to one-word answers, in the company of his very expensive solicitor. Each

3

time he had been polite, cooperative as far as it went, and utterly unhelpful. Each time he had been released without charge. Circumstantial evidence, including his mobile phone number appearing on the itemised phone bill of three men who were eventually charged with armed robbery and conspiracy, had never amounted to enough to justify an arrest. Nevertheless, the links were there and officers in a number of departments were watching and waiting for him to make a mistake. In the meantime Nigel went about his legitimate day job, running his farm and maintaining his expensive golf club membership, the horses, the Mercedes and the Land Rover and the Porsche convertible, and stayed one step ahead.

'Mrs Maitland's in charge of the stables, leaves all the rest of it to her husband,' the Area DI said. 'The victim worked for them as a groom, lived here in the cottage rent-free. I gather she was a family friend.'

'Any word on an offender?'

'Nothing, so far. Apparently the victim lived on her own.'

'What happened?'

'She's at the bottom of the stairs. Massive head trauma.'

'Not a fall?'

'Definitely not a fall.'

'Weapon?'

'Nothing obvious. CSI are on the way, apparently.' He indicated the patrol officer standing guard. 'This is PC Dave Forster. He got the short straw.'

PC Forster grinned.

DI Carter disappeared shortly after that, back to the station.

Yonder Cottage was a square, brick-built house separated from the main road by an overgrown hedge and an expanse of gravel, upon which a dark blue Nissan Micra was parked. The scene tape stretched from the hedge to a birch tree and outside of this was a roughly tar-macked driveway which led up to a series of barns and outbuildings. Beyond this, apparently, was the main house of Hermitage Farm.

'Right,' Lou said, more to herself than to PC Forster, 'let's get started.'

Her phone was ringing. The cavalry was on the way.

```
Email

To:          DCI 10023 Louisa SMITH

From:        DSupt 9143 Gordon BUCHANAN

Date:        Thursday 1 November 2012

Subject:     Op Nettle - Polly Leuchars

Louisa,

Hope the MIR is coming together. Ops
Planning have given us the name Op Nettle
for the murder of Polly Leuchars. Let me
know if you need any further help.

Gordon

Email

To:          Central Analytical Team

From:        DCI 10023 Louisa SMITH

Date:        Thursday 1 November 2012

Subject:     Op Nettle - analytical
             requirement
```

Could someone please contact me asap about
providing an analyst for the Major Incident
Room of Op Nettle. I have a full MIR team
with the exception of an analyst and I have
failed to reach anyone by phone.

DCI Louisa Smith

Major Crime

11:29

Julia Dobson, fifty-eight years old and current Ladies' Golf
Champion at the Morden Country Club, pulled the heavy velvet
curtain slightly to one side and peered out. From where she stood
in the bay window of Lentonbury Manor – which was not actually
a manor house, in much the same way as Seaview Cottage, a few
yards further towards the village, did not actually have a sea
view – she could see some distance up Cemetery Lane towards
the entrance to Hermitage Farm on the left, and Hayselden Barn
on the right.

'That makes three,' she mused. 'Good Lord, what on earth is
going on?'

Ralph, her husband, murmured in reply from behind his copy of
the *Financial Times*, delivered by the newsagent's van an hour ago.
They didn't have a paperboy any more. The last one had nearly
been run over by a tractor, and his mother had insisted he went and
got a Saturday job at the greengrocer's instead.

'Ralph, you're not listening,' she said peevishly.

'Three, you said,' and then a moment later he shook his paper
and looked up: 'Three what?'

'Police cars, Ralph. Three police cars in the lane. The first one had the siren going. You must have heard it! I wonder what's going on?'

He put the paper down and joined her at the window, mug of coffee in one hand, in time to observe an ambulance driving at speed down the lane. It turned into the driveway of Hayselden Barn, which was just within sight before the road bent sharply to the left. A police car rounded the bend from the opposite direction, and followed the ambulance into the driveway.

'Barbara must have had one of her turns,' Julia murmured.

'"Turns"?' he snorted. 'That's a new word for it.'

Julia set her lips into a thin line. 'Well, there's only one way to find out.' Without further ado she retrieved the phone handset and dialled the number for Hermitage Farm.

12:45

Taryn stared at her screen, trying to catch the reflection of the activity that was going on in her boss's office, behind her and to her left.

'They're talking,' Ellen said. She was sitting at the desk opposite and had a commanding view.

'Have they all sat down?' Taryn asked.

'No. Reg is sitting behind his desk, but the two police are just standing there. Oh, hold on, here we go ... '

Taryn heard the office door open and couldn't help turning round to look. Reg was heading in her direction. The two police officers were still in the office. One was a woman, which indicated that whoever they were here to see was about to receive some bad news.

'Taryn, would you step into my office, please?' Reg said, giving

7

her a look that should have been empathetic but was somehow the wrong side of slimy.

Please, let it not be about Chris, she thought. Prayed. Reg scuttled off in the direction of the kitchen. Maybe they'd told him to go and make a cup of tea – *first time for everything*, Taryn thought.

She entered the office and shut the door firmly behind her.

'Mrs Lewis? I'm PC Ian Richardson from Briarstone police station, and this is PC Yvonne Sanders. Would you like to take a seat?'

They sat too and she wanted to say: Tell me now, tell me straight away. But the words wouldn't come.

'I'm here about your parents, Mrs Lewis. I'm afraid it's bad news.'

'My parents?' That was a word she hadn't heard used with any degree of accuracy since she was eleven years old.

'Mr and Mrs Fletcher-Norman—'

'Barbara Fletcher-Norman isn't my mother.'

This obviously was news to the young police officer and he seemed to momentarily lose his thread.

'I'm sorry,' Taryn said, 'please go on.'

'I – er – your father, Mr Brian Fletcher-Norman, is in hospital and I'm afraid he's seriously ill. Your stepmother, Mrs Barbara Fletcher-Norman, was found dead earlier today. I'm very sorry.'

Taryn looked at her hands. 'Oh. I see. Thank you.'

Now it was the female officer's turn. 'Is there anyone we can contact to be with you? I understand this must be difficult for you.'

'No. Thank you.'

They seemed to be waiting for her to say something more, so she looked at them in turn and said, 'Can I get back to work now?'

The officers exchanged glances.

Taryn felt sorry for them. 'I don't get on with my father,' she said patiently. 'I haven't seen him for ... a long time. Thank you for your kindness, but really, I'm fine.'

She stood and the officers got to their feet in unison. At the door she stopped and turned. 'Do you need me to do anything?'

The policewoman shook her head. 'Not at the moment, Mrs Lewis. But if you did decide to go and visit your father, he is in intensive care at Briarstone General.'

'Thank you.'

Taryn slid back into her seat just as Reg slopped a coffee onto her desk. I don't drink coffee, she thought, but Reg had never offered to make her a drink before so how would he know? She was trying to think when she had last been at the Barn. Maybe April? It had been the argument about the bike, and instead of making the effort to put things right she had left it, and left it. It was the longest they'd gone without speaking.

'Well?' Ellen said, eyes eager. 'What was all that about?'

'Oh. My father's in hospital, that's all.'

'That's all? Goodness, are you all right? Shouldn't you take the rest of the day off?'

'No.' She took a swig of the coffee despite herself, because it was there, and because her throat was horribly dry. 'I haven't seen him for ages. We don't get along. So really, I'm fine. And I'm sure he will be too.'

Ellen had no reply to this, so she left it, although she did continue giving Taryn the occasional odd look over the top of her screen.

Despite her desire to get on with things, it was quite hard to concentrate, after that. Only half an hour later did she remember what they'd said about Barbara. Had they really said she was dead?

13:02

Louisa sat on the edge of a table, her mobile pressed to her ear. All around her was chaos and next to her a telecoms engineer plugged in a phone, which rang immediately. One of the DCs picked it up.

'Incident room. She's on the phone, I'm afraid. Can I help? Who? OK, what's your number there? Hold on; let me find a piece of paper. Right. OK, I'll get her to call you.'

It was amazing how quickly the room was coming together.

The first desk set up had been the reader-receiver's. Barry Holloway was there, monitoring everything coming into the room. Initial witness statements, intelligence reports, transcripts of calls from the public; nothing came in without first going through Barry. He checked everything, gave it an audit log number, decided how urgent it was and who should get it next.

Who should get it next was still up in the air. Desks were being pushed together, people arriving minutes after being assigned to the operation.

On a whiteboard behind her, Louisa had written a notice in foot-high black letters:

OP NETTLE
BRIEFING 1600hrs.

She checked her watch, wondering if it was out of order to task one of the DCs with going to the canteen to get her a double espresso, when finally the phone was answered.

'Senior analysts.'

'Ah, so there *is* someone alive in there?'

'Yes, there is.' The man's voice was decidedly chilly, and

with an unexpected accent. American or Canadian? 'Can I help you?'

'This is DCI Lou Smith. I'm waiting in the MIR for Op Nettle in the hope that we might get an analyst.'

There was a pause.

'I'm sorry. Bear with me.'

He didn't sound sorry. He sounded pissed off. There was a longer pause.

'Les?' Lou said, putting a hand over the mouthpiece. 'Can you save my life and go and get me a double espresso? And a KitKat. Cheers.'

Then, in her ear: 'I'm afraid there's no one available today – they're all out.'

What the fuck? Lou took a deep breath. 'This is a murder investigation. What do you mean, there's no one available? There must be sixty bloody analysts and I only want one!'

'Actually, since the reorganisation there are in fact only thirty-two analysts and they are all assigned to other duties. I'm the only senior here, and—'

'What's your name?'

'Jason Mercer.'

'Jason, *please*, find me someone in time for the briefing at four, and someone else who's prepared to do the late turn.'

A heavy sigh. 'For sure.'

Definitely Canadian, Lou decided.

13:15

After.

Flora had spoken to her father and at the time she'd been calm, almost serene. She'd asked the right questions: When? How? And then she had put down the brush that was still in her hand, stared at the canvas that she knew already she would now never complete, and left.

When she drove past Yonder Cottage there were police cars blocking the drive, an ambulance on the gravel outside the house. The PC who was standing beside the fluttering tape in his fluorescent jacket regarded her closely.

She went on to the next turning, the main entrance to the farm. She headed up the driveway, which, at the top, curved round through the yard and back down towards the cottage. She parked outside the farmhouse.

Flora's mother, Felicity Maitland, was sliding into comfortable oblivion. Nigel Maitland had poured her a tumbler of brandy in the hope of calming her down before she made it into a full-on panic attack.

Following her call to the police, Felicity had been looked after by the ambulance crew and the police had taken an initial statement from her at the cottage. Then she'd been walked back to the farmhouse by someone in a uniform.

Now, hours later, Felicity was still in a state, vacillating between shuddering sobs and unnatural, staring stillness.

'It was so utterly horrible,' she said now. 'Blood all over the walls, everywhere! The whole place will have to be redecorated, and we only did it last summer.'

There were times Flora wanted to slap her mother, hard. She went to make toast for everyone, not least to soak up the brandy. The plain-clothes police officer who'd been assigned to them was leaning against the breakfast bar, fiddling with her mobile phone.

'Would you like me to do that?' she asked, when Flora came in.

'No, it's fine, thanks. Do you want some tea?'

12

And at that moment Felicity's voice rose again in a wail: 'Oh God! Who's going to do the horses?'

'I'll do them,' said Nigel.

'Oh God! I'll have to put an advert in the paper, then it will be interviews! I can't bear it, I can't!'

'What about Connor, Dad?' Flora shouted. 'I thought he was supposed to be a groom?'

Nigel didn't reply. Other than the phone call, he had not spoken directly to Flora.

'He can't be trusted,' Felicity wailed. 'Polly said he was always sloping off. I don't know why you insist on having him here, Nigel, he's more trouble than he's worth, and—'

'Oh for God's sake!' Flora called sharply. 'I'll do the bloody horses.'

The toaster popped up and Flora applied herself to the task of buttering, slicing into halves. Tea. Must make the tea. What had the police officer said to her offer, yes or no? She couldn't remember. She would make one anyway, not wanting to ask again; aware of the way the woman was watching her. Pretending to be here to help, but they were being watched, that was the truth of it. And right now the policewoman was watching *her*.

Flora could remember the exact moment of the exact day when she fell in love with Polly Leuchars. It had been on the fifteenth of December, almost a year ago. Half past ten in the morning and Polly was sitting at the kitchen table in the farmhouse, her long blonde hair pulled back in a tight ponytail, wearing a jumper, jeans and thick socks. Her boots were on the mat.

'Where's my mum?' Flora asked, wondering who this was.

'Are you Flora? My, you've grown up since I last saw you,' the person said, with a beautiful smile. 'I'm Polly. You probably don't remember me. I've come to work.'

It turned out that Felicity had known Polly was coming but had neglected to tell anyone else. Polly was the daughter of Cassandra Leuchars, an old school friend of Felicity's. Polly needed a job for a year or so before she went travelling. And when she was reminded, Flora remembered her from years ago, from family holidays when Cassandra had been abroad and had left Polly with them.

She was twenty-six, and the most beautiful thing Flora had ever seen. It was hard to believe that the thin, quiet blonde girl who lurked on the fringes of her childhood memories could have turned into this lithe, confident, always-smiling young woman.

Who on earth would want to hurt Poll? Who could do it?

15:37

Nearly time for the briefing. Lou had asked Barry Holloway to do most of the talking for the first one. Not, strictly speaking, the way it was usually done, but to his credit he didn't argue or ask her to explain. She wanted to watch the room, keep an eye on them all, see their reactions – gauge from it who she could use, who she would need to keep an eye on.

The room was almost ready – it had previously been the central ticketing office, but they'd been moved to the new traffic unit two weeks ago. Fortunately, as it turned out, because the room usually reserved for MIRs was already in use. There had been three armed robberies in the space of a month, a bank manager and a member of the public shot dead, and the investigation for that was well underway.

In a way this room was better, Lou realised; the area briefing

14

room was right next door, which meant they could use it without having to lug all the equipment backwards and forwards, and the canteen was just up the corridor. The downside was that the only windows looked out onto a brick wall and a few had bars on them because it was the former cell block. The nearest custody suite was now a few miles away in Briarstone nick, which wasn't ideal, but no one asked anyone who was ever actually affected by these management decisions what they thought.

A knock on the door of her goldfish bowl office, which was right in the corner; Mandy, one of the HOLMES inputters. 'More for you,' she said, handing over another pile of papers to add to the collection.

'Thanks. How's it looking out there?'

'Well,' Mandy said, with a discreet cough, 'were you expecting DI Hamilton?'

'Oh, shit.' Lou felt the blood drain from her cheeks. 'What's he doing here? I asked for Rob Jefferson.'

'Apparently DI Jefferson's done his back in. Sorry. Thought you should know.'

Lou pulled herself together and managed a smile. 'Thanks, Mandy. All the photos ready?'

Mandy nodded, and left her to it.

Fucking Andy Hamilton – that was all she needed. Another knock at the door, and Lou looked up to see Andy's bulky frame filling the glass window. She took a deep breath and beckoned him in.

'Guv,' Andy acknowledged, giving her his best charming smile.

She regarded him steadily. He'd put on weight since she'd last seen him, but he was still attractive, that dark hair and dark, neatly trimmed goatee. Eyes that were wicked, that suggested imminent misbehaviour.

'Andy. How are you?'

'Great, thanks. You're looking . . . well.' His eyes had managed to travel from her new shoes, up her legs, to her face, within a fraction of a second.

She gave him a smile so tight it pinched. 'We've got a briefing in twenty minutes. Have you got a desk?'

'I'll find one. It's going to be great working with you again, Lou.' He was disarmingly relaxed. Not fair.

'How's Karen? And the kids?'

Andy's expression tensed, but only slightly. 'They're all fine.'

'Is Leah sleeping through yet?'

'Not quite. We have the odd good night here and there.'

'This is going to be a tough case, Andy. If you're finding it difficult fitting it around home, I want to know about it, OK? I can't have you not with us a hundred per cent on this.'

'You know me, boss. Loads of energy and up for anything.' He finished with his cheekiest grin, and a wink.

Lou felt something twist inside her. She looked up at him. 'Strictly work, Andy, OK?'

'Sure thing.' And he was gone.

But he had always had trouble taking no for an answer.

15:40

Flora pulled her cold wellington boots on over her thick socks in the mudroom at the back door.

'Can I come with you?' the policewoman asked, appearing in the doorway.

'Sure,' Flora said, her tone unnaturally bright. 'You'll need boots. Here, try these.'

The woman slipped off her shoes and pulled Felicity's old

boots over the top of her smart grey trousers. 'They'll do,' she said.

'What's your name?' Flora asked, giving in at last.

'Miranda Gregson,' came the reply.

As soon as she heard the name Flora remembered it. 'Of course. Sorry.'

'That's OK. It's a difficult time.'

She gave Miranda one of her father's jackets to wear and they set off towards the stables. It was already starting to get dark, a wind blustering and swirling around the farm buildings, tugging at their clothes.

'I used to go riding when I was younger,' Miranda said. 'I helped out at some stables at the weekends. Loved it.'

Flora didn't answer. Given a choice, she would much prefer to work with this woman than Connor Petrie. Nigel had phoned him twenty minutes ago and told him to get his arse down to the stables. He'd been somewhere else, clearly, even though he was supposed to be working.

Petrie, leaning against the horsebox, gave them a wave as they approached. 'Who's this, then?'

'This is one of the police officers,' Flora said quickly. 'Miranda.'

'You here about Polly?' he asked. 'Boss told me. Lots of blood everywhere, right?'

'Shut up!' Flora snapped at him. 'Have some bloody respect. You're here to work.'

'I'm the Family Liaison Officer,' Miranda said, her tone even. 'Here to help, if I can.' She offered her hand and after some shuffling and wiping, Connor gave it a brief shake.

Oh God, this was no good. The ugly little bastard was going to have her crying in a minute. She had come out here to try and take

17

MG11 WITNESS STATEMENT

Section 1 – Witness details

NAME:	Felicity Jane Elizabeth MAITLAND		
DOB (if under 18; if over 18 state 'Over 18'):		Over 18	
ADDRESS:	Hermitage Farm Cemetery Lane Morden Briarstone	OCCUPATION:	Farm manager/housewife

Section 2 – Investigating Officer

DATE:	Thursday 1 November
OIC:	DS 10194 Samantha HOLLANDS

Section 3 – Text of Statement

My name is Felicity Maitland and I own and run Hermitage Farm, together with my husband Nigel. My main role is running the stables. We have five horses, three of which are liveries, the remaining two belong to us.

Polly Leuchars is a family friend and has been working with us since December last year, looking after the horses. As part of the arrangement we allowed Polly to live at Yonder Cottage, which is part of the farm estate. She was expected to be working with us for another few months, after which she was planning on travelling. I do not know where to.

On Wednesday 31 October Polly came to work as normal. She asked if she could go into town at lunchtime, and I agreed. She offered to do some shopping for me as well. She left in her car at about 12.30. I did not see her again until 3, when I saw her riding out in the top field.

I saw her return a couple of hours later through my kitchen window and I went to the stables to talk to her. She said she had been unable to get the things I wanted. I was very disappointed, as I could have gone into town myself if she had told me sooner. We had a bit of an argument about it. She left without finishing off the work in the stables, claiming she had a headache. The last time I saw her alive was around 5.30.

The next morning Polly was due to start work at 7 but at about 9 I noticed that the horses weren't out in the back field, so I went down to see what was happening. Polly wasn't there. The horses were quite agitated as they usually have breakfast by 8. I fed them and let them out into the field. After that I went to Yonder Cottage to see where she was. By the time I got there it was probably gone 9.30.

I noticed Polly's car was in its usual place and the back door to the cottage, which we use as the main entrance since it is nearer the road, was wide open. It opens into the kitchen and I could see blood there. I called out several times but there was no response. I was very frightened. I went to go through to the stairs. The door to the hallway was not completely shut, but I needed to push it open in order to go through.

I could see a body on the floor, right by the door, and a lot of blood everywhere. I almost fell over the body, which I recognised as that of Polly Leuchars by the colour of her hair and her build.

I went back into the kitchen and used the phone there to dial 999.

I did not notice if anything was missing from the house and I do not know why anyone would want to kill Polly.

Section 4 – Signatures

....
WITNESS: (Felicity Maitland)   OIC: (S Hollands DS 10194)

her mind off the subject of Polly's death, lose herself in mindless physical activity. She walked away from them to the hay store. Connor could talk to the police all he wanted, she wouldn't be there to listen. Didn't care any more, in any case.

15:57

'Right, let's have some hush, please,' Lou said, raising her voice above the conversation going on all around her. The briefing room was packed. Andy Hamilton was sitting right at the front; next to him was Barry Holloway. Her Detective Sergeant, Sam Hollands, was at the back, her mouth set in a determined line. Lou knew she would probably never have so many people at a briefing again; by the time the first week was over, she would start to lose people to other duties and would have to beg, borrow or steal to get them back. If, heaven forbid, the case was to drag on into months, she would end up with only a couple of the people here now.

She needed a quick arrest.

A few moments before, her mobile had rung. The display said it was the Superintendent, probably calling for a pre-briefing update, or maybe to wish her luck with it. Whatever it was, she would have to ring him afterwards. Being late for the briefing would not be a promising start.

She was quietly relieved at how quickly silence had descended on the room. She wasn't going to get too many chances to find her place at the head of this team.

'For those of you I've not met, I am DCI Louisa Smith. I'm going to give you some background, and then I'll hand over to Barry who will get us all up to speed on where we are now. Firstly, let me say that if you have any problems here I want you to feel you can come and see me or call me at any time. We all need a swift result with this one. And, as you're aware, this is a murder enquiry, and anything you hear in this briefing may be of a sensitive nature, so please keep it to yourselves.' The standard warning.

Clicking the down arrow on her laptop, the first slide:

OP NETTLE
Murder of Polly LEUCHARS

With a picture of Polly herself, taken earlier in the year; it was a poignant photograph because she looked so young, so alive, beautiful, in a fresh, carefree sort of way, with long white-blonde hair and tanned skin from spending the summer outdoors.

'This morning at just after nine-forty, Polly Leuchars' body was found by her employer at her home, Yonder Cottage, Cemetery Lane, Morden. Polly worked as a groom at Hermitage Farm and lived in the cottage because she was a family friend of the Maitlands, who, as we all know, own and run Hermitage Farm.'

A few murmurs.

'Polly was on the floor in the downstairs hallway and had been severely beaten. She was wearing pyjamas and her bed had been slept in. Early estimates from the pathologist put the time of death as between midnight and four, although this needs to be confirmed.'

Lou looked at the sea of faces. She still had their undivided attention and some of the Late Turn were busy making notes. 'Right, over to you, Barry. For those of you who don't know, Barry Holloway is our reader-receiver.'

'Guv.'

Lou stepped to one side of the projection screen, watching the room.

Barry fiddled with the laptop. 'Anyone not happy with scene

photos, look away now, folks. Otherwise I'll warn you when we get to the really grim ones.'

The first slide came up, a picture of the kitchen of Yonder Cottage. Blood on the floor, on the work surfaces.

'Good news and bad news so far. The good news: we've probably got forensics all over the place. Nothing confirmed until we get the CSI report back, but for now spatter marks indicate the main attack took place downstairs in the hallway. No sign of forced entry but apparently the back door wasn't routinely locked. No sign of the murder weapon, and we're waiting for confirmation of what that could be. Something solid and heavy in any case.'

The slides clicked over to the stairs. 'We've got some good shoe marks, and a smeared handprint. Likelihood of fingerprints is pretty good. Brace yourselves for the next few, if you're squeamish.'

Next slide, the hallway, stairway to the rear. Body in situ.

Click. Close up onto what remained of Polly Leuchars. She was face down, one arm up near her head, the other by her side, one knee brought up, wearing cotton pyjamas, patches of pink still visible in all the dark brown and red; flashes of still-blonde hair; white bone showing through.

Click. The side of Polly's face, swollen, purple skin in the places where you could actually see the skin. What could have been bruising under a still perfect shell-like ear.

Someone in the room let out a long breath; otherwise there was silence.

'As you can see, this is a nasty one. There's not a lot of Polly's head left. We had to get initial identification from the Maitlands via some jewellery, although Felicity Maitland assumed it was Polly from her size and her hair. Extensive blood loss here, here and over here.'

Lou looked across at the faces, earnestly looking at the bloody scene on display and trying not to show emotion. They'd all seen stuff like this before, but it didn't mean they were unaffected by it.

'Post mortem hopefully tomorrow. We'll have to wait until then for the first thoughts. Guv.'

'Thanks, Barry.' Lou resumed her place and flipped on to the next slide. 'This is where we are now. We have an initial witness statement from Felicity Maitland. Sam's been in touch with Miranda Gregson, who is our FLO. She's been with the family all afternoon. How are they, Sam?'

Sam Hollands, stockily built with a sweep of heavy blonde hair, spoke up from the back. 'Felicity Maitland is in a bad way and her husband keeps feeding her alcohol which isn't helping. Flora, their daughter, has been looking after everyone, not saying much. She's got a flat in Briarstone.'

'What about Polly's parents?'

'The mother, Cassandra Leuchars, died a few years ago. I asked about Polly's father but nobody seems to know who that is.'

A hand went up at the back. 'Ma'am?'

'Yes?' Lou didn't know this one. A brown-haired chap, older.

'DC Ron Mitchell. We just had reports come in of another body being found this morning, might be linked to this – did you get that already?'

Lou hated to be wrong-footed, especially in a briefing. 'Thanks, Ron; could you enlighten us, please?'

'I got a report from PC Ian Richardson from Briarstone nick. He's been dealing with a suspected suicide, complicated by the husband of the deceased keeling over with a heart attack when a patrol went round to break the news. Dog walker saw a car had gone over the quarry cliff at Ambleside, called it in. Initial patrol and paramedics went down via the access track. Too ropey for cars unfortunately, so they got down there on foot. After that it took a while to get the rescue team to get some abseil gear down there. Anyway, there's a woman's body in the driver's seat of the car. Bit of a mess. The car's a silver Corsa, new shape. Index goes down to a Mrs Barbara Fletcher-Norman, address Hayselden Barn, Cemetery Lane, Morden – right across the road from Hermitage Farm.'

That got everyone's attention.

'What happened with the husband?' Lou said.

'They got to the address and the old man was getting out of the shower. Says he thought his wife had gone out early, that he got back from work late last night and went to bed, assumed she was out with friends. So he hadn't seen her since yesterday morning when he left for work.'

'Right,' said Lou, not sure where this was heading.

'Well, then it gets interesting.' Ron, loving the attention, flipped over the pages of his notebook with a flourish. 'Ian Richardson went into the kitchen with him, and there's what looks like blood in there. Not all over the place, but the kitchen's a mess and there's blood on a tea towel by the sink. Husband seems dead shocked by this. Claims he never went into the kitchen last night or this morning. Pretty soon he started having trouble breathing, then all of a sudden he went grey and collapsed. They called for Eden District Ambulance Trust and did CPR in the meantime but it was a few minutes before the ambulance got there. I think it was the one that had been up at the cottage.'

Lou looked across the faces for someone reliable and unfortunately her gaze alighted on Andy Hamilton. The call from Buchanan must have been about this. What were the chances? Two bodies from adjacent properties, on the same morning, in a tiny place like Morden? They *had* to be linked.

23

'Andy, they'll probably open a second case for this, even though it might be part of our job. Can you find out who's in charge and see if you can take it on? We won't be able to get a search team or CSI in there but we need to make sure the Barn is sealed off until we can treat it as a scene. We don't know it's linked, but I think for now we should assume it is.'

'Ma'am.' Andy smiled warmly, clearly pleased with himself for landing a juicy job.

'Ron, anything else?'

'Briarstone ran a next-of-kin check through the old boy's work and the only name they came up with was a Mrs Taryn Lewis, daughter of Brian Fletcher-Norman, the husband. Turns out she's not spoken to her father for months. That's about where we've got to.'

'Where is this place in relation to our cottage, exactly?'

'A hundred yards or so away, no more.'

'Right.' Lou digested the information, working out the best step forward with it. 'Thanks, Ron. How's Mr Fletcher-Norman doing, do we know?'

'He's in intensive care in Briarstone General. Not looking too bright. Be lucky to get an interview any time soon.'

'And what about the body in the car?'

'Waiting for PM.'

'Thanks, Ron. I'll leave that one with you.'

Ron was slightly red in the face. Lou guessed it had been a good few years since he'd been able to play a trump card in an initial briefing. They were on the home straight now, at least.

'Barry? Back to you. How's the intel looking?'

Barry Holloway was the most experienced member of her team as far as Major Crime was concerned. He'd been the reader in more MIRs than she could count.

'Thanks. Right, pin your ears back, chaps. We've got a witness who thinks he saw a car going over the cliff last night. That came in on the box while you were talking, ma'am. And something from Crimestoppers. An anonymous caller saying Polly Leuchars was having an affair with someone in the village. Another Crimestoppers, suggesting we might want to look closer at the Fletcher-Normans – well, we're ahead of the game on that one. Mrs Maitland says that Polly went on a shopping trip to Briarstone yesterday lunchtime, was gone three hours or so. We'll get CCTV, see if we can track her movements. I had a look on ANPR for Polly's vehicle, no results unfortunately, but then the back road into Briarstone isn't covered unless the mobile camera unit happens to be there. We've got a sighting of Polly in the Lemon Tree last night. She left before closing time, so we'll need to interview the regulars, see who she was meeting. And two reports of a car revving and driving away at speed during the night not far from the cottage. We'll get more tomorrow morning after the press conference.'

'Right.' Lou had almost forgotten that she was going to be broadcast to the nation tomorrow morning and felt a lurch of nausea at the prospect. It would be nice to be able to go to the press conference with a firm picture of what had happened to their victim.

'Can we see what the latest is on Nigel Maitland?'

'Already checked that,' Barry said. 'Nothing recent. I've put a source tasking in.'

'What about the house-to-house?'

'Jane Phelps is organising that; she's still out there with Les. I spoke to her before we came in and it's all village gossip so far, no dramas. She said she'd ring in when they're done. Patrols did most of it this morning before we got there, anyway. She's going round again to make sure.'

'Thanks. Well, that's about it for now. Any questions?'

Murmurs, everyone itching to get on with it.

'Right. Next briefing tomorrow morning, eight sharp. I'm talking to the press at nine, so let's see if we can stay ahead of them. OK. Let's go.'

A brief second, and then the shuffling of chairs, rustling of papers, laughter, voices. A few handshakes, people who'd been off working other areas and found themselves back on the team together.

Lou let out a long, slow breath, dealt with the few people who came up to her afterwards with comments, suggestions, or ideas that they hadn't felt brave enough to pipe up with in the briefing.

Then there was only one person left, someone she didn't know, leaning casually against the back wall, arms crossed, giving her his complete and undivided attention. He had dark hair, broad shoulders and – most disconcerting of all – a black eye.

'Can I help you?' she asked, wondering with a snap of fear if someone had been in the briefing who shouldn't have been.

'I'm Jason Mercer.'

She'd forgotten the name but there was no mistaking that accent. Shit! Had she been really rude to him on the phone earlier? A warm flush spreading across her cheeks, she decided there was only one way to play this: pretend it never happened.

'Hi. Did you have any luck finding me an analyst?' she asked, shaking his hand. His was warm, his grip firm. He looked her in the eye, held her gaze. The dark bruise, a smudge across the bridge of his nose, made the green of his eyes more striking.

'Yes and no – I'm afraid you've got me.'

'Well, thank you. I'm glad you're here. Did you get everything you needed from the briefing?'

'I think so. Presumably you want a network, timeline, that sort of thing?'

'Yes, please.'

'What about the phones?'

'Jane Phelps is going to be the exhibits officer. When she's back later I'll get a list of them for you. She's already put the applications in for the billings of all of the phones we have. We didn't find Polly's phone at the cottage, unfortunately, but we've got the number from the Maitlands.'

She led him out of the briefing room, stopping at Barry Holloway's desk to introduce them. But they had worked together on a case before and shook hands briefly. 'We've got you a desk sorted out and the workstation's all loaded and ready to go,' Barry said.

'Can you brief me tomorrow morning?' Lou asked. 'Before the press conference?'

Jason looked her straight in the eye once again. 'Sure. I'll see what I can do.'

Turning away, walking back to her poky little office, Lou wondered why her heart was pounding and her skin felt as if it was on fire.

16:10

When Flora got back, Miranda Gregson and Petrie were nowhere to be found. She began mucking out the stables, managing to hold herself together as long as she didn't think about Polly doing this and now never doing it again. She kept her eyes on the wet straw and horseshit, shovelling it into the wheelbarrow and then over to the heap.

'Flora!'

Flora groaned. He was back. Connor-bloody-Petrie.

'Where have you been?' she said, not looking up until his green wellington boots appeared in her line of vision, directly in her way.

He was standing with his hands in his pockets, looking casual and jolly as if he owned the stables and felt the need to supervise his own personal shit-shoveller. 'I was giving that nice police lady a tour of the farm,' he said. 'None of you lot bothered to do that, did you?'

'Where is she now?'

'Back in the kitchen.'

'You're in the way,' she said.

He didn't move, but his weasel smile dropped from his face, making him look decidedly nasty – which he was. But as well as being an evil bastard, he was also a foot shorter than Flora and she wasn't afraid of him.

'What you doin' here anyway? You don't even live here.'

She put down the fork and leaned on it. 'What does it look like I'm doing?'

'Looks like you're taking your time about it, if you ask me,' he said.

'I'm not,' she said. 'And you should be doing this. It *is* your job. Grab the barrow and give me a hand.'

'Not me. Your dad's got important stuff for me to do today.'

'What important stuff?'

He tapped the side of his pointed nose conspiratorially. 'None of your business, Flora. You keep mucking out like a good girl and I'll come back later and check you done it right.'

That was it. Enough.

She dropped the fork. It clattered and bounced off the concrete

28

yard, but Flora didn't even hear the noise because by that time Petrie was face down in the dung heap, Flora's knee in his back. She had him by the scruff of his too-big, hand-me-down waxed jacket that made him feel so self-important. He was shouting as best he could, calling out: 'No, no! Lemme up! You stupid bi-bi-bitch!'

'Flora! Let him up.'

She took her knee off his back and turned to see her father in the yard.

'Nige!' Petrie was shouting, wiping his face and pulling bits of straw and dung from the front of his jacket. 'You see what she did? Did ya see? Bitch!'

He made a move towards Flora but Nigel stepped forward and Petrie backed off immediately.

'You're fine, Connor,' he said, calmly. 'Go and wash your hands and face.'

Petrie complied, looking daggers at Flora as he made his way round the yard towards the offices at the end. 'Fuckin' cow,' he muttered.

'Feel better?' Nigel asked, when Petrie was out of the way.

'He's a piece of crap. Why do you bother with him? He doesn't want to work, he's a lazy little bastard.'

'I know. But he has his uses.'

'Polly hated him,' Flora said, and then stopped short.

'Polly tolerated him,' Nigel said.

A single tear fell, taking her by surprise. She turned back to the stables, wiping her face angrily. She wasn't going to cry in front of him, that was for sure.

'Come on, Flora. Let's go and have a drink. All right?'

'I need to get this done,' she said. 'Nobody else is going to do it, are they?'

He stood for a moment watching her, haunting her peripheral vision, and then he turned and left her to it.

One more stable to do, and then she could go and walk. Clear her head.

17:54

Over the course of the afternoon, police came and went at Hermitage Farm. Flora finished at the stables and left Connor to bring the horses in. It was dark by that time, so she gave up on the walk and stayed in the kitchen, making endless cups of tea.

Felicity sat holding court as various neighbours came to call and talk about the trauma. Miranda Gregson loitered, making detailed notes of all the visitors, who they were, where they lived, taking contact phone numbers should the police wish to ask them further questions.

At a quarter to six the one Flora remembered as Sam came back again. She had an air of kindness about her, patient with Felicity despite all the dithering and rambling.

When the madness had isolated itself in the room that held her mother, Flora slipped upstairs to the bathroom and tried to phone Taryn. She wanted to tell her about Polly, but also that it seemed something was going on at the Barn too. None of the police officers had said anything, but there had been an ambulance and police cars over there since late morning. Maybe Polly had been the victim of a burglary that went wrong and the same thing had happened over at the Barn?

It was pointless to speculate. Taryn's phone number went unanswered, and her mobile phone was switched off.

'Flora? Flora?' shouted her mother. 'Flora? They want to take our fingerprints – and our DNA!'

She returned to the kitchen, heart thudding.

'It's fine,' said Sam, gently. It was as if she could tell that Flora was feeling the loss more than the rest of them. 'It's routine. We expect *your* prints to be in the cottage; it's the ones we don't expect to find that we're interested in. We need to take yours for elimination purposes.'

And there, on the table, an ink-pad, a roller, sheets of paper, plastic sealable bags. Her mother at the sink, already scrubbing at her finger tips with the Fairy Liquid and a pan scourer.

Nigel came in as Sam was explaining the process to Flora: fingerprints, then cheek swabs for the DNA.

'You can forget about taking mine for now; I want to speak to my solicitor first,' her father said and went to the office to make a phone call. By the time he came back Flora was washing her hands.

'I'd like it to be noted that I'm cooperating fully,' he said to Sam.

'I'm happy to note that.'

Flora watched her father as he allowed the officer to manipulate his fingers, one by one, against the ink-pad. He must be hating this, hating having them here. He was hiding it well, though, and it was something she had always grudgingly admired – the more difficult the circumstances, the more he turned on the charm, the easy, relaxed confidence.

And the oddest thing: Flora, with nothing at all to hide, felt nervy and guilty and afraid while Nigel, with the most to fear, was as relaxed and confident as she'd ever seen him.

MG11 WITNESS STATEMENT

Section 1 – Witness details

NAME:	Richard John HARRISON		
DOB (if under 18; if over 18 state 'Over 18'):		Over 18	
ADDRESS:	35 Priory Acre Morden Briarstone	OCCUPATION:	Retired

Section 2 – Investigating Officer

DATE:	Thursday 1 November
OIC:	DC 8745 Alastair WHITMORE

Section 3 – Text of Statement

I am a retired accountant and I live in the village of Morden. On the morning of Thursday 1 November I was walking my Jack Russell, Lima, on the Downs outside the village. Our usual walk takes us across the fields to the old quarry at Ambleside, skirting round the top of the quarry, and then back home.

I left home at around 6.30. It was still quite dark but by the time we reached the quarry it was fairly light. I estimate that we were there no later than seven.

When we reached Ambleside Quarry Lima ran off into the bushes, barking. I believed she was chasing a rabbit and I followed her because I didn't want her to go over the edge of the quarry. When I cleared the bushes I noticed that there was a car lying on its roof at the foot of the cliff on the far side of the quarry. I believe this is directly under where the car park is situated.

I could not see what make of car it was, except that it was silver in colour. I do not believe the car had been there yesterday when we took our walk as I would have noticed it.

I called out in case someone was trapped in the car, shouting that I was going to get help.

I walked back to the path where I found Lima waiting for me. I attached her lead and walked quickly home, where I phoned for the police and an ambulance.

Section 4 – Signatures

WITNESS: (R Harrison)   OIC: (A Whitmore)

It was heading towards nine, and Lou was reaching the point where nothing more could be usefully done until the morning. She would grab a takeaway on the way home – her stomach was growling and she realised she hadn't eaten anything since the KitKat she'd had in the morning.

'I thought you said the witness saw the car go over the cliff?' she asked Ron when the statement came back.

'Sorry, ma'am, it was third-hand info by the time I got it. We know it definitely happened overnight, though. The countryside warden says it wasn't there at six the night before. PM on the body should tell us more.'

'Do we have any idea when that's going to be?'

'I've asked for it to be prioritised and linked it to Op Nettle. Might have it by the morning if we're lucky. They recovered the body and the car.'

Back in her office, she braced herself to phone Andy Hamilton's mobile. Went through the motions of looking it up on the Force Directory, even though she knew it off by heart.

'Andy, it's me,' she said, when he answered.

'Yeah,' he said.

Of course. He knew her number as well as she knew his. God, this was so awkward; she was glad she'd managed to push him aside to the other body. With a bit of luck, the two cases would be completely unrelated and she could get another DI in.

Could she ever be that lucky? Of course not.

'Area are desperate to get rid of this one, boss. They've been on to Mr Buchanan, claiming it's definitely linked to Hermitage Farm. I think we're going to have to take it.'

Shit, shit! She'd completely forgotten to phone the Superintendent back. She would have to do it the minute she got off the phone.

'Have they got any actual evidence linking it?'

'Witness statements to say that Brian Fletcher-Norman was having an affair with Polly Leuchars. Witness statements going on about how unstable Barbara – that's our body in the quarry – was, how she was jealous, an alcoholic.'

'Evidence, Andy? Rather than village gossip?'

'Nothing yet. I reckon Barbara went over to confront Polly about her affair with Brian, got riled up enough to kill her, then went back to the Barn. Washed her hands, was overcome with remorse, drove drunk to the quarry and went over. Accidentally-on-purpose.'

'Thanks for that, Sherlock.'

'You're welcome.'

'If you know anything more by tomorrow morning, come to the briefing?'

'Wouldn't miss it.'

Every little thing felt like flirting where Hamilton was concerned. Did he do it to everyone, or just to Lou? And how did you stamp your authority on the working relationship when there was this sort of history between you? Two months ago, she'd been a DI and his ranking equal. When it had happened, she'd been his sergeant. Her swift rise to DCI was all to do with her grim determination to get her head down and concentrate on work rather than let herself be distracted by men, or one man in particular – Andy Hamilton.

Sooner or later she was going to have to have a chat with him. It wasn't going to be pleasant, but it had to be better than this.

She dialled the number for Mr Buchanan's secretary. No answer, of course, not at this time of night. She tried the mobile, and got the answering service.

'Sir, Lou Smith. Sorry I didn't get back to you earlier. I'm guessing you were calling about the second case in Morden. I've sent Andy Hamilton over to establish links, if there are any. Hope this is OK. If you need me, the mobile's on, otherwise I'll brief you tomorrow first thing. Thanks. Bye.'

With luck, Buchanan wouldn't phone back tonight.

The next person on the list was Jane Phelps, who had finally made it back to the office. Lou had worked with Jane before, had confidence in her.

'How's the house-to-house?'

Jane waved a small pile of papers. 'All done for now. Area had covered most of it before we got there. Lots of people seem to be away on holiday – it's that sort of place, weekenders and well-off families. And I tell you what, some of these women who sit at home all day planning lunch parties – it feels like all they want to do is gossip about their neighbours. You wouldn't believe some of the things they've come up with.'

'I think I know what you're going to say, but carry on, I like a good goss.'

'Well ... ' Jane riffled through the pages, handwritten at this stage. 'Mrs Newbury at Willow Cottage, she seems to think Polly was having an affair with Nigel Maitland. Apparently he's the reason she came here to work.'

Lou raised her eyebrows.

'Marjorie Baker from Esperance Villa – honestly, I'm not making it up – seems to think it was Brian Fletcher-Norman that Polly was seeing. Saw Brian coming out of Yonder Cottage once late at night when she went round there to deliver a Christian Aid leaflet or something.'

Just as Hamilton had said: Polly Leuchars and the man from the Barn across the road. But Nigel Maitland as well?

'Have we got anything we can actually use?'

'The next house along, towards the pub, is Rowe House. Occupant's a Mr Wright, a weekender from London. He's staying for the week with his two children because of it being half term. Says he was woken up at two-fifteen by the noise of a car driving along the lane at speed. Didn't look out of his window, went back to sleep.'

'OK. Let's get a proper statement from him. Remind me, where does that lane end up if you follow it in that direction?'

'Takes you to the crossroads, then straight over would be towards Briarstone. The other way would be out towards Baysbury.'

'Any ANPR cameras on that road?'

'Afraid not.'

'Too much to hope for, I guess.'

'It's really quiet, that area. I've been looking at the crime data – hardly anything goes on down there. Most of the traffic seems to be related to the farm.'

'I need to get a nice map,' Lou said absently, wondering whether the analyst had gone home already.

21:04

Drifting in and out of consciousness was at times a delicious and a devastating thing, Brian thought. You saw faces, not knowing if they were real or imagined, a thought came and then it was gone, voices came and went . . .

'Have we located any next of kin?'

'Police found a daughter, we are waiting for more from them.'

Music ... light and dark ... pain ...

Taryn. Where was Taryn? Suzanne ... Polly ... ?

And darkness.

21:05

Andy Hamilton pulled out of the hospital car park and headed through the rain towards home, wondering if there was any chance Karen would have cooked something for him, or if he should stop and get a kebab. He could have phoned her, of course, but that would risk waking Leah who might, with a bit of luck, have gone off to sleep. He'd sent a text an hour ago letting Karen know that he was going to be a bit late. No reply had been forthcoming.

In the end his car seemed to pull in of its own accord to the parade of shops where the Atilla Kebab House and Pizzeria's bright lights beckoned, and a few minutes later he was back in the car, a steaming polystyrene carton warming his thighs. He picked at bits of grilled chicken, wiping them in the chilli sauce that dribbled out of the edges of the pitta, thinking about Detective Chief Inspector Louisa Smith.

It wasn't the first time he'd seen her since it happened, but it was the first time they'd worked together. Was it awkward? Not for him. She was looking even better these days, or was it because she had that new, brisk air of authority about her that made her even more of an exciting challenge?

I'd go there again, he thought.

Outside the off-licence a little crowd of the usual halfwits had gathered and he kept a contemplative eye on them while he crammed the pitta in. They were here all the time. Patrols got bored with coming out here night after night, sending them on their way, getting all the verbal abuse that went with it, only to be called out again by the shopkeeper an hour later because they were back, throwing stones and beer cans around and shouting obscenities. It was putting off her regular customers, Mrs Kumar complained. It was bad for business.

Neighbourhood were supposed to be putting together a dispersal zone. In the meantime, the local arseholes sat on Mrs Kumar's storage unit, spat great gobs of phlegm at the pavement and shouted incomprehensible twaddle at each other and at passers-by.

If they did something really bad, he'd have to get out of the car, kebab or no kebab.

He watched one of them, a skinny lad with a shaved head, wearing a vest – a *vest* for crying out loud, it was November – push one of the girls on the shoulder, hard enough to knock her off her perch on the metal barrier. She kept to her feet but immediately turned to square up to him, her fist brought back behind her ear.

'Oh, no,' Andy groaned, 'don't be a muppet.'

The skinhead in the vest, one of the Petrie family, judging by the extensive monobrow and weaselly chin, was laughing at the girl, pointing. Her mate, squeezed into too-tight white jeans with some appropriate word sequinned across the arse, shouted back at him, wobbled her head and waved her hands, ghetto-style; and for some reason that seemed to be more of a legitimate challenge because the halfwit backed off then, hands up in mock surrender.

Two minutes later the skinhead was snogging the face off the girl who'd nearly punched him and Andy had finished his kebab.

21:53

There was no one in the Intel Unit. The Late Turn officers were all out on a job and Lou went back to her desk and sent an email to the

Source Handling Unit to try and hurry up the latest on Nigel Maitland, copying in Ali Whitmore.

It would be a bonus, Lou thought, if she could be the one to nail Maitland, the smarmy bastard. She had met him once, and charming and handsome as he was – hair greying at the temples, light blue eyes with plenty going on behind them, a warm smile – she'd been wary of him. And it might have been a whopping great coincidence that this young woman, who may or may not have been having sex with her employer and 'family friend' who was not quite twice her age, ended up with her skull smashed to pieces on Nigel Maitland's property: or it might just be the mistake that would finally see him brought down.

The MIR was still active, but there weren't many people left. Jane Phelps and Les Finnegan were writing up statements, crosschecking details.

Behind some screens and a long table which supported a fax machine, scanner, colour printer and black and white printer, Jason Mercer was still hard at work. There was something about him that was making her feel ... odd. Yet he wasn't especially good-looking, although he was tall and probably had a good body underneath his meticulously ironed shirt. He held himself with an easy confidence, as though he was here for fun, yet at the same time he was clearly very focused on what he was doing. And he had agreed to work on her team even when he obviously hadn't wanted to.

'Hello,' said Lou, smiling as he started. 'Sorry – didn't mean to make you jump.'

He leaned back in his chair and stretched his arms above his head. 'I hadn't noticed it getting dark.' He checked his watch. 'My God!'

'What time did you get to work this morning?' Lou found herself perched on the edge of the desk opposite, tugging at her skirt.

'Half past seven. Oh, well.' He gave her a smile. 'I daresay your day has been at least as long and twice as stressful. Are you going home?'

Lou nodded. 'The mortuary first to see if there's any update or if they need anything from us. After that, home. I need sleep, otherwise I won't be able to function at all tomorrow. How are you getting on?'

'Fine so far,' Jason said. 'Do you want me to brief you now, or can you wait for the morning?'

'Tomorrow will be fine. I will have to find some way to contain my excitement until then. By the way, what happened to your eye?'

It must have been a corker when it was still swollen but now it was a purplish smudge under his right eye with a tiny cut on the bridge of his nose. She'd been dying to ask ever since she'd first laid eyes on him at the briefing.

'I play hockey,' he said. And then added, as he must have had to do every single time someone asked, which was probably several times a day: 'Ice hockey.'

'Ah,' Lou replied, as if that explained everything.

'Did you find out about the phones?' he asked.

Shit. 'Sorry. I saw Jane briefly but we were talking about the house-to-house. Have you checked the comms folder on the computer?'

'Still empty.'

'I'll give her a call, hold on.' Lou headed back to her office to grab the mobile but he called her back.

'Don't worry, it can wait till morning. I don't especially want to start on it at this time of night, anyway.'

He stood up and stretched, pulling his jacket off the back of his chair.

The reception desk at Briarstone General Hospital was empty, the flower kiosk shut, the only activity around the vending machines; but Lou knew where she was going. The public mortuary.

She rang the bell on the door that was tucked away, its only identification the simple word 'Mortuary'. After an age, an assistant appeared. She recognised Lou but still checked her warrant card before letting her in.

'Dr Francis has just finished. You're lucky to catch her.'

Adele Francis was in the staff room, changing out of her scrubs and wellies into a smart skirt and high heels.

'Hi, Adele,' Lou said. 'Sorry, I don't want to keep you. I know it's been a long day. I wanted to check if you've got everything you need.'

Adele did look tired, but she managed a smile. 'Yes, thanks. You can walk me to the car park if you like and we can talk on the way. I've got a date with a bottle of wine and I'm late already.'

They went out of a door marked 'Fire Exit Only', which was a short cut out to the fresh air.

'Not bad going, two bodies already. How's your first MIR?'

'OK so far, I think. And the second body isn't officially mine yet.'

'Well, I'm not convinced the two are linked by anything more than location. You're going to have to wait for the blood results to confirm it.'

'Anything you can tell me that might help? I've got the press conference tomorrow morning.'

'Polly Leuchars died of head injuries, multiple trauma with a blunt instrument, plenty of force needed, very aggressive. Someone had had a go at strangling her first. Bruises around the neck, possibly

41

enough to render her unconscious. She was still alive when the head injuries occurred.'

'Time of death?'

'I'd say between midnight and two, no later. There was some evidence of older injuries which may be worth considering in your investigation.'

Lou stopped. 'Older injuries?'

'Healing bruises, mainly. Some around the wrists, barely visible unless you've got the best sort of light.'

'So she'd been restrained?'

'Possibly. Not recently but within the last week or two. She was a horsewoman, wasn't she?'

'She worked as a groom, yes.'

Adele considered this. 'I saw similar bruises around the wrists and lower arms of a child, once. She'd been thrown at a gymkhana. Had wound the reins around her wrists. So don't go jumping to any premature conclusions, Chief Inspector.'

'I'll try not to,' Lou said, then added: 'What about Mrs Fletcher-Norman?'

'Yes, that one was interesting. I only got her late this afternoon. Do you happen to know if she was wearing her seatbelt when she was found?'

'I'll ask. We're waiting on the CSI photographs.'

'I did phone earlier; someone was going to call me back. Never mind. I'll do the PM tomorrow and let you have the report as soon as I can.'

'Thank you.'

They had stopped beside a silver BMW, parked in a designated bay in the staff car park, the one reserved for consultants and senior management.

'Enjoy your wine – I think I might pick some up myself.'

Lou paused at the main entrance, then on a whim walked all the way back to the Intensive Care Unit. She showed her warrant card, said she was here to check on Mr Fletcher-Norman's progress. She waited for twenty minutes while they found someone who was prepared to commit to an update, even a vague one.

Still unconscious. Nothing further.

That's it, she thought. I'm going home.

23:14

After work, Taryn had phoned the hospital to check if her father was still alive. They'd suggested she should come in, that he was still in a critical state but might respond to her voice. Fat chance of that, she thought, but after speaking to her husband, Chris, she had gone in anyway.

She was surprised at how old he looked without his glasses on, his eyes closed and tubes and monitors everywhere. He was wearing one of those hospital gowns and his skin was pink, the hair on his head was white and tufty, not neatly groomed. He looked frail and vulnerable, not like him at all. From this position she could see there were marks like yellowing bruises on the top of his right arm. Maybe he got them when they were trying to keep his heart going – wasn't it supposed to be really brutal? Or maybe Barbara had been beating him up; Taryn wouldn't have put it past her.

The last time she'd seen him had been at the Barn. He had been complaining about the bike she'd bought him last Christmas. It wasn't right for his needs, apparently, even though it had been the one he had chosen from some enthusiast's magazine, and she had gone round to look at it.

Barbara had opened the door to her.

'Oh. It's you. Well, you'd better come in.'

Her father was in his armchair reading the *Telegraph*, paisley-patterned feet up on the footstool.

'Good heavens,' he'd said, peering at her. 'What the hell is that thing you're wearing?'

'It's a poncho, Dad. I've come about the bike.'

'It makes your legs look enormous,' he said. 'You'd be better off with a long coat.'

She'd taken a deep breath in, and repeated slowly: 'I've come about the bike.'

'It's outside, next to the garage,' he said. 'You'll have to take it back.'

'What's the matter with it?'

'Gears keep slipping,' he said, from behind the newspaper.

'What? What do you mean?'

He lowered the newspaper slowly and looked at her over the top of his reading glasses. 'It's a road bike, Taryn.'

She remembered the feeling bubbling up inside her, the frustration and the misery of being spoken to like that. How long would she have to put up with it? 'I know what it is. It's the one you asked for. The one you picked out of the magazine!'

'I don't want a road bike, I don't enjoy cycling on the roads; if I wanted to cycle on the roads I would have asked for a road bike, wouldn't I? I can't ride that thing through the countryside. It's not suitable. It's not appropriate.'

His voice rose over the course of the outburst until he was on the verge of shouting, his face flushed to a deep crimson.

She stared at him for a moment, counting to ten. Then fifteen. Then she looked away, defeated. 'All right. I'll see if I can trade it in for a different one.'

Her father shook the creases out of the newspaper. The matter was closed, resolved to his satisfaction, for the time being at least. He always won. If he didn't win, he would carry on and on until he could claim the victory in another way.

She'd gone out to the garage and looked at the bike, leaning miserably against the wall with the front wheel turned out at an odd angle, as though it had been casually tossed aside and had slumped down under the weight of its own inadequacies.

It had started to rain by then and she was wondering whether she could fit the bike in if she put the seats down in the car, when Barbara came to the back door with a bag full of bottles for the recycling bin.

'I'll see you, then,' Taryn had said, with an attempt at a cheerful wave.

'What? You're not coming back, are you?'

'No. I just meant – never mind.'

Head down against the rain, she'd gone round to the front as the back door slammed shut. She spent a good twenty minutes trying to fit the bike into the car, scraping the skin on her ankle with a pedal, getting grease on her hands and her new wool poncho and the fabric of the back seat, blinded by tears and hating herself for bothering with them; the pair of them, they were as bad as each other. Hateful people!

The next day she had taken the bike back to the shop where she'd bought it, at considerable expense since it wasn't the cheapest.

'He says the gears keep slipping,' she'd said.

They took the bike back to examine it and then phoned Taryn at work to tell her the good news. The gears were fine.

When she went back to the shop she asked if there was any way she could exchange it for a mountain bike. The manager showed her round the mountain bike selection and told her he would give her a trade-in value for the road bike. Less than half what she'd paid, and the mountain bikes were much more expensive.

She had wheeled the bike out of the shop and spent another twenty minutes fighting to get it back into her car. Subsequently she chose a Friday lunchtime, when she could be reasonably certain that Barbara would be playing tennis and her father would be at his office, and dumped the bike round the back of the Barn. Then put a note through the letterbox, explaining that she couldn't exchange it, she had tried, and if he wanted to buy himself a mountain bike that was up to him. She had signed it with a 'T', no niceties. And that had been it.

But she'd been working up to seeing him again, working up to contacting him, knowing that the immovable boundary of Christmas was approaching and that someone would have to break the silence and say something about letting bygones be bygones, blood being thicker than water, the wrong time of year to be holding grudges, all of that old nonsense that would still be directed at her as though she were the guilty party.

And now Barbara was dead, and her father was breathing through a machine. She tried to feel sorry. She even tried to feel happy, but that didn't work either. She couldn't seem to feel anything apart from tired.

What she had wanted to hear was that he was dead. It was bad of her, very bad, to wish something like that, but it didn't stop her wishing. And if he was going to die, she wanted it to happen soon so she wouldn't have to keep going back, day after day. She wanted it to be over with.

Day Two – Friday 2 November 2012

00:52

Flora was in a bar in town, numbing everything from her lips to her heart with alcohol and loud music. At some point she would walk back to the studio, sleep there. Not the flat. It was too full of Polly's presence, the ghost of her.

Flora could have stayed at the farm; her mother had specifically asked.

'What if I need you, Flora?'

'Need me for what, exactly?' It was like speaking to a petulant child. When she'd been at the wine, their roles were often reversed.

'But what about the horses?'

'The horses are fine. Dad's here, and that Petrie idiot, if you need him.'

'But Flora ... Polly ...'

More tears. It wouldn't have been so bad if the tears had been for Polly but they were selfish ones; Felicity was cross that her life had been thrown upside down, that her home had been invaded by police, that Polly had gone and got herself killed and made such a mess in the cottage. And the only way to deal with it was to make it all about *her*.

Her mother was pathetic, frustrating, but her father was worse. There was a calmness about him that felt dangerous. The more pressure he felt, the more relaxed he seemed, and today, when they had been taking his fingerprints, police in his house, he had been almost casual. Flora knew how his moods worked, how his temper built, masked by the composure, until a point of no return had been reached. Then his fury was explosive.

Flora left the farm without saying goodbye. They were all busy, anyway.

She'd been approached in the bar, several times, propositioned, turned them away. The last one, a bloke twice her size who had also consumed more than his fair share of alcohol, got aggressive when she turned him down, called her a 'frigid fucking bitch'. The door staff ejected him, and then came back and asked her to leave too. She'd had enough anyway by then.

The studio was echoing in silence, the only sound the buzzing inside her own head. She curled up on the old sofa, pulled a dust-sheet over herself and sobbed until sleep took her.

05:30

The alarm rang at five-thirty, too early, still deeply dark. Lou pressed the snooze button and allowed herself another few minutes. She would feel better when she had been in the shower. As soon as the alarm rang again she got out of bed. If she were late today she would never live it down.

Her mobile was charging downstairs, and already there were two missed calls. One from Andy Hamilton's mobile, late last night, and one from the office. Nothing on voicemail, so nothing urgent.

Her mind was starting to race ahead. Results from the initial enquiries would be pouring in to the MIR today. Once she had finished the press conference and the results were aired, broad-cast, printed and published, even more would come in. Of course, a lot of it would be worse than useless – the cranks, the would-be investigators, the psychics, the people who only wanted to be helpful and somewhere, in amongst it all, would be the crucial bits of information that would lead them to the person who took Polly's life.

Briefly she wondered about the Fletcher-Normans. Of course, it could be something straightforward, with no connection to the Polly Leuchars murder other than a horrible coincidence of time and location. But it felt like an uneasy tangle of events. The forensics would help to sort out one case from the other, and Jason's reports, once they started to come through. She was lucky to have him; not any old analyst, since they were in such short supply, but one of the seniors. Unhelpful as he'd been during that initial phone call, it was clear that he knew what he was doing and he was committed enough to the investigation to put in the hours. They weren't all like that.

Let's hope I get to keep him, Lou thought.

07:14

From somewhere far away, Flora could hear her phone ringing. In her dreams she kept answering it, only for there to be no one on the other end.

'Polly?' She woke herself up saying the name out loud, then, as she realised that her mobile was ringing, it stopped.

Moments later it rang again.

'What.' Her voice sounded like it was a long way off, even to her.

'Flora. It's me. Are you OK?'

Taryn, at last! Her best friend, the only person who would understand the devastation . . .

'Oh, Tabby . . . ' Tears started. Only moments since she'd opened her eyes and everything was there despite the headache thumping inside her skull. Polly was dead, Polly was dead . . .

49

'Flora? What's the matter? I know about Dad, if that's what you were calling about. The police came round to work yesterday. I got your messages and—'

'Polly's dead.'

'Polly? What? Flora, how?'

Flora took a moment, a few deep breaths to steady herself, prepare her voice. 'She was murdered, Tabs. Someone hit her on the head. The night before last. They don't know who. I've been trying to ring you, but there were so many people at the farm, and Mum's gone mental, of course.'

Shocked silence, then, 'Barbara's dead, too!'

'What? How? And what's happened to your dad?'

'I don't know about Barbara, I didn't wait for them to tell me. I suppose it was a car crash or something. Dad had a heart attack. He's in the hospital – they said he's critical but they don't know him, do they? He's a tough old sod . . . ' Her voice trailed off. And then: 'I didn't realise. Poor, poor Flora, I'm so sorry about Polly.'

'There's been nobody I can talk to about it. Mum – well, you know what she's like. And she found her, Polly, I mean. Oh Tabs, I missed you so much yesterday.'

'Where are you? Do you want me to come round now?'

Flora ran a hand through her hair. 'No, I've got to go back to the farm. Maybe – could I come round to yours later? I can't go back to the flat and I certainly don't want to stay with *them*. Would you mind? And what about Chris?'

'Chris won't mind at all. Have you still got the spare key?'

'Yes.' She had moved in for a fortnight in the summer, when Chris and Taryn had gone to France on holiday, to water the plants, keep an eye on things.

'Well, go round whenever you like. I'll make the spare bed up later. And Flora, it will be all right, OK? Everything will work out.'

No, it won't, Flora thought. How could it be? Nothing could ever be all right again. But what she managed to say was, 'OK. Thanks.'

'Deep breaths, Flora. Yeah? You have to get through this bit. This is the difficult part.'

'At least you haven't said I told you so!'

'What do you mean?'

'You always said she would break my heart . . . '

There was a pause. The tears were blinding Flora, pouring down her stinging cheeks. She rubbed them away with the back of her hand, sniffed.

'I didn't mean like this,' Taryn said quietly.

'You never really liked her, did you?'

'You know why that was,' Taryn said, with emphasis.

'She wasn't flirting with Chris,' Flora said, remembering Taryn's house-warming dinner party.

'She absolutely bloody was. She flirted with *everyone*, Flora, you know she did.'

'That's – that's simply how she was.'

'She wasn't good enough for you. There. I've said it.'

Flora couldn't speak. It was too much. She hated herself for the high-pitched wail that she couldn't hold in any more.

'Oh, Flora, I'm sorry. But you know what she was like; you deserve to be treated better than that. She was beautiful, but you deserve someone who is going to put *you* first, someone who is going to love you properly. I'd rather be honest with you – and I know she hurt you. It wasn't fair.'

51

After a moment Flora got control of herself again. 'Yes,' she said. Not meaning it.

'Will you be OK?'

'Yeah, sure.'

'I'll see you later? And you can ring me any time.'

Flora said goodbye and rang off, just in time for the tears to overwhelm her again.

07:52

The Op Nettle MIR was buzzing, full of people, and it wasn't even eight.

The press pack for the briefing was the first item on Lou's agenda. The Media Officer had started preparing it yesterday; had obtained photographs of Polly Leuchars and her car, written up a statement. First thing this morning the colour copiers on the command floor would be churning it out for the press conference.

Back in the incident room, the first bit of news from Forensics was a pile of fingerprint idents.

'Right, what have we got?' Lou asked, flipping through the pages. Jason was peering over her shoulder. He had on some very subtle aftershave. God, what was the matter with her? It wasn't as though she needed any distractions.

The first three pages were fingerprints taken from Yonder Cottage. Fingerprints identified were those of Polly Leuchars (all over the house), Felicity Maitland (downstairs only, including the downstairs bathroom), Flora Maitland (all over the house). Several other sets, some recent. And three clear prints made in blood, indicating someone present in the house when Polly was already dead or dying.

'Oh, crap!' Lou said, reading the final sentence again.

Prints in blood belong to Mrs Barbara Fletcher-Norman (print idents taken from cadaver). Others unidentified.

'Well, at least we know it's definitely connected,' Lou said.

A few pages further on, mention of shoemarks, badly smudged, at Yonder Cottage; a small size, indicating a child or a woman.

A few pages further on, fingerprints taken from inside Polly Leuchars' car, which had been parked, locked, in the driveway to the cottage.

'Prints belonging to the victim, Nigel Maitland, and three unidentified sets. That's a bit odd, don't you think?'

'Is it?' Jason replied.

'Well, how many different sets do you think would be in your car?'

Jason thought for a moment, his skin flushing. 'Well, quite a few. I had the car fixed a couple of weeks ago. Could have been several mechanics working on it, right?'

'Hmm, fair point I guess.' Lou made a note; someone would have to check the car's service history, get a list of people who were insured to drive it. 'Wonder why Nigel's prints are in there? He has better cars to drive than hers.'

'Maybe it was in the way and he moved it.'

'Maybe.' Next report, forwarded from Andy Hamilton – the prints from inside the kitchen of the Fletcher-Normans: two sets, his and hers. No others.

'We need Brian to wake up,' Lou said.

'The phone data is coming through,' Jason said. 'I need to start work on that.'

'Will it take long?'

'You're a hard taskmaster.'

When she looked up he was giving her a smile. Cheeky.

53

'Too right I am. You'd better get busy before I start thinking up penalties for slacking.'

07:57

Detective Superintendent Gordon Buchanan had descended like the Lord Almighty from the Command Floor to attend Lou's second briefing.

A small man, he made up for his lack of stature with a personality that demanded full attention, rewarded it with hearty good wishes and punished the lack of it with a merciless bellowing that put the fear of God into all those unfortunate enough to find themselves on the receiving end. Lou had worked for him on a previous case, had been lucky enough to spot something that should have been glaringly obvious, but which everyone else had missed. She took it to her colleagues first, who were grateful that she'd not taken the matter straight to Buchanan himself. They'd worked through the case but somehow Buchanan had got wind of what had happened and had had a soft spot for her ever since. He valued hard work and bright intelligence, and she was there ready to dish out both in spades.

In addition, she wasn't half bad-looking either, and as everyone knew, Gordon Buchanan liked his ladies.

He sat at the front, facing the room, a reminder that there would be hell on a stick if anyone made any unfortunate cock-ups and that if things went well, there might be future glory for whoever made the vital breakthrough that helped bring Polly Leuchars' killer to justice.

Lou was supposed to have offered him some sort of pre-briefing briefing, but she had been too busy. As she strode into the room ahead of everyone else she mouthed an apology. Buchanan pointedly

54

looked at his watch as though things were running behind schedule and he was a very busy man, but Lou was on time and she knew it. Her priority was the investigation, in any case, not sucking up to the boss.

'Sir,' she said, 'thanks for coming. I appreciate it.'

'Not at all,' he said, melting. For someone with such a lot of front, he was very easily buttered up. 'How's it going?'

'Rather well, I think,' Lou said, 'but it's very early days.'

'Thanks for your voicemail last night. I'm afraid you're going to get the other case too, by the look of it. However, I've managed to get you a couple more DCs, for now.'

Andy Hamilton was sitting behind Buchanan, chatting happily to Ali Whitmore, one of the DCs who'd been working on the Fletcher-Norman case yesterday. Who was the other one?

Lou had a PowerPoint presentation that Jason had knocked together for her with bullet points which had already emerged from the investigation.

'Right, thanks everyone, let's get on with it,' she said.

First slide, the Op Nettle title slide.

'OK, we've got the initial pathology report back which tells us that Polly was killed between midnight and two, no later than that. Priority for me is to trace her exact movements on the evening before she died. Andy, can you give us an update on the Fletcher-Normans?'

Andy coughed to make sure he had everyone's full attention. 'Right, well I understand we're working on the possibility of the cases being linked. If you weren't here yesterday, come and see me and I can give you an update after the briefing. To summarise: Barbara Fletcher-Norman was found around the same time as Polly. She was in her car at the bottom of Ambleside Quarry.

We're still waiting on the full PM report which should be later today. PC Richardson reported that when he went to give the death message to Brian Fletcher-Norman, there was blood in the kitchen of Hayselden Barn, as if someone had washed their hands in the sink. The Barn's been sealed since then, but until now we've not had the powers to go in. However, the CSI report from Yonder Cottage shows Barbara Fletcher-Norman's bloody finger-prints in the kitchen and the hallway. So she was in the cottage when Polly was dead or dying and we have a suspect, albeit a dead one.'

There was a little murmur from the people in the room.

'Thanks,' Lou said. 'Les, did you get back to Dr Francis about the seatbelt?'

Les peered round Andy Hamilton. 'Yeah. She had half fallen out of it when she was hanging upside down, but it was in place. I'm off back to the hospital in a minute for the rest of the PM.'

'When can we get CSI into the Barn, do we know?'

'Later today. Simon Hughes is going to be the Senior.'

Lou had all but forgotten that Buchanan was there; this was one of her favourite bits of the job, bringing everything together, prioritising, making sure that things got done and nothing was left out.

'OK. Our priority for today is to find out what the connection was between Polly Leuchars and the Fletcher-Normans. How's Miranda getting on with the Maitlands, anyone know?'

Jane Phelps said: 'She's still there. There seems to be plenty of people paying visits to the farm. Nigel Maitland claims he was out all day, came home late, last saw Polly a few days ago. He won't say anything else without his solicitor.'

'And the daughter?'

'She seems to be the most sensible one in the house, shame she doesn't live there.'

Lou thought for a moment. 'We should talk to her properly, I think. Get to know her a bit.' She looked around for a suitable person, aware that allocating tasks was something she should trust to her sergeant – old habits were dying hard. 'Andy, can you take that for me?'

He looked up in surprise. Did he think he'd done his bit?

'I've got meetings – I was going to brief the CSIs, sort out the Fletcher-Normans.'

He was trying it on, Lou thought. She took a deep breath. 'Nevertheless, since you're going to be across the road from the farm most of the day, I'd appreciate it if you'd take a moment to talk to Flora.'

'Jane's going to be at the farm all day.'

An embarrassed hush descended on the briefing room and for a moment they all faded into the background, even Buchanan, until it was just her and Andy, facing each other. It reminded her of the last confrontation they'd had, when she'd been in tears and he'd been tender, gentle with her, pleading. She hadn't backed down then, either.

There was a cough and Ali Whitmore raised a hand. 'Ma'am, I'd like to take that one if I can? I've worked on Nigel Maitland before so I might be able to bring something to that line of enquiry ... if it would help?'

Andy kept up the hard stare but didn't say anything else. It was tempting to push him to take the job but he'd been thrown a lifeline by Whitmore. Really, that had been embarrassing and unprofessional. He should have known better, and the room was charged with excitement now, as if they'd all enjoyed the little argument.

'That would be really helpful, Ali, thank you. Which brings us neatly on to intel,' Lou said briskly. 'Barry – anything useful?'

'We should be getting some stuff in this morning. One thing that did stand out for me, though, is that on the list of the farm employees is one Mr Connor Petrie. He's showing as a casual farm-hand-slash-groom. Been there since March.'

'Connor Petrie?' Lou echoed.

'One of the younger Petries. Son of Gavin Petrie and Emma Payswick, charming couple that they are.'

Lou smiled. 'Well, at least this one seems to have a job. But Ali, can you find out how Mr Petrie came to be employed by Nigel Maitland? That seems like an odd combination. You might need to put in a request for more intel. Anyone else interesting on the list, Barry?'

He shook his head. 'They've got a cleaner for the farmhouse, comes twice a week; various people who work with Nigel on the farm side of it, mostly casuals, but nobody jumps out. We're working our way through them.'

She had one eye on the clock – half an hour to go until she was in front of the press.

'Jane, how are we doing with the phones?'

'We don't have Polly's phone – wasn't in the cottage – but we've got Felicity's and Nigel's, although from the casual way he handed it over I would imagine it's clean. I don't know about the ones from the Barn, though.'

'Andy?'

He looked pissed off. 'I'll get back to you on that one. Leave it with me.'

'I will,' Lou said. 'I want billings and cellsite for both their mobiles. Landline billing, too.'

'I've already applied for billings from the farm,' Jane said.

'Thanks, Jane. Can you make sure Jason's down as the appointed analyst?'

'I've done that.'

'Great. Where are we up to? I'm conscious of the time, so any urgent questions?'

She scanned the room looking for hands, for confusion in the faces, and her eyes stopped when she got to Jason. He was looking right back at her, attentive, interested. That was a good sign, at least.

08:21

BT151 – Message left on 01596 652144

'Hello, this is a message for Mrs Taryn Lewis from Sister Roberts of the Lionel Gibbins Ward, Briarstone General Hospital to let you know that your father has regained consciousness. Could you call me please on 921000 extension 9142. Thank you.'

PRESS RELEASE

Statement prepared by Eleanor Baker, Media Officer for Eden Police, Briarstone police station

Briarstone police are appealing for witnesses following the murder of Polly Leuchars in the early hours of 1 November. Polly was a regular at the Lemon Tree public house in Morden and had visited the pub on the evening of 31 October, Halloween. Police would urgently like to speak to anyone who saw Polly in the pub that evening, or who may have any other information that might help the investigation.

'We're trying to build up an accurate picture of Polly's last day,' said Detective Chief Inspector Louisa Smith, leading the investigation. 'In particular, we don't know who Polly was meeting. Was it you? If so, I urge you to come forward now so that you can be eliminated from our enquiries.'

Twenty-seven-year-old Polly Leuchars was found at her home, Yonder Cottage, Cemetery Lane, Morden, on the morning of 1 November. She had been brutally assaulted and was pronounced dead at the scene.

Anyone with any information is asked to contact the Incident Room directly on 01596 555612. Alternatively, you can call Crimestoppers anonymously on 0800 555 111.

- ENDS -

08:58

'Andy,' Lou said.

He was disappearing out of the briefing room, quicker to his feet than any of the others. He froze when he heard his name.

'My office.'

She went back to the MIR next door, hoping he was following but determined not to look back at the arrogant piece of shit.

He came in behind her and closed the door. He didn't move to sit and she didn't request it. Instead they stood facing each other, the space in the small office made still smaller by his bulk. Even though she was wearing heels, he towered over her.

She waited for a moment, composing herself and wondering

how on earth she was going to do this, and at the same time as being angry with him – *furious* – she realised that this was the closest they'd been since everything had happened and she could feel the warmth from his body, and her body was reacting to it in spite of herself.

'I'm sorry,' he said, unprompted. 'It was unprofessional.'

'Yes,' she said. 'It was.'

He started to say something else, then stopped.

'What?' she said. 'Say it.'

'You should have known Ali Whitmore would have wanted to take that side of it. He did the last job on Maitland when he was in Intel.'

'I'm not bloody psychic!'

'Well, it all worked out for the best, then, didn't it?'

'I don't want you playing games like that again. I don't do pissing contests.'

In spite of her fury, Andy smirked. Damn the man! How was it possible to hate him quite so much and still find him attractive?

His shoulders had relaxed and he leaned forward slightly. 'It wasn't that long ago that we were proper friends, Lou . . . '

She didn't need reminding of it. 'Is that what you call it? Felt more like betrayal than friendship.'

'I didn't mean that. I just meant – sometimes I forget you're in charge. And I'm sorry.'

'It doesn't matter what rank I am, what rank you are,' Lou said. 'We're here to do a job, aren't we?'

'Sure.'

She waited for more, half-expecting him to bring up the one big subject that they were both ignoring, but he remained silent.

'I think we should leave it there. Now are you doing the press

61

conference with me, or are you too busy?' She smiled, to soften the sarcasm, and to her relief he took a deep breath and smiled back.

Opening the door of her office, the silence in the main room despite the number of people crowded into it made her realise that they'd probably all been watching through the glass, straining to hear.

She took five minutes in the Ladies to apply some lipstick and run a brush through her hair. Her cheeks were pink, her eyes staring back at her, challenging her to admit to the crushing weight of self-doubt that she was feeling. Why this case? Why not something nice and straightforward, like every other Major Crime job that had turned up in the last few months?

You asked for it, her reflection suggested insolently.

The main conference room at the Police Headquarters was full: lots of cameras being set up at the back, press of varying types chatting happily together as if they were all best friends.

Lou had had media training as part of the three-week Senior Investigating Officer's programme. They'd staged a press conference at which various police staff pretended to be members of the press, asking the most awful questions they could, with some sort of internal competition to see who could be the one to 'break' the poor trainee. They'd got the police photographer in with his big camera to flash away while they were talking. Part of the test was to see if you could remember to set the ground rules for the press conference before it started – no flash photography until the end, all mobile phones turned off, no questions until the end of the briefing. If you failed to do this, you'd have mobile phones going off left right and centre, flashing in your eyes the whole time, questions fired at you from the back of the room with no warning. You'd lose control of the room, lose your thread, lose your marbles.

'Good morning, ladies and gentlemen,' Lou said in a voice that sounded more confident than she felt. 'Thank you all for coming. My name is Detective Chief Inspector Louisa Smith and I am the officer in charge of this investigation. Before we begin, can I ask you please to turn all your mobile phones off? Thank you. There will be time for photographs at the end of the press conference, so I would ask you to refrain from flash photography until then. I would like to introduce my colleague, Detective Inspector Andy Hamilton – I will run through a brief summary of the pertinent points of the investigation, and then DI Hamilton and I will be happy to take your questions. We will also be issuing you with a press pack at the end of the briefing which contains photographs that can be used in your reports, together with a written statement. There are also telephone numbers for the incident room, which I would be grateful if you could make public for the benefit of those people who may have information for us to contact us directly. Thank you.'

She moved to the chart stand on one side of the table where she and Andy were sitting and flipped over the top sheet to reveal a photograph of Polly Leuchars, happy, smiling, blonde hair blowing away from her tanned face. How fortunate it was for the investigation that the murder of good-looking people always received more press attention than the murder of the unlovely. Lou had worked on the killing of a middle-aged prostitute and drug addict, back in the days when she was a new DC at the Met. They'd held a series of press conferences, and after the first one almost nobody came. None of their readers would be likely to know anything that would help anyway, one arrogant old hack had told her, as though they moved in certain circles and remained untainted by the detritus of life that floated past.

'We are currently investigating the brutal murder of a young woman,' Lou began, turning to face her audience and standing in front of the table behind which Andy sat. She knew it was much harder to be intimidated by your surroundings when you were standing up with no barrier between you and your audience.

'Polly Leuchars was twenty-seven years old, and was working as a groom at Hermitage Farm in Morden to earn some money to go travelling. In the early hours of Thursday, the first of November, Polly was violently assaulted in the hallway of her home, Yonder Cottage, which is part of the Hermitage Farm estate on Cemetery Lane. We are anxious to get a clearer picture of the events of Wednesday, thirty-first October, particularly in the evening, and we would like to appeal to anyone who has any information concerning where Polly might have been, and who she may have spoken to, on the day before she died. If anyone saw Polly's vehicle, which is a blue Nissan Micra, I would ask them please to come forward and speak to a member of the investigation team as soon as possible.'

There was silence as Lou scanned the journalists, some watching her intently, some busy scribbling notes.

'I would like to emphasise that we are dealing with the murder of a popular young woman who had her whole life ahead of her. Her family and friends are needlessly dealing with her loss, and our feelings and thoughts are with all of them at this tragic time. If anyone has any information that might help us find out who was responsible for this crime, I would ask them to come forward and contact us as soon as they can.'

Lou paused. Then, 'Thank you for your attention. Are there any questions?' While she waited for them to decide which was their most pressing question, she took her seat next to Andy. They'd agreed to take it in turns answering, and the Media Officer was in charge now.

'Yes – lady in the pink top.'

Hers hadn't been the first hand to go up, but Lou knew that this particular journalist had been promised the first question because of a recent favourable article she'd written regarding the Force's response to anti-social behaviour.

'Alison Hargreaves, *Eden Evening Standard*. DCI Smith, can you tell us anything about the death of Mrs Barbara Fletcher-Norman? Are the two deaths connected?'

Lou felt her cheeks flush.

'Thank you,' she said, 'we are not connecting the two incidents at this time. Next question.'

There was a sudden buzz as all the other journalists started wondering who the hell Mrs Barbara Fletcher-Norman was.

'Do you have any suspects at this stage?' This was from the local BBC Radio reporter.

Andy answered. 'At this key early stage of the investigation, we are keeping an open mind about who the perpetrator of the crime was.'

'Roger Phillips, *Daily Mail*. Any idea of a motive at this stage?'

Good question, thought Lou, and Andy was going to deal with this one too.

'Again, we are keeping an open mind. We cannot rule out the possibility that Polly woke in the night to find a burglary in progress.'

'Were there signs of a break-in?' Roger Phillips again.

'Next question,' Lou put in. She was only being fair – there were several other people with their hands up and she didn't want the enquiry to be pushed in one direction, especially not at this early stage.

'What about forensics? Have you got any fingerprints, stuff like that?' This one was from Lucy Arbuthnot, from the local ITV news network.

'Several sets of fingerprints have been identified at Polly's home address. We are in the process of eliminating them as we speak. If anyone visited Polly in the days before her death, we would be grateful if they would come forward so we can eliminate them from our investigations.' Lou was ready for something made of chocolate. It felt like the longest day of her life, and she was only a tiny bit of the way through it.

'This is a question for Ms Smith. Can I ask about your personal qualifications to lead a murder enquiry?' It was Roger Phillips, revenge for her failing to answer the break-in question.

Both Andy and Ellie the Media Officer looked like they were going to try and fight her corner, but she silenced them with a look.

'Thank you for that question,' she said with a wide smile that made it look as if she meant it. 'I have been a police officer for fifteen years, the last eight of them spent working on major crime investigations. Although this is the first time I have led a murder enquiry, I have worked on several murder investigations, both with Eden Police and the Metropolitan Police. I am proud to be running this case with a highly professional, highly trained team behind me and I am confident that we will bring Polly's killer to justice very soon.'

Ellie stepped in, despite more hands being raised. 'Ladies and gentlemen, thank you for your time. I have the press packs here . . .'

Andy and Lou posed behind the desk for a couple of photographs and did a couple of TV and radio interviews outside the front of the main building, saying the same things over and over again for the benefit of viewers and listeners on the BBC, Sky News, Five Live, Eden County FM and ITV local news. They would be lucky to get one or two lines out on air, so better make them good ones.

As soon as it was all over, Lou whispered to Andy: 'I really need a drink.'

'Coffee or something stronger?'

'Ideally coffee followed by something stronger, but I guess I'll have to settle for coffee.'

As they walked to the rear of the building to get access to the staff canteen, Andy said, 'I thought you did really well.'

'Thank you,' she said, still wary of him. 'So did you. Thank you for being there.'

Lou paid for three coffees and a KitKat for herself, a bacon sandwich for Andy, and then they walked back down to the MIR.

'One thing's for sure,' she said as she pushed open the heavy fire door, balancing her paper coffee cups on the back of her KitKat, 'we need to get to the bottom of the whole Fletcher-Norman thing before they do.'

If Andy thought he was going to accompany her into her office for more cosy chat, he was mistaken. 'Jason,' Lou said, passing his desk, 'can I borrow you for a sec?'

He ran a hand through his hair. 'Sure.'

Andy called after her, 'I'm going to go and catch up with Flora Maitland, boss. OK? I'll be on the mobile if you want me.'

Thank God for that.

'I got you a coffee,' Lou said as Jason shut the door.

'Thanks,' he said.

'How's the timeline?'

'It's OK. There's more coming in all the time, should be a lot more by the end of today, thanks to the press conference. I'll make sure it's up to date before I go tonight. Do you want me in tomorrow?'

'No,' she said. 'You deserve a weekend and I need to hang on to my overtime budget.'

'I don't mind.'

'Have you got nice things planned?'

Oh, subtle, she thought to herself, feeling her cheeks warming. What the hell was she doing? Wasn't it awkward enough with Andy Hamilton?

'Nope. I'd rather be in here getting on with it.'

Well, that was honest – give him credit for that.

'Really?'

'Sure. There's a ton of stuff to do – I don't really want to spend the whole of Monday catching up. I can take it as hours instead of overtime, anyway.'

'Well, thanks. See how you get on today and I'll leave it up to you, Jason. You know I'm really grateful for your help.' Lou slipped the lid off her coffee and emptied a sachet of sugar into it.

'Are you having briefings over the weekend?'

'Depends on what comes in. We'll have one this evening when the shift changes, then maybe an informal catch-up when we need one, until Monday.'

'Well, if you need my input you know where I am.'

'Thank you,' she said.

'No problem. Been a while since I worked a major incident.'

'What do you make of the whole Fletcher-Norman connection?'

'I'm trying not to get drawn on it. You realise that Polly is turning into quite something, don't you?'

'In what way?'

'Well, if any of the gossip is to be believed, she was having or had an affair with just about everyone in the village, male and female.'

'Really? God, the press are going to love this. Do you think it's simply gossip? Jealous wives, that sort of thing?'

'Might be, if there weren't such a lot of it. We've heard from a couple of her ex-boyfriends – there are intelligence reports and two statements already – and both of them were unceremoniously dumped after she refused to stop sleeping with other people.'

Lou sighed, taking a swig of coffee. 'This makes the whole motive question rather interesting, at least,' she said. 'I almost wish it were a simple burglary.'

'Nothing's ever that simple,' he answered softly. 'You know that.'

10:04

The worst thing was the smell. That was how he knew he was in hospital. His throat was sore from the tubes that were down it, his skin felt dirty, clammy, and he could smell himself. He couldn't speak because of the tubes, but his eyes were open now. And there was that bloody nurse, the loud one. He remembered her voice from somewhere. Somewhere he'd been that was dark.

'Brian? Are you all right there, Brian? Are you in any pain?'

Irish, of course. They all were. That, or Malay. And the doctors would all be Indian. All the good British nurses were earning a

MG11 WITNESS STATEMENT

Section 1 – Witness details

NAME:	Simon Andrew DODDS		
DOB (if under 18; if over 18 state 'Over 18'):		Over 18	
ADDRESS:	18 Oak Rise Brownhills Lewisham LONDON SE15	OCCUPATION:	Sales Manager

Section 2 – Investigating Officer

DATE:	Friday 2 November
OIC:	DC 13512 Jane PHELPS

Section 3 – Text of Statement

My name is Simon Dodds and I live and work in London. I heard from a friend who lives in Briarstone that Polly Leuchars had been murdered.

Approximately two years ago I had a relationship with Polly Leuchars. She had joined the company I worked for at the time, SVA Consultants Ltd, as a receptionist. A few weeks later I asked her out and she accepted. I thought she was a fantastic girl and I enjoyed being with her a lot.

A few months into our relationship she told me about someone else she was seeing. She said it very casually, as if it was no big thing, but I was upset. She was surprised at my reaction and explained that she was not into monogamy and I could not expect her to be faithful.

I was very upset by the whole business, although I was in love with her and could not end the relationship. I asked her about the other person she was seeing and she admitted that she was seeing more than one person, and that one of them was a woman. I asked her to stop seeing them and she told me she could not, and that it was better if we ended our relationship.

I tried to win her back but she was adamant, and the next day she handed in her resignation. I never saw Polly after that, although I have often thought about her. She was a hugely charismatic person and was very attractive. I am sorry Polly is dead, and I have no idea who killed her, although I do feel her lifestyle was unusual and may have contributed somehow to her death.

Section 4 – Signatures

....
WITNESS: (Simon Dodds)   OIC: (J. L. Phelps)

fortune in the Middle East. Where the hell was Barbara? Off playing bloody tennis or something. Never there when you needed her.

Why did they bloody keep asking him questions? How the hell did they expect him to answer when he had a mouthful of plastic tubing?

He raised a hand feebly to his mouth and the nurse slapped it down.

'Ah, no, Brian. Mustn't touch. We'll see about getting those taken out later, if you're up to it. Doctor will be around shortly.'

It was easier with his eyes closed, after all. The light was too bright, too loud. But in the darkness bad things waited for him. Something had happened – he couldn't quite grasp it – an accident? Had he been in an accident? He could see Barbara, and ... was that blood? He felt sick, the same way he'd felt when he'd hit his head on that bloody doorframe at the golf club. He must have had a head injury, or something.

And her? Of course, she would have no idea that he was in hospital. A tear slid unbidden and silent from the corner of Brian's eye. *I wish I could tell her*, he thought. *I wish she were here.*

11:50

Andy Hamilton considered himself to be easy-going and positive, but today was trying his patience almost to breaking point.

First off, Leah had chucked up all over his last remaining clean, ironed shirt and Karen had laughed when he'd asked if she had any idea where his clean shirts were. He'd had to drag one out of the washing basket and iron it while Karen got Ben's breakfast. And then he'd had to watch both of the kids while Karen had a shower.

71

Consequently he was nearly late for the briefing and wasn't giving it his full attention until he realised Lou had started picking on him.

He felt like he was being deliberately shown up in front of the others. Of course, the sensible way to handle it would have been to agree and then have it out with her later on. But he wasn't sensible, was he? He was an idiot, clearly, because he enjoyed picking verbal fights with people, especially women he fancied. He'd sorted it out anyway, told Ali he'd take on Flora to keep the boss sweet. Ali had looked disappointed, but he'd said nothing.

Waiting at the lights on Forsyth Road he closed his eyes slowly and pressed the flat of his palms onto the edge of the steering wheel.

Still fancied her, despite all the shit she'd given him last year. Maybe that made it worse, in fact, and in that moment he knew it to be true. He was more turned on by her anger than he'd ever been by her flirtation. What sort of a man did that make him?

Fourteen Waterside Gardens turned out to be a smart Victorian villa in the nicer end of Briarstone. Steps led up to two front doors, side by side, each with a neat sign indicating Flat 1 and Flat 2. Flat 1 had a small typed label which read 'Martin'. Flat 2 had nothing to indicate who might live there.

He tried Flat 2 first and couldn't hear any sound from within to indicate whether the bell actually worked. There was no reply.

The upstairs flat was in darkness, no sign of the red Fiesta on the gravelled area passing for a front garden, only a sleek black Mercedes.

Giving up on Flat 2, he tried the bell for Flat 1. This one he heard ringing from somewhere within. Through the frosted glass door he saw lights on towards the back of the house and after a long while a middle-aged woman wearing a navy-blue nurse's uniform answered the door. She was holding a coat and a bag, as though she was on her way out. He saw the uniform first, the fob watch above the curve of her breast, the way the dark cotton fitted close around her body, and then he raised his eyes to take in her attractive face, the short, ash-blonde hair, the ice-blue eyes. He produced his best smile.

'Sorry to trouble you,' he said, holding out his warrant card. 'Detective Inspector Andy Hamilton, Eden Police. I'm looking for Flora Maitland, from the flat upstairs. Any idea where she might be?'

'None at all,' the woman said in a voice that would freeze vodka. She'd taken Andy's wallet so that she could get a better look at the photo; when she'd examined it to her satisfaction she handed it back.

Andy watched as she pulled on her coat. Red gloves were pulled briskly on to her slender hands. As she shut the front door behind her he had a sudden mental picture of her snapping on a pair of surgical gloves and smiled to himself.

'Is she in some sort of trouble?' the woman asked.

'No. Just need to ask her something. If she comes back, could you ask her to call me, please?' He pressed his business card into her gloved hand.

'Of course,' she said, looking at him curiously. 'Although I'm unlikely to see her. She comes and goes at odd times, as do I.' She pressed her key fob and the central locking system of the Merc clunked invitingly.

He turned to go, wondering how she could afford it on a nurse's salary, but her voice, low, called him back: 'Inspector Hamilton?'

She waited until he was standing in front of her again, so he had plenty of time to appraise her. As well as the appeal of the uniform, she

MG11 WITNESS STATEMENT

Section 1 – Witness details

NAME:	Anthony MORTIMER		
DOB (if under 18; if over 18 state 'Over 18'):	Over 18		
ADDRESS:	Newbury House Bedlam Lane Baysbury Briarstone	**OCCUPATION:**	Corporate Lawyer

Section 2 – Investigating Officer

DATE:	Friday 2 November
OIC:	DC 13512 Jane PHELPS

Section 3 – Text of Statement

Polly Leuchars was my girlfriend before she moved to Morden. She had been living with me at my home in Baysbury, Newbury House, from January 2010 until December 2011. We met through mutual friends at a New Year's dinner party in Briarstone. Polly was living in a bedsit in the city at the time. I fell in love with her almost immediately. She was honest with me from the start and explained that she wanted an open relationship. This suited me because I have had partners in the past who have been very possessive; I thought Polly would be different, and she was.

Polly and I became involved with the swinging scene in London and we attended a couple of parties together where we both had sex with other people. We also met up with another couple a few times and had sex. Polly was very liberated and incredibly attractive. Because of this I felt I had met my life partner and I asked her to marry me in November last year.

She was upset by this and turned me down. I tried to explain that I was happy with our lifestyle but she didn't want to listen. We had a long discussion about it and we were both rather upset. In the morning she was gone. She left a note to say she had gone to stay with some friends and that our relationship was over.

I saw her about a week later when she returned to the house to collect her possessions. I tried once again to ask her to stay, but she refused. She seemed very happy and relaxed, I presumed by this she had met someone else, although she didn't say she had.

I saw Polly again in Briarstone a few times this year, but on neither occasion did I speak to her. The last time I saw her was in May or June. She was walking with another girl through the precinct near where I work.

I am now involved in another relationship.

I was very upset to read about Polly's death in the newspaper and I do not know who may have killed her.

Section 4 – Signatures

WITNESS: (A J R Mortimer)   OIC: (J. L. Phelps)

was very attractive; her eyes, although they were cold and an unnerving pale blue, were bright and focused on him. He felt the hairs stand up on his arms.

'She has a studio. I'm not sure of the address, but she's probably there.'

'A studio?'

'She's an artist. A very talented one.'

'Thank you. Mrs ... ?'

But she was already heading for the car, her back to him. He had been dismissed. Charming, he thought. Bet she was a winner with the patients.

He went back to his own car, spent some moments jabbing with his massive fingertips at the screen of his non-work-issue iPhone, trying to persuade it to Google 'Flora Maitland artist'.

Proves my point exactly, he was thinking. That woman had been cold to the point of rudeness and now all he could think about was what she might be like in bed. He'd always had a bit of a thing for nurses.

The phone wasn't going to cooperate, and the signal here was crap. Quicker to go back to Hermitage Farm and ask the Maitlands. Flora was probably there anyway.

12:40

Miranda Gregson answered the door to the farmhouse.

'Are they up to seeing me?' Andy asked. 'Don't suppose Flora's put in an appearance?'

'She was here earlier. Left about half an hour ago.'

'Bloody typical, that is. Just my luck.'

Felicity Maitland was having coffee in the kitchen with two other women. They were huddled around a cafetière and three bone china mugs, looking to Andy's eyes rather like *Macbeth*'s three witches, no doubt discussing the case and solving it all by themselves.

'Mrs Maitland, sorry to trouble you again.'

'Oh! It's you, Inspector Hamilton. No trouble at all. Would you like some coffee?' Felicity Maitland had taken a shine to him, not something he was unused to. Under normal circumstances he would have declined the offer, but he felt that this conversation might be valuable. 'I'd love a coffee, thank you.'

Sitting down, he was aware of the subtle changes in the body language and posture of the three ladies: stomachs pulled in a little, sitting up a little straighter, turning oh so slightly so that all three of them were facing him.

'Have you met Marjorie and Elsa, Inspector?'

'I'm afraid I haven't had the pleasure . . . ' He knew how to turn on the charm and he enjoyed all the attention, even if there was part of this flirting that slightly turned his stomach.

'Marjorie Baker, my bridge partner, and Elsa Lewington-Davies, Ladies' Captain of the Seniors' Tennis.'

They cooed up at him. Wasn't Marjorie the old trout who had suggested Brian Fletcher-Norman was having an affair with Polly?

'It must be a very difficult life for you, Inspector. Do you get much time off?'

'Please, call me Andy. Yes, one sugar, thank you.' He was wondering how quickly he could steer the conversation around to a point where he might learn something useful. 'It's not so bad. There are quiet periods as well as busy ones. But of course you get to meet some lovely people.' Smiling round at present company.

'And some nasty ones too, no doubt,' Marjorie Baker added. She must have been pushing seventy, but still looked after herself: unnaturally blonde hair that was being allowed to meld gently with the grey; a complexion that had seen the benefit of many expensive treatments over the years. Make-up that was subtle and did justice to her age as well as her fading beauty.

'Have you made much progress? We all think it's a simply dreadful thing to happen, and in Morden of all places! Shocking really.' This last from Elsa. She was younger, dressed more casually, looking like she was fighting to stay in touch with the generation that came after her.

'We're still working on several lines of enquiry,' he said noncommitally, but allowing a lingering look to pass between him and all three of his companions.

'And, may I ask,' Marjorie said with a slight cough, 'would the Fletcher-Normans be one of those lines?'

Andy smiled at her, as though in deference to her sharp mind. 'I really shouldn't,' he said conspiratorially, 'but yes, we have been investigating recent events at the Barn in case they might be linked to the murder.'

'I knew it!' Marjorie said triumphantly. 'He's a dreadful man, that Brian Fletcher-Norman, I've always thought so.'

'Rubbish,' interjected Elsa. 'You used to fancy the pants off him.'

'Nevertheless,' Marjorie continued, 'I saw him coming out of Yonder Cottage late that night. And when I knocked at the door, there was poor Polly in her dressing gown. He took advantage of an impressionable young girl, there's no doubt about it. He probably killed her when she started to see sense.'

'Marjorie, really!' Felicity was looking slightly uncomfortable because Andy was there. 'I'm sure Inspector – I mean – Andy, doesn't want to hear about our theories.'

77

'On the contrary. You ladies know more about this village than I'll ever know. Something you've seen, something seemingly minor, might be the key that cracks this case. Tell me, what was Mrs Fletcher-Norman like?'

They paused, and the replies when they came were a little too measured for Andy's liking.

'She was a reasonable bridge player,' said Marjorie.

'Her tennis wasn't bad either. Especially after she had those lessons,' Elsa added.

'I thought her common,' said Felicity, and got an admonishing look from the other two. 'Well, she was! Even though she tried hard to act like the Lady of the Manor. Remember that dinner party we had, not long after Polly arrived? She was perfectly beastly when she'd had a few glasses of wine and poor Brian had to take her home, saying she wasn't herself. Don't you remember, Elsa? You were there. Marjorie, I rather think you were in Spain – or was it Jamaica?'

Andy's phone rang at that moment. He mouthed 'excuse me' to the women and went outside.

'DI Hamilton.'

'Andy, it's me,' Lou said. 'Can you talk?'

'Yes, it's fine.'

'The hospital phoned. Brian Fletcher-Norman is awake and they say we can talk to him briefly. I'm sending Sam down with Ali Whitmore because everyone else is busy. Thought you should know.'

'Sounds good to me,' he said. 'I'm at the farm.'

'How are you getting on with Flora?'

'Haven't managed to track her down yet.'

'Well, you don't need to worry about the phones for Hayselden

Barn. Jane's got all the numbers and she's put the billing application in already. For now, you're down as the officer in the case.'

'Right.'

The call ended. Was she deliberately trying to make him look like he didn't know what he was doing? Because it felt exactly like that. He was a DI, for fuck's sake; he'd been a DI when she was still a probationer. What was she trying to prove?

He went back to the kitchen. Whatever it was they'd been talking about, they all stopped when he came in and turned and looked at him. Felicity was looking very pink. He took a deep breath.

'You all keep yourselves very fit,' he offered as an opening gambit. 'Did Polly play tennis?'

Elsa made a noise. 'I don't believe she did.'

'She kept fit in other ways,' said Marjorie, meaningfully.

Felicity cleared her throat. 'She was very busy at the stables most of the time. When she had time off, I think she went to the pub, or she was off out with friends.'

'Anyone in particular?' Andy asked.

'Oh, Lord knows. She didn't tell me anything.'

'What about Connor Petrie, was she friends with him?'

'You all seem very interested in the Petrie boy, don't you?' Felicity said sharply. 'Why's that, I wonder?'

Andy leaned back in his chair. 'Well, they must have spent a lot of time together at the stables. I thought they might have been friends.'

'She was perfectly pleasant with him, but I wouldn't have said they were friends. He followed her around like a little puppy until she gave him something to do. I remember her telling Flora about it.'

'What about Flora, was she friends with Polly?'

'I suppose so, they went out into town occasionally, although not for a while. Flora's been spending more time at the studio recently.' She gave a strange, high-pitched sort of laugh. 'Actually, I was starting to think she was avoiding me.'

'Why would she do that?' Marjorie asked, before Andy had a chance to.

'I have no idea. She used to stay over at the farm all the time in the summer, every day. I asked her why she'd gone back to her flat and she said she was busy with her painting. But I don't know.'

Andy saw a glance pass between Elsa and Marjorie and wondered what it was they weren't saying. He decided to risk stirring things up, see what might float to the surface.

'Mrs Newbury at Willow Cottage. Is she someone you know?'

Felicity straightened in her chair. 'That old witch,' she said. 'You don't want to pay any attention to her.'

'She's a nasty old gossip,' Elsa said. 'Her husband ran off with one of the partners at his firm two years ago and she couldn't deal with it.'

Andy made a note. They were watching him like hawks now.

'She was very pretty, wasn't she?' Andy coaxed. 'Polly, that is. I'm surprised she was single.'

There was a silence, then eventually Elsa said: 'Well, *I* liked her. She was fresh and bright and always seemed to be happy.' She bit her lip and continued, 'I'm sorry for her, sorry she's gone. She was a nice girl, despite everything . . .'

'Despite what?' Andy asked, unable to help himself.

But after Elsa's glowing recommendation, none of them seemed willing to elaborate on this. They had all fallen quiet, and Andy thought he had probably reached the limits of their sociable conversation. The rest of it was up to Miranda Gregson, who had tactfully left him alone to do his thing.

'Mrs Maitland, thank you very much for the coffee, but I'm afraid I must leave you. It's been lovely to meet you all.'

They cooed their goodbyes and Felicity rose to show him out. 'You simply must call me Felicity – all my friends do.'

Andy treated her to his best smile. 'Felicity, I did want to ask one thing. I've been trying to get in touch with Flora but I keep missing her. Any ideas where she might be?'

'Oh,' Felicity said, her voice quavering as it tended to do when people demanded something of her, 'I'm not really sure. She might be at the studio.'

'Where's that?'

'On the road to Briarstone, just past the fire station. There's a few industrial units, her studio is on the upper floor, above the printing shop. I'm afraid I'm not sure of the actual address.'

'Don't worry,' Andy said, soothingly, hiding his rising impatience. 'Do you have a mobile number I could catch her on?'

13:21

Flora wasn't in her studio. She was sitting in the car outside, looking up at the big windows, thinking of the canvas in there and wondering if she'd ever be able to look at it again.

Crying again, of course. How long would it take before she could think of Polly and not cry? It wasn't even as if they'd been together when it happened. It had finished months ago. But that didn't stop the hurt, didn't make it any less; didn't make any bloody difference.

The canvas was huge, swirls of green and gold, flashes of navy, dots of bright red.

It was an abstract, and it was based on the memories of what had happened in the top field at Hermitage Farm. The field where, on that hot spring day when the world had seemed so suddenly full of promise, Polly had kissed Flora for the first time. And then, when Flora had looked at her in amazement and kissed her back, Polly had pushed her gently into the shade of the trees, the buttons being undone one by one whilst Polly met her gaze and smiled at her surprise.

Flora had been breathless, stunned, unprepared for how she would feel the moment Polly's cool hand slipped over her burning skin. She didn't wear a bra – nothing worth putting inside one – so when Polly's fingers met her bare nipples they reacted instantly.

The taste of Polly, the coldness of the lemonade they'd shared, the smell of the hot, baked earth, the horses on Polly's clothes, her own sunburned skin, the salt of her sweat on Polly's fingers, the softness, the incredible softness of her mouth . . .

And she had lain back, the ground hard beneath her shoulders, breathing hard while Polly's hand inside her jeans brought her to orgasm, looking up at the pattern made by the sunshine through the leaves on the trees, such a bright, bright green, and somewhere nearby a blackbird sang a song of uplifting joy whilst Flora writhed, clutching Polly's wrist with one hand, the other buried in that thick blonde hair.

That was what she had been trying to paint.

It had been a way of dealing with the way things had finished between them at the end of August. She had stayed away from the farm, avoided Polly as much as she could. And it had hurt that Polly hadn't really pursued her, hadn't asked her why, had seemingly carried on with her life as though nothing had happened. Finishing the painting had been like a catharsis and Flora had believed that when it was completed she would have what they called closure.

But this was different. How could she ever finish it, when Polly had been taken from her? How could she ever even look at it again?

No point staying here – she wasn't going to be able to paint today. She turned the key in the ignition and drove back out towards the town.

13:25

'Slumming it a bit, aren't we, Sarge?' Ali Whitmore said with a smile on his face, as Sam Hollands crossed the car park towards him.

'What's that?' she said, not hearing him – or maybe pretending not to.

'Interviewing with me.'

'Boss clearly thinks you can't manage on your own. How are you getting on?'

Ali dropped his voice, although there was nobody near enough to hear them. 'Bits and pieces coming in on Maitland; still the same stuff he was up for when I was working on him – you know, all the trafficking, the links to the McDonnells. We had a couple of arrests and convictions – drivers, dealers, none of the big nobs though. Whatever we did, Nigel Maitland came up clean. Felt like he'd been tipped off, it was that obvious, but we couldn't get any further with it.'

'Happens a lot,' Sam said. 'Karma says one of these days we'll get to put him away.'

'Yeah,' Ali said. 'Fingers crossed for this job, then. I can't wait to see that smarmy bastard locked up.'

The Intensive Care Unit sister looked them up and down appraisingly, as though she could sense them bringing germs into her domain. They were shown to the antibacterial hand gel, and she watched them closely as they rubbed the stuff into their hands.

'He only woke up this morning,' she said, 'and had the tubes removed a couple of hours ago, so he's still very tired and out of sorts. I don't want you upsetting him if you can help it.'

'Is he aware that his wife is dead?' Ali asked.

'Yes, but I'm not sure how much you'll be able to get out of him, so don't expect miracles.'

'How is he, physically?'

'He's fine, for now. We take things one day at a time with heart attacks. And his was particularly nasty, you should be grateful he's here at all.'

More grateful than you could possibly realise, thought Sam.

Brian Fletcher-Norman was propped up at an angle of about forty-five degrees, connected to various machines. His eyes were closed and monitors attached to the wires coming out from underneath his blue hospital gown kept reassuringly steady beats. Sam looked at the grey chest hair at the neck of the gown and wondered idly how much it would hurt when they took off the sticky pads. Maybe they'd shaved those bits underneath . . .

'Mr Fletcher-Norman? Brian?'

The eyes opened and swivelled round to Sam's face. He managed a smile, although he was pale.

'I'm Detective Sergeant Sam Hollands, and this is my colleague, Detective Constable Alastair Whitmore.' She took Brian's hand, resting on the white sheet that reached up to his waist, half shook it and half gave it a gentle squeeze. 'I wonder if we could take up a few moments of your time.'

'As you can tell,' said Brian, 'I'm not exactly busy.' His voice was a little hoarse, but otherwise strong and with a resonance that was curiously attractive.

'I wish we were meeting under other circumstances, Mr Fletcher-Norman. I'm very sorry about the death of your wife.'

His gaze fixed at some point in the middle distance. 'You must call me Brian.'

'Thank you. How are you feeling, Brian?'

He gave a little shrug. 'Quite tired ... Do you know any more about what happened to my wife?'

'That's why we're here, I'm afraid. Can you tell us a bit more about that day? About what happened?'

Brian cleared his throat weakly. 'I said goodbye to her in the morning as usual. Well, she was still in bed asleep when I left. I don't – don't remember much about the evening. I got home late. Barbara – she's often out in the evenings, playing bridge or tennis, or at dinner parties or whatnot.'

He paused for a moment, brows furrowed.

'I've been trying to remember. I sat in the living room, drank a whisky. Read some papers from work. Then I went up and had a bath, went to bed.'

'So you didn't see Barbara in the evening?'

A long, long, pause. For a moment Sam wondered if he was drifting off to sleep.

Then he sighed: 'I don't remember. It's very hazy. I wasn't feeling well.'

'And in the morning?'

'I didn't set the alarm because Thursday isn't one of my working days. I woke up some time after nine, had a shower. I was going down the stairs when I heard the door knock, and it was the – the police officers.'

'So you didn't go into the kitchen at all?'

'I don't think so. No. I didn't.'

Sam took his hand again, gave it a little squeeze. There had been a tremor in his voice, his eyes filling slightly. He was a handsome man, despite his circumstances and still looked strong, fit. No wonder Polly had been attracted to him – if that rumour was true.

'Brian, I'm not sure if you're aware of this, but Polly Leuchars was murdered in the early hours of Thursday morning.'

She'd kept hold of his hand, knowing that his reaction to this news was fairly crucial. The monitor tracking his heartbeat noticeably speeded up. He was looking at Sam again, eyes wide.

'Polly? What – what on earth happened?'

'She was attacked at Yonder Cottage. Brian, I am so sorry about this, but you realise there is a question I have to ask you.' Sam's voice was gentle. 'Is there any reason why Barbara might have wanted to harm Polly?'

The eyes closed. There was a long pause. Sam was desperate for him to say something, as she could sense the approach of the sister and knew she did not have long.

'Brian?'

'Barbara was a very jealous woman. Polly and I were friends. She'd given me riding lessons at the stables in the summer. We had – we had some arguments about it, so I gave them up. But I never thought ...'

His hand gave Sam's a little squeeze.

As expected, the ward sister's footsteps squeaked across the lino towards them. 'Now, Brian, are you feeling all right?' She started fussing around the monitors, checking things.

'Quite well, thank you.'

'Just a few more minutes, then,' she said, with a strong warning look towards Sam before she headed back to the nurses' station.

'Barbara was suffering from depression,' Brian continued without any prompting. 'Had it for ages. Finally got some drugs from the doctor a few months ago. She didn't drink a lot, but it affected her badly when she'd had a few too many.'

'Do you think she had been drinking that night?' Sam asked.

86

'Probably. She drank most nights.'

'OK.' Sam took Brian's hand in both of hers and held it for a moment. 'Thank you for your time, Brian, I understand this must be very difficult for you.'

He gave her a weak smile.

'Is there anyone we can contact for you? A friend, a neighbour?'

Brian shook his head sadly. 'You could try my daughter, but I doubt she'll come.'

Sam wanted to ask him about that, too, but the sister was back again. 'I'll show you out, officers,' she said, in a voice that invited no argument.

At the door, she asked: 'What about his daughter? Have you spoken to her?'

Ali said: 'We spoke to her briefly; we'll go back to her now Mr Fletcher-Norman is awake.'

'See if you can persuade her to come. He needs somebody and this would be a good time for a reconciliation.'

'Is he likely to make a full recovery?' Sam asked.

'You'll need to speak to the doctors, but he isn't out of the woods yet by any means.'

'Please do call us if he remembers anything, won't you? Please?' Sam asked, handing her a business card.

Then Sam was marching down the corridor, heels sounding loudly, Ali having trouble keeping up. 'I hate hospitals,' she said passionately. 'I'll see you at the station later,' she said, without even looking back.

14:12

Flora's studio bore little resemblance to Felicity's description, the building being a converted mill rather than a purpose-built industrial unit – and the office downstairs was a management consultancy, not a printer. A nice place to work, Andy thought, admiring the landscaped lawns and flowerbeds around the building. The door that led directly to the stairs and the upper floor had a handwritten sign taped to the inside of the glass which said 'No junk mail thanks'. There was a buzzer, which also had a handwritten note: F MAITLAND STUDIO.

F Maitland was not there. The buzzer remained unanswered, and the car parking space reserved for the studio was empty. The office downstairs was also locked.

Andy Hamilton sat in the car and dialled the mobile number he had been given for Flora Maitland. It rang several times and went to answering machine. He thought about leaving a message, but decided against it. Waited for a few moments and dialled again. This time it was answered.

'Hello?'

'Is that Flora Maitland?'

'Yes. Who is this please?'

'Detective Inspector Andy Hamilton. I'm working on the Polly Leuchars murder investigation.'

There was silence on the other end.

'I'm sorry about Polly. She was a friend of yours, wasn't she?' He had an instinct that being official wasn't going to get him anywhere with Flora, so he decided to try sympathy instead.

'Yes,' came a small voice.

'Flora, I wondered if I could meet up with you today? I need to get more of an idea about what Polly was like, who her friends were, what she liked to do. I get the feeling you would be the best person to help me out with that.'

A longer pause.

'Are you in Briarstone? I could meet you for a coffee, if you like?'

'I guess so,' Flora said.

Like pulling teeth. 'How about if I meet you in the Caffè Nero on the corner by the old post office? About three? How does that sound?'

'OK.'

'Flora? You won't stand me up, will you?'

He thought he could almost detect the hint of a smile in her reply: 'No, I'll be there.'

He was on the outskirts of Briarstone now, joining the back of the queue to the town centre car parks. He wondered what sort of day Lou was having, whether she was making progress and whether she would bother to keep him updated. He still had a lot of ground to make up with her, he knew, but despite her best efforts to persuade him to the contrary, he could not quite believe that everything between them was over. She had been one of the best shags of his life. She hadn't been the first of his trips 'over the side', as his colleagues put it, and she probably wouldn't be the last. He didn't think of it as cheating. There had been no real emotional connection with any of his sexual partners. The one who had come closest, however briefly, was Lou, so it was probably a good thing that it had ended when it did.

He remembered the moment Lou had found out that he wasn't single at all, the fury in her eyes. She had made him promise that he was going to come clean with his wife and tell her he'd had a fling, ask for her forgiveness, otherwise she would do it herself. He believed her.

'Why?' he'd said. 'If it's all over between us, Lou, why do I have to tell her? She'll ... she'll be devastated.' He'd been going to say 'She'll kill me,' which was nearer the truth, but realised that Lou would probably have been even more in favour of it if she knew that would be the reaction.

There were tears in Lou's dark eyes but her voice was cold. 'You have to tell her, Andy, because you have to start learning that there are consequences to your behaviour. And if she knows about this, then it's much less likely that you'll feel inclined to try and resurrect things with me. Do you understand?'

The following morning he told her that he'd confessed to Karen. 'How did she take it?'

As if you care, he'd thought, but he'd answered: 'She was pretty upset. She's gone to stay with her mother for a few days, taken Ben with her.'

She'd seemed satisfied, which was a relief, because it was all a complete fabrication. In reality he would have no more confessed to Karen than he would take up a vow of celibacy. Karen might only be five foot one, but she had a fearsome temper on her and he was genuinely scared of her reaction. Besides, Karen was fine just as she was. She had no need to know; as long as Andy had no intention of actually leaving her for someone else, why trouble her with information that was only going to hurt them both?

Of course, Lou had been partly right; he still had this feeling like they had unfinished business. He thought of her sometimes, late at night, when Karen was asleep, her back to him.

TEXT MESSAGE

07194 141544 To 07484 322159
02/11/12 1416hrs

Police want to interview me later. Can u be there with me? 3pm in town. Call if u get chance. F Xx

14:19

The MIR was quiet when Lou got back from an update meeting with Buchanan. He'd bid for additional resources on her behalf at the Tactical Meeting, and she now had a tiny overtime budget. And even more pressure for a quick result.

She'd thought the office was empty but Jason was there, focused on the computer screen. From her office, sitting at her desk, she could glance to the side of her screen and see him in profile: good cheekbones, a strong jawline and a straight nose, short, dark hair that would have been curly if he'd let it grow. He moved abruptly and she looked quickly back to her own screen, feigning fascination with it as he tapped on the doorframe.

'Hi!' she said brightly.

'I wondered if you'd like a coffee?' he said.

She stared at him for a moment, as if he was a figment of her hormonal brain.

'I've got a better idea,' she said. 'Would you like to see the scenes? I think it helps to see where everything is.'

'Sure, that would be great.' He gave her a smile, then, and it lit up his face.

14:52

'We can go to Reg's office,' Taryn said. 'He's not here today. What do they want to see you about, Flora, do you know?'

Flora shook her head. She looked rough, Taryn thought, her hair unwashed, dark circles under her eyes. 'They haven't interviewed me yet. The guy that wants to meet me – he said he thought I could give them some more information about the sort of person Polly was.'

Taryn almost laughed at this. 'Never a truer word, huh? You know her better than almost anyone. If only they realised.'

'What on earth am I going to say to him, Tabs?'

'You answer his questions as truthfully as you can. You don't have to tell him you had a relationship unless he asks you. And if he does ask you, tell him the truth.'

'The truth?'

'Flora, you don't have anything to be ashamed of.' She put her hand on Flora's knee, squeezed it reassuringly. 'You fell in love, that's all. And Polly loved you back, in her own way. What's wrong with that? You're less likely to be the one who killed her than someone who didn't love her, after all, aren't you?'

'Did she, Tabs? Did she love me back?'

'Of course she did.'

'They'll suspect me, then, won't they? After all it's usually the victim's partner. They just don't know who the victim's partner was yet.'

Taryn bit her lip to stop herself saying it out loud. *You weren't her partner.* 'I thought it was all over between you two?'

Flora was rubbing the palm of her hand over her jeans, over and over again, as though her skin was itching. 'It was. I mean, we weren't together. But she wasn't with anyone else. I was the last one. The last proper relationship she had.'

Taryn let the words 'proper relationship' hang in the air between them like a tattered piece of tinsel.

'Are you sure? You hadn't seen her for ages.'

'I saw her a couple of weeks ago, only briefly. I went to the farm to see Mum. You know I'd been avoiding them. Polly saw me as I was leaving. She wanted to talk but I – well, I didn't want to listen. I was too scared of falling for her again.'

'What did she say?'

Flora shrugged and said nothing.

MG11 WITNESS STATEMENT

Section 1 – Witness details

NAME:	Ivan ROLLINSON		
DOB (if under 18; if over 18 state 'Over 18'):		Over 18	
ADDRESS:	The Lemon Tree Cemetery Lane Morden Briarstone	OCCUPATION:	Publican

Section 2 – Investigating Officer

DATE:	Friday 2 November
OIC:	DS 10194 Samantha HOLLANDS

Section 3 – Text of Statement

I am the landlord of the Lemon Tree public house, which is situated on Cemetery Lane in Morden, about half a mile away from Hermitage Farm.

Polly Leuchars was known to me as she visited the pub regularly, probably once or twice a week at least. She met friends in the bar, and she was well known to the other regulars too.

On Wednesday 31 October I recall Polly came into the bar at around 8.30. She ordered a vodka and Coke and sat with it at one of the tables to the rear of the bar area. I did think she would be meeting someone because she was sitting alone, and because she was wearing smart clothing. She was usually more casually dressed. She had black trousers on with a white blouse, and she was wearing make-up. Unless she was meeting a friend, Polly usually stayed at the bar and chatted either with me or with Frances Kember, our barmaid.

At 9 Polly was still on her own and came back to the bar for another drink. I joked that it looked like she'd been stood up, and she replied 'Seems that way, Ivan' or something of that nature. She did not look very happy.

Much later on, I'm not sure of the exact time, I saw Polly outside the pub talking on her mobile phone. You need to go outside as there isn't much of a signal. I didn't hear her speak. She sounded upset. I was putting some rubbish out into the bins and when she saw me she ended the call and went back inside.

Soon afterwards I noticed she had gone. I think it must have been between 11.30 and 11.45 that she left. I did not see her again after that.

Section 4 – Signatures

....

WITNESS: (Ivan Rollinson)   OIC: (S Hollands DS 10194)

Taryn tried again. 'How did she seem?'

'She was happy. As always. Happy and bouncy and completely at ease with life.'

The very opposite of the Flora who now sat opposite Taryn in the office, in fact.

Taryn found herself wondering how this policeman would react when he realised who she was. Would he be the same one who had been here yesterday, the one who had broken the news? Well, there was no need to explain anything. She was only going to be there in support of her friend. She didn't have to say anything, did she?

15:00

'That's got to be him,' Taryn said. 'He looks like a policeman.'

'How do you know what a policeman looks like?' Flora countered, eyeing the man in a suit who had come into the coffee shop and was looking around.

'He's on his own, and he's looking for someone. And it's not exactly busy in here. He's looking for a girl on her own; he's not expecting there to be two of us. It must be him.'

Flora got up and crossed to where Andy Hamilton was standing. 'Hello,' she said. 'Are you – I mean, are you looking for me?'

'Flora?' He held out his hand. 'I thought you'd be on your own.'

'I was meeting a friend. I hope you don't mind.'

'That's fine. I'll grab a coffee and I'll be with you in a sec. Can I get you anything?'

He seemed all right, Flora thought, as she went back to sit with Taryn. 'It's him. He's getting a coffee.'

'He looks like a rugby player,' said Taryn, and Flora smiled. Tabs had always had a bit of a thing for well-built men, and this one was

94

certainly well built and at least six foot tall. He had kind eyes, too. Flora felt a little bit better. But thank goodness Tabs was here.

'Detective Inspector Andy Hamilton,' he said when he got to the table, holding out his hand to Tabs. 'Your name is?'

'Taryn Lewis,' she said.

His expression told Flora that he'd not made the connection.

'I hope you don't mind,' Taryn said. 'I thought Flora could do with a bit of moral support.'

'No, no, that's fine. As long as you're happy?' This to Flora, who nodded.

'I'm going to take a few notes, if you don't mind,' Andy said, pulling his notebook out. 'Right. How about you tell me a bit about Polly. What was she like?'

Flora hesitated, biting back the tears that were ready to fall at the sound of that name. She cleared her throat. 'She – she was full of life. She was clever, witty, always smiling. Always happy.'

Flora fell silent, remembering.

'Did you know her too?' Andy asked Taryn, as though to give Flora a moment to collect her thoughts.

'I met her a couple of times. As Flora said, she was very bubbly and fun to be with.'

'Was she seeing anyone, that you know of?'

Both girls looked at each other.

'She saw lots of people,' Flora said slowly. 'Nobody serious. Not that I knew of, anyway.'

'Anyone recently? Or maybe she *spoke* of someone in particular?'

Taryn stepped in. 'She didn't talk about who she was seeing, ever. She was always discreet. But you can guarantee there was at least one person. More likely two or three.'

Andy, furiously scribbling, looked up. 'You mean she slept around?'

Flora made a little sound, like a sigh, but cross. 'No, she didn't sleep around. She had friends and she usually ended up having sex with them, that's all. She was always honest about it. But she had lots of partners. It's not a crime, is it?'

'Not at all. But maybe someone she was seeing didn't like it.'

He took a swig of his coffee, grimaced, added two sachets of sugar and stirred; all the while they watched him intently, not speaking.

'Flora, do you know the Fletcher-Normans? They live at the converted barn across the way.'

'I know where they live,' Flora snapped back. Taryn let out a nervous cough. This was getting into awkward territory. 'Yes, I know them.'

Before Andy could ask his next question, Tabby was standing. 'Excuse me,' she said. 'I'm going to the Ladies.'

Flora watched her go, understanding completely why she wanted to leave the table, and yet desperate for her to stay. 'Sorry, were you going to ask me . . . ?'

'Yes. I wondered whether the Fletcher-Normans also knew Polly?'

'Everyone knew Polly. It's a small village, Inspector. And one with a very active social life. Whenever Mum had one of her dinner parties, she included Polly. Polly played some golf at the golf club, sometimes drank in the golf club bar with my father and his cronies. Polly used to use the gym at the country club and half the village is in there most days. Just about the only thing she didn't get involved in was the bloody WI.'

'And the Fletcher-Normans?'

Flora's brow furrowed. 'I think Brian Fletcher-Norman came for riding lessons. I was living in Briarstone by then and not around much. But I remember Polly saying that he was fawning all over her.'

'Did she mind?'

Flora snorted. 'Polly *never* minded that sort of thing. She thrived on attention.'

'Do you think she had an affair with him?'

She wouldn't meet his eyes. 'Probably.'

'And Mrs Fletcher-Norman?'

'I don't think she was Polly's type.'

The policeman looked startled. 'I meant, did she know Polly too? Can you remember seeing them together at any stage?'

Flora managed a smile. 'I'm sorry, I knew what you meant. It was a little joke. I don't remember Barbara and Polly specifically. But Barbara was always at Mum's parties. They both were. Barbara used to get a bit loud when she'd had a few drinks and we always tried to make sure she didn't have too many. I believe Brian used to get her to drive whenever they went anywhere that was driving distance, so I think coming to the farm was Barbara's chance to get let off the leash, as it were.'

He smiled, and then he put in the blinder. 'And you, Flora?'

'Me?'

'You and Polly were friends?'

Flora blushed, stared at him. Tears were in her eyes before she could help them. Damn the man. 'Bit more than that,' she said, in a very small voice. Two fat tears fell into her lap; she rubbed at her eyes furiously.

'I'm sorry,' he said, his voice as gentle as he could get it. He put a hand to her knee. She didn't brush him off. 'I'm really sorry. This must be very difficult for you.'

'Yes,' she said again.

'So you were in a relationship?'

'Yes. I suppose you could call it that.'

'Had you been together long?'

'We weren't really "together" as such. She was with other people. It's – it's the way she was. It was very difficult to deal with. But I was in love with her. I hadn't seen her for a while. Since late August. I went back to my flat in Briarstone and I was busy with work. I only saw her once or twice since then. So it was all over, really.'

'Right.'

Although Flora strained to look, she could not decipher what he'd written.

'Was that why you moved out of the farm?'

Flora swallowed. 'Partly. I had some arguments with my dad. He wanted me to get involved in the farm more. Help out with the business. I – I didn't want to do that.'

'What about Polly? What did she think?'

That brought a smile to Flora's lips. 'She thought I should tell him to shove the farm up his arse. She thought everyone should follow their dreams. Not let anyone tie them down.'

'But you didn't see her, after you moved out?'

'She was – she was involved with other people. I just couldn't deal with that any more. So I let things come to an end. There wasn't any argument, nothing like that.'

'Did you speak to her on the phone?'

'Sometimes. We kept in touch. Like friends, you know. But that was all.'

'So . . .' he said, flipping back through his notebook, 'you moved into the flat in Waterside Gardens?'

'I've actually had the flat there for years. I stayed at the farm a lot when I was with Polly, but after we . . . after it ended, I avoided coming to the farm and stayed in Briarstone instead.'

'And you have a studio?'

'Yes.'

'I've never met an artist,' he said.

I'm not surprised, Flora thought. He didn't look like he had much appreciation for the aesthetic.

'You said Polly was involved with other people, when you moved out. Can you tell me who?'

'I didn't want to know.'

'But you must have had an idea, Flora.'

He waited again. Let him wait. He would hear about Polly from everyone else in the village, let them gossip about Polly – she wasn't going to.

They were still staring each other out when Taryn came back. She cast a glance at Flora and saw the expression on her face.

'I told him about me and Polly,' she said.

15:14

They'd driven for almost three miles before he spoke.

'Are you OK?'

She was watching the road with a fixed expression, eyes forward. The weather was closing in and it was almost dark. Rain spattered on the windscreen and reflected on her face as they waited at traffic lights.

'Louisa?'

'Hmm? Sorry, I was miles away.' She turned to look at him then and for a moment could not look away.

'I asked if you're OK. You seem a little distracted?'

She managed a smile that didn't quite go up to her eyes. 'It was something somebody said earlier, I can't even remember what. But it's making me think about other things.'

There was a long pause as the traffic lights changed to green. The queue of traffic, however, did not move. They were waiting to join the long ranks of the commuters on their way home.

'I'm sorry,' she said at last, 'this was probably a bad idea. Bad timing, anyway.'

'I can think of worse places to be.'

She laughed. 'Are you sure?'

'So,' he said resignedly, 'if we're going to be stuck in traffic for an hour, you can tell me all about what's really bothering you.'

Another pause while she decided whether she really wanted to go there or not. After all, she had nobody else to talk to. Jason was as good a bet as any.

'Parental responsibility.'

'Ah.'

'Nobody is ever good enough for their parents, I find. Do you get on with yours?'

'Sure. I talk to them all the time. It's difficult being so far away sometimes.'

'Are they in . . .' she thought for a moment and then risked it: 'Canada?'

He smiled at her. 'Yeah. You know you wouldn't believe the number of people who assume I'm American.'

'Really? But the accent's completely different,' she said, glad that she'd made the right guess.

'I think so. But most Brits seem to get them easily confused.'

'How come you're here?'

He hesitated, looking out of the window. 'Kind of a long story,' he said. 'I've been here six years already.'

He hadn't actually answered the question but she let it go. 'Do you have brothers and sisters?'

'One brother, older. He lives over here too, works in IT. You?'

'I have a sister and a brother. My sister is happily producing babies. My brother is bumming around Europe at the age of twenty-nine, having never held a job down longer than four months. And they are both utterly wonderful in the eyes of my parents, whereas I am always sadly lacking. I've never been able to work it out.'

'Maybe their expectations of you are higher?'

'You're probably right, but how is that fair? No matter what I do, they always make me feel like a failure.'

'At least it keeps you striving.'

She laughed. 'Are you trying to make me feel better, Jason? Because it's not working.'

'You're probably too tough on yourself. I've no doubt they must be really proud of you and what you've achieved. But you're always pushing yourself to achieve more, and I'm sure that drive is in you, rather than in them.'

He had a point, of course. 'I think my mother will be happy when I'm married with two point four children, and my father will be happy when I've done that *and* got to Chief Constable.'

'Save that for next year.'

She looked at him, smiling because already she felt better, and the eye contact between them went on until the traffic began to move on and someone beeped behind her.

'So what about you? Don't you feel under pressure to start having kids?' It was the sort of flirting that you could almost get away with when you got to your mid thirties.

'I've fallen behind the field with that one,' he answered. 'I guess I've been single a bit too long.'

She waited, knowing that if he really did want to participate in this particular conversation, more would come along.

The traffic ground to a halt again. The rain was coming down so fast now the wipers were having trouble keeping up. There was a tension in the air that had nothing do with the storm. Lou felt the warmth of the air, almost thought she could feel him breathing. She felt his eyes on her face again and turned to look.

'Can I ask you something personal?' Jason said then.

'Go on.' She turned her gaze back to the road ahead.

'You and Andy Hamilton – is there something going on?'

'Shit. That *is* personal.'

'Sorry.'

'Why do you ask?'

He shrugged. 'Just curious.'

Lou sighed, wanting to be honest but also wanting not to rake over what she still thought of as something sordid. 'Yes, there was something going on, but there definitely isn't any more. And that's something I'd like to keep quiet, if possible. How's that?'

'So you're not seeing him any more?'

'No. He neglected to tell me he was married, I found out by accident, and that was that.'

Jason nodded slowly. 'Figures.'

For a moment she couldn't speak.

'Look, I'm sorry,' he said. 'I wasn't going to mention it. And you know I won't say anything, right? This is between you and me.'

'I'm sorry that you're seeing me in a really unprofessional light here. I did everything I could to do the right thing ... '

'I can see that,' he said. 'I'm sorry if I embarrassed you.'

'You didn't,' she lied. She thought she had detected a note of amusement in his voice.

102

'Good. Is this the place?'

Hardly realising it, Lou had driven all the way to Morden and they were pulling up on the driveway of Yonder Cottage. There wasn't a lot of room; two cars and a CSI van were already squeezed onto the gravel. Polly's car had gone for forensic examination.

They got out of the car. The rain had stopped, and the sun was trying to force its way through the breaking clouds.

'This is Yonder Cottage,' Lou said, although he could have seen that for himself by the slate sign hanging on the wall. 'There are two entrances to the farm – you can go further up this driveway which goes through a farmyard with barns and outbuildings, then curves round to the left and eventually you get to the farmhouse itself. There's another drive about a hundred yards further down the road, which also goes to the farmhouse.'

High heels sinking into the gravel, picking her way between the puddles, Lou led the way up the road to a five-bar gate on the opposite side. This time a handsome oak sign with gold lettering proclaimed it to be Hayselden Barn. From the road the driveway stretched between manicured lawn and flowerbeds up to a vast horse chestnut tree, and beyond it a black-timbered former barn.

'There you go,' she said. 'Not far, is it?'

He shaded his eyes against the sunshine. Lou was only aware that she was gazing at him like a teenager when he turned his head towards her and smiled.

'They must be seriously loaded,' he said. 'All of them. What does Fletcher-Norman do for a living?'

'Some sort of executive, shipping I think. Although he's supposed to be semi-retired.'

They walked back to Yonder Cottage. The road was quiet and Lou could hear birds singing. She unlocked the car but stood for a moment, looking from the cottage up the driveway towards the out-buildings. Somewhere a horse neighed. From the map, you'd imagine that there would be a view of the cottage from the upper floors of the farmhouse, but there were several big trees obscuring the line of sight.

'You want to go someplace else?' he asked.

She was lost in thought, hardly heard him. Then her phone rang and she pulled it out of her jacket pocket. She recognised the number on the display, stared at it for a moment. She wasn't ready to talk to Hamilton. If it was important, he would leave her a voice-mail.

'I think we'd better get back to the office,' she said.

There was silence between them for the rest of the journey. To try and distract herself, she turned on the radio to catch the local news headlines, but she wasn't listening to it. Their earlier conversation was going round and round in her head. His easy confidence had taken her by surprise, the relaxed way he'd asked her questions that were so personal. And now she was suddenly uncomfortable in a different way, not knowing what to do with herself, believing that he could see right through her: arousal, confusion – and sorrow that there was no way on earth he could possibly feel this attraction the same way she did, that it was all a game to him.

A game that she already knew she was going to lose.

15:17

This time Taryn saw her coming, shown up to the sales floor by the receptionist who looked far too excited for this to be a regular vis-itor. With Reg away, there was no intermediary. They approached Taryn's desk.

'Taryn, this lady is here to see you,' said Juliet, and scooted back off to reception.

Taryn stood up uncertainly. This one was younger, on her own, dressed in a smart linen suit with short, honey-blonde hair and green eyes behind rectangular-framed glasses. 'My name is Detective Sergeant Sam Hollands. I'm working on the Polly Leuchars murder investigation. I wondered if I might have a word with you? Somewhere private?'

As she showed Sam Hollands into Reg's office, Taryn was partly worried that she was going to get told off for failing to tell Andy Hamilton who she was, and partly worried about what on earth Polly's death had to do with her.

'Thanks,' Sam said as Taryn indicated Reg's small conference table. 'It's not bad in here, is it? I can imagine worse offices to work in. I gather my colleagues came to tell you the news about your father and his wife. I am sorry you had to hear about it under such circumstances.'

Taryn gave a tiny shrug. 'As I explained to your colleagues, I am not really in contact with my father, so the news was probably less upsetting to me than they were anticipating.'

'So I gather. Have you been to visit your father at all?'

'Yes. I went last night. He was still unconscious.'

'You know he's come round now?'

'The hospital left me a message. I might go back after work, if I get a chance.'

'I think he might appreciate that.'

Taryn made a noise, and Sam Hollands tried a different tack. 'Are you aware of the circumstances of Mrs Fletcher-Norman's death?'

Taryn shook her head. She wanted to say, actually, I'm not

105

especially interested in that, either, but a part of her somewhere was certainly curious. 'Car crash?'

'Mrs Fletcher-Norman was found in her car at the bottom of Ambleside Quarry. We're trying to establish whether there might have been any connection between her death and the murder of Polly Leuchars.'

'She was found at the bottom of a quarry? You mean she drove off the edge and killed herself?'

'It's possible.'

'How strange.'

'Why?'

'I can't think of anyone less likely to commit suicide than Barbara.'

'What do you mean?'

Taryn thought about Barbara being mean, vindictive and rude; thought of her voice getting louder when she'd had a drink. 'I guess she was always a bit flaky. But I never realised she was unhappy. You said you're linking her suicide to Polly's death? Does that mean you think she killed Polly?'

'We can't rule anything out yet, but it's one of the lines of enquiry.'

Taryn took a deep breath. She had a sudden mental picture of the bruises she had seen on her father's arm, last night. 'I didn't think she was prone to violence. Has my father said anything?'

'About what?'

'About – oh, maybe she was violent at home, or something. You don't simply turn psycho and kill people overnight, do you? Even if you have a reason.'

'Not usually. You know, your father may tell you things that he wouldn't feel comfortable telling the police.'

Taryn gave a short laugh. 'Have you met my father?'

'I saw him earlier.'

'Well, then. He tells you what he wants you to hear. That goes for you as well as me.'

'I realise things are – difficult between you. Can I ask how that came about?'

Taryn was useless at fibbing, even when she was doing it with good intentions; she would blush, fluster, get things muddled up. The safest thing to do would be to not answer.

So she took a deep breath, tried to be calm. 'It's nothing in particular. He left my mother when I was quite small. Ever since then I've been a bit of an inconvenience to him. Having to see me was always a chore. It was hurtful. But it's only in the last few years that I can't seem to put up with it any more. He's not used to people standing up to him; he doesn't like it. So these days we steer clear of each other.'

'And Barbara?'

'She was a complete bitch. I know I shouldn't speak ill of her after she's died in a horrible way, but she was. She was always hostile towards me, which is bad enough when you're an adult; when you're a small child it's very difficult to deal with.'

'I can imagine,' Sam said. 'I'm sorry.'

Taryn was taken aback by the sympathy, more so because she could tell that Sam Hollands meant it. 'Are you?'

'Of course. You can't choose your family, can you? And you can't really escape it, not when you're too young to be able to speak up for yourself.'

'No. Exactly.'

'Can you remember when you last visited them?'

'Months ago. I can't remember exactly. April, sometime. That was the last time I saw him until last night in the hospital.'

'Did you speak to them on the phone in that time?'

'No. The last time I went to the Barn, with the bike, they weren't in and I left a note.'

'The bike?'

Taryn sighed. It sounded so stupid, this. 'He'd taken up cycling, for some reason. I got him a bike for Christmas. It wasn't right. Long story.'

There was a pause. Taryn wondered if she was supposed to say anything else. Then Sam smiled at her, and produced a business card. 'I've taken up enough of your time. Will you give me a call, if you think of anything that might help us?'

'I don't think there's anything I *can* help with,' Taryn said quickly. 'I only met Polly once or twice.'

'But your father might mention something to you that would be helpful. After all, they were right across the road from Polly. Who knows what they might have seen, or heard.'

'Surely he would tell you that himself.'

'Nevertheless. You never know if you might need to talk,' she said. Her voice was calm, soothing. Taryn wondered at the woman's patience.

'Thank you,' she said at last, giving in. 'You've been really kind.'

She watched Sam Hollands heading back towards reception and thought about the other police officer, the great hulking rugby player, and she knew which one of the two she preferred.

16:05

The MIR was busy when they got back. Jane Phelps collared Jason as soon as he got through the door, and when Lou logged on to the workstation she saw that she had received a hundred and fifty new emails.

She left her door open to listen to the buzz from the room, trying to catch up on all the stuff that had come in, and as a result Andy Hamilton thought it was OK to walk straight into her office and sit down. She deliberately ignored him until he gave a discreet cough.

'Have you got an update for me?' she asked, still looking at the screen. Deleting emails.

He looked surprised, when she finally managed to look at him. 'Everything OK?' Andy asked.

'Everything's fine. What have I missed?'

'We've had intel back on Maitland. Only the same stuff we had last year about him and the McDonnells doing people trafficking. Special Branch were looking at it but they've got other stuff on their plates right now. Mandy says there should be some more later this evening, she's putting it all on HOLMES.'

'Good – it's something, anyway. Would be excellent if we could get another phone number for Maitland.'

'I met up with Flora. She's pretty done in by Polly's death, seems she had a relationship with her earlier this year. She said it ended in the summer when she moved out of the farm.'

'What do you think?'

'I think there's more to it than she was telling me, but whether she bumped her off I couldn't say.'

Lou realised he was jumpy, excitable, beyond what might have been caused by her bad mood. 'What else?'

'The PM is done for Mrs Fletcher-Norman.'

'And?'

He smiled. 'Multiple head wounds. Multiple trauma. Excess blood alcohol, consistent with her being rat-arsed. And some of the blood she was covered in wasn't actually hers.'

TEXT MESSAGE

07484 322159 to 07194 141544
02/11/12 1732hrs

Going to go to hosp see dad. Not sure what time will be back. Hope OK T xxx

17:45

He saw her before she saw him, stopping at the nurses' station and waiting patiently for them to pay attention to her. She'd put on weight, of course. Impatience nearly made him call out to her but, oh, what was the point. Everything just felt too exhausting. She would find him eventually, and if she'd just turn her head slightly she would see him anyway. Like a sensible person would do. He despaired of her.

And at that moment she looked round and, very briefly, there was the happy, girlish smile of recognition before she put the mask back on.

'Hello.'

She approached the bed but did not kiss him. Did not touch him at first, then after a moment or two took his hand in hers.

'Taryn. I'm glad you've come. Thank you.'

'How are you feeling?'

He gave a light cough. His throat was still dry from all the tubes. 'I'm fine. I don't know how long they're planning to keep me here, though.'

He wanted her to say something about Barbara, but knew she wouldn't. She wasn't one to hold with convention, his daughter. 'How are you? How is Chris?'

Taryn's husband had only been to the Barn once. Likeable

110

enough – heating engineer, or something like that. For a while Taryn had tried to organise meetings; had invited Brian and Barbara to dinner in that godforsaken terraced box they lived in, tiny rooms and flatpack furniture, until they'd made it clear that they had other things to do. Chris, the husband, was as uninterested in their lives as they were in his. They had absolutely nothing to talk about, and on those rare meetings it had been nothing short of awkward.

Taryn had married him quietly in the register office a couple of years ago, which suited Barbara, who'd not been at all happy at the prospect of them having to pay. He'd slipped Taryn some money towards the honeymoon. Where had they gone? Cornwall, that was it. Cornwall, in October. Of all places. They'd had to save up, apparently.

'Chris is fine. I'm fine. Is there anything you need me to do?'

His eyes closed, just for a moment, in concentration. 'Yes, lots of things. Can you go and see if the house is all right? I don't trust the police to set the burglar alarm and lock up properly. Sister Nolan, the Irish one? She's got some of my things somewhere. The door keys, car keys. Can you go inside, make sure it's all in order? Check the post, that sort of thing?'

'If I get time. I'm busy at work. Do you need me to bring you anything? Clothes?' Her tone was flat.

A voice came from behind, loud and Irish. 'He needs clean pyjamas, a towel, a flannel, toothbrush, all of those things. With a bit of luck he will be on the ward before Monday and we can't have him there without him being nice and clean. You should also find him a set of clothes, it would be good to get him up and dressed before too long. OK now? I have the keys for you.'

For a moment Brian and his daughter locked eyes, years of things unsaid passing between them. Then she turned and walked away.

111

5x5x5 Intelligence Report

From: Karen ASLETT – Source Co-ordinator

To: DCI Louisa SMITH

Subject: Nigel MAITLAND

Date: 02/11/12

Grading B / 2 / 4

Nigel MAITLAND is currently involved in money-laundering enterprises using offshore accounts.

5x5x5 Intelligence Report

From: Karen ASLETT – Source Co-ordinator

To: DCI Louisa SMITH

Subject: Nigel MAITLAND

Date: 02/11/12

Grading B / 2 / 4

Nigel MAITLAND was responsible for a recent shipment of illegal immigrants. They travelled into the country via Dover aboard a Lithuanian-registered lorry. The shipment was due to travel to London but was diverted elsewhere following a tip-off.

5x5x5 Intelligence Report

From: Karen ASLETT – Source Co-ordinator

To: DCI Louisa SMITH

Subject: Nigel MAITLAND – Harry MCDONNELL – Lewis MCDONNELL

Date: 02/11/12

Grading B / 2 / 4

Harry McDONNELL and Lewis McDONNELL are working with Nigel MAITLAND to operate a people-smuggling enterprise. The younger females are forced to work in a brothel in London, and are threatened with violence. The males are put to work on farms in the north of England until they have paid their transportation costs.

5x5x5 Intelligence Report

From: Karen ASLETT – Source Co-ordinator

To: DCI Louisa SMITH

Subject: Nigel MAITLAND – Harry MCDONNELL – Lewis MCDONNELL

Date: 02/11/12

Grading B / 2 / 4

The McDONNELL brothers and Nigel MAITLAND are still bringing illegals through Dover. MAITLAND organises legitimate shipment of goods to and from the continent via his farming business. One in five of the lorries is carrying immigrants. They are housed in a special container between the lorry cab and the refrigeration unit.

5x5x5 Intelligence Report

From: Karen ASLETT – Source Co-ordinator

To: DCI Louisa SMITH

Subject: Nigel MAITLAND – Harry MCDONNELL – Lewis
MCDONNELL

Date: 02/11/12

Grading B / 2 / 4

It is believed that the recent shipment of illegal immigrants that
Nigel MAITLAND and the McDONNELL brothers arranged
via Dover ended up in the Briarstone area following some
problem at the original drop-off location. Lewis McDONNELL
was not happy about this and it is likely that MAITLAND will
get into some trouble over it as the brothers see it as his mistake.

TEXT MESSAGE

From 07122 912712 to 07194 141544
02/11/12 1742hrs

We need to talk. Can you come to office later? Dad

17:50

Since returning to the MIR Lou had barely stopped for breath.

The blood found on Barbara Fletcher-Norman's clothing had
been taken to the lab by Les Finnegan personally for further
analysis on the premium level of service, which cost the taxpayer
a small fortune but would steer the investigation one way or the
other. With a bit of luck the results would be back in a few hours.

Buchanan had called her in for a meeting with the Assistant Chief Constable, which had been brief, and surprisingly jolly. They both seemed convinced that the blood was going to be Polly Leuchars' and were therefore happy with her blowing a large chunk of the operation's budget on the lab work. It was going to be a quick result after all, they joked, even if they didn't have an arrest. And with a bit of luck, this would disrupt Nigel Maitland's criminal enterprises for a while. Who knows, he might even let something slip over the interview process, something that could unravel things for Special Branch.

Buchanan hadn't even asked her about the details of Barbara's post mortem report and she was grateful. She hadn't had a chance to read the report properly and for the rest of the meeting she waited to be caught out with a question that would show up this oversight.

But there were no dramatic revelations about the way Barbara had met her death. As Andy had said, there were multiple injuries consistent with being inside the car as it fell. Adele Francis had asked her about the seatbelt, and reference was made to that point, something Andy hadn't mentioned: ' . . . broken ribs consistent with pressure from the seatbelt during impact.' She read through the report in detail, looking for other things that Andy might have missed. Although there had been multiple injuries, death had most likely been caused by an open skull fracture to the side of the head. Lou looked at the pictures. The side of Barbara's head was concave, most likely from the car's doorframe, which had been pushed inwards on the quarry floor. She looked at the pale skin of the woman's face, criss-crossed with rivulets of blood which had dried to a black lacy pattern that was almost beautiful. Her eyes were closed, her expression almost serene. Sometimes their faces registered traces of the expression consistent with the manner of death –

fear, pain – but not in this case. Lou wondered if it had something to do with the amount of alcohol in her system. Had she parked at the top of the quarry, left the handbrake off and passed out and had the car then rolled over the edge?

There was to be no easy explanation from the post mortem, in any case.

On her desk was Jason's first report into the phone analysis he was working on as well as the timeline of events, the network associations and the intelligence. She flicked through it, looking blindly at tables and paragraphs until she got to the end. He'd done a summary. Fantastic.

Preliminary Phone Analysis on Numbers ending:

774 – attributed to Felicity MAITLAND

712 – attributed to Nigel MAITLAND

544 – attributed to Flora MAITLAND

920 – attributed to Polly LEUCHARS (note the handset is still missing)

Summary of Findings

774 (Felicity MAITLAND)

– call traffic during the day, little in the evenings

– little contact with the number ending 920 (Polly LEUCHARS) – final contact with this number was on 31/10/12 at 11:15hrs

712 (Nigel MAITLAND)

– little call traffic on this number

– all contacts are with numbers attributed to family members

– only additional numbers dialled/contacts are landlines and open source research shows these to be local businesses connected with farming

– should be considered that this is likely not MAITLAND's only phone

544 (Flora MAITLAND)

– regular, frequent contact with number ending 920 (Polly LEUCHARS) until 27 August 2012

– regular contact with 07484 322159 which is attributed via HOLMES to Mrs Taryn LEWIS (daughter of Brian FLETCHER-NORMAN).

920 (Polly LEUCHARS)

– contacts with phones attributed to Flora MAITLAND, Felicity MAITLAND but notably not that attributed to Nigel MAITLAND. As his employee and given intelligence that he was in a relationship with Polly LEUCHARS, again this may indicate that he has at least one other number in regular use.

– there were two outgoing calls made to 07484 919987 (unattributed number) at 22:15 and 22:20. Cellsite for both calls is on the route between Morden and Briarstone. (Possible that one of these calls was that observed by Ivan ROLLINSON at the Lemon Tree.) At 22:58 there was a further unanswered call to the same number, but the cellsite location for this contact was Briarstone.

– at 23:49 an incoming call was received from the same unattributed number, 07484 919987, with a duration of 3 minutes 42 seconds. Cellsite location was Morden. (This may indicate that Polly LEUCHARS received the call when she was back at Yonder Cottage and was therefore alive at 23:49.)

<u>Morden 719643 – Yonder Cottage Landline</u>

– this line was only used once in the entire billing period. The only call registered was at 23:43 on 31/10/12 – an outgoing call to 07484 854498 (unattributed) – duration of 23 seconds.

Recommendations:

– billings/cellsite data to be obtained for 07484 919987 and 07484 854498 to enable attribution

– interview Flora MAITLAND / Taryn LEWIS to determine nature of their association

– identify other phone(s) for Nigel MAITLAND

When Lou looked up from Jason's report, he was standing in the doorway, hands in his pockets, watching her.

'This is good stuff,' she said.

'I've got something else,' he said.

'Have a seat. I'm on the last page.'

He sat and waited for her to finish, and when she got to the end he was tapping an inaudible rhythm with his fingers on his right knee. Lou looked at him expectantly.

'I've been looking at Polly's cellsite data some more, comparing it with the maps, trying to trace her movements on the last day.'

'And?'

'You saw from the data that the phone travelled from Morden to Briarstone around eleven, and then was back in Morden just before midnight, right?

'Yes.'

'Well, the cellsite in Briarstone ends up at Forsyth Road.'

She thought for one horrible moment he was going to wait for her to make the connection, the way her geography teacher used to stare at her expectantly, demanding an answer that she was unequipped to provide, but thankfully Jason didn't seem to want to play that particular game.

'Forsyth Road is the nearest cellsite phone mast to Waterside Gardens.'

This time she knew what he was getting at before he could say it. 'Where Flora lives?'

'Exactly.'

Lou stood, looked past Jason out to the main office, and the person she most wanted to see had just walked through the door. 'Sam!' she called, and beckoned her over.

Jason stood up as Sam came in, offered her the seat. Sam looked at him with amusement in her eyes. 'No, you're all right,' she said. 'I can manage.'

They all stood in the tiny office while Jason repeated what he'd just said about the cellsite.

'What do you think?'

'It's not enough to arrest her,' Sam said. 'But we can bring her in and take a statement, at least.'

'I agree it's a bit feeble,' Lou said. 'If we can bolster it up, it would be very good. And if we could get a search warrant for the farm – who knows what else we might get from that.'

'We still need to find the murder weapon,' said Sam. 'Chances are it hasn't gone far from the cottage. And we still haven't found Polly's phone handset, either.'

'I want Nigel's dirty phone,' Lou said. 'This is the best chance

119

we've got. What about that other call, the one made from the land-line? Any ideas?'

'I've already emailed Jane about it,' said Jason. 'Hopefully we'll get a result from the checks. In the meantime, at least we might get something from the search of Flora's place.'

'Right,' Sam said. 'Well, I can try for a Section 8 search warrant, at least. Let's hope I don't get Boris.'

She went back out into the main office to start putting the warrant request together.

'You want me to give her a hand?' Jason asked.

'Everything you've got, thank you.'

'One question – who's Boris?'

Lou smiled. 'Your friendly local magistrate, Jan Bryant. Also known as Battleaxe Bryant, never raises a smile, never looks pleased to see you under any circumstances. And to keep us all amused, she wears her hair like Boris Johnson.'

18:05

Taryn had phoned Chris when she got back to her car, sitting in the hospital car park with the fan heater on, trying to get the windscreen to clear.

'Flora's been here,' he said. 'She's gone off to see her father, said she'd be back later. Are you on the way home?'

'I'm going to stop off in Morden. He needs some things.'

'You want me to meet you there?'

She thought about it, just for a moment. 'No. I'm probably better off doing it alone. Thanks though.'

Twenty minutes later, she was pulling into the driveway of Hayselden Barn. Morden, being a village, wasn't particularly well lit, but here, out in the sticks, it was black as black could be. When she parked and turned the lights off, the world outside disappeared. For a moment she sat listening to the wind bend and stretch the horse chestnut tree which towered over her, wishing she could have just gone home and forgotten about everything. The door key was on a silver key ring with car keys, what looked like a locker key, and one for something else, a padlock maybe?

She took a deep breath and stepped out into the blackness. Almost instantly a bright light came on and Taryn almost jumped out of her skin. Of course, a security light, triggered by a sensor of some kind. She headed for the front door and opened it. As she did so, she wondered what she would do if the alarm actually went off, but fortunately there was no sound at all from inside. Everywhere was in darkness. She found light switches by groping along the wall, knocking something off the hall table and treading all over the post on the floor in front of her.

Taryn gathered up the envelopes and shuffled them into a pile. One letter, addressed to Barbara. Handwritten. It was so unbelievable. One day she'd been living her life as normal, and then she left this house and never returned. Here were letters she would never get to open, bills she would not pay, laundry in the basket she no longer had to bother with.

For a moment she stood in the hallway listening to the silence broken only by the ticking of the enormous grandfather clock. How strange it was to be in this house on her own. She had never lived here, never even spent a night here, and yet the place was furnished with antiques she remembered from her gran's house, all the pictures and ornaments and dark wood she had grown up knowing so well. A glass-fronted mahogany bookcase under the stairs held her grandmother's collection of dolls from around the world, old and faded. As a child she had been allowed to take them out and look at them, had given each of them a name and treated them with such reverence and care when all she had wanted to do was set up tea parties and hunting expeditions into the wild corners of the garden. They had probably never been taken out of the case since then.

She was wasting time. Upstairs, then: into the bedroom at the far end of the long hallway that stretched the length of the Barn. It was neat and tidy in here, but the bed was unmade. On the back of the bedroom door she found a dressing gown. She draped it over one arm and had a look in the chest of drawers for something that looked like pyjamas. Underwear, socks, trousers, a shirt – God, this was a hideous task. There was a leather holdall in the top of the wardrobe. She pulled it down and inside was a black leather travel washbag, containing various male-smelling things, a toothbrush and toothpaste. The dressing gown went into the bag, along with a handful of pants and socks, a pair of khaki trousers and a polo shirt, a pair of worn-looking brogues in the bottom of the wardrobe that he probably never wore. She gave up on the pyjamas. Perhaps he didn't wear them.

Going back out into the bland, beige-coloured hallway, Taryn was struck by the transition from the maleness of the room she had just left. There was nothing feminine about it, nothing at all. And at the other end of the hallway, she could see through an open door into another bedroom. Curious now, she dropped the bag at the top of the stairs and carried on, pushing open the door at the other end and reaching along the wall until she found a light switch.

This must be Barbara's room. How strange, that they had separate rooms! And yet, why wouldn't they? When you had five bedrooms to choose from and visitors only infrequently, why not spread out a bit more? This room was in a curious amount of disarray, the wardrobe doors open, revealing clothes draped over hangers and in piles on the floor. The bed was made, but a large rectangular indentation was on the plain white duvet as though someone had been packing a heavy case and had only just removed it.

She turned off the light and took the bag back downstairs. On a whim, she took the envelope addressed to Barbara Fletcher-Norman, Hayselden Barn, Morden, away with her. Barbara wasn't going to get to read it, so Taryn decided she should read it instead. It might help her understand this woman after all, might help her get some answers about why she had always been so unkind.

30 October 2013

Dearest Bunny,

I hope this letter finds you well and happy? I must admit the tone of your last worried me a little. I understand that what you feel for Liam at the moment surpasses what you feel for Brian, but you have to try and keep things discreet for the time being or else you might end up with nothing. Goodness knows we all know what Brian's like when he's cornered! Do you remember that time in Rome when you told him we all wanted to leave early? He was just unbearable.

Darling girl, don't do anything rash – I know Liam has been putting pressure on you to leave but really, there's no need. I'm sure he can wait just a little while longer, until you are sorted out financially and ready to make your move. You never know, if Brian is seeing the stable girl as you suspect then he might be happy with the arrangement!

All is well here. Andrew is finding the commute very hard again – I am trying to persuade him to try for more part-time hours, but it's a big ask. We will see what they say. I live in fear of the hospital calling to say he has had another heart attack.

All for now, Bunny, dear, write soon and we will talk at the weekend,

Love from your

Lorna

X

5x5x5 Intelligence Report

From: Karen ASLETT – Source Co-ordinator

To: DCI Louisa SMITH

Subject: Nigel MAITLAND – Connor PETRIE – Harry McDONNELL

Date: 02/11/12

Grading B / 2 / 4

Connor PETRIE has been working at Hermitage Farm for a few months as a groom. Nigel MAITLAND gave him a job as a favour to Harry MCDONNELL, whose wife is Emma PAYSWICK's (Connor's mother) best friend.

5x5x5 Intelligence Report

From: Karen ASLETT – Source Co-ordinator

To: DCI Louisa SMITH

Subject: Nigel MAITLAND – Connor PETRIE – Harry McDONNELL

Date: 02/11/12

Grading B / 2 / 4

Connor PETRIE has been working at Hermitage Farm for a few months as a groom.

Nigel MAITLAND also has PETRIE doing other small jobs for him in relation to the criminal association with the McDONNELL brothers. This includes running messages between MAITLAND and the McDONNELLs, as PETRIE sees them at home.

18:18

By the time Flora got back to Hermitage Farm, it was dark. The halogen lamps that lit up the main farmyard showed the yard was glossy in the way that meant it was turning to ice. It would be slick as a skating rink tonight.

She drove through the yard and up into the secluded turning circle in front of the farmhouse. Most of the lights appeared to be on inside.

The kitchen was warm and steamed up from whatever had been in the Aga for the past few hours; Felicity was sitting at the dining table with one of her cronies, an empty bottle of wine and a half-full one on the table between them. Her mother's cheeks were red, as were her eyes.

'Hello, Mum,' Flora said, bending to kiss the fiery cheek.

'Flora, dear. Check the roast for me, would you? Of course, I never knew what to think,' – this last directed at the elderly woman in the pink tracksuit, seated across the table.

'Well, she was always a bit of an unknown quantity, for all you knew her mother,' said the visitor, and Flora knew that they were talking about Polly. She opened the Aga door and inspected the meat. It looked decidedly pink. Taking a pair of oven gloves, she moved the joint up to the hotter part of the oven.

The woman's voice dropped to a coarse whisper, 'Of course you know that she swung both ways, don't you?'

'Swung both ways?' echoed Felicity, aghast.

Flora would have smiled if the situation hadn't been quite so grim.

'You mean she – she liked *gels*?'

Flora stood, and of course the visitor looked from her to Felicity and back again. Her short hair, inevitable jeans and T-shirt, lack of make-up and lack of a boyfriend had not gone unremarked upon in the village. Although not yet within Felicity's earshot.

'Where's Dad, Mum?'

Felicity looked up, her eyes unfocused. 'Hmm? Oh. In the garage, I think.'

Outside, the wind had picked up again. A sleety drizzle had started and Flora pulled her jacket around her chest, folding her arms to keep the wind from blowing it open again. Right around the side of the house, a former barn was used as a garage housing Nigel Maitland's collection of vehicles. When he wasn't in the farm office, or visiting 'associates' in London, he was most likely to be found here.

The side door to the barn was unlocked, the fluorescent lights bright within. At the far end of the barn, the old tack room had been converted into a second office – one that most of the 'associates' were never invited to. If Felicity wanted him when he was in the garage, she usually phoned his mobile.

'Dad?' Flora called out from the doorway, knowing full well that he would have reacted when he heard the door open at the far end of the barn.

'In here,' he called back. That was her permission to approach.

He had a laptop open on a desk that was cluttered with paperwork. She didn't look too closely, knew better than to be nosy where her father was concerned. It was one of the reasons why she was admitted where few others were.

The ladder to the hayloft, in the roof space above them, was down. Normally it was stowed away out of sight. In the loft, on a specially reinforced floor, was a second safe – a much larger one than the small safe holding paperwork and his wife's jewellery, which was to be found in the main house. Flora didn't know what it contained, didn't want to know: but for a brief moment she thought of Andy Hamilton and wondered what he would give to view what was inside.

Pictures of the family and various horses lined the walls, and a Pirelli calendar, two years out of date.

At the bottom of June – the page that never seemed to get turned over – was a scrawled list of names and phone numbers. One of the names on the list was 'Flora' but the mobile number listed next to it wasn't hers. In fact, it was the combination to the safe. He'd told her that, one afternoon, out of the blue. He'd said that one day, if anything happened to him, she might need it. She had been surprised that he had trusted her with something as important as the contents of his safe, but thinking about it afterwards Flora realised that he didn't have anyone else. Who could he tell? Not Felicity, who was flaky at her best and downright unstable at her worst. Certainly not Connor Petrie. Despite the amount of time he spent on the farm, Flora didn't trust him and she suspected Nigel didn't either. What the hell he was doing working here at all was anyone's guess. Nigel must owe someone a bloody big favour, she thought.

Against one wall, next to an oil-filled radiator that was on full blast, was an old, threadbare sofa. Nigel waved towards it. 'Want something to drink?'

'No thanks. I'm not staying long.'

A bottle of ten-year-old Benromach single malt came out of the bottom of the filing cabinet, and a tumbler on Nigel's desk was half filled. He drank from it as though preparing himself for something.

'So, Flora-Dora. What's new?'

She'd not been called that in years. What was that about? Suddenly over-friendly, trying to catch her off guard? He regarded her with those bright, electric-blue eyes. Polly had once told her that she'd thought he was wearing coloured contact lenses. But they really were that colour. Flora's were brown, like her mother's.

Flora wished she hadn't bothered coming. 'Is there something specific you wanted to see me about? Because if there isn't, I'd rather go home.'

Nigel drank some more, watched her, clearly deciding his next move. 'Have the police interviewed you yet?'

She nodded.

'And?'

'And what? Do they think I killed Polly? Probably. I couldn't give a fuck any more to be honest.'

'You should have phoned me. I could have got Joe for you.'

'I didn't think I needed a solicitor, thanks,' Flora said. 'Especially not that little turd.'

Nigel fished through the papers on his desk and found a small box full of business cards. He rooted through it and handed one over to her. 'Keep this handy. You never know. Whatever your opinion of him, he's good at his job.'

Giovanni Lorenzo, known to his close friends as Joe, had been

Nigel Maitland's solicitor for the last twenty years. Flora personally found him uncomfortably familiar, and always thought he wore too much aftershave, which meant that in confined spaces like interview rooms people rarely wanted to keep him there for long.

'So have they got you pegged as a suspect?' Flora asked, thinking that she already knew the answer. Of course, Joe wasn't paid a fortune for nothing, and he'd always managed to get Nigel out of any sticky situation that he'd failed to avoid.

'If I'm a suspect, I'm in big trouble. It's all about the wording. To them, we're "nominals". Know what that means?'

Flora shook her head.

'We're on their system, in connection with this particular case. We're a number to them. The minute they start to refer to us as suspects it means they're about to make an arrest, no more talking nicely – it all gets very official. So for the time being, let's be happy that we're nominals and not suspects. In any case, they're probably building up a nice meaty case against me. Trouble for them is, I didn't do it.'

He poured another tumbler of whisky.

'Where were you?' he said, his voice rough from the whisky. 'The night Polly died. Have you got an alibi?'

She thought back, trying to remember what she was doing. She remembered the next day clearly enough . . .

'It was Halloween night, wasn't it?' she said at last. 'Mum phoned me up about six. I painted. Went to bed. Woke up, painted some more and got your phone call. So – no alibi.'

Nigel grimaced. 'Me neither. At least, not one that I'd be prepared to share with the fucking police.'

'You were out, then?'

Nigel nodded. 'With some friends. But they wouldn't thank me

129

for mentioning their names, and in any case I was back here at midnight. Crawled into bed about two. Your mother was snoring her head off, as usual. If I'd known I was going to need an alibi I'd have shaken her awake.'

'Would they believe her as an alibi anyway?'

He snorted. 'Probably not. She doesn't come across as entirely lucid at the best of times.'

Flora raised a smile at this, just for a moment, and then remembered where she was and who she was talking to, and let it die on her lips. 'Was there anything else?'

He looked sad for a moment, if that was even possible. 'Flora,' he said. 'I know things have been . . . awkward. But I want you to know that if anything kicks off, I'm still your father—'

'What's going to kick off? What do you mean?'

'I don't mean anything in particular. I just think we should present a united front.'

That was bloody typical, Flora thought. She felt the anger rise up to meet the misery she'd been feeling all day. But there was nothing she could say to him, of course, because he was entirely right. They were in this together, for better or worse – the Maitlands against the force of the law. Just as it had always been. Except this time, she was right at the heart of it, instead of watching from the sidelines.

18:24

Andy Hamilton was waiting for Flora outside 14 Waterside Gardens, even though he knew she wasn't there. Doing as he was told, because Lou had asked him to keep an eye on Flora while they got the warrant together. Andy was pretty much convinced they were all barking up the wrong tree – it was going to turn out to be Barbara Fletcher-Norman, of course it was.

Phoning Lou for an update, no answer – no answer to the text he sent her either. Not work, just checking she was OK. Mildly flirtatious. When he'd seen her in her office, the first day of the case, he had seen that same gleam in her eye and had thought that he was in with a chance. She still wanted him. She would fight it, but in the end he would win.

Now, he wasn't so sure. Briefly he wondered if she had found someone else, and then quickly dismissed the idea. She was too busy here, didn't have time to meet anyone outside the job – and there was nobody else on this case that he could see her being interested in. Ali Whitmore? More likely to want to go home to his slippers than wind up in bed with an energetic girl like Lou. That weird American analyst? More keen to go home to his PC and fiddle with his web cam, probably. That left Sam Hollands. Andy smirked a little at the thought – that was something he'd pay to see. Pay even more to join in with.

If he didn't find Flora he might get another chat with the nurse he'd seen here yesterday, Flora's very attractive downstairs neighbour. She must be a sister, he thought – they wore the navy-blue uniforms, didn't they? They were the ones in charge – and the thought of it was curiously arousing.

He frowned. There was something not quite right about 14 Waterside Gardens and for a moment he couldn't quite place what it was. Flora's flat was in darkness, the curtains drawn, and downstairs ... downstairs the front door to Flat 1 was slightly ajar.

He got out of the car and walked up to the house, standing for a moment at the bottom of the steps, looking up to the front door. It wasn't open by much, just enough to tilt it slightly into shadow, which is what had attracted his attention.

He climbed the steps and stood listening. He should call it in. He should get back-up. Maybe she'd been burgled – or maybe she was lying in a pool of blood in the hallway, like Polly.

He gave the door a little push, letting it swing soundlessly into the hall. He could see down a long corridor into a kitchen at the bottom. A light was on, but no sign of anyone inside.

'Police! Anyone in here?' he called. Alarm bells were ringing so loudly in his head he thought they must be audible halfway up the street, but still he stepped inside. This was wrong, all wrong. He kept telling himself that he had legitimate concerns for the welfare of the occupant, and yet he didn't want to call out again, didn't want her to know he was in here.

Holding his breath, he walked down the corridor into the kitchen. On the table a copy of today's *Eden Evening Standard* was open to page two, the continuation of an article about Polly's murder. There was a picture of Yonder Cottage with that PC – whatever his name was – standing gamely guarding the driveway.

He hadn't heard her, but suddenly she was behind him.

He spun round to see her standing close to him, those blue eyes regarding him. Beyond his surprise at how he had managed to find himself in this woman's kitchen came the sudden shot of desire. She wasn't wearing the uniform this time but somehow she looked even more sure of herself: a skirt, short, showing tanned, well-toned legs and sharp sandals with a killer heel. Her white shirt was open at the neck, showing cleavage.

'You took your time,' she said.

Andy felt his skin colour. 'Sorry – what?'

She smiled at him, taking a step closer. 'You've been sitting outside in that car for over half an hour. And you know as well as I do that Flora isn't home. Therefore you must be waiting for me. What do you want, then?'

He couldn't think of anything to say.

She put one hand on his chest, sliding under the fabric of his suit jacket and over his cotton shirt, her fingers pressing into the skin underneath. Her other hand joined in and she pushed the jacket off his shoulders, letting it fall onto the kitchen table.

She brought her face close to his, so that he could feel her breath on his cheek. He was about to take a step back, ask what the fuck she thought she was doing, when he felt her hand run down the front of his trousers, curving around the hardness of his erection. Her grip on him was strong, and deliberate. Jesus!

He stumbled back, knocking into the table, staring at her in shock.

'Next time, I expect more from you than this,' she said.

'I'm – I'm sorry?' He had no idea why he was apologising. What she'd done was pretty much sexual assault – even if he had been about to kiss her.

She laughed at his expression, turned at the kitchen door and gave him an amused little smile. 'Shut the door behind you on your way out, Inspector.'

For a moment he stood there, dazed, wondering what the hell just happened. Then he retrieved his jacket from the table and did as he was told.

19:14

Flora was lying on Taryn's spare bed, scrunched up into a tight ball. Downstairs, Sky Sports was on and Chris was sitting in front of it. Tabby was at the hospital. Maybe if Flora was asleep by the time she got home, they wouldn't have to talk about it.

If only she could stop thinking, just for a moment, she might be able to sleep. Still, every thought led back to Polly.

That morning in August, the sun already hot although it was barely nine, the air smelling of ripe wheat from the field opposite; the sound of the tractor trundling up the lane. There was no car parked on the drive of Yonder Cottage. Sometimes there had been a car parked there; different cars. If there had been a car, Flora would have turned around quietly and driven away.

There was no car.

Just the sunlight, and the morning. By now Polly would have seen to the horses, would be back for a shower and breakfast. If Flora was lucky she would catch her in her dressing gown, hair damp from the shower, skin glowing, the bed still unmade . . .

The back door was unlocked the way it always was.

Flora didn't call out. She wanted to surprise her.

Only when she was halfway up the stairs did she hear it – laughter, gentle, light – Polly's voice. And another voice, low, one that made Flora's heart pound and the bile rise in her throat.

She couldn't stop herself then, although she already knew what she was going to see. She could hear the voices properly now, at the top of the stairs.

'. . . you're silly. You always were.'

'Polly. Come here. Where are you going?'

'Nowhere. I'm staying – right – here . . . '

Flora pushed the door to the bedroom just enough to see her father lying splayed on Polly's bed, the single white sheet covering a leg, an ankle, and Polly completely naked, the masses of blonde hair falling like a golden river over Nigel Maitland's lap. Polly was too occupied with the task in hand to see Flora turn, slowly, and go back the way she had come. But Nigel had met his daughter's eyes, briefly, before she had turned away.

She had gone back to the flat she rented in town, avoided the

134

farm where she had been every single day. Polly had called, and sent texts. Flora had not responded. Her father had called, several times, and then turned up at the studio. She had not opened the door. Felicity was by far the most persistent. Flora returned her mother's calls and texts with brief, conciliatory responses. Nothing was wrong. She was busy working. It was all fine; she was just busy. Eventually her mother had sent her one of those ultimatum texts she was so good at, and Flora had reluctantly come back.

'What on earth's the matter with you?' Felicity had said, sitting in the garden with a cup of tea because the kitchen was too damned hot with the Aga on.

Flora had lost weight; all her clothes were hanging off her already thin frame. 'Nothing, Mum. I've been busy working.'

Felicity snorted. She'd never considered Flora's art as real work, even when the exhibition she'd had last year had netted several thousand pounds in sales.

'Is it a boy?'

'What?'

'Are you having problems with a boy?'

Flora stared at her, not sure whether to laugh or cry. 'No, nothing like that. Where's ... ' Flora hesitated over the word, tried again: 'Where's my father?'

'Daddy? In his office I shouldn't wonder.'

Flora considered. It was time. 'Perhaps I'll drop in and say hello.'

He wasn't in his office, he was behind the main barn, talking on his mobile phone the way he did when he didn't want to risk anyone in the house overhearing.

'Tell him I won't have it. It's the whole deal or nothing.' Nigel Maitland saw his daughter approaching and tried to end the call as

135

quickly as he could. 'I don't give a fuck. *You* sort it out. It's what I'm paying you for.'

He snapped the phone closed and stood a little straighter. 'Flora.'

'Dad.'

They stood for a moment regarding each other. It was cool here, in the shade, no sound but the occasional neigh or snort from the horses in the field behind them.

'I remembered,' Flora said at last.

For a moment Nigel hadn't a clue what she was talking about. 'What?'

'Seeing you with Polly. It brought something back to me. Of course, when you're just eight you don't always understand things that you see. It's only afterwards when you realise.'

A glimmer of realisation was starting to creep across his rugged features. 'Oh. And what was it that you saw? When you were eight?'

'We were on holiday in Spain with Polly and her mum and lots of other people. I'd completely forgotten. I remembered you playing in the pool with Polly.'

There was a pause while Flora remembered, and Nigel tried to remember the moment.

'You were . . . you were tickling her, and she was laughing. She must have only been fourteen. There was nobody else there. I was watching from the window. *And you were tickling her.*'

There was a long moment. Nigel looked at the floor. 'But you know what she's like. She was like that even then. It wasn't about sex, not then. She was just so bright, so vivacious. She was – addictive.'

Flora felt tears, fought them back. 'Have you been sleeping with her all these years?'

Nigel gave a short laugh. 'No! God, no.' He took a step towards Flora, who took a step back. 'Flora! There was nothing between Polly and me until about a month ago. I promise you.'

She couldn't stop it now. A sob, a gasp – and he stepped forward as if to embrace her. At the same moment she took a step back, shaking her head. Something had broken.

He was staring at her, unmoving, his jaw clenching. 'I won't see her again,' he said.

'It doesn't matter,' she sobbed. 'You do whatever you like. I don't care!'

And the tears fell, then and now, in the privacy of Tabby's spare room. And what she had been unable to say to him then: the true hurt, the ultimate betrayal lay not in the fact that the woman Flora loved was unfaithful, she already knew that; nor that her father had been intimate with Polly for longer than she had, probably – despite his denials – long before it was right or appropriate for him to do so, even putting aside the fact that he was a married man. No, the pain that tore her apart came from that secret, terrible knowledge in her own heart that, as an eight-year-old girl, she had seen the secret moment between her father and Polly and had been burned raw with the acid of jealousy. She had been envious of them! How stupid, how foolish she had been.

Later, walking back past the barn at the top of the drive, she had seen Polly getting out of her car at Yonder Cottage. Always at a rough angle, wheels turned, as though she'd just tossed the car to one side instead of actually parking it. Polly had seen her and waved.

Flora had continued walking. Then she heard Polly call out, and when she looked round again she was running up towards her.

'Flora! Flora, wait for me!'

She stopped and waited, heart thudding, pounding in her chest. She didn't feel ready for this, so soon after her father. Polly was wearing tight jeans, a clinging T-shirt, her hair tied back in a messy bun. She was breathless when she reached Flora.

'Where have you been?' she asked. 'I've been trying to call you.'

Flora tried out several possible responses in her head, eventually settling on: 'At the flat.'

'Why didn't you answer your phone? Have you been avoiding me?'

How could she not know? 'You – and him. My father.'

'Oh, that!'

She said it cheerfully, dismissively, as if it was such a trivial thing. 'But Flora, you know I see lots of people. You've always known. I've never kept it a secret from you. And I thought you were OK with it!'

'Not him. Not with my dad.'

'Oh, Flora. My lovely girl ... ' She had put out a hand towards her, and Flora shrank back.

She was already walking away when Polly said:

'I'm not seeing him any more, Flora. I've stopped all that now. There's someone else, someone important ... '

'I don't want to know,' Flora said, over her shoulder. 'It's nothing to do with me.'

'Don't be like that, please, Flora!'

Flora got to the car, stopped and waited, took a deep breath. 'Why are you doing this?' she asked quietly, not even sure if she was talking to Polly or to herself.

Polly had caught up with her, her eyes bright. 'Everything's changed. My whole life has changed.'

'What are you talking about?' Flora turned to look at her, moved

138

round to the driver's door, keeping the car between her and Polly as if she needed it for protection.

'I'm sorry,' Polly said, at last. 'I'm sorry if I hurt you. I didn't mean to.'

They stared at each other. Flora couldn't think of anything to say. Polly was looking radiant, beautiful, even more than normal. And she was smiling, a wistful smile that could have been genuine, sorrowful for how things had turned out, or maybe it was just pity. Eventually, wanting a way to bring this to an end, Flora said: 'Thank you.'

Then she opened the car door and got in, shutting the door and, at last, breathing out in a long, gasping breath.

19:25

The hospital car park was a lot quieter than it had been earlier. Taryn found a space near the entrance and didn't get a pay-and-display ticket, despite the sign saying that charges applied 24 hours. Bollocks to that, she thought. If she got a ticket, that meant she was really here. And she couldn't see that there would be any security staff looking for ticket flouts at this time of night. They were all tucked up in their cabin watching *EastEnders* and drinking tea.

The ICU was quiet, too, although a few of the beds had visitors. Not many of the patients were conscious. At first Taryn thought her father was asleep, too, but when she approached the bed he opened his eyes and turned to look at her, a half-hearted smile on his lips. The machines beside him beeped quietly. They had been turned down so people could sleep; those that weren't unconscious, at any rate.

'Taryn,' he said, with a cough. 'I didn't think you'd be back tonight.'

'I can't come tomorrow,' she said. 'I have a visitor. Maybe not the day after. So I thought I'd bring this stuff.'

'Thank you.'

She stared at him for a few moments, then dropped the leather holdall by the bed. There was nothing on the cabinet next to him, no flowers or cards. Taryn wondered vaguely if any of his friends knew he was in here. Did he have friends?

'Is the house OK?'

Taryn gave a tiny shrug. 'Looked fine to me. I locked the door.'

His eyes closed slowly. Taryn thought his breathing sounded a bit funny. She wondered if he was asleep and turned to leave, but he raised his hand as if to touch her. She was too far away from the bed, though.

'Taryn,' he whispered. She had to come closer to hear him.

I don't want to hear this, she thought. Whatever it is, I know this isn't going to be something I am going to want to hear.

'I need you to do something for me.' He coughed again, a low rumble from inside his chest.

'What?'

'I need you to phone someone. Just to tell her what's happened, and where I am.'

'Who?'

'Her name is Suzanne. I don't know her number off hand; it's in my mobile. The number is listed as "Manchester Office" in the address book.'

Taryn raised her eyes to the ceiling. 'Who is she, this Suzanne?'

'Will you do it? Will you phone her? My mobile should be in my briefcase, it will be in the office at home.'

'Who is she?'

140

Brian gave a deep sigh, turned away for a moment. Taryn thought there might be a tear in the corner of his eye.

'Don't tell me you were cheating on Barbara, Dad? Wasn't she good enough for you in the end?' This confrontation felt good, and yet bad at the same time. What was this? Was she starting to feel sympathy for him, this tired old man, lying here all alone with no one to care for him? Nobody left? Where were all his golfing friends? Bridge partners? Mistresses galore, going back through the years like a line of Tiller Girls, all legs and tits and sarcasm?

'She was going to leave me,' Brian said, in a small voice. 'She was having an affair with her tennis coach. She was planning to go to Ireland with him.'

'So you thought you'd beat her to it?'

'Suzanne is different. It's not what you think. She – she's special. Will you phone her?'

'What about Polly, Dad?'

'What about her?'

'Did you have an affair with her, too?'

Brian managed to raise a smile at this. 'Of course. Didn't everyone?'

Her heart grew colder towards him again. The poor girl was dead. She might have broken hearts everywhere she went, but someone had taken her life from her in a brutal way. And taken Polly away from Flora, who deserved better.

'What happened with Polly, Dad?'

'Tabby, please. I am so tired. Will you call Suzanne for me?'

'Tell me about Polly.'

Brian sighed. 'If I tell you, will you call Suzanne?'

'Yes.'

He looked away for a moment, remembering. 'Polly came on to

141

me at one of Felicity's dinner parties. Not long after she moved in to the cottage. I'd taken Barbara home – she'd had a few drinks too many – and as soon as I came back, Polly sat next to me and, well, she flirted. Made me feel good. That was the start of it.'

'Barbara found out?'

'She was suspicious, but she could never prove anything.'

'She might have followed you, or something.'

He shrugged, as if it didn't matter any more. 'I didn't see her for long.'

'So why did you stop?'

Taryn wondered if it was her own curiosity leading her to ask these questions, or whether Sam Hollands had put the idea into her head.

'She introduced me to Suzanne.'

'The woman you want me to phone? She was a friend of Polly's?'

Brian nodded.

'Like I said,' Taryn said, her voice cool, 'I've got a visitor. I don't know if I'll get back to the house again this week. If I get a chance, I'll find your phone and let Suzanne know.'

Brian's eyes closed, and his breathing deepened. That was her cue to leave. She had had enough, anyway.

19:50

Les Finnegan took the call on his mobile and by the expression on his face and his frantic hand signals to those that were left in the office, everyone stopped what they were doing and waited in silence for him to finish. Lou got up from her desk and stood in the doorway.

'Right. Thanks. Yeah, I'll wait for the details, thanks. Bye.'

He looked around, a big grin spreading on his face. 'Blood

results back. The DNA on Barbara Fletcher-Norman's clothes is definitely Polly's.'

Some of them cheered. Jason was smiling and suddenly everyone was talking at once.

Lou went back into the office to ring Buchanan, and when she came out again they all had their coats on and were waiting for her.

'King Bill, is it?' she asked, somewhat redundantly. 'I'll catch up with you.'

She spent a few minutes working her way through emails, writing a brief report for Buchanan that he could take into the Chief Officers' Briefing tomorrow morning.

She tried Sam's mobile, but it went to voicemail. Sam had called to say Boris had put up a bit of a struggle and then caved in, possibly due to the fact that she was having a dinner party that evening and was making a soufflé.

Flora Maitland or Barbara Fletcher-Norman ... The stronger evidence pointed to Barbara, who was dead and could not therefore be arrested and interviewed. But whatever the reason that Polly's phone had been used in the immediate vicinity of her former lover's home address just before she had been murdered, it wouldn't hurt to ask her about it. And have a good old rummage through the farm while they were about it.

Sam arrived a few minutes later and looked crestfallen when she came in to the MIR and found only Lou in attendance.

'Oh, let me guess,' she said. 'King Bill?'

'Sam, I've just had a thought – did you specify all the outbuildings on the warrant?'

Sam grinned and waved the piece of paper. 'All properties on the land pertaining to Hermitage Farm, Morden,' she said with triumph.

Definitely cause for celebration. 'First thing tomorrow, we'll bring her in.'

'Do we know where she is?'

'Mr Hamilton's in charge of keeping tabs on her. Shall we go and have a little drink, Sam?'

She logged out of the system and told Sam to go on ahead while she took a copy of her report upstairs to the management corridor and slotted it into Mr Buchanan's pigeon-hole. After that, she went to the Ladies and stared at her reflection, criticising her hair and her tired face and the state of the make-up she'd applied that morning. If it hadn't been for Sam, she might not have bothered going to the pub after all, but it wouldn't hurt to show her face across the road. If they were to get a quick result, it warranted a drink or two. And if this *was* a blind alley, then it would serve as a consolation.

20:14

Andy was tired. He'd called in to the MIR to report back to Lou and found they'd all buggered off. A note in Les Finnegan's handwriting on his desk read 'King Bill'.

One of the phones was ringing. It was an outside line and he wanted to ignore it, wanted desperately to pretend he wasn't here so that he could fuck off to the pub with the rest of them, start the weekend even if it was going to be a working one.

In the end, his conscience got the better of him and he answered it.

'Incident room, Andy Hamilton speaking.'

'Can I speak to Detective Sergeant Sam Hollands, please?'

The voice on the other end was familiar. Andy searched through the catalogue of people it could be – someone he'd met recently, someone he'd liked.

'DS Hollands has left, I'm afraid. Can I help? Take a message?'

There was a long pause. 'No, I'll ring tomorrow.'

'Who's speaking, please?'

'My name is Taryn Lewis.'

The link clicked into place between the voice and the curvy blonde who'd been at the café earlier in the day. Taryn – Tabby. Bugger.

'Mrs Lewis. You didn't explain who you were when we met earlier.'

'You didn't ask.'

'Are you sure there's nothing I can help with?'

'Tell Sam Hollands to call me as soon as possible, would you?'

It could wait. It could all wait. Apart from one thing: 'Mrs Lewis, there was something else I needed to ask Flora. She's not answering her phone and she doesn't seem to be at home. You don't happen to know where she is?'

'She's staying at my house. I didn't think she should be alone at the moment, until she's had a bit of time . . . you know.'

Bingo. 'I understand. She's going through an incredibly difficult thing.'

'Exactly. And she can't go to the farm, of course.'

'She's lucky to have such a good friend,' Andy said. He should be on some therapy talk show, he thought. He couldn't half spout some bollocks when the situation demanded it.

'Thank you,' Taryn said. 'Do you want me to ask her to call you?'

'It's fine. I'll catch up with her tomorrow. As long as she's OK,' he said. As long as she's not planning to leave the country or disappear, is what he meant.

When she rang off, Andy sighed with relief. The day was ending favourably and he had earned the right to finish off with a pint or two with the lads. With a bit of luck, Louisa might be in there too. With a lot of luck, she might be ever so slightly pissed already and therefore less immune to his charms.

20:19

Brian's eyes closed. Talking to Taryn about Suzanne and Polly had brought back all the memories of how tangled his romantic life had become. He'd had many affairs over the years, had lost count somewhere along the line of all the one-night stands he'd had, the expensive prostitutes paid for by clients overseas, the women he'd met in bars, hotels, the women he'd met socially and seen regularly: Emma, a sports therapist at the gym; Andrea, the wife of one of his colleagues, hungry for some danger; Sheila Newton, Barbara's friend who'd wanted to set Barbara up with her corpulent stockbroker husband, Derek, and try and engineer a foursome – that had brought that particular liaison to an abrupt end as Brian couldn't imagine anything less sensual or appealing. And then there was Christine, Barbara's bridge partner. He'd had her on more than one occasion.

The first time he'd cheated on Jean, Taryn's mother, it had been difficult, shameful, and he'd sworn he would never do it again. But the second time it was easier. The third time, it was with Barbara, and she hooked him good and proper. When he married Barbara, he promised briefly that he would mend his ways. That lasted three months, until one of the stewardesses on a transatlantic flight slipped him her New York phone number.

Infidelity was only an issue if you let it be. He was happy to come home to Barbara, happy to share his life with her, happy to have an attractive woman on his arm at parties, even if she did fail to behave herself when she'd had more than three gins.

And then, just when everything was simple, there was Polly to complicate things.

She had curled up beside him on the sofa in Felicity's conservatory at one of those interminable drinks parties, put her hand on his knee and laughed, throwing her head back and baring her throat. She told him she liked sex, a lot, couldn't get enough of it. She liked people. And she was so young, so *alive*.

Later, walking back to the Barn, the silent moon lighting the way, he had heard a low whistle behind him. Polly had followed him out. She was running across the tarmac with no shoes on, her short, sequinned dress swishing against her naked thighs. She threw her arms around his neck and kissed him, giggling softly.

He brought her into the garden and, in full view of the house, he pulled her dress above her head. Underneath, she was naked, her skin silver in the moonlight. Aside from the noises they made themselves, everything was silence. She pulled at his trousers to get at what she wanted, and from then on it was a mad tangle of limbs – the smell of the grass, the thought of the grass stains on his clothes; even if he took them off now it would be too late ... She climbed on top of him, her hair around her like a cloud. He looked up into the night sky, at the moon watching them without comment, and laughed, not believing the madness of it. He knew Barbara would be asleep, snoring off the effects of the gin, but still the dare of it, the challenge of fucking this beautiful girl, twenty-something, full of life and energy and the bold confidence of her own sensuality, overwhelmed him completely. Who cared if anyone saw? He would never live like this again, never.

He wasn't naïve.

He knew Polly's type, although he'd never met anyone really like her. She was what they used to call a nymphomaniac, needy for sex in the same way that many women were needy for emotion. She had sex as often as possible. She was depressed if she went without it for more than a few days. She cared about the people she slept with, some of them at least. But that was as far as it went – Polly could no more be faithful to someone than she could fly to the moon.

He also knew, because she told him, proudly and excitedly, that she had been involved with the swinging scene when she had lived in London; that she still met up with some of the people she had played with from time to time. He remembered lying in Polly's bed, upstairs at Yonder Cottage, while Barbara was drinking tea at Hermitage Farm with Felicity. He loved the whole danger of Polly. She was dangerous and intriguing. She was lying next to him, her hands idly playing with him, teasing. She was telling him about this woman who was nearly as insatiable as she was.

'Her name is Suzanne,' Polly said, and a wistful look came over her face that Brian had never seen before. 'I met her when I was travelling, but she's here, living in Briarstone now. She is so amazing! One of these powerful women, you know? All about power.'

'What sort of power?'

'Control. I didn't think it was my thing, but there's something about the way she does it. She makes me feel scared, and safe, all at the same time.'

'Can't be good, feeling scared, surely?' he murmured.

Polly laughed. 'It gives me the most incredible high the way she does it. I've never had orgasms like that, Brian. You wouldn't

148

believe how it feels – it's like flying. She's my idol. My goddess.' Her eyes went back to his face. 'Want to meet her?'

'Yes,' said Brian, before he had time to think about it.

'Did you ever do a threesome, Brian? Fancy it with me and Suzanne?'

He had done a threesome, years ago. Well, of a sort. In a hotel room in Bangkok. One of his clients had paid for a show – two girls licking and fingering each other enthusiastically. Once he'd given up watching and joined in, they'd left each other alone and concentrated on pleasuring him. They weren't really into it – it was all just acting – enjoyable for that, mind you, but not exactly real.

A few weeks later, Barbara away visiting her friend in Norfolk, he had gone with Polly to a flat in town to meet Suzanne.

To say the woman was charismatic was an understatement. She was animated, confident like Polly, but witty and intelligent, even intellectual. And completely insatiable. They had dinner, wine, and then fucked the night away, all three of them. He flagged long before Polly and Suzanne did. Polly had been right, there was something dangerous and yet addictive about relinquishing control to another person. And when the two of them finally fell asleep, he knew that something had changed. He wanted to see Suzanne again. More than that. He had never thought for one minute a woman would come along who would be sensational enough to make him want to leave Barbara, with all the hassle and financial costs that would incur. But as he slipped in and out of consciousness, his thoughts strayed to how on earth he would persuade Barbara to leave him without it costing him any money.

And now, as Brian felt himself drifting towards sleep, he smiled. He'd done it. He belonged to Suzanne, now, in every sense. And Barbara was gone.

The pub was noisy and warm, the windows steamed up from the beery breath of a hundred or so patrons, fifty per cent of them Job from one department or other. When they'd shut the subsidised bar at the station two years ago, the landlord of the King William had suddenly found his takings up by nearly a hundred per cent. He'd lost a few of his old regulars, the ones who didn't fancy sharing their pint with the likes of the local CID and who had used the nickname 'Old Bill' for the pub, rather than the King Bill – but the huge leap in profits more than compensated for it.

You couldn't miss Andy Hamilton in a crowd, Lou thought. He was a head taller than anyone else, propping up the bar with Les Finnegan and some of the others. She almost ducked back out of the door when she realised Jason wasn't there, but by that time Hamilton had beckoned her over. 'Here she is, look,' she heard him saying to someone else.

'What are you having?' Ali Whitmore was at the bar, most of a round of drinks lined up in front of him.

'Just a Coke, please, Ali.'

Hamilton made her a space on the bar stool next to his, gave her a warm smile. The others were all laughing and joking, the tensions of the case forgotten. She realised she had forgiven him, because suddenly the anger she'd felt this afternoon wasn't there any more.

'You look great,' he said, quietly, leaning towards her so the rest of them didn't hear.

She smiled. 'I feel like shit.'

He laughed. 'In that case, I'd like to see you on a good day. Guess who I just spoke to?'

'Who?'

'Taryn Lewis. Brian Fletcher-Norman's daughter. She rang to speak to Sam.'

'And?'

'She didn't want to leave a message. Just that I recognised the voice, is all. She was with Flora this afternoon when I met her in the coffee shop. Didn't tell me who she was.'

'What's she like?'

Hamilton hesitated and she knew that he was thinking about how she looked rather than what sort of a personality she had. 'She was all right, I thought,' is what he said. Eventually. 'Anyway, Flora is staying at her house so she's all tucked up safe and sound, and we can pull her in first thing tomorrow. I told Sam to call her back, anyway.'

His eyes looked tired, and Lou wondered how he was sleeping. He'd once told her that he never slept a full night, needed tablets to catch up on sleep during the day when he was on nights.

'Just like old times, huh?' he said, raising his glass and only just stopping short of giving her a wink.

She pulled a face at him. 'Yeah.'

Across the bar, she saw Jason coming out of the Gents and making his way through the bodies back towards the table. He met her eyes and gave her a smile.

Andy had edged closer, having followed her gaze across the pub. 'We should go to the Palace of India,' he said. 'I fancy a curry. Don't you? Fancy a curry?'

A year ago, they were in the Palace of India celebrating the end of a case. The drug dealer they'd been targeting for months had been arrested; the search teams had seized eight kilos of heroin and nearly a quarter of a million pounds in cash. The interview teams, led by Lou, had managed to get not only a confession of sorts, but evidence links to other organised crime gangs across the county and the whole team had headed into town, drinking from one place to another, Andy flirting with her as he had done through the case, both of them not letting it get any further because they were both too busy, too focused, to let something get in the way. Now that was gone.

In the Palace of India Andy sat next to her, his thigh pressed against hers, the smell of his aftershave, faint after a long day, driving her mad. While everyone was too drunk, too loud to notice, he slipped his hand under the table and between her knees, sliding her skirt up her thighs, stroking her skin. Lamely she pushed him away, once. Then everyone was going, heading off to a club or something. He'd hung back, the others hurrying ahead to get in the queue. He pulled her into a doorway, pressed her tight against the glass door, his body pressed against hers. She pushed her hands inside his jacket, feeling the warmth of him, while his mouth invaded hers. She felt the pressure of him through the fabric of his jeans, his hand up her skirt at the back, on the verge of pulling aside her underwear until she noticed over his shoulder that they were about to fuck in full view of a restaurant full of people.

Instead of turning left towards the nightclub, they turned right to the taxi rank, took a cab back to her house. He left at half past three, when she was just falling asleep. Kissed her goodbye so tenderly she barely felt it, only the smile that went with it.

'No thanks,' she said now. 'You guys go ahead. I've gone right off curry.'

Finishing the last of her drink, she gave him a smile that didn't quite go all the way up to her eyes. 'Night everyone. Thanks for the drink, Ali. See you tomorrow.' As a parting shot she palmed Ali forty quid to get a round or two in, then went out into the cold to find her car.

The wind was tugging at the corners of her coat while she fished in her bag for her keys. She didn't hear the footsteps behind her until a second before she wheeled round, and there he was, behind her. He grabbed her arm to steady her.

'Jesus, Andy. Don't sneak up on me like that.'

He leaned forward a little, pinning her against the car. 'Don't go,' he said, his face close to hers. 'I wanted to spend a bit of time with you. Like the old days.'

'Andy,' she said sharply. 'We're in the bloody station car park. Right under the CCTV. Get off me.'

His hand was around her waist, strong and firm. He fitted against her exactly, his whole body warm and solid and safe. She felt her heart give, just a little bit. Then she felt the unmistakable hardness of his erection and the feeling passed in a sudden, nauseating rush.

'Inspector, get the fuck off me. NOW.'

He moved quickly, almost stumbling back. 'I'm sorry,' he said. 'Sorry. Don't know what came over me.'

Lou looked at him, his face shadowed in the half-light from the arc lights by the exit.

'I'm telling you,' she said, her voice soft, carried away on the wind, 'it's not going to happen. If you pull a stunt like that again I'll put in a complaint.'

His expression changed, grew cold. 'You wouldn't do that to me, Lou. Would you?'

'You seem to be having trouble getting the message. I'm telling you again, it's not going to happen. Can we just call an end to it now – please?'

He attempted a smile. 'Sure. I'm sorry. I just – well. You're beautiful, and I won't stop wanting you. That's all.'

'You're *married*,' she said, with an air of finality, opened the car door and got in. He stood there for a few moments, then he turned away.

Lou exhaled, rested her head against the window, trying with long deep breaths to stay focused. As she felt herself calming, the car parked two spaces away from her beeped and flashed its indicators. She watched as a familiar figure crossed the car park in front of her and she took a sharp breath in.

He stopped when he saw her sitting there. He even chanced a smile and a wave but then he hesitated, changed direction and walked instead over to her car.

Shit. Not now, not right this minute.

He was right by her window. She looked straight ahead, thought too late about rooting in her bag and bringing out her phone so she could pretend she was taking an urgent call.

What the hell, there was no point pretending, was there? Not when all she wanted to do was go somewhere Hamilton wasn't, get drunk and spend the night with someone who was not, just for a change, married to someone else.

By the time she glanced up at her window he'd gone, and at that precise moment the passenger door of her car opened and Jason Mercer climbed in beside her.

21:55

'What's wrong?' he asked her.

She laughed at this and even to her own ears it sounded forced. 'Nothing, everything's fine.'

And then his hand on her shoulder and he was pulling her across into his arms and holding her tightly. The warmth of his body, through the thin cotton of his shirt, against her hot cheek; the smell of him, his masculine warmth, so good that she realised she was taking deep breaths on purpose.

'It's OK,' he said. 'It's all right. I've got you.'

And for a moment it was all right, and then it was completely not all right and she pulled away from him.

'Oh God. I'm sorry. What am I thinking?'

For a moment she couldn't look at him and then she did and she was lost in the way he was looking back at her. *I don't want to do this. I don't want to make these stupid mistakes all over again.*

He broke off the eye contact and looked straight ahead, out of the windscreen at the cars and the darkness and the rain spitting on the windscreen. He cleared his throat.

'So, I'm going to go get in my car,' he said. 'You're welcome to follow me, if you like. I'll cook you dinner and we can get drunk together and you can tell me all about what's happened to you and why you're unhappy.'

She made a sound as if to say something – thanks, but no – you're kind – I'm your SIO, it's not appropriate – I can't –

But he wasn't quite finished.

'Or you can drive home on your own and I won't mention it again. Does that sound OK?'

She nodded dumbly. Christ, what on earth was she doing? He was giving her the option to walk away from this horribly embarrassing encounter and yet she already knew what she was going to do.

He opened the door.

'Jason,' she said.

He looked back at her.

'Are you sure about this?'

He smiled as if that was a reply and shut the door. She started the engine immediately, thinking that she was going to drive away now, right now, before he even got back to his car and she would have to exit through the barriers behind him, thinking that if she did it quick enough he would have got the message properly and there would be no more flirting, no more lingering looks, no more intense silences.

And then he was reversing out of the parking space and her chance for that particular dramatic gesture had gone.

She waited for a moment and then turned on the lights and the windscreen wipers, and eased the car out. His car went through the barrier and waited at the junction while she swiped her pass. Then he indicated left.

After just the briefest hesitation, she followed him.

22:12

Jason parked on the driveway of a house about two miles across town, and Lou pulled in to the kerb outside. He was waiting for her in the doorway. He took her hand to lead her inside, and then didn't let go of it. She stood in the darkness of his hall, the door still open behind her, looking at him. He pushed the door closed, slowly, purposefully, with one hand, without taking his eyes off her.

His hand threaded through her hair and pulled her close to him and then he kissed her. Oh, it felt good. Like a huge sense of release.

She kicked off her shoes and that felt good, too, even though she didn't quite make it up to his shoulder without her heels. He took her through to his living room, turned on a table lamp next to the sofa, kissed her again.

There was a pile of laundry folded on the sofa, newspapers and a cereal bowl and a mug on the coffee table.

'Sorry,' he said, 'wasn't expecting ... this.'

'It's a nice room,' she said, to make him feel better.

He put the laundry on the other chair and pulled her down onto the sofa with him. There was no debate about it, no hesitation. It was a this-needs-to-happen-now moment; his arms pulling her close against him, one of his hands at the small of her back, one in her hair.

As they kissed, his hands moved over her body, exploring her. Lou thought distractedly how it was good precisely because he didn't just get his hands straight up her skirt or into her blouse – he was getting to know her body, all of it, even the parts most men tended to miss: the back of her neck, her throat, the insides of her elbows, the small of her back. She pressed her fingertips into the muscles on his chest, feeling the beating of his heart as he breathed into her hair; ran her fingers down the back of his head, feeling his short hair.

Her phone bleeped loudly to signify an incoming message. She ignored it but a second later he pulled his head back and said, 'You need to get that.'

'No,' she said. And then her stomach gurgled loudly and they both laughed.

He extricated himself and sat up. His shirt had become untucked at the back and she pushed her fingers up inside, over his warm skin.

'I should get us some food,' he said, looking down at her.

'I'm not hungry, really,' she said.

'You should still eat. I haven't seen you eat anything except KitKats.'

'I think it counts as one of my five a day, or at least the orange ones do.'

He went to the kitchen that was separated from the living room by a breakfast bar, turned on the lights. The text was from Hamilton. Just a single word: Sorry.

She watched him moving around his kitchen, cutting slices of wholemeal bread that looked home-made, then bringing out lettuce, radishes, olives and cucumber from the fridge and chopping and mixing.

'Tell me how come you're in the UK,' she asked again.

He stopped for a moment, looked at her. That blue-eyed gaze again, so intense. 'It's a long story,' he said.

'I'm interested.'

He got a plastic container out of the fridge and when he pulled the lid off the tub, a waft of garlic and lime and chilli came out of it.

'So I was working in Toronto and I got talking to a girl in the UK online,' he said. 'I came over here and kinda stayed put.'

Lou waited for him to continue, expecting there to be more. He took chicken out of its marinade and added it to a wok that started up an immediate, fragrant sizzle.

'I thought you said it was a long story,' she said.

'Felt like it at the time.'

'What happened to her?'

If she'd stopped to think about it she would probably have changed the subject, because he was looking increasingly uncom-fortable. But that was the trouble with being a police officer. You started off with the little things and sooner or later there was a nugget of information that was too interesting to ignore, and you dug and dug at it until what you eventually found was the great big mine of information that lay buried beneath. It was addictive – and easy to lose sight of the fine line between professional curiosity and tactless intrusiveness.

'She wasn't serious about it.' He was looking at her again, his hands spread on the breakfast bar, facing her.

'That's a shame.'

'Yeah, well. Doesn't matter now. I'm over it, a long time ago.'

He turned back to the stove, flipping the pieces of chicken with a pair of tongs, then adding them to the two plates that already had salad on them. The smell was wonderful. He got two forks out of a drawer, a bottle of red wine from a rack under the breakfast bar, two glasses from the cupboard. He opened the wine and poured it. The discussion about his love life was clearly at an end.

'Let's eat, hey?'

5x5x5 Intelligence Report

From: Crimestoppers

To: DCI Louisa SMITH

Subject: OP NETTLE – Polly LEUCHARS

Date: 02/11/12

Grading E / 5 / 1

Call from MOP [Member of the Public] to Crimestoppers at 2153hrs on 02/11/12 regarding Op Nettle.

Caller reports seeing Polly LEUCHARS on the night of 31/10/12 in a small dark blue car. The car was parked halfway into the driveway of one of the houses on Cemetery Lane with the rear end of the car sticking out into the road. Caller had to swerve to avoid it.

Caller states he parked up in the lay-by just ahead of the driveway and walked back to the car to remonstrate with the driver. Driver described as young woman, aged late twenties, long blonde hair. Woman was in a distressed state and was arguing with a man who was in the passenger seat of the vehicle. Caller states he decided to leave it and went back to his own car and drove home.

Time of sighting of car was approximately 2325hrs as he states the news was on ITV when he got home shortly afterwards.

Caller saw press briefing regarding the murder earlier today and felt he should report this sighting.

No description of male seen in vehicle.

Caller wishes to remain anonymous.

23:58

I shouldn't fall asleep here, Lou thought. But it was a battle she was losing – already her eyes were closed. She was lying on the sofa with Jason, both of them still fully dressed, if a little dishevelled. His breath was heavy and deep against her hair, and if it hadn't been for his fingers still gently stroking her shoulder, she would have thought he'd dozed off.

Dinner had been great, the bottle of wine was great, and she'd managed to restrain herself from inappropriate conversation, like quizzing him about previous relationships. In fact, back on the long deep sofa that seemed just the right size and shape for two people to lie face to face, when he'd touched her hair and then whispered 'You're beautiful' in her ear she even forgot that she wanted to ask him about ice hockey and didn't they wear some sort of face protection these days?

And now it seemed much too late to mention it, and the most important thing seemed to be remembering not to fall asleep here – and then it was too late for that, after all.

Day Three – Saturday 3 November 2012

08:50

The briefing room was busy, despite it being Saturday: full of people talking at the tops of their voices. Jason was logging on to the computer, preparing the slides that would take everybody through the main points.

Lou snuck in at the back. She felt flushed, like the first day back at school, waiting to see the boy you fancied.

She'd left his house at six, having woken up chilly and with an ache in her shoulder. At some point in the night he'd covered them both with a fleece blanket, but it had half-fallen off the sofa. He was still fast asleep, still fully clothed. When she moved, he stirred and woke.

'Hey,' he said, sleepily.

'Morning. I should go.'

'In a minute.' He moved and stretched, pulled her tighter against him. 'We should have gone to bed, you know.'

'I shouldn't have fallen asleep.'

She eased herself out of his embrace and went to find her shoes. 'I might see you a bit later, then? Only if you don't have anything else planned . . .'

'You kidding? I'll be there for the briefing.'

He was not only there, he was looking smart and refreshed and fully in control. In contrast she felt half-awake and, despite her shower and change of clothes, hopelessly crumpled.

This is ridiculous, she thought, checking out the room to see who was there, who was ready to go. No sign of Andy. He'd better turn up in time for the start of the briefing or she'd have him.

Sam Hollands approached her. 'Ma'am. How are you today?'

'I'm fine, thanks, Sam. How are things with you?'

Sam smiled. 'Going well, I think. I spoke to Taryn Lewis last night. She went to see her father in the hospital and quite a lot of info came out of it. Seems Brian was seeing Polly after all.'

'Really?'

'Polly introduced Brian to swinging, through a woman called Suzanne. Yesterday Brian asked Taryn to phone this Suzanne to ask her to come and see him in the hospital.'

'Do we know any more about her?'

Sam shook her head. 'CSIs are due to start work on the Barn this morning, now we've identified Barbara as a suspect. Search teams are going in first. We know where Brian's phone is, thanks to Taryn, so we'll get started on it as soon as we've got it in an evidence bag.'

Lou made her way through the tangle of chairs and gave Jason a brief smile.

'Right, let's have some hush,' Lou called, got everyone's attention. 'Just a few things to bring you up to date. As most of you know by now, today's priority is to get a statement from Flora Maitland. Sam's managed to secure a Section 8 warrant for Flora's flat and for the farm, so we'll have another briefing this afternoon once we know what we've got from that. Sam, who's going to bring Flora in?'

'I'm going to go with Les,' Sam said. 'Miranda Gregson is lined up to do the interview but she's not coming in till later. Dentist.'

'Right, thanks, Sam. And as for Flora, we haven't got enough to

164

nick her, but at least if we bring her on board we can get her account down on paper. Any questions so far?'

Nothing other than rapt attention.

At the back of the room, the door opened and Andy Hamilton came in. He stepped over toes, jackets and bags, muttering apologies, found a seat.

'Sorry,' he whispered.

She gave him a look, but didn't reply.

Lou ran through the events for the previous few days, up to the discovery of Polly's body and on to the discovery in Ambleside Quarry. Confirmation now that Polly's blood had been found on Barbara Fletcher-Norman's clothing, and forensics from Yonder Cottage, meant that she was officially a suspect in Polly's murder. The sighting of the car on Cemetery Lane provoked some murmurs – not all of them had seen the information report.

Lou was nearly done. 'Now, I know it all looks very much like Barbara was responsible, but we still need to evidence it. By the end of today I want to know who that man in the car was, what that argument was about. Can we sort out another press release?'

Sam nodded. 'I'll see if I can get the witness to come forward – see if he can ID anyone.'

'Thanks. I want to sort out Polly's relationships, I want to know exactly who was sleeping with whom and when – and did any of them get jealous? We need to follow up everything that came in yesterday, even if it sounds trivial. I know we've finished the house-to-house but half term's over with now, people who were on holiday will be coming back so we need to go back and check all the houses we missed. When that's done, I need someone to get Barbara Fletcher-Norman's medical notes. See if she was as unstable as Brian's trying to make us think. Andy, I'd like you to liaise

165

with CSI at the Barn today. Anything useful that comes out of that, you can follow up, OK? Right. Thanks everyone. Next briefing this afternoon.'

The room cleared quickly and noisily, Andy Hamilton waiting at the back for her. Lou saw the way he was looking at her.

'How are you today?' she asked Jason.

'Fine,' he said. 'Could have done with a bit more sleep.'

'Ah. The case going round and round in your head, was it?'

'Something like that.'

She smiled at him. 'I'll catch up with you later.' Then, as an afterthought: 'I nearly forgot. Sam Hollands has got some info from Taryn Lewis – make sure you get her to tell you about it before she disappears off.'

By the time she turned away from Jason, Andy had gone. Lou made a mental note to talk to him at some point during the day, knowing at the same time that she would put it off.

09:05

When Sam Hollands arrived with a ginger-haired man whose name Taryn instantly forgot, Flora had been sitting at the kitchen table eating toast. Chris had left the house early, going with his dad to watch Spurs at home to Wigan.

'We need a witness statement,' Sam said.

'Why can't she do that here?' Taryn wanted to know.

'It would be very helpful,' the man said. He was standing in the doorway, arms folded, in his long wool coat. His light-reactive glasses were taking their time to adjust to being inside the house and as a result he looked like he was trying to be Sam Hollands' enforcer.

'You could have told me about this when I spoke to you last night,' Taryn said crossly.

Sam gave her an apologetic smile but turned her attention back to Flora. 'We're not treating you as a suspect at this time, Flora. It's just easier at the station. Less distracting.'

Flora clearly didn't want to make a fuss. She looked shattered, as though she'd not slept at all. She went with them, leaving the half-eaten piece of toast behind.

After they'd gone Taryn wondered whether to phone Felicity, or Nigel. And then she remembered that she had agreed to phone that Suzanne, her father's whatever she was – fancy woman?

Reluctant as she was to fall into that passive-aggressive trap of being at his beck and call and feeling that even her best efforts would always go unacknowledged, the lure of disobedience was feeble compared to the tug of guilt she felt inside. It wouldn't take long, then she would go to the police station and wait for Flora.

She drove out of Briarstone and on to Morden. As she rounded the bend on Cemetery Lane she could see that the driveway to the farm was blocked with police cars, three of them this time, and a van.

She carried on to the Barn and parked. It felt like her world had suddenly shifted on its axis and left her off-balance. Everything felt wrong. What did they want with Flora, when it was so obviously Barbara who had killed Polly? Who else could it have been?

The Barn was silent, but warm. The heating must have come on. In fact, it felt stuffy inside; Taryn spent a few moments opening windows to let in the fresh air. More post had arrived, along with another letter for Barbara, and one that looked like it might be a bank statement.

Upstairs in Brian's study she found his open briefcase, the mobile phone lying on some files. She picked it up and examined it. It was turned off. She wondered if the battery had died, and pressed the on button fully expecting no response, but it lit up brightly.

It took a moment to work through the menu options until she found 'Contacts' and there, under 'Manchester Office' was a mobile phone number.

Taryn found a pen and wrote the number down on her hand. As she did so, the phone vibrated and beeped in her hand and she nearly dropped it in shock.

It wasn't a call though, it was a text. Three of them.

TEXT MESSAGE

07252 583720 'B MOB' to 07252 583200
31/10/12 2229hrs

youfucking bastard, i hate you i hate you i hae you youll b sorry

TEXT MESSAGE

07484 919987 'Manchester Office' to 07252 583200
01/11/12 0105hrs

Did you get home safe and sound? Let me know.

TEXT MESSAGE

07484 919987 'Manchester Office' to 07252 583200
02/11/12 0950hrs

Hope you slept well. I'm looking forward to seeing you soon.

For a moment Taryn sat at her father's desk, in her father's house, and contemplated how strange a turn events seemed to be taking. Just a few days ago she was living in blissful ignorance of her father's doings and now, it seemed, she knew more about him than she would ever hope to know about another living soul.

Before she could chicken out of it, she dialled 'Manchester Office' and waited, breathless, wondering what she would hear from the other end of the phone.

'Hello?'

'Is that Suzanne?' Taryn said, her voice trembling slightly in spite of herself.

'Who is this, please?'

'My name is Taryn Lewis. I'm Brian's daughter.'

'Oh. I see. How can I help you?'

She was certainly cool, this Suzanne, Taryn thought. She'd given nothing away, absolutely nothing. Almost as if she were expecting someone else to be phoning her using Brian's mobile.

'Brian is in the hospital in Briarstone. He had a heart attack on Thursday morning. He asked me to call you.'

On the other end of the line Taryn could hear voices – an office?

'Thank you for letting me know.'

And, abruptly, the phone was cut off.

She took her own mobile out of her back pocket, scrolled through to find Sam Hollands' number, and dialled. But the call never connected; at that moment a loud banging came from the front door, along with the doorbell chiming.

She opened the door to a whole team of police officers wearing black boiler suits. She didn't know who was more surprised.

REPORT

To: Op Nettle

From: DC 13512 Jane PHELPS

Date: Saturday 3 November 2012 09:42

Subject: Medical Disclosure – Summary

Details of Barbara FLETCHER-NORMAN's medical records received from GP Dr Thomas SUTCLIFFE at the Village Surgery, Morden.

Mrs FLETCHER-NORMAN had been suffering from depression and insomnia diagnosed in March 2012. She had been prescribed various anti-depressant medication, anti-anxiety medication and sedatives and had been taking these sporadically (according to prescription collection data) since. Additionally she was prescribed hormone replacement therapy (HRT).

On 19 September 2012 Mrs FLETCHER-NORMAN was admitted to Briarstone General Hospital following an overdose of medication combined with excess alcohol. She admitted this was a suicide attempt and she was discharged two days later. She was offered counselling but declined. After that she had been taking her medication regularly.

09:45

The wind continued to howl and now, as if to make the whole day worse, occasional showers of sleet and hail began to fall, driven horizontally into the faces of the early Christmas shoppers in the town centre.

Brian Fletcher-Norman was oblivious to the weather. Following the ward round by the ICU consultant, a man Brian had met once, on a golf course, it seemed Brian was well enough to be transferred to the Coronary Care Unit. Most of the monitors had been removed; just his IV drip remained so they could continue to pump him full of 'clotbusters' as Sister Nolan affectionately termed them, and a wire attached to his finger that was monitoring his oxygen levels. Last night they had been at 90%, but this morning they hadn't fallen below 98% since he'd been woken, which had been at six-thirty.

He didn't suppose being on the ward was going to be any more pleasant than being in the ICU; in fact, it would probably be much worse, but at least it would be a change of scene. And moving to the ward was a step closer to going home.

Plenty of time for thinking about things, sitting here, waiting for those brainless porters to come and wheel his bed away to the ward. Surely they must want to clear the space for some other poor bastard?

How long would it be before he would be back at the golf club? Would he have to sort out Barbara's funeral, first? Surely nobody would say anything if he put in a couple of rounds, something to take his mind off things.

After all, it had been undoubtedly the worst week of his whole life.

As he settled into the warm cosiness of a true bout of self-pity, he was interrupted by a porter, helpfully wearing a name badge which proclaimed him to be RON, who unhooked his drip and unplugged the oxygen monitor, dumping it casually between Brian's feet.

'You OK there, mate?' Ron asked cheerily. 'Where to? CCU? Right-oh.'

Passing the nurses' station, Brian's load was added to by Sister Nolan, who dumped his notes, files and charts on the bed and removed the oxygen monitor. Before he could ask, she gave Ron a pretend sour look. 'You're a cheeky one, Ronald. Don't you be taking our kit away. This is staying right here. Don't worry, Brian, they'll plug you in to a new one when you're on the ward.' She gave his arm an affectionate pat. 'Good luck,' she said softly, and then Ron wheeled the bed through the ward doors.

Good luck? Brian thought. Am I going to need it for the CCU? Or does she just think I'm going to die after all?

10:02

Buchanan had kept her waiting, of course, but she'd expected that. It was a control thing. He liked her to be sitting down in his office, trying not to nose around the room, trying not to fidget, so that she would have to stand when he entered, like a schoolgirl in the head-master's office.

'Good morning, sir,' she'd said as he finally blustered in, stand-ing up whilst holding on to all the loose bits of paper she'd been scanning, waiting for his appearance.

'Ah – how's it going? Progress?'

'As you know, we're in the process of getting a statement from Flora Maitland. Meanwhile, we've got search teams all over the farm, so with a bit of luck we'll find something we can put to her in interview. For the time being, we need to establish her movements on the night Polly died, since the cellsite data from Polly's mobile seems to indicate that she visited Flora at home that night.'

'What about the – er – suicide?'

Barbara Fletcher-Norman: the only person Lou could legitimately

172

identify as a suspect, and she was lying on a big metal tray in Adele Francis's mortuary.

'We've got several strong lines of enquiry. Her husband Brian is looking promising – at least for further information. He told his daughter that he was having an affair with Polly Leuchars. And we have forensics linking Mrs Fletcher-Norman to the murder scene.'

'Hmm.' Buchanan was reclining slightly in his big leather chair, which dwarfed him. 'So you think the wife killed Polly out of jealousy and then went to the quarry to commit suicide?'

'That does seem the most likely explanation at the moment.'

There was a pause. Buchanan was skimming through his emails. Come on, Lou thought. Some of us have work to do.

'What do you think?' he asked.

Lou hesitated. Although she trusted her instincts, she never liked to share them with other people until she had good solid evidence to back it up.

'I think there's a lot more to it than that. And we still need to establish whether Nigel Maitland has anything to do with it.'

Another pause. Something he'd read on his PC was making him chuckle.

'Sir? Was there anything else?'

He gave a short cough and returned his attention to her. 'No, no. Just checking how things are going. Got everything you need? Resources?'

'For now, we're managing. As long as I don't start getting abstractions.'

'I'll hold them off as long as I can.'

Of course, he was still doing her favours and making sure she knew it, Lou thought as she hurried back to the MIR. It didn't feel right, the way he oversaw her investigation and granted her things she needed to run it as though he was her Lord and Master granting her largesse. At some point she was sure he would start asking for some sort of favour in return. She'd heard from Sarah Singer, a DCI who'd gone to the Met last year, that Buchanan had taken more than his fair share of credit for her investigations when they'd got a good result.

The MIR felt warm and more than a little stuffy by the time she finally made it, two coffees and a KitKat from the vending machine balanced on top of her stack of paperwork.

Jason was on the phone when she passed his desk. She gave him a smile, indicated the second coffee with a nod of her head and he nodded back. She went on into her office and sat down.

Already on her desk was another pile of information reports, witness statements and charts. Jason was working on a new network chart indicating the various people involved in the case and their relationships to each other.

She looked up at the knock on the door, felt her heart lift slightly as she gave him a wave to come in. He didn't waste time with a greeting:

'I've got some news. Well, three things.'

'Go on,' Lou said, although he hadn't paused.

'Firstly Jane got the medical history for Barbara Fletcher-Norman. Suicide attempt in September, not a serious one, but she was on anti-depressants when she died.'

'Well,' Lou said, 'that puts a different slant on things.'

'Secondly, Mandy just took a call from the hospital. Brian's been transferred to a regular ward.'

'And the third thing?'

'Not such good news. The search team went in to the Barn this

174

morning. Taryn Lewis was there, playing with her dad's mobile phone.'

'Shit! I thought the Barn was supposed to be sealed off?'

'Brian gave her a key, asked her to check the post. Nobody thought about that one.'

'What's happened to the phone?'

'The search team bagged it and took it straight to Computer Crime for download. Let's hope they haven't got too much of a backlog.'

'Where's the DI?' asked Lou.

'He went out after the briefing,' Jason said.

'Thanks, Jason. The coffee and the KitKat's for you,' she said.

Something was going on with Hamilton. He had always been a bit of a risk-taker, it was one of the things she'd liked about him, but that – whatever it was – last night in the car park, that was something completely different. It was like he'd crossed the line into reckless. And she had crossed a line, too: from being still attracted to him, despite his behaviour, into a nagging concern for his welfare. He had been a little drunk. Maybe that explained it: but it still felt like something was wrong.

10:17

For a moment she stood waiting at the access door to the ICU, looking through the glass door, past the posters encouraging healthy living, avoiding drink-driving, and advertising self-help groups, to where the bed Brian had previously occupied was being made by two healthcare assistants.

Taryn hadn't rung the bell yet, to gain access.

Maybe he had died in the night. She considered how this made her feel, searched for something, but found nothing. She turned to go.

There was to be no escape, though. Sister Nolan was coming towards her, wearing a thick wool coat buttoned up to the neck.

'Ah, you'll be disappointed now if you're looking for your dad,' she said, her voice loud in the quiet corridor. 'He's been moved down to Stuart Ward. Ground floor. Much better this morning, he was. All right?'

Taryn tried to arrange her face into an expression of gratitude and relief. Back on the main corridor, which connected the different wings of the hospital, the traffic was unrelenting, porters pushing people on beds, relatives carrying magazines and Sainsbury's carrier bags. Further down, past the maternity wards, mothers-to-be going for walks to try and encourage labour, leaning against the wall every so often as another contraction hit. Oh yes, whatever you were here for was done entirely in public these days.

At last Taryn located Stuart Ward. It was far from peaceful, a world away from the ICU, with a constant flow of people coming and going. The nurses' station was unoccupied, so Taryn consulted a huge whiteboard that listed everyone on the ward, who their consultant was, and what they were in for. Everything from 'appendix' to 'hip replacement' – and there he was: Brian Fletcher-Norman, Bay 3, coronary.

He looked so miserable that Taryn felt a curious rush of both pity and joyous revenge.

'Tabby. Good to see you.' He was still wearing that hospital gown, she noted, one of those ones that opens at the back so everyone can see your arse if you need to go somewhere. Good job I didn't find any pyjamas, she thought. But then she noted the dressing gown she'd brought last night, slung over the chair next to the bed. She moved it and sat down.

'They moved you, then,' she began.

'Ah, that's my daughter. Mistress of the Bleeding Obvious.'

She pressed her lips together tightly.

He must have seen her expression and remembered that he needed her, because he said quietly, 'Sorry. Been a tough morning.'

'Right,' she said.

He was twisted awkwardly in the bed, trying to turn to see her. It would have been better for her to sit on the edge of his bed, but she didn't want to get any closer to him.

'Did you get hold of her?' he asked quickly.

In the bed to Taryn's left, an old man was fast asleep, snoring like an elderly pig, wheezing and rasping. The curtain was pulled slightly across, but she took a quick peek behind it. The man's mouth had fallen open, revealing pale gums. On the lap trolley next to the bed, a plate of congealing shepherd's pie lay untouched. As she watched, a fly buzzed past and settled on it.

'Taryn. Did you phone her?' His voice had a sharp edge to it.

The more he spoke to her like that, the less inclined she was to be helpful. 'Nice here, isn't it, Dad? I thought you were better off upstairs, myself.'

'They were going to put me in the Coronary Care Unit, but they didn't have enough beds. This is the "leftovers" ward. Fucking unbelievable.'

'Mmm. I expect you'll be glad to go home, won't you?'

Brian stared straight ahead at the curtains around the opposite bed. If they'd been opened, Brian might have had a chance to see a bit of window. 'Apparently they want to keep me in for a bit.'

'Jolly good thing too,' Taryn said brightly.

He shot her an evil look. 'How do you work that one out?'

'Well, at least the police will go easy on you while you're in here.'

He looked away again, concentrating on the curtains. 'What do the police have to do with anything? And keep your voice down.'

Taryn relaxed a bit more, leaning back into the armchair. Although the bay was bright enough, there was a distinct smell of something – urine, probably. A bag of it was hanging below the curtain, attached to the bed next door. 'I should imagine they're just desperate to talk to you. Your lover and your wife, both dead on the same night? Good Lord.'

'For your information,' he growled, his cheeks reddening, 'they've already seen me. They know I had nothing to do with Polly's death, for Christ's sake.'

'But you didn't tell them Polly was your lover, did you?'

Slow realisation crossed his face. 'You told them?'

She shrugged, wondering if he could tell just how much she was loving every minute of this conversation.

He was so angry he couldn't look at her any more, but his cheeks were pale now. 'Did you phone her?' he asked again, quietly.

'Yes, I did.'

'What did she say?'

'Nothing much. I just told her where you were, and she said thanks. That's all.'

'Did you bring the phone with you?'

'No, I didn't.'

'Why not?'

'Well, firstly, you didn't ask for it. And secondly, the police took it and put it into an evidence bag.'

'What?'

'They turned up at the Barn while I was there. They've got a search warrant. Or something. I didn't really look. After all, it's not my house, is it?'

The snoring stopped abruptly. Taryn waited for it to resume. A minute passed, during which she'd been wondering if she should go and find someone, but then the bed creaked and it resumed as a low, throaty rumble.

'Polly's death,' Taryn said.

'What?'

'You said you had nothing to do with Polly's death. Does that mean you had something to do with Barbara's?'

'Are you stupid? Of course I didn't. She killed herself, didn't she? Isn't it obvious?'

Taryn stood up to go, buttoned up her jacket, fished around inside her bag for her car keys. She'd entirely had enough of being called stupid.

'Are you going? What about – look, Taryn, can't you go and buy me some pyjamas? From M&S?'

Her heart was as cold as her voice, when it came. 'I don't think I'll have the time.'

On the way out, thinking about how she could make Flora feel better, Taryn just missed the striking woman who was making her way to Stuart Ward, having first tried the ICU. They passed in the corridor, each entirely unaware of the other, Suzanne having never been shown a picture of Taryn, and Taryn having no knowledge of what her father's lover looked like.

11:37

'Stop,' said Ali, pulling out of the police station car park into the traffic. 'Tell me that again, bit by bit.'

Jane Phelps had started off the conversation by passing on the news from Sam Hollands about Brian's daughter, and Ali had only been half listening. Now, though, something Jane had said had dragged him back to full awareness.

A rustle of Jane's notebook as she consulted what she'd scribbled earlier, the phone receiver tucked behind her ear. 'Taryn Lewis said her father had told her that he had been Polly's lover, but wasn't any more. And that he had a new lover, a woman called Suzanne. He asked Taryn to phone her to tell her about his heart attack. No mention of whether she also had to tell her about poor old Barbara, but there you go.'

'Good Lord,' Ali muttered. 'It's all going on in Morden, isn't it? So that's why she was at the Barn this morning, phoning this Suzanne?'

Jane shrugged. 'I guess so.'

Silence fell for a moment while Ali waited at the traffic lights. 'How do you want to play this?'

'By ear. He should be on the mend if they've moved him to a regular ward, so I think he's up to a few more robust questions. But we really need to get him on his own so it depends how private the ward is.'

Not nearly private enough, was Ali's first thought when they found their way to Stuart Ward. The curtains around Brian's bed were partly drawn, so only when Jane pulled them slightly aside did she see the view of Brian's bare back as he sat on the edge of the bed, his feet dangling a few inches above the polished vinyl floor. He looked around sharply. 'What the—?'

Jane apologised but held her ground. 'Sorry to intrude, sir. How are you feeling?'

Brian sat back on the bed and Jane pulled the thin sheet and blanket over his legs, giving off the professional air of someone who has seen it all before.

'We're police officers, Brian, as you might have gathered. My name is Detective Constable Jane Phelps and my colleague there is Detective Constable Alastair Whitmore. Hope you don't mind if we have a chat with you?'

'Not at all,' he replied, although he looked far from comfortable.

'How are you feeling?' she asked again, keeping her voice low.

He cleared his throat. 'I was feeling much better, but I just had a visit from my daughter. She really is a piece of work.'

'In what way?'

'She's gloating at my predicament. We don't get on and she's refused to get me any pyjamas, which is why you find me in this state. And, to cap it all, I understand she's told you that I was romantically involved with Polly Leuchars!'

Brian was clearly upset. Ali defused the situation by changing the subject: 'You don't mind if we take some notes while we talk?'

A brief hesitation. 'No, I suppose not. It's all lies, what she told you.'

'Are you happy to talk here, Brian? I'm sure the sister might be able to arrange something more private.'

Brian considered this for a moment. 'No, no, this is fine. As long as you're not going to shout about it all.'

Jane gave him a sweet smile. 'May I?' and without waiting for a definite response, perched on the edge of the high-backed chair by the head of the bed.

'Why don't you tell me about Polly, Brian? When did you first meet?'

181

'I went to the stables for horse riding lessons. Nigel Maitland and I played golf together and we've been to dinner at the farm a few times. He suggested I should have some riding lessons to keep fit, get me out into the fresh air.'

Jane sat completely still, trying to maintain eye contact, letting the vacuous sweet smile remain on her lips, listening to what she could already tell was a complete load of bollocks. 'And did you have lessons with Polly?'

'A couple. I didn't know her name then. She was at a dinner party we went to at the farm a few weeks later.'

'You had lessons with her and you didn't know her name?'

'No – yes. I mean, she told me her name, but I didn't really pay attention.'

'And did you carry on with the lessons for a while?'

'I had a couple, as I say. Then we were away on holiday, and I was busy at work, and it sort of tailed off. I can't say it was really my thing. I'm too old to be starting things like that.'

Jane made a little sound to suggest that he was far from decrepit, managing to get him to raise a slightly suggestive grin in response. He leaned towards her a little.

'I do believe she was a bit of a naughty girl, though. I heard a rumour that she was seeing a married man in the village, but I can assure you it wasn't I.'

'Come on, Brian. You must have a good idea – who do you think it could have been? Nigel Maitland?'

Brian tapped the side of his nose conspiratorially. 'I'm saying no more,' he said.

Jane leaned back in the chair, satisfied. He was lying through his teeth about Polly, of course.

'What about Barbara? What did she think?'

Brian's face flushed a little. He took too long over his answer. 'My wife was a jealous woman. She was always ready to believe rumours in that respect.'

'She believed you were having an affair?'

He let out a sigh, raised his eyes to the ceiling as he spoke. 'Someone made a comment about Polly and a married man, she put two and two together and made eighteen, the way she always did.'

'You argued about it?'

'More than once.'

'Was your relationship ever a violent one, Brian?'

'No.' His answer was quick, his voice raised. Then he added: 'At least, never on my part.'

Jane leaned forward again a little to make sure she didn't miss anything. Ali had been scribbling furiously in his notebook the whole time, had barely looked up.

'What do you mean?' Jane asked.

'Barbara was always – er – physical when she had had a drink. She would lash out at me sometimes. Never hurt me, of course, but she would get tongue-tied, slur, and then she would resort to slaps, pushing me away, that sort of thing.'

'And how did you respond?'

'I would walk away.'

Brian's eyes met hers, unfaltering this time. He'd been lying about Polly, but he was telling the truth about the arguments. Whether he was lying to protect his reputation, his integrity, or to distance himself from Polly's murder, the outcome would be the same. Lying to the police was never a good idea.

'We understand that your wife had been diagnosed with depression, anxiety. That must have been quite tough on you.'

183

'Oh, it was. She tried to kill herself a couple of months back, you know. Not seriously. Just enough to make it bloody awkward for me when I had some important meetings coming up at work.'

'How was she recently?'

'All right on some days, bad on others, especially when she'd had a drink.'

'Did she ever drive when she'd had a drink?'

'If she needed to get somewhere. Most of the time, though, she got drunk at home.'

Jane sat back again. 'Thank you, Brian. Have they said how long it will be before you can go home?'

He breathed out in a long sigh, visibly relaxed. Jane wondered what it was he'd been expecting her to ask.

'It can't be soon enough as far as I'm concerned. This place is appalling.'

Jane gave him a reassuring smile, remembering the irony that his wife was actually lying in a cold storage compartment not a million miles away, and he'd not mentioned the loss of her at all, or shown any concern for the violent way she'd apparently chosen to die.

'Will your daughter be coming back to see you?'

Brian shrugged. 'Who knows? I wouldn't be surprised if she comes back to have another gloat.'

Jane stood, raised the strap of her handbag over one shoulder. Ali took the signal and stood too. Jane took hold of Brian's hand and gave it a friendly squeeze.

'Don't listen to her,' Brian said, his voice a low whisper once again. 'She's just making things difficult for me, that's all.'

'Your daughter?' Jane asked.

Brian nodded.

'We will need to interview her again,' Jane said reassuringly, 'but I promise I'll bear in mind what you've said.'

With that they said their goodbyes and left. On the way back to the car, Ali phoned Sam Hollands to report on their progress and see if they had another tasking.

'Head back to the incident room for now, guys,' Sam told them. 'I'm on my way to the quarry with the DCI. Les Finnegan says they've found something that might be the murder weapon.'

'In the quarry?' said Jane into the hands-free kit. 'What is it?'

'No idea. Les is being all secretive, canny old git. It's like he lives for moments like this. I'll let you know later, OK?'

13:52

Being on Stuart Ward was not unlike being in Piccadilly Circus in the rush hour, Brian thought to himself. First of all there had been the initial confusion about where he was to go: the porter had taken him to the cardiac ward, where he was left by himself reclining on his bed in a draughty corridor for half an hour before another porter had turned up and wheeled him along to the far less attractive Stuart Ward. Then there was the ordeal that was Taryn's visit. He'd been harbouring hopes that she might have got over whatever foolish tantrum it was that had caused her to go off in a huff, but obviously this was not the case.

After Taryn, Suzanne. Oh, he'd felt so much better, seeing her beautiful face looking for him – hearing her voice was the best tonic he'd had for days. Then, of course, the conversation that needed to be had. What was to be done. He wished someone would take it all away from him; leave him be to concentrate on getting better. Instead he found he was once again working to a detailed, precise set of instructions.

And then, minutes after Suzanne had left, just as he was gearing himself up to head off to the bathroom for the first time, the two police officers had turned up for one of their friendly chats. He'd had to think quickly, worrying less about what it was he needed to say and concentrating instead on what he absolutely shouldn't. When he spoke to them again he would make sure it was on his own terms.

Now, though, the ward was quietening down. Official visiting time was a few hours away, and it was entirely likely that he wouldn't have any visitors at all. He could just relax, close his eyes and think about how he was going to recover.

```
Email

Date:              Saturday 3 November 2012

Officer:           DC 13521 FINNEGAN

To:                DCI Louisa SMITH /
                   Op Nettle MIR

Re:                Taryn LEWIS / Op NETTLE

CC:                Computer Crime Unit CCU

Visited Mrs LEWIS at home at 1415hrs today.
She confirms she has visited her father in
hospital three times now but has no
intention of visiting him again. She is
quite scathing in her opinions of him.

She confirmed that her father told her that
he HAD been in a sexual relationship with
```

Polly LEUCHARS (Op Nettle). There was no
indication when this affair had begun or
ended, although it seems that her father
has recently been involved with another
female, known to Mrs LEWIS only as
'SUZANNE'. Brian FLETCHER-NORMAN asked Mrs
LEWIS to telephone this SUZANNE and ask her
to visit him in the hospital, which she
duly did. Mrs LEWIS used Mr FLETCHER-
NORMAN's mobile to do this, which she
handed over to officers at Hayselden Barn
this morning.

I would respectfully request that a contact
number for 'SUZANNE' should be obtained
from this phone as a matter of urgency and
subscriber check completed.

13:52

In Briarstone police station, Flora sat in what she couldn't possibly know was the most comfortable of all the interview rooms.
When difficult interviews needed to be conducted with trauma-
tised people, this was the room they used. It had a window, albeit
too high up to see out of unless you stood on tiptoe; carpet that
was stained here and there with various spillages, but nevertheless it was carpet. The chairs were the sort you might find in an
office reception waiting area, low and padded, with a coffee table
in the middle and a further table against the wall upon which was
the obligatory tape recorder.

She had been sitting huddled on one of the chairs, waiting for Andy Hamilton to get back from wherever it was he'd gone. He'd explained that they were performing a search of her flat, and the farm, and that they were looking for Polly's mobile phone. Flora had looked at him as though he were slightly mad. Why would she have Polly's phone? Andy had told her they had a search warrant, but for all of their sakes it would be much easier if she were to give him the keys to her flat and save them having to break in.

She handed them over without a word, and now she was sitting here waiting for them to come back.

They'd asked her if she wanted a lawyer, offered to provide one if she didn't have one of her own, like a solicitor was a handy gadget you carried around in your pocket. She had said no automatically but now she was starting to wonder whether it would be worth calling the number on the card her father had given her. She went over the same arguments in her head: she didn't need a solicitor, because she hadn't done anything wrong. She should get one anyway, because she was her father's daughter and who knew what the police would try and pin on her, even if only to get at Nigel? Joe Lorenzo was phenomenally expensive, and if he wasn't needed, then she would have wasted a lot of money, and Nigel would know she'd been giving them a statement. Until she knew what it was they wanted, then she was better off playing it by ear.

The door opened abruptly and her thoughts were interrupted by the arrival of Detective Inspector Andy Hamilton. To Flora, huddled into her chair, her knees tucked up under her chin, he seemed mountainous. A few moments later the door opened and Miranda Gregson came in. She gave Flora a smile. That was encouraging, at least.

'Sorry to keep you waiting,' Hamilton said, although he didn't sound very sorry and he wasn't smiling. 'I'd just like to remind you that you're under caution, but you haven't been arrested at this stage, and you're free to go whenever you choose to. We asked you if you wanted a solicitor present while we speak to you, and you declined. If you change your mind at any time, we can get a solicitor for you.'

'I understand. I don't want a solicitor, not at the moment anyway.'

Miranda spoke next. 'When we spoke to you yesterday, you told us that you'd been in a relationship with Polly Leuchars. Can you tell us how that came about?'

Flora looked from one of them to the other. They wanted to know? Right then. That wasn't something she needed Joe Lorenzo for. Flora tilted her chin, just slightly, and assumed an air of quiet defiance.

15:25

Les Finnegan was waiting for them in the car park, leaning against the bonnet of an elderly BMW, smoking, looking for all the world like an extra from *The Sweeney*.

'Ma'am,' he acknowledged when Lou got out of the car, 'Sarge,' to Sam Hollands.

'Hold on a sec, Les. Won't be a minute,' Lou said. She beckoned Sam round the back of her car. 'Just stand there, Sam. I'm going to get my jeans on.'

She opened the boot of the Laguna. The first thing out was a piece of old carpet, about a metre square, which she flopped down on the gravel of the car park, and then stood on to remove her shoes. Fishing around in the boot, she found a carrier bag containing a pair of jeans, muddy at the bottom, and some trainers. Sam stood with her back to the DCI, giving Les Finnegan a look, whilst behind her Lou wriggled into the jeans under her skirt, which she then unzipped and stepped deftly out of. A pair of trainer socks over her stockinged feet, and then the trainers. From another bag she pulled out a new pair of latex gloves which she pushed into the pocket of her jacket. Lastly she picked up the square of carpet, shook it down, and threw it back in the boot.

The wind was strong and cold as they walked towards Les, the sky grey and menacing above them. It was still early afternoon, but it was already getting dark.

Les gave her a yellow smile. 'They're about finished down there, to be honest. Just thought it might be worth a visit.'

As he spoke, three members of the party came into view, climbing back up the slope. One of them was a CSI, the other two members of the Tac Team – but they were all dressed in white protective suits. Les introduced Paul Harper, the CSI.

'We found it further down the slope, towards the bottom of the hill. Half buried in the sand. You can track it back up to where it landed – it must have been thrown a fair old way.'

He held up a plastic evidence bag, containing what looked like a black orb of some kind. Grey sand clung to half of it. The way it was pulling down the plastic of the bag, it looked heavy.

'It's a shot-put,' Les said helpfully.

Paul added, 'There's a stand for it on the small table in the hallway, with a little plaque. Apparently Felicity Maitland was a county champion when she was at school.'

'The hallway ... ?' Lou asked.

'Yonder Cottage. I think it was a repository for all the ornaments Mrs M didn't want to keep at the farm.'

Lou took the bag from Paul. It was heavy. And the sand clinging to the side of the shot-put – 'Is it blood under there?'

'Yes, ma'am. We've got a sample – been biked over to the labs already. Hair, too.'

'Prints?'

''Fraid not.'

Lou turned to Paul Harper again. 'So where was it, in relation to the car?'

Paul pointed vaguely over the edge of the cliff, the wind making the white suit flap against his arm. 'About fifty yards further on. Although it was thrown from up here – it didn't fall out of the car.'

'You're sure about that?'

'I'll take some proper measurements and check it all, but yes, I'm sure. We're going to have a look at analysing the trajectory to see if we can work out where it was thrown from.'

'You want to show me?'

The Tac Team officers exchanged a glance which said, actually, no we don't, but Paul Harper gave a nod and took Lou back towards the edge of the slope. 'Wait for me, Sam,' Lou called over her shoulder. 'I won't be long.'

There was a steep path running around the edge of the quarry, and they followed this, a sheer drop to their left. Lou watched her feet, choosing her way carefully. When Paul Harper stopped in front of her, she nearly ran into his back. He indicated the quarry floor, small flags marking the place where the car had been found. Other markers indicated the path of the vehicle through the undergrowth, the locations of bits and pieces that had fallen off the car on the way down.

'You can see it best from here. If we go all the way down you won't get a sense of the perspective,' he told her. Just to the right of them, at the very bottom of the quarry, a small red flag flapped from within a patch of nettles. 'That was where we found the ball. Right down there.'

Lou tried to get a feel for whether the weapon could have fallen out of the vehicle on the way down, but since it had gone so much further it seemed somehow doubtful. 'Did it roll far?'

Paul nodded. 'There's a definite track. That's why I want to trace it back properly, but it's going to take a while to do it with all the foliage, and the light's starting to go. We'll get back onto it first thing.'

Climbing back up to the edge of the quarry, gingerly picking her way through the nettles and scrub, Lou stood for a moment feeling the wind trying to free her hair from the ponytail, whipping it round her cheeks. Sam was waiting, shivering, at the top.

'Dreadful place to choose to end it all,' Sam said, her voice all but lost in the gale.

16:20

Even though she was under caution and therefore free to leave at any moment, Flora agreed to help police with their enquiries until late afternoon. They'd written down all their questions and all her answers to them, had got her to sign several times to say that she agreed with what they'd written. Then she had written out her statement and signed it.

All the searches were complete. Flora's flat had revealed nothing of any interest; Polly's phone was still unaccounted for. Now the shot-put had turned up at the quarry, the investigation had once again veered off in the direction of Barbara Fletcher-Norman. The opportunity to search the farm and all its outbuildings had been thoroughly exploited.

Unfortunately, nothing had come to light there, either. Nigel's solicitor had been called as soon as the team turned up. He observed

MG11 WITNESS STATEMENT

Section 1 – Witness details

NAME:	Flora MAITLAND		
DOB (if under 18; if over 18 state 'Over 18'):		Over 18	
ADDRESS:	Flat 2 14 Waterside Gardens Briarstone	OCCUPATION:	Artist

Section 2 – Investigating Officer

DATE:	Saturday 3 November
OIC:	DC Miranda GREGSON

Section 3 – Text of Statement

My mobile phone number is 07194 141544, it has been my number for the past two years and it is the only mobile phone number I use.

I have known Polly LEUCHARS for a number of years as she was a family friend. In December 2011 Polly started working as a groom at Hermitage Farm, which is owned by my family. I helped out in the stables often and we became very close. Around April 2012 our relationship became more serious, although I knew Polly was not monogamous and was involved with other people at the same time. She was the only person I was involved with. I believe she would have told me who else she was seeing if I had asked, but I did not want to know.

Our relationship came to an end around the end of August when I realised I wanted our relationship to be exclusive, and Polly was not prepared to continue on this basis. We did not argue but I moved back to my flat in Briarstone, partly because I wanted to be on my own for a while. Polly tried to contact me by phone a few times but after a while this stopped.

I last saw Polly when I visited the farm at the end of September or beginning of October. I spoke to her briefly in the yard and we parted on good terms. Polly told me she had found someone special she wanted to be with, but I did not ask who this was. I said goodbye to her and went straight home. This was the last time I saw Polly and I had no further contact with her either by email, phone or in person after that.

On 31 October 2012 I spent the day painting in my studio. I do not remember what time I went to sleep. I slept in the studio and carried on working the next morning until my father telephoned me to tell me that Polly had been found dead.

I do not know of any reason why someone would want to harm Polly and I do not know who might have killed her.

Section 4 – Signatures

....
WITNESS: (F Maitland)

....
OIC: (A Gregson DC 9323)

every part of the process and commented on everything. Their warrant was in relation to Flora Maitland, who did not work at the farm and did not even live there any more. He tried his best to argue that there was no justification for the police to remove anything pertaining to farm business, including computers, files or paperwork. With the warrant they could have taken whatever they wanted, computers, files, the lot. But in the event, Nigel's offices – including the second office at the far end of the barn housing his 4x4 and his Mercedes and the Porsche convertible – had yielded nothing they could use. In the loft above the office, a large safe stood empty, its door open. Whatever had been in there had been moved.

The frustration in the MIR, when Lou returned to it after a visit to the farm to discuss progress with the search co-ordinator, was evident.

'He must have been tipped off,' Les Finnegan was saying. 'That's all there is to it.'

'Well, at least you got him to give a statement,' Ali said. 'That's bloody impressive, if nothing else.'

'It was hardly worth bothering,' Les muttered.

Hamilton came in at that moment, interrupting the debate.

'Andy,' Lou said. 'How are you getting on with Flora?'

He leaned back on the edge of Sam's desk, unbuttoning his jacket. 'Well, the good news is she never called out that wanker of a solicitor.'

'He was busy with us at the farm,' Ali said gloomily.

'That's the good news? Did we get anything useful out of her at all?'

Andy sighed. 'She claims the last time she saw Polly was weeks before she died, and that was at the farm. Flora said she hadn't been near the farm since then.'

'What about the phone?'

Jason said, 'We still don't have a subscriber for that number that Polly was calling.'

'Why not? Have we chased it up?'

'They've been having computer problems at the service provider. No subscriber checks are going through – I chased it up an hour ago.'

That was typical, Lou thought. 'Well, how long's it going to take, do they know?'

'They said they would update me, but I'll ring them back if they haven't got back to me in an hour.'

'I don't think it'll help,' Andy said. 'So she was visiting someone in Briarstone on the night she died. That's not so surprising, is it, given what we know about her? She went for a fuck somewhere, came home, and in the meantime the mad old woman from across the road had decided to confront her. Got herself covered in blood, pissed up, drove to the quarry full of remorse and there you go. Over the edge. Job done.'

'Incredible,' Sam muttered.

'I'm talking about evidence,' he said. 'You've got the weapon, the blood, the motive for it, everything. I think we should stop wasting resources on the Maitlands and concentrate on Barbara and Brian. I wouldn't be surprised if it was Brian that Polly was meeting that night. She met up with him somewhere in Briarstone – away from the farm and the Barn – for a quick shag, Barbara caught them out somehow and saw red.'

He might not be putting it in the nicest of terms, Lou thought, but he had a point.

'So Flora was seeing Polly,' Sam said. 'But so was half the village, including Brian. We don't know who else she was involved with, do we?'

There was a momentary silence.

Lou sighed. 'I think we need to bear in mind that it's still really early days,' she said. 'We've found out a lot already, and yes, it would be nice to have an arrest but we have some good strong leads and plenty to keep us busy, right?'

Everyone looked as tired as she felt.

MG11 WITNESS STATEMENT

Section 1 – Witness details

NAME:	Nigel MAITLAND		
DOB (if under 18; if over 18 state 'Over 18'):		Over 18	
ADDRESS:	Hermitage Farm Cemetery Lane Morden	OCCUPATION:	Farm owner

Section 2 – Investigating Officer

DATE:	Saturday 3 November
OIC:	DC 8244 Les FINNEGAN

Section 3 – Text of Statement

Polly LEUCHARS was employed by my wife, Felicity MAITLAND, to assist at the stables which are part of the farm business. I saw Polly infrequently and I cannot remember the last time I saw her. I do not know of anyone who might have wanted to harm her.

Section 4 – Signatures

....

WITNESS: (N R Maitland)   OIC: (L Finnegan DC 8244)

196

Lou had been running through the intelligence and comparing it with Jason's latest charts and timelines, which he'd left on her desk. They went from the last sightings of Polly in the days before her death, right up to the discovery of the possible murder weapon in the quarry. Adele Francis had already been shown the shot-put and agreed that it was 'likely'.

Of course, if the shot-put *was* the murder weapon, then pretty much everything was still pointing to Barbara Fletcher-Norman as the offender. Tomorrow she would get Jane and Ali to pay another visit to Brian and try to get more out of him about the fatal night. She made a mental note to put in a medical disclosure form to Brian's doctors – it wouldn't do to put pressure on him when his health was so fragile. The last thing the case needed was another death.

She thought Jason had gone home, long ago – or gone over to the King William with the rest of them – until the gentle knock on the doorframe made her jump.

He looked tired, the black eye was yellowing a bit around the edges.

'Hey,' he said.

'Hey, yourself. Come in.'

'I was hoping for some results from the download of Brian's phone,' he said, sitting down, 'but they won't have anything until Monday at least. They've got a backlog, apparently.'

'They've always got a backlog,' she said a tad sourly.

'It would have been a whole lot easier to just check the phone before we handed it over to the CCU.'

Lou smiled. 'Unfortunately, we have to comply with RIPA. Can't have anyone accusing us of tampering with evidence, can we? I know it feels like we've been doing this for weeks but really we're only into the second day.'

'Two days, huh?' he said. 'You're right. Feels longer.'

'Are you finished?' she asked. 'You should get home. You've done a brilliant job and I'm really grateful. And it's Sunday tomorrow, so you are definitely taking the day off.'

He smiled at her. 'I guess I should stop hanging round here late at night. I'm looking way too keen.'

Lou looked up in surprise. 'Keen? You mean on me?'

He looked back into the empty office behind him. 'Yeah, keen on you. Nobody else here right now.'

'Oh.'

'You're really sexy when you blush, Lou.'

She tried a stern look. 'Jason. This isn't happening here, OK?'

'Sure. Just – you know. Whenever. You want me to make you some dinner?'

God, how tempting, how very tempting to just go home with him again. And maybe, this time, stay the whole night and not on the sofa either.

'I'd like to ...'

'I can hear a "but" coming on.'

'I'd like to. But I can't do this. Not at the moment. I need to focus on this case, and I'm spending too much time distracted, thinking about other things ...'

' ... like what we could be doing if we went back to my place?'

Lou looked at him for a long moment, drinking him in while there was nobody else watching. He matched her gaze and the longer she looked, the more tempting it was.

'You know Hamilton is a huge asshole, right?'

'What brought that on?'

'It's just the way he speaks to people. Arrogant piece of shit.'

'He gets the job done, Jason,' Lou said, wondering where this was coming from.

'He'd do it much better if he could stop showing off all the time.'

Lou sighed. 'Unfortunately he's still my DI. Much as I wish he wasn't sometimes.'

'Right. Just know that we're not all shits like that, huh? And when this case is over, or when it quietens down, or when you just need a bit of moral support, I'll be here waiting for you. For whatever it is you want, or you need.'

21:44

Flora was thinking about lying in Polly's bed in Yonder Cottage, the late summer heat drifting lazily in through the open window with the scent of the farm and the white lilies in a vase on the windowsill, naked, too hot for covers. She was gazing at Polly, the almost unbearable beauty of her.

'Flora, don't look at me like that,' she said, smiling.

'Like what?'

Serious, all of a sudden. 'Don't fall in love with me, Flora. I'll break your heart if you do.'

Of course, it was too late. Flora only found out what she meant a month later.

I can't stand it, she thought. I miss her too much.

She heard Tabby coming in, heard the door bang. Heard her muffled conversation with Chris, the kettle going on, mugs clinking in the kitchen.

'She's upstairs. Been there since you phoned.'

' . . . try to talk to her?'

'I don't know . . . thought she was asleep.'

All those text messages between Polly's phone and hers. They were always texting, even when Flora was working at the farm and Polly at the stables. It was like a secret between them, a delicious secret that nobody else could be involved in. At the stables, once, Connor, who had a crush on Polly like everyone else did, was mucking out while Polly brushed Elki's coat and Flora kept interrupting her with messages:

You look so sexy when you bend over

And she'd laughed and Connor had demanded to know what she was laughing at, and that had made her laugh harder, shaking her head so her blonde ponytail swished from side to side like Elki's tail.

And the replies Polly sent, late into the night, all of them saved on Flora's phone:

You are all mine. Later. Wear your red shirt. P x

This weekend I am planning to not get dressed at all. Shall we go to the Lemon Tree naked? What will yr Mum say?? P x

Well, the police had her phone now. They would have seen all those messages, everything that had been private between them. Would they tell Felicity?

Polly was always teasing Flora about coming out. It was time, she said, for Flora to come clean to the world, release herself from the chains of parental expectation. For a while Flora thought this was because Polly wanted to be able to go out in public as partners and lovers, not just as friends. But in reality, of course, it was neither here nor there to Polly whether Flora came out as gay or stayed firmly in her little closet, because from her point of view there wasn't a relationship. The word simply wasn't in Polly's vocabulary. After all these weeks of agonising over what went wrong, Flora realised that it was simply because there was nothing Polly

200

found more depressing than people who weren't true to themselves. She'd phrased it exactly like that once, when they'd been talking about Felicity, whose inhibitions were more of the social class variety.

I wish I could talk to her, thought Flora. Just once more. I just want to tell her I love her, that I miss her, that I don't care that she didn't love me back. I just want to let her know I'm still here and I will always love her . . .

The weekend after that first afternoon in the top field, Flora had taken Polly out for the evening to meet some of her friends. They had drunk too much, giggled like schoolgirls and when the last of the friends disappeared off home, Polly had pushed Flora gently but insistently against a wall and kissed her hard. Flora had responded, at first uncertainly, and then with a force that surprised her. Polly's hand cupped her firmly between her legs, while all Flora could think of was how soft was her mouth, how sweet her taste.

They'd stumbled their way back to Flora's flat.

'Is this where you live?' Polly asked, astonishment on her face, as Flora felt through her pockets for the key.

'Yes, why?'

Polly's face opened into a big, beaming smile. 'No reason. It's lovely, that's all.'

Inside, Polly took Flora by the hand and led her straight to the bedroom, as if she had been in the flat before, as if she knew exactly where everything was. And there she had stripped Flora gently, of her clothes first, and then her inhibitions, and held her as the tears finally came, hours, hours later when the sky was turning grey.

I never knew, she thought. All those years, I never knew it could feel like that. My heart and soul, so complete. So happy.

22:40

Andy Hamilton's crap day had not been improved any by the transition into evening. Quietly sinking the last of his pint, he wondered whether Karen was in bed yet and whether he really should have phoned her – he checked his watch – about three hours ago.

'Time to go home, gents,' the barman said, to Andy and some other poor souls who should also have made their way out a long time ago.

The rest of the squad had gone looking for a curry house at least an hour ago. He'd stayed, claiming he just wanted to finish this one off and he was heading home, but the truth was he didn't want to. He wanted to be with Lou. Not for ever, just for one more night.

He wasn't used to not getting his own way where women were concerned. Every time Lou kicked up a fight he felt a twinge of humiliation – and wanted her all the more. If she would just give in, let him fuck her one more time, he would be able to get her out of his system.

Twice in the last few days he'd felt rejected by women he fancied: Lou last night, and that blonde nurse. Although that wasn't so much of a rejection as a tease. What made it worse was that he knew that if he went home to Karen now, four hours after the end of his shift, reeking of beer, he wouldn't get much of a welcome there, either.

Still, beggars couldn't be choosers. He tipped the dregs of his last pint down his throat and made his way outside.

The night air was brisk and he debated going to fetch his car and taking a chance on the five miles between here and his house, but even with his judgement clouded by alcohol he knew it was a risk too far. He wandered off in the direction of the High Street, got lucky with a taxi driver who knew him heading back towards the rank.

'All right, Andy?' Geoff said, as Andy collapsed into the back seat. 'Big night out, was it?'

'Something like that,' Andy said. 'I'm getting too old for these things.'

All the lights were off in the house. That was a bad sign. Andy walked up the driveway, tried his key in the lock. He couldn't work out for a while why the door wouldn't open, then he realised it was deadlocked and he didn't have a key for that one.

He banged on the door with his fist and a light went on somewhere across the street. Then he saw a piece of paper Blu-Tacked to the doorframe. He ripped it off and took it over to the street light so he could read it.

TOOK KIDS GONE TO SARAH'S.

Why had she bloody double-locked the door? She knew he didn't have the mortise key. He groaned, slowly, and lifted his head to see Geoff's cab coming towards him. He'd been to the end of the road to turn the car around. Seeing his fare standing forlorn by the side of the road, the cabbie stopped, wound down his window.

'Locked out, are you? Need a ride somewhere?'

'Waterside Gardens,' Andy said, almost without thinking, and climbed back into the warm cab out of the drizzle that had developed in the cold, misty night.

22:40

Flora had managed to eat some of Taryn's spaghetti Bolognese. It tasted great, the first proper meal she'd had in days.

'I still say you need to go and see your father,' Taryn said.

'He can wait. If they'd found anything at the farm, we'd all know about it by now.'

'Even so! They had you in custody, Flora.'

'It was a caution, that's all. Helping them with their enquiries. And if they had anything on me, they would have arrested me, wouldn't they?'

After they'd finished eating, Flora went to help Taryn with the washing up.

'I need to go home,' Flora said. 'I've got no clothes, Tabs, and I'll be all right tonight. Thank you for letting me stay. You've been such a good mate. But honestly, I need to go home. And I feel so much better, you know that.'

Taryn shot her a wry grin. 'I know my Bolognese is good, but I didn't realise it could mend broken hearts.'

Having consumed three glasses of wine with dinner, Flora caught a cab back to her flat an hour or so later. She let the cab drop her off at the end of the road, then walked the hundred yards up Forsyth Road to the small cul-de-sac where the flats were. She hesitated when she got to the end of the garden wall separating the small car park from the road and saw a figure standing on the top step. In the faint orange glow from the street light she recognised that hulking great police officer, Andy Hamilton. Flora was indignant. Surely he wasn't going to try and talk to her at this time of night? She was about to turn back when, to her astonishment, the door to the ground-floor flat opened and, without any sound that she could hear, Hamilton was admitted.

She waited for a moment, holding her breath, looked at her watch: it was nearly eleven.

Then, as fast as she could, she ran across the gravel on tiptoe to her own front door, slid the key in the lock, opened the door and shut it quietly behind her. At first, no sound came through the wall separating her hallway from the one of the ground-floor flat; she stood there for several minutes in the dark, the dark staircase leading up to her flat in front of her, standing on a small pile of post and junk mail, listening. She even moved her ear to the wall; then, she heard just two words. The inspector's voice, low, quite close: 'Can I . . . ?'

No reply, but then footsteps, heading towards the back.

And then silence.

23:15

It had been inexcusably late when Andy appeared at 14 Waterside Gardens, that much was clear. By the time the taxi dropped him off for the second time since leaving the pub, the cold air had sobered him up enough to realise that what he was about to do was pretty serious. He'd misbehaved in the past, but every time it had happened had been with someone he knew well. This was uncharted territory.

In his wallet was the packet of three he'd paid over the odds for in the machine in the Gents' toilet of the King Bill, last night. His intention then had been Lou; but now his needs were different. And after all, he thought, his mind wandering back to the encounter on Friday evening, he was nothing if not obedient. She expected more from him, that's what she'd said. And that's exactly what he intended to give her.

He'd stood for a moment outside, the air chill and damp, his breath in clouds around him, contemplating his choices. If she didn't answer, he'd head for the Travel Inn.

He didn't want to end up in the Travel Inn. He wanted a bed, and a warm body to share it with. He'd been thinking about Lou, how her body felt, for so many hours today that it seemed the height of cruelty to be denied it. Now, though, there was another option: that tight arse, those breasts, small but firm, and that smart mouth. To be taken in hand by Sister, told what to do, devolved of all responsibility for himself and his actions.

He knocked quietly, although there were no lights on in Flora's flat, and her car wasn't outside. He assumed she was staying at Taryn Lewis's house in town. After a moment the door opened, and before he could say anything she was already standing aside to let him in, shutting the door behind him with a soft click.

To his great delight she was wearing the uniform, although her feet were bare; neat, tanned feet with toenails painted pink. She was looking at him enquiringly.

'Can I . . . ?' he said. Further words failed him. He must stink of alcohol.

Without saying a word, she led him down the hallway, opening a door halfway down. The bedroom was dark, and quiet, and cool. He looked at the bed and suddenly he was exhausted.

He undressed while she was somewhere else in the flat, crawled naked between the cool white sheets, and, listening to the sounds of her running water, the television in another room, and absolutely not intending to let himself doze off, instantly fell asleep.

What seemed like hours later he half woke and realised he was not in his bed at home, and the woman who was next to him was not Karen. It was not Lou, either.

He reached out a hand and touched naked skin. She stirred, turned towards him, and he folded his arm around her waist and drew her to him. Her body was warm, her skin soft. To his surprise he felt her hand close over his penis. It hardened quickly, and it didn't take long before he was wide awake.

A few moments later she pushed him firmly onto his back and sat astride him, her shape just visible from the small amount of light coming through the blinds. She put a condom on him expertly while he lay between her thighs, wondering whether he was dreaming.

As she lowered herself onto him, her head fell back and he heard her gasp. She put both of her hands flat onto his chest, pressing into him with all her weight. Light as she was, it was hard to breathe. But oh, this felt good. He was holding her waist, lifting her and pulling her back, trying to take some of her weight off his ribcage and moving faster, when she suddenly smacked him with the flat of her hand. 'Listen to me. Do not come. Do not. You do *exactly* what I tell you to do.'

This was more of a turn-on than anything, and in order to obey he had to almost throw her off him. For a moment he lay on his back, wondering if he could hold off when he was so close.

Instead of mounting him again, he felt her hand threading through his hair, and without warning she pulled him roughly round to face her. Her breath in his ear was loud, and fast. 'Fuck me with your mouth,' she said. She pushed his head down, down her body. While he licked her, she encouraged the pressure by digging fingernails into his shoulder. The pain was intense, and erotic. He held off his own pleasure, counting random numbers, concentrating.

'Stop. Stop.' Her voice was quiet, calm. Not angry. He raised his head, trying to see her in the darkness.

'Lie on your back,' she said.

He moved back up the bed and lay back. The pillows were whipped away from under his head. She sat astride him again, but this time higher up, over his face – my God! – really? She pulled at his shoulders and tucked her calves behind them, kneeling over him, tantalisingly out of reach. His hands were on her buttocks, trying to pull her down to him, moaning softly. And as she lowered herself onto him one of the pillows was pulled over his forehead, covering his eyes, denying him the pleasure of the view. For a crazy moment he thought she was going to smother him. But as hard as it was pressed over the upper part of his face, his nose and mouth were clear.

'Can you hear me?' she asked. Her voice was quiet, but clear. He could imagine her barking orders at the junior nurses, expecting an immediate and compliant response.

'Yes, Sister,' he said, unable to help himself. Smiling.

'This is what's going to happen. I am going to sit down and I expect you to try your hardest to make me come.'

'Yes, please.'

'Don't interrupt me. I expect you to make me come. You will find it hard to breathe while you're doing it. Do you understand?'

'Sorry. Yes. I mean—'

'I will be in control of when you can take a breath. You will need to trust me. Do you understand?'

'Yes,' he said.

'Raise your right hand straight up if you want to stop. Do it now, to show me you understand.'

He raised his hand obediently into the air, left it there for a second, and then reached forward blindly until he found her skin, her bare arm, the muscles on it flexed and holding the pillow tightly over his face.

'Good. Are you ready?'

He answered with a sound. He was absolutely ready. And then he felt her against his mouth, and nose, and he kissed and nuzzled and licked as best he could while his heart thumped; she was pressing into him, moving very gently, and there was no way he

208

could have taken a breath. At first it was fun, if a little strange. Then it became intense, urgent; his lungs began to burn and just at the moment he thought he was going to have to push her off him, she lifted herself away from his face. He gasped in a fresh lungful of hot, damp air that smelled like sex. Another long breath in and she was back against his face again, and this time his tongue worked faster against her, and as well as the fear that she would not get up in time for him to breathe he felt something else – a thrill, a buzz, a surge of vast erotic delight that rose and swelled within him. Oh, this was good, this was so good . . .

Sooner this time she raised herself, and, muffled by the pillow, he heard her make a sound that might have been one of pleasure. Barely time, then, to heave a breath in and she was on him again. He felt the panic building together with the desperate need to do this right, to get her to come quickly so that he would be allowed his own satisfaction – but even more so to please her, to impress her. He blocked out the voice in the back of his head that was becoming shrill – *fuck she is going to kill me like this* – and his brain was bursting with stars and lights, with the pounding of the blood in his ears, the slick wetness of her skin sliding against his face. Sensation surged through his whole body like a drug, like pure energy.

When everything started to spin, he began to raise his hand feebly; and at that moment she tensed, the muscles of her legs closing around his shoulders with a grip that was painful. He held on for another few seconds while he floated inside himself, observing his lack of oxygen in a way that was now almost calm, that almost made him want to laugh. Who needed air, after all, when this was what lay beyond it?

She lifted herself away from him. The air surged painfully back into his lungs in a long, noisy, uncontrollable rasp that was followed with a choking cough. His throat was raw with it. Another breath, another. The stars were colliding behind his eyelids. She untangled her legs from his shoulders and moved away. The pressure on the pillow lightened and he could have moved it off his face, but his arms didn't work.

Andy had managed perhaps three or four recovery breaths before her hand closed over his erection.

'Hold your breath,' she said.

I can't, I can't do it, he thought, at the same moment knowing he wanted to. He reached out blindly and caught her other hand, pulled it up to his mouth and nose and pressed it against his wet face. And after a moment of her denying him breath again, the stars were back, the panic died away at the same moment as the floating sensation returned and this time the stars were brighter and denser and he felt like he could almost reach out and touch them. And his body sang with it, every part of him burning. He didn't even know what she was doing any more.

The stars began to fade and a darkness approached, sidling up to him like sleep. She took her hand away from his face and for a moment nothing happened. Space. Then she slapped him, hard, across the cheek, and he heaved a breath in. With it came sudden panic, his eyes wide open. She had stopped everything.

'Please,' he gasped.

'Take some breaths. You need to be fully conscious.'

When he could speak, he said again: 'Please.' Not even knowing what it was that he wanted.

'As this is clearly your first time, I will permit it.'

Permit it?

'There are rules. Do you understand? Say "yes" if you understand.'

'Yes,' he coughed. His limbs, his body – everything was liquid. He could barely move.

'You do not touch me unless I tell you to do so. You ask for permission before you come. As you will be silenced, you will have to gain permission from me now.'

'Please can I—'

'Please *may* you what?'

'I need to come – *please*.'

'I am going to restrict your breathing again. Remember you can raise your hand. Do it now to show you are in agreement.'

He lifted his hand. It was like dragging a weight from the surface of the bed, his fingers feebly curled.

'Very well. Let's see what you've got.'

This time it was the pillow, over his face, held down with one of her hands. Her grip was so strong, both on the pillow and on his cock. It wasn't going to take long, and, although it was difficult, he could get shallow breaths through the fabric. There was more panic this time, less bliss, until the moment when he came. It almost took him by surprise. He felt the orgasm in the whole of his body at once, a jerk that pushed him physically off the mattress and crackled through his nerves and muscles and sinews like an electric current. His head was spinning. The sensation of it lasted longer than he had ever, ever experienced. Minutes, hours maybe. He was soaring. The pressure on his face did not let up.

And then, after the thudding in his ears, silence.

Day Four – Sunday 4 November 2012

08:10

Lou woke up and before she opened her eyes she had a headache. It was dark except for the bright light coming from the digital alarm clock beside the bed, and looking at it felt like looking into the sun.

Time to get up.

Downstairs, her mobile phone bleeped intermittently, signalling that a message had come through. Lou groaned. It shouldn't be legal to have to be awake this early on a Sunday morning. Unfortunately that was one of the hazards of working incident rooms, particularly this early in an investigation.

She showered in the dark, not daring to put the light on, but when she got out of the shower her head had eased a bit. By the light of the orange street lamp outside, she found a blister pack of paracetamol, popped two and swallowed them, cupping her hand under the tap to get enough water to wash them down.

Downstairs the kitchen light felt unnaturally bright, the tiled floor freezing under her stockinged feet. In her living room she fished around for her phone.

The message was from Ali Whitmore, timed just after seven: *Did you see msg re: Lorna? Really useful. Call when you get chance.*

She dialled. 'Ali? It's me. Who's Lorna?'

REPORT

Re: Lorna Paulette NEWMAN DOB 18/02/1962
of 11 Downsview Road, Winterham, Norwich

Sunday 4 November 0745hrs

From: DC 9952 Ron MITCHELL

To: Op NETTLE

Phone call received from Mrs Lorna NEWMAN. Mrs
NEWMAN claims that Barbara FLETCHER-NORMAN has
been a close friend of hers for a number of years. She last
spoke to Barbara by telephone on the night of 31 October at
about 2100hrs.

Mrs NEWMAN states that Barbara FLETCHER-NORMAN
had been having an affair with her tennis coach named as a
Mr Liam O'TOOLE and was planning to leave her husband
for him. However it seems that the tennis coach had
apparently run away with some of Barbara's money and this
was the cause of Mrs FLETCHER-NORMAN's upset that
evening.

Mrs NEWMAN claims to have in her possession a number of
letters written to her by Mrs FLETCHER-NORMAN and
believes the letters provide some insight into the state of mind
of the deceased.

R Mitchell

08:52

Flora's eyes opened and for a moment she wondered where she
was. The last time she'd slept here was less than a week ago but

already it felt like a lifetime. So much had happened, so many changes, her life no longer felt like her own.

Polly was dead.

She tested the thought, rolling it around in her head, realising that it was somehow less panic-inducing than it had been even yesterday.

Her watch told her it was nearly nine. Surprised at how well she'd slept, she suddenly recalled the peculiar events of last night. It seemed unreal, dreamlike, in the bright sunlight that filled the room. Had that really been him? Surely it could have been anyone. She often had visitors, the woman downstairs.

Since Flora had moved in a couple of years ago, she'd seen her downstairs neighbour a few times but they had never exchanged more than the occasional polite 'hello'. Flora had seen her in the small courtyard garden at the back from her bedroom window. She was much older than Flora, but still beautiful with a good body, fit. Flora had often wondered if she went to a gym somewhere.

Pulling on a pair of tracksuit bottoms and a hooded top, she padded down to the kitchen to put the kettle on. And then she reached for the phone.

It was the answering machine – probably too early for Taryn or Chris to be awake on a Sunday. 'Tabs, it's me. Give me a call later on if you can. I saw the strangest thing last night – still can't quite believe it. I'll come over and pick up my car this afternoon if that's OK. Oh, and thanks again for everything. See you later.'

09:02

Finally, after weeks of cold, grey days, wind and rain driving the last reluctant leaves from the trees, Sunday had burst into bright, cold sunshine. The light streamed in through the blinds, over the

215

white duvet, up to the closed eyes and sleep-crumpled face of Andy Hamilton. It disturbed him, but instead of opening his eyes straight away he turned his head, glancing across the bed to see if it was empty. Determining that it was, and that he was alone, he pulled the other pillow over his pounding head and plunged back into darkness again.

Oh God. What had all that been about? He had never had sex like it, never experienced a thrill like that before. He had been too drunk to refuse, of course, or too intoxicated to realise that being smothered by a woman he'd only just met was possibly not the cleverest thing to do. And yet – if he hadn't done it, hadn't allowed her to control him like that, he would never have known how it felt. He was twice her size and possibly twice as heavy, he could have thrown her to one side if he'd wanted to. And yet – and yet, she had controlled him utterly. At that crucial moment when he felt like he was flying, he could not have moved or spoken or asked for help if his life had depended on it.

You will have to trust me, she had said. He hadn't understood what she had meant, then, still pissed from the beers; thinking it was funny. Thinking he was going to get a shag and a warm bed to sleep in after all. She had even told him what she was planning to do, and the roaring in his ears must have drowned out the alarm bells that should have been ringing; but the drunk, the thrill-seeker, the Andy who relished a challenge, particularly when a woman was involved, went with it.

He must have passed out, last night. He knew this because she brought him round from it. He heard her talking to him, saying things like, 'Open your eyes. Andy, look at me . . . ' and the funniest thing of all was that he thought he was in hospital. She had that tone of voice that said 'nurse' even more than the uniform did. He

216

had opened his eyes and the room was still dark, but he could see her leaning over him. She did not look concerned.

She did not need to, after all: she was a nurse. She knew he was fine. Of course he could trust her – he was in the safest hands possible, wasn't he?

Half awake, he became aware of sounds. He moved, stretched, felt the soreness on his back. He opened his eyes to see her lithe, brown legs as she came back into the room. A steaming mug of coffee was placed on the bedside table beside him. He raised his head, his eyes travelling up her body, taking in the ironed uniform, the blonde hair shiny and blow-dried, the make-up.

He reached out a hand towards her but she did not come closer. She sat on the chair in the corner of the room, facing him, crossed her legs elegantly. 'How are you feeling?'

He thought carefully about his response. 'Tired,' he said.

She smiled. 'That's to be expected.'

Hard to know what to say that didn't sound idiotic. In the end, he settled on: 'I've never done anything like that before.'

'Yes, I could tell. But you liked it.'

This time his response was instant. 'Yes. I did.'

Her smile changed from benevolent to faintly lascivious. 'What we did was quite tame. There are plenty of other new experiences to try, if that's what you would like to do.'

Andy grinned at her. 'Will you teach me?'

Suzanne, for that was her name, stopped smiling then and said: 'You'd better get up. You're going to be late, Inspector.'

09:30

The briefing had the lowest number of officers in attendance since the investigation had begun. On the face of it, this wasn't

217

surprising: many of the major crime specialists who had been temporarily deployed to the investigation worked regular office hours, leaving the weekends for the core team. If anything came up which required additional resources, Lou could bid for more bodies.

It felt like things were slowing down, as far as Polly's murder was concerned. Practically everyone who had the vaguest connection with the case had been interviewed at least once; the most promising of leads had already been followed up, paperwork was now churning through the incident room like a constantly flowing stream.

No Jason today. It was going to be a long slog of a day, even if she didn't spend all of it here. Looking on the bright side, it should be a hell of a lot easier to concentrate.

Altogether there were seven people in the room. Lou, near the front, legs neatly crossed at the knee, daybook and pen poised; Les Finnegan and Ron Mitchell; Sam, even though Lou was fairly sure she should have been off today; Barry Holloway was in, too – when was he due for a rest day? Lou scribbled a hasty note to remind herself to check. Paul Harper, the Senior CSI, was there; and finally, late, Andy Hamilton had entered and sat at the back.

His hair was still damp as though he had only just fallen out of the shower, and out of the corner of her eye she observed that he looked even more dishevelled than usual, but she directed her attention to Barry.

'The key focus for the investigation remains the Fletcher-Normans,' he said. 'Forensic evidence links Barbara Fletcher-Norman to the scene. We know she had a suicide attempt in September and the medical disclosure indicates that she was still on medication. We now have further intel that Barbara was having a relationship with a man believed to be her tennis coach, which seemed to have ended on the day of Polly's murder. We should get more on that once the witness has been interviewed fully, but the indications are that on the night of Wednesday thirty-first, Barbara was extremely upset and had been drinking heavily.'

A few murmurs. Lou glanced at Hamilton. He was scribbling notes, head down. She sighed, wishing not for the first time that Rob Jefferson's back had not chosen this particular time to fail him.

Lou caught Barry's eye and interrupted. 'Ron and Sam are going to Norfolk today to interview Mrs Newman. We should be able to take all the letters that Barbara sent to Lorna for the coroner.'

Barry nodded.

'Paul?' Lou said, 'can you give us an update on forensics?'

Paul Harper cleared his throat. 'So we now have three scenes that are being worked on.' He indicated Jason's map, taped up to the whiteboard. 'Yonder Cottage, Hayselden Barn and the quarry. We are working at the quarry again today, trying to establish if the shot-put that was found yesterday was thrown from the top of the quarry before the car went over, or if it fell out of the car as it went down.'

Les Finnegan raised a hand.

Paul nodded to him.

'Are we definite on the shot-put being the weapon yet?'

'No, but it's looking the most likely bet at the moment. Any other questions before we carry on?'

Silence in the room. There was a faint odour of stale beer and Lou hoped it wasn't coming from the big man at the back.

'OK,' Paul continued. 'So that's the quarry. We've finished at Yonder Cottage for now, awaiting results of blood tests and a few other things there. Hayselden Barn is still being worked on.'

'Any results?'

'Bits and pieces. Yesterday Brian gave his key to his daughter and asked her to make a phone call from his mobile phone. So we've had some unexpected complications. We've managed to retrieve blood from the kitchen sink – likelihood is that it's Polly's. Should get that back today.'

'Thanks, Paul. You'll let us know when you have any more?'

Paul Harper nodded. He looked relieved to be done.

Lou went on: 'Sam spoke to Mrs Lewis yesterday. Can you give us the update, Sam? I think some people might have missed it.'

'Her father – Brian, that is – told her that he was no longer sleeping with Polly because she had introduced him to another woman. Brian asked Taryn to go and use his mobile to ring her, to let her know where he was. Mrs Lewis kindly handed the phone over to us and it's being downloaded. Should be done later today. We're still waiting for the billings and the cellsite data on it, though. The service provider is still having computer problems so we can't get the subscriber check done on that number Polly was calling the night she died.'

'What about that other number, the one called by the landline in Yonder Cottage?' Lou asked.

'Unfortunately it's the same SP. We'll have to wait for that one, too.'

Lou smiled at Barry again. 'Nearly there. Just a few intel requirements remaining. We still need more on what happened at the Lemon Tree on the last day. Statement's gone out about that today.'

Barry Holloway nodded his assent to this and added: 'We've not had anything more about the car that was seen – that guy from Crimestoppers. We appealed for him to come forward again, but nothing so far.'

'Shame,' Lou said.

'If we're working on the theory that Barbara Fletcher-Norman was the killer, we need more information about that last night. Was she drinking at home? Did anyone else speak to her on the phone – we should get that from the landline billing, at least. And we need to locate this man she was supposed to be seeing, Liam O'Toole. See if he can corroborate the story put forward by Mrs Newman in her first statement. That's about it for now. Just awaiting the results of the key interviews from today, really.'

'Thanks, Barry. Right then. We need to crack on, folks,' she said, standing and straightening her skirt. 'Ron and Sam – you're going to see Mrs Newman today. Try and get back as soon as you can, and give us a call if there's anything we can action straight away. Les, we also need a check on CCTV. Keep you out of the cold wind, eh? We've got another press conference booked for Monday, unless anything earth-shattering turns up over the weekend. Anyone got anything else they'd like to say?'

Quiet in the room, although chairs were squeaking and shuffling as everyone made ready to get out and get on with it. Barry was cleaning off the whiteboard.

Hamilton cleared his throat. 'You got anything specific for me?'

Lou looked at him, mentally checking off her list of urgent tasks and wondering which of them she could bear to devolve to someone who looked like he'd had a particularly spectacular night on the town.

'You can find out what's happened to Brian's computer. How about that?'

'It's Sunday,' he said.

'And?'

He didn't answer, just maintained the eye contact. They were on shaky ground again, Lou thought. 'I know it won't take you very

long. So maybe you could find out some more about Liam O'Toole.
All right with that?'

'Yes, of course.'

'Right, let's get on with it. Ron, Sam, can I see you both please –
my office? Thanks everyone.'

The room emptied quicker than water down a plughole.

MESSAGE

For: DC Jane Phelps c/o DCI Smith Op Nettle

From: Brian FLETCHER-NORMAN

Tel: hosp

Message: Please call back. Has remembered further.

09:45

Lou picked up the message from her crowded desk as she went in,
pocketed it. Ron Mitchell was waiting for Sam by the door, his coat
already on. Sam was shutting down her workstation. Neither of
them looked happy.

'I don't know why you two are looking so bloody grumpy,' she
said. 'The sun's shining, it's a lovely day. Just right for a nice drive.'

'A nice long drive,' Ron said sadly.

'You never know,' Lou said, 'this might uncover something crucial. You two could be heroes.'

'Yes, boss,' Sam said. 'It'll be great.'

'And you might even finish early and then you can relax. OK?'
Lou regarded them both for a moment, knowing that sending her
sergeant off to conduct an interview was not generally considered
to be the best use of resources. But Sam had a knack with witnesses

222

and suspects; she listened, and was intuitive, picking up on things that other interviewers missed. If she couldn't go up to Norfolk and meet Lorna Newman for herself, sending Sam was the next best thing. 'You got a car sorted out?'

'Yes, we've got one of the Volvos booked.'

'OK. Call me later?'

'Yes, boss,' Sam said, and they left.

When they had gone, Lou looked at the message again and dialled the number for Briarstone General Hospital, and asked for Stuart Ward.

10:15

Flora was thinking about going back to the studio. Something about the sunshine had made her want to go back and look at that canvas, the one of Polly, even if she wasn't going to be able to complete it. She was just pulling on her leather jacket when there was a knock at the door.

Fearing it was Hamilton, she froze at the top of the stairwell, not making a sound.

A few moments later, another knock and an imperious voice suddenly through the letterbox. 'Flora? Let me in, for Christ's sake.' It was her mother.

'Mum,' said Flora, going down and opening the door.

'Where's your car?'

'I left it at Taryn's.'

She could tell straight away that Felicity was upset, given the outfit she was wearing: blue jeans, pink trainers and her waxed jacket over the top of it, accessorised with a ridiculously large designer white handbag. Normally her mother took more care with her outfit, if she was planning to leave the farm.

'Aren't you going to let me in?'

'Sorry,' Flora said, and stood aside as her mother marched on up the stairs. 'I was just off out, actually.'

Felicity ignored this, and took a seat on one of the kitchen chairs, looking flustered.

'Are you all right, Mum?' Flora asked, laying a hand on Felicity's shoulder. For a moment she had a passing thought that her mother had come to confront her about her sexuality, a scene she had often imagined and long dreaded.

Felicity slipped the waxed jacket off her shoulders and Flora took it to hang up in the cupboard in the hallway. 'It's your father,' she said. 'I'm worried about him.'

'Worried?' Flora said, coming back into the room. 'Why?'

'This business over Polly. He's been – different – ever since. Oh, I don't know. I can't understand it. You know the police were round yesterday? Searched the whole place. They had a warrant. Heaven alone knows what they were looking for.'

'Some sort of evidence, I expect,' Flora said.

'Oh, Flora, don't be flippant! Daddy was beside himself.'

Flora doubted that. He would have descended into that level of Zen-like calm that was somehow even more terrifying than anger. 'Did they find anything?'

'I don't think so. Daddy thinks they were on a fishing trip, whatever that means.'

Flora was never quite sure if it was possible for Felicity to be that naïve, or whether an act she had carried on for so many years had become her natural state.

'He was always very close to Polly, even when she was a little girl,' Felicity said, in a small voice. 'I did wonder ...'

'What?'

She shook her head. 'No. No, you'll think I'm foolish.'

'Go on, Mum. What did you wonder?'

Tears formed in the brown eyes and rolled down the cheeks. 'I did wonder whether Polly – whether maybe Nigel had had an affair with Cass, years ago.'

'With Polly's mum?' For a moment Flora didn't understand, then a wave of cold fear gripped her from the inside and held her tightly.

Silence. Felicity fished a tissue from the pocket of her jeans and wiped under her eyes.

'You – you think Polly might have been Dad's . . .' Flora's voice trailed off. She couldn't manage to say it.

'Oh, it's too silly. He'd never be unfaithful. But I couldn't see why he would be so different all of a sudden, and then I just got thinking – you know how it is. I had thought it before, to be honest. We used to see Cass and Polly quite often – you were very tiny – and Polly used to pull your hair when she thought nobody was looking. Daddy always seemed so pleased to see them. I thought that was so peculiar, he was never normally pleased to see anyone, you know how he is.'

'Mum,' Flora said, her voice barely under control.

'Of course, I always wondered where she got her colouring from. Cass had such dark hair, and there was Polly, blonde, with those lovely blue eyes—'

'Mum!'

'Cass always seemed to have some man or other in tow, never the same one from one week to the next. I suppose that's where Polly got it from – you heard that she was having an affair with Brian Fletcher-Norman, didn't you? Julia told me. Whatever next? I ask myself. He's twice her age. Maybe that's what brought his heart attack on. You never know . . .'

225

'Mum!'

'Hmm?' Felicity paused.

'I'm sure that's not right,' Flora said, with more conviction than she felt. 'I'm sure Dad wouldn't . . . I mean, he would have told you, surely?'

Felicity had grown older in the last week, the lines on her face standing out more, her hair greyer at the roots, as though the horror of finding Polly's body had drained the colour and the life out of her. 'I don't know, Flora. I've been thinking it over for days.'

'And Cass never said anything about Polly's father?'

'Never. Well, she led me to believe she'd been to a sperm bank. She said the time was right for her to have a baby, and all of a sudden she turned up one weekend and announced she was pregnant.'

'Was Dad there, then?'

Felicity frowned. 'No, he was away on one of his business trips and Cass and I had a girlie weekend, got quite drunk. Well, I did. Cass did manage to cut down a little.'

'Dad would know, though. Wouldn't he? If – if he was? Surely Polly's mum would have told him?'

'Oh, I don't know, darling. She could be funny, Cass. One minute she was your best friend and then she'd take off and you'd not hear from her for months. I never knew what she was up to. And she loved having secrets.'

Flora took a deep breath, laid her hand over Felicity's and gave it a squeeze. 'Mum, I'm sure you're imagining it. Dad would never be able to keep something like that private. Have you asked him?'

'Of course not, don't be so utterly ridiculous! How do you recommend I bring that topic up? "By the way, darling, is there a chance that the corpse in the cottage might be your love child?" But if it's not that, then what is it?' Felicity wailed plaintively.

'What is what? What do you mean?'

'If it's not something to do with Polly, then why is he acting so strangely?' Felicity looked at her daughter and stuck out her chin, demanding some sort of answer.

For a moment Flora was lost in thought, pondering why it was that, at so many points in her life, her mother would come up with a passing comment which devastated her so utterly – whether it was a mere mention of her school grades, or how she was expected to remain at the farm and work instead of wasting time on art, or how one or other of her cronies had remarked that Flora would never get on in life if she insisted on dressing like a tramp and never combing her hair.

Flora shrugged. 'Maybe he's just worried about the business, or worried that the police will ask him too many questions about Polly's death.'

Felicity's gaze became suddenly more penetrating. 'Suspect him of the killing, you mean?'

'Maybe. You know how much the police love Dad.'

Felicity shook her head impatiently. 'Why haven't they been round to interview him, then? He's just as likely to be guilty as any of the rest of us. I mean, he had plenty of opportunity.'

'I thought he went out? Somewhere in town with his friends?'

Felicity shook her head. 'But that was earlier. He came home about eight, had told me not to make dinner and then got all cross because it wasn't waiting for him. Told me I'd got the dates wrong. We had a bit of a row about it, even though I'd written it on the calendar. Seems silly now.'

She looked at the table, running her thumbnail along a groove in

227

the grain of the oak surface. 'I *know* it was that day. I'd given Polly a telling off about the shopping she'd promised to buy me in Briarstone. I told Daddy he should go and have a talk with her, and he did. He went down to the cottage. It was raining by then and he was gone for about an hour. I was about to go down and find out where the hell he was when he came back. Said Polly had made him cheese on toast.'

She gave a small sound, half a laugh, half a sob.

Flora's heart had started beating faster. Something wasn't adding up. Why had he told her he was out? And he'd not mentioned going to the cottage. He'd not said he had been with Polly that night. Why would he lie, unless he was hiding something?

Flora put her hand over her mother's. 'Mum, I've really got to go out now. Can we talk about this another time?'

'Hmm? Oh, of course, darling. Sorry to hold you up. I just needed – someone to talk to, I guess. Thank you for being so under-standing.'

'That's all right, Mum.' Flora got the waxed jacket for Felicity then steered her gently towards the staircase.

'Flora dear, will you come over tonight and have dinner? Come and see if you think Daddy's any different. Will you?'

'I'll do my best,' Flora said.

At the front door, Flora said goodbye quickly, shutting the door almost in her mother's face, not wishing to risk a meeting with Andy Hamilton, just in case he was still inside the flat downstairs.

11.12

It was nearing lunchtime by the time Lou made it to the hospital. She wasn't supposed to be interviewing people, but everyone else was out and besides, she fancied having a look at Brian herself.

228

While she'd been parking the car a text message had come through on her job phone from Jason.

Hope u don't mind me texting work phone. This is my no in case u need anything today. Not busy. Jason

It felt as if there was a coded message in there somewhere. She thought about texting back straight away, but there were more pressing things to attend to.

The hospital was busy with visitors – the WRVS shop buzzing with people buying bottles of Lucozade, newspapers and magazines. The paracetamol she'd taken had finally started to kick in, although somewhere at the back of her head the headache lurked like a malevolent creature, waiting for an excuse to take over once again.

PC Yvonne Sanders, casually dressed in jeans and a fleece, was waiting for her near the reception desk. 'Ma'am,' she said. 'I'm sorry to be dressed like this, I wasn't expecting . . .'

'Don't worry,' Lou said. 'I'm just glad I got hold of you. You got your PNB handy?'

Yvonne patted her bag. Her pocket notebook, or PNB, was what Lou needed more than anything else. If she was going to be talking to Brian, she wanted a careful note of everything he said.

'You were there when he had the heart attack, weren't you?' Lou asked, as they eased their way through the throng and headed up the corridor towards Stuart Ward.

'Yes, ma'am.'

'You did CPR on him?'

'Yes – well, we both did. Ian did a lot of it.'

'Good job,' Lou said. Short on officers, Lou had gone back through the case files to find someone who had a vague bearing on the case and who might actually be on duty – and had found Yvonne Sanders. Lou hoped she was a fast writer.

'Er – anything you want me to do, apart from writing up?'

'I know it's a bit irregular, interviewing with a DCI,' Lou said. 'I'd rather just get on and do it though, while the ward's quiet. So I'll do the talking, you take notes and type up a statement for me back at the nick, OK?'

'Of course.'

So much for preparing the evidence for the coroner. At this rate she would still be working until midnight to get things ready. Under her breath she muttered a fervent prayer to whichever god was listening for this trip not to be a waste of time.

Eventually they found Brian Fletcher-Norman in the day room, sitting up in an armchair watching television. He was sporting a smart-looking pair of burgundy pyjamas, covered with a dark green towelling dressing gown, and some matching slippers. On the day-room door a sign had been taped: PRIVATE MEETING IN PROGRESS.

'Hello. Brian, isn't it?' Lou asked, offering him her hand.

'Yes.'

'I'm DCI Louisa Smith. You've got me, today, I'm afraid.'

'A pleasure.'

'You might remember my colleague, PC Yvonne Sanders?'

Brian shook Yvonne's hand but didn't make the connection.

'PC Sanders was there when you were taken ill. I believe she saved your life, Brian.'

'Ah,' he said. 'Thank you, my dear.'

Lou decided she could see the appeal. He might have been far too old for her, but he had a deep, resonant voice and a presence about him even wearing pyjamas and a dressing gown. Dark eyes in a tanned, surprisingly unlined face, and a good head of silver hair. He looked every inch the business executive.

She sat on a lower chair and pulled a low coffee table closer, treating him to a close-up view of the swell of her breasts under her black cashmere sweater. 'You don't mind if Yvonne takes notes, do you, Brian? We can ask you to check through them when we're finished, and we can get a statement typed up for you. All right?'

'I'm sure it's fine, my dear. I don't need my solicitor or anything, do I?'

Lou pulled a face: 'Lord, no. Not unless you're planning to confess to something?' She gave him a smile and a wink, and watched him start to relax.

He used the remote control and turned off the television.

Lou glanced across at PC Sanders to make sure she was ready with her notebook and pen. Yvonne smiled back at her, keen.

'Now, when we spoke on the phone this morning you mentioned that you'd had some further recollections regarding the evening of your wife's death. Would you mind going over exactly what it is you recall?'

Brian paused for a moment. 'Where shall I start?'

Lou gave him an encouraging smile. 'Start from when you got home from work. Was Barbara there?'

Brian nodded. 'Yes, she was upstairs. I didn't realise she was there at first. I assumed she must have been watching television because she didn't answer when I called.'

'What time did you get home?'

He looked away before answering vaguely. 'Eightish, maybe nine. I left town at gone seven, anyway.'

He looked as if he was concentrating hard, trying to bring the memory back. He's a sly old goat, Lou thought. She was quite aware that he'd remembered all along. Was it because they'd had contact with Lorna Newman that he'd changed his story? Had she been in contact with Brian at the hospital?

231

'I poured myself a drink and sat down to read the paper. Barbara came downstairs much later. It must have been about eleven, twelve, and we had an argument.'

'What was the argument about?'

Brian sighed deeply. 'Much the same as usual. I was late home from work, and so she accused me of having an affair. She said I smelled of women's perfume; I said she smelled of gin. It got quite heated. She stormed off back upstairs; I heard her talking to somebody on the telephone, I don't know who.'

'And why were you late home?'

Brian looked a little cross at this interruption. 'Can't remember,' he said vaguely. 'It was work, nothing unusual.'

'I understood you were semi-retired – is there still a call for you to be working late? That seems a little unfair.'

Brian shrugged. 'Unfair or not, the work's there. And to be honest, Barbara wasn't always that much fun to come home to. Miserable, most of the time.'

Lou thought of Barbara's depression and recent attempt at suicide and suddenly felt rather sorry for her. 'Sorry, I interrupted. Barbara was upstairs.'

'Yes. I finished my drink and went into the kitchen to wash up the glass. I checked on the gin – we keep the bottles in a cupboard in the kitchen – and found it was nearly finished. That was a pretty bad sign.'

'Did she drink every day?'

He shook his head. 'Sometimes she'd go for several weeks without a drink. Those times were quite pleasant, really. I think they coincided with the times she was less depressed, less – low, I suppose you'd say. Also, I think she was aware that people thought she might be an alcoholic, and she was always trying to present everyone with evidence that she could manage without a drink, that she wasn't a slave to it.' Brian looked Lou in the eye. 'Her mother was an alcoholic, you know. Died of liver failure. And her father died of a heart attack at fifty, and he was also a man who liked a drink. So she was very aware of it.'

'So lately, had she been particularly depressed?'

Brian nodded again. 'We've been having rows fairly often. Usually we only ever argued when Barbara had had a drink or two – she's too easy-going otherwise.'

'Was there any particular reason for it, that you were aware of?'

Brian looked wary for a moment, then shrugged. 'I can't think of anything in particular. In fact, I thought she'd been doing rather well. She'd been getting out more, playing golf with her friends. She'd started playing bridge again. Having tennis lessons three times a week at the country club – cost me an arm and a leg, that one, but she said she was determined to be fit by the summer.'

Lou thought it unlikely that Brian was unaware of Barbara's infatuation with the tennis coach, but chose to let that one go. It could have been something as simple as it being a huge attack on his ego to admit that Barbara had chosen to go elsewhere. Doing it himself was no doubt just a bit of fun – for his wife to indulge was a different matter entirely.

She gave him an encouraging smile. 'So, Barbara was upstairs and you were in the kitchen. Can you remember what happened next?'

'I went and had a bath. Fell asleep in the tub. I often do that if I'm late. Anyway, I've no idea what time it was when I got out again, but the water wasn't cold, so it can't have been hours. Barbara wasn't downstairs, so I assumed she'd gone to bed. The bedroom door was shut.'

Lou watched him, eager for him to get on with the story, but waiting while he had a sip of water. Yvonne Sanders flexed her wrist.

'I went back downstairs to turn all the lights off and lock up. Then all of a sudden, Barbara came barrelling into the hallway from the kitchen. I couldn't work out where she'd been, but I suppose she must have come in through the back door. She was hysterical, shouting and yelling about something. I told her to calm down and tell me what was wrong. She pushed me and I fell back onto the stairs. She kept saying, "It's done now, I've done it now, it's too late." Something like that. Over and over.'

'"It's done now, I've done it now, it's too late?"' Lou repeated.

'Yes.'

Yvonne was scribbling fast. Lou hoped she was getting every single word of this. He'd already changed his story once, they needed to make sure he could be pinned down somehow.

'What do you think she meant by that?'

Brian shrugged. 'At the time, I hadn't a clue. She was pretty drunk, almost incoherent. Thinking about it now, of course, I'm wondering whether she'd been over the road to see Polly.'

'Do you have any idea what time this was?'

He shook his head. 'Well after twelve, I think.'

'OK. So then what happened?'

'After she pushed me, I got up and went to bed. I told you, I don't put up with that sort of behaviour. Everyone has a breaking point, and that's mine. I heard the door bang, but I thought that was her locking it – sometimes the front door doesn't lock properly until you've given it a good bang.'

Something was being left out, Lou was sure of it. There was a tension in the air that hadn't been there just five minutes ago.

234

'Did you not notice any blood on her hands, her clothes?' she asked.

'No. It was dark in the hallway because I'd already turned the lights off.'

'Before locking the front door?'

He shrugged, looked at her defiantly. 'That's just my regular routine.'

'So you went up to bed and you assumed she'd locked the front door and come up to bed herself?'

He nodded, seeming to relax again. 'I didn't hear anything else. If she hadn't gone to bed she was probably passed out on the sofa. I was thinking I'd see her again the next morning, and she'd be right as rain.'

'You sleep in separate rooms?'

'Yes. Have done for years.'

'So when you woke up, you didn't notice anything unusual?'

He shook his head again. 'I'd just got up when there was a knock at the door. I was already feeling a bit unwell. My chest hurt – I thought it was from where she'd pushed me. Then when the police officers came in – you,' he said, smiling at Yvonne, 'and the other chap – it was suddenly excruciating.'

A pause. 'Go on,' she said.

'That's all I remember,' he said with finality, sitting back in the chair and, to all intents and purposes, breathing a heavy sigh of relief.

Yvonne continued writing. Lou paused, to give Yvonne time to catch up and to give herself a moment to think. This version was a completely different story to the one he'd told immediately after the incident, before he'd had the heart attack. However poorly he was feeling, surely his memory wasn't affected at that point? And in hospital just a few days ago, acting like the whole thing was a blur. Surely you'd remember such a dramatic confrontation with your wife?

She looked up at last. 'Thank you, Brian. I know this must have been very difficult for you. I appreciate your efforts.'

He gave her a wan smile, showing that he was prepared to battle through any adversity to make her happy. It just wasn't right, though. Bits of it probably were. There were undoubtedly bits missing. And other bits that were complete fabrication.

For a start, the amnesia thing. Lou had had dealings with amnesia when she'd worked a stint in Traffic Division; amnesia was an occasional side effect of head trauma. Retrograde amnesia, usually caused by injury or disease, resulted in a chunk of memory being lost. Usually this would return after a period of time as the injury healed, but the process would be gradual, with bits of memory re-emerging as fragments until they could be placed in context, eventually forming a complete picture once again. Sudden wholesale return of memory like the one Brian seemed to have experienced was, as far as Lou was aware, rare. Of course, he'd not actually had a head injury, although there had been a period of unconsciousness, which could also be a factor.

'It's great that your memory has come back,' Lou said, with a bright smile designed to deflect any suspicion. 'It's really helpful to us. Gives us a better picture of events.'

Brian did not seem to be at all suspicious. 'Do you think she did it? Killed Polly?'

'It's a bit too early to be coming to conclusions, Brian. But let's just say I think what you've told me today has moved things forward a great deal.'

Lou gave the nod to Yvonne, who was flipping through the pages

236

of her notebook. 'Brian, does the name Lorna Newman mean anything to you?'

His face registered surprise, and Lou was about as certain as she could be that it was genuine. 'Of course. She's a friend of Barbara's. A very old friend. They came to us in the summer – August, I think. Why do you ask?'

'She called the incident room. Saw the news about Barbara on the television, I believe. Just wanted to check with you that she is who she says she is.'

Brian nodded with satisfaction. 'Yes, she's a game old bird, Lorna. No nonsense. Always liked that in a woman.'

So. His memory hadn't been jogged by any contact with Lorna. And he didn't view her contact with the police as any sort of threat. Did that mean he'd been telling the truth about that night, after all? Lou was confused. It wasn't that the whole story was wrong – more that there were some parts that were muddled, out of place.

Of course the usual way that stories like this were untangled was through repeated interviewing, going over the same questions, the same story again and again until things changed, or until things started to make sense. Or until new information came to light that changed the perspective on the investigation. It didn't mean he was somehow implicated in Polly's death. It didn't necessarily mean that he was lying.

At some point, of course, she would have to confront him about the affair with Polly. For the moment, though, she believed that he would just deny it further and accuse Taryn of lying to make him out to be a bad person. They needed some corroborative evidence, or at least firm proof that he'd lied about something else.

'Can I ask you to read through my notes, Brian,' Yvonne said,

237

'and sign each page to say you agree with what I've written? I'll type things up back at the office ...'

Lou watched him as he scanned the pages of the notebook, frowning. Several times he seemed to pause and she thought he was going to dispute something, but then he would continue. Come on, she thought, some of us have work to do, and then chided herself. This statement was going to be crucial, it would take as long as it needed to take. It had been a long time since she'd taken a statement herself – years – and she'd forgotten what a drag it could be. Add in the pressure of making sure you'd got everything you needed; she was glad that particular responsibility wasn't on her list any more.

When Brian got to the end of the notes Yvonne handed him a pen and showed him the various places he needed to sign. Lou picked up her jacket and got to her feet. She held out her hand and found his handshake was now surprisingly warm, his grip firm. Overall, he had the appearance of a man for whom a great weight has been lifted from his shoulders.

'I'll be in touch if anything else comes to light, of course.'

'Certainly. Thank you, Inspector.'

As much as she dearly wanted to correct him, part of Lou held back. It might disrupt the balance of their relationship if he suddenly saw her as a senior rank, even if that was the case. And this, despite the fact that she'd given him her business card, which clearly stated her rank. If he wanted to persist in addressing her as 'Inspector', then there were other ways of tackling it.

'Call me Lou,' she said. 'After all, I've been rather cheekily calling you Brian.'

'Lou,' he said, testing the word, still holding the handshake, maintaining eye contact in a way that, in another place and time, might have been flirtatious.

She let him hold it until he relaxed his grip, and gave him another of her bright, slightly vacuous smiles. 'Take care of yourself, Brian. Hope they let you home soon.'

'Goodbye.'

Lou juggled her bag and her coat, and together with Yvonne Sanders made her way back along the endless corridor to the front entrance, where they parted company.

'Thanks,' Lou said. 'Really appreciate your help.'

'Any time,' Yvonne said, shaking Lou's hand. 'I'll send the statement through as soon as it's done. If there's anything else you need, please give me a shout.'

Lou drew in deep lungfuls of cold, clear air. The sun was about as high in the sky as it was likely to get, and still not a cloud to be seen. She hadn't realised until she was out in the grand space of the car park, cars circling slowly, competing for the next vacant space, just how stifled she'd felt in the day room of Stuart Ward.

12:16

Brian watched Lou's arse appraisingly as she walked to the door of the day room. She was a nice girl, he thought. Brighter than she pretended to be just as he was brighter than she gave him credit for. She knew he hadn't told her the full story, and yet he felt like she'd believed him, which had been the key to it. Of course, he remembered every single detail of what had happened that night, gone over it a million times, lying here in the hospital.

From the pocket of his dressing gown he pulled out the mobile phone that Suzanne had slipped him when she'd visited. He turned it on, waited, then hit the speed dial that she'd programmed in.

'It's me. Yes, they've just been. A female inspector and another

239

one who just took notes.' He listened to her voice, relishing how she sounded, just a voice, a long way away, but next to him in the room.

'It all went well, I think. She didn't ask me anything I couldn't handle. No, nothing. Well, she asked if I noticed any blood. I said no, it was dark. It's all right,' he said, trying for reassurance. 'I'll be home soon, and then we can . . .'

He listened to her telling him what he had to do. Finally, he chanced his luck and asked: 'When will you come in?'

Then, a pause. 'I love you. Goodbye, my darling. See you soon.'

12:19

Ron's phone rang when they were still some way away from Lorna Newman's house. He put his hand over the phone and mouthed, 'it's the boss' at Sam before pulling his notebook out of his inside jacket pocket, biting the top off a biro and scribbling something down. 'Right. Gotcha. Uh-huh.'

He shut the phone with a snap. 'Apparently Brian's memory has come back. Quite a lot, by all accounts.'

Sam raised an eyebrow.

'Seems he remembers Barbara coming back into the house all hysterical, late that night. Then she disappeared off again and he went to bed.'

'That's a bit odd.'

He nodded. 'Boss thinks he's not lying exactly, but not telling the full story either. She's going to have another go, maybe when he gets out of the hospital.'

'She's not treating him as a suspect, then?'

'Nah. More likely it's her, isn't it?'

'You mean Barbara?'

He gave her a look which said of course fucking Barbara, but simply nodded. 'You can't tell me she went and topped herself covered in Polly's blood because she was a bit depressed. She went over there to confront her husband's bit on the side, got the red mist on because she was half cut, and then took herself off over the quarry because of what she'd done.'

Case closed, Sam thought to herself. He had a way of simplifying things which was by turns deadly accurate and horribly misplaced.

'What about if Brian did it – killed Polly – and Barbara saw him?'

'What – and then she topped herself?'

'No, he pushed her over the cliff. Might explain the heart attack. That level of stress.'

He shook his head. 'The woman was depressed, suicidal. You've got to stick with the evidence, Sarge, don't go off half-cocked with complicated theories. It's usually the most obvious explanation. Sometimes people just act funny, don't they?'

You got that right, Sam thought, turning her full concentration back to the road.

12:41

Lou parked in the station car park, pulled out her job phone and checked for messages – nothing – and then, on a whim, found her personal phone. It was turned off, as it often was, since nobody ever used it to phone her. She turned it on and sent a text to Jason's number:

This is my pers number FYI. All good here. Hows your weekend going? Quiet without you. Lou

Almost immediately a reply bleeped:

241

Hockey this morning. Bored now. Could meet 4 lunch ... ? X

Lunch – what a great idea. And it gave her another idea. She sent a reply:

Great. Meet you in the Lemon Tree? Soon as?

5x5x5 Intelligence Report

Date: Sunday 4 November 2012

Officer: PC 9921 EVANS

Re: Op NETTLE

ECHR Grading: B / 1 / 1

Phone call received from Mr Dean LONGFORD, DOB 27/01/87, address 15 Castle View, Briarstone.

Caller states he was the person who phoned Crimestoppers last week having seen two people arguing in a vehicle in Cemetery Lane on the night of the 31/10.

States he has seen the police appeal for him to come forward with further information, although he hasn't got anything further to add. Is willing to make a statement but is going on holiday next week.

In case the statement doesn't get taken, he gave the following details:

Small car, dark in colour, like a Peugeot or a Fiesta size.

Parked in a lay-by or driveway entrance in Cemetery Lane, right before a sharp bend.

There was a lorry sticking out of a driveway on the opposite side so the inft had to slow down to pass – hence noticing the car.

Female with long fair hair in the driver's seat.

Male figure (larger) in the passenger seat, no description.

Couple appeared to be arguing, lots of finger pointing etc.

Interior light was on but headlights off.

Definitely Halloween night as Wednesday night is when the inft works in town.

No idea what the time was exactly but inft left work at 2315hrs and arrived home about 2345hrs.

13:24

Number 11 Downsview Road was a smart bungalow, set back from a quiet road by a long, open driveway. The front lawn, along with all the others in the road, was neatly trimmed.

It was the sort of silence that indicated an elderly population, cars put away in garages reserved for that purpose; smells of dinner cooking from somewhere.

Ron and Sam parked against the kerb opposite the house and got out. Sam resisted the urge to have a good stretch. It had been a long drive, the last part especially tedious.

The door was opened almost immediately.

'Mrs Newman?' Ron asked of the woman who answered the door. Her dark hair was cut neatly in a bob and grey eyes examined his warrant card closely.

'I'm Detective Constable Ron Mitchell; this is my colleague, Detective Sergeant Sam Hollands.'

'Come in,' she said. Her voice was clear and steady. 'I've got the kettle on.'

She showed them into a large front room which was rather more modern than either of them had been expecting. Two huge leather sofas dominated the room, matching the cream which covered three of the walls. The fourth wall, mainly an archway into the dining room, was painted a colour that might have been purple.

On one wall a handsome gas fire played pretty flames over realistic-looking bricks of coal. A low hiss from the gas flame could be heard above the noise of the kettle rattling into a boil from the kitchen.

Sam perched on the edge of one sofa. Ron sat next to her and sprawled backwards into the leather, knees apart, displaying hairy white calves above diamond-patterned grey socks and pale brown loafers.

Sam looked elsewhere.

Lorna Newman brought a tray through from the kitchen. A cheerful brown teapot, large enough for them all to have at least two cups, with three small mugs – Denby, Sam thought – a milk jug, and a sugar bowl. Matching.

'Thank you for seeing us, Mrs Newman. I'm sure you must be busy.'

'Oh, not really. Andrew's playing golf. My husband, that is. I do all of my chores in the mornings. Usually by now I would be either visiting friends or at the shop.'

'The shop?'

'I volunteer at a charity shop in the town. Closed on Sundays, though.'

'Mrs Newman, I wanted to thank you for calling us,' Sam said. 'I'm sure you might be able to help us build up a clearer picture of what Barbara was like, which will be of great help to the enquiry.'

'Which enquiry would that be?'

Sam looked up from her pad, where she had written the date and time but nothing else. 'We need to gather evidence for the coroner's inquest into Mrs Fletcher-Norman's death,' she said. 'The inquest is due to be held next week. That will determine the cause of death, so it's important we are able to present any evidence that might be relevant. Particularly if the evidence you have supports or refutes the theory that Mrs Fletcher-Norman might have taken her own life.'

Lorna nodded. Looking directly at Sam, she added: 'But you are working on the murder case, aren't you? That Polly – what's her name?'

'Polly Leuchars,' Ron said helpfully.

'Yes, Mrs Newman,' Sam said. 'We're both working on that case. However, we also work on other unexplained deaths in the Briarstone area, one of which is that of Mrs Fletcher-Norman.'

'So you're not linking them, then?'

'We don't have any direct evidence to support a link.'

Lorna was silent for a moment. 'That's good. I'd hate to think of Barbara mixed up in all that. She was a good girl, you know. We've been friends for years.'

'Can you tell me how you met?' Ron was having another go at conducting the interview.

'We were at school together. Kept in touch ever since, although there were long periods where we didn't write. Not for any bad reason.'

'And you visited them recently, in Morden?'

'Beginning of August. Spent a week there.'

'What was your impression of Mrs Fletcher-Norman at that time? Did she seem in good spirits?'

Lorna hesitated before replying. 'I think so. There were a few times – we went out for dinner, and she'd had a few drinks. Got a

245

bit overexcited, I think. On the last night we were there, she and Brian had a stinking row. We had gone to bed and you could hear them shouting from downstairs.'

'What was the argument about?'

She shook her head. 'Couldn't tell you. Just a lot of shouting and banging. She didn't seem depressed, although I know she had been. The doctor had her on medication. She used to tell me about all the various pills she had to take.'

'I gather she was hospitalised in September?' Ron said.

'Yes. She took an overdose. I think she had had a particularly difficult week with Brian.'

'They argued often?'

She nodded. 'Brian had had a number of affairs going back over the years, always with women he'd met through work, usually while overseas. Barbara tolerated those because she could pretend to herself that they weren't really happening. A friend of mine – Andrea – her husband used to work with Brian, years ago. Apparently they got up to all sorts when they were on their overseas trips.'

Sam was scribbling furiously.

'She'd always been quite a jealous woman,' Lorna said. 'She was quite nasty to Brian's daughter, saw her as a threat, I believe.'

'So when Brian semi-retired . . .?'

'Barbara believed he was having affairs closer to home. First of all it was some physiotherapist woman at the health club they belong to. That was just after they moved to Morden. Then it was all about the stable girl, Polly Leuchars.'

'Mrs Fletcher-Norman mentioned Polly in her letters to you?'

Lorna nodded. 'Yes, and over the phone. At first it was just a suspicion, but Barbara has a way of latching onto an idea and going over it so many times in her head that it becomes the same thing as a truth. She said Brian was having an affair with Polly. Other women in the village had confirmed it to her.'

'Did she confront Brian?'

'Yes. He denied it, of course. Even stopped having riding lessons to appease her. I felt quite sorry for him, really. I think going riding had been doing him some good.'

'Do you know when it was that Barbara confronted her husband?'

'It was around the beginning of September. On the Monday before she was admitted to hospital she said he had denied it. She sounded very low about it. It was as though his denial made it worse – if he'd owned up to it, she might not have felt so bad. He'd admitted his foibles in the past, so it felt to Barbara as though he was really lying to her as well as cheating.'

'You seem doubtful that he was having an affair?'

She thought about this, and nodded slowly. 'I just can't see it somehow. I've seen pictures of that Polly on the television, what was she, twenty-something?'

'Twenty-seven,' Ron said.

'And pretty, too. Forgive me for saying so, but Brian's not usually the sort to appeal to young girls. And I don't think he would be so foolish as to do it right under Barbara's nose like that. Far more likely he was seeing someone else and using Barbara's suspicions about Polly to cover up the real mischief.'

For a moment the only sound was Sam's pen moving across the notebook. Ron seemed lost in thought.

'More tea?'

The mugs were duly topped up and Sam paid a visit to the bathroom. It was light and airy and she washed her hands with a purple soap that smelled of lavender, and dried them on a white fluffy towel. The bathroom was spotless. She wondered whether they employed a cleaner, or whether Lorna did the housework herself.

Ron seemed to have found a way in. When she went back into the living room, both of them were chortling with laughter. She wondered what it was that had got him into Lorna's good books, but it seemed the joke wasn't going to be shared.

'Right,' he said with a deep breath. 'Where were we?'

Sam retrieved her notebook and flexed her right hand, which had started to ache.

'You mentioned a phone conversation with Mrs Fletcher-Norman on Monday last week. Did you phone her, or was it the other way round?'

'She called me,' Lorna said. 'It was about Liam O'Toole.'

Ron said, 'This was the man she was seeing? The tennis coach?'

'Yes. She'd written me a few letters about him, and the last one had indicated that they were planning to run away together. She'd been saving up money for years, money Brian knew nothing about. She called it her Rainy Day Fund.'

'Do you have any idea how much money we're talking about?'

Lorna gave a little shrug. 'Thousands. Every time Brian had an affair she used to get jewellery from him – keep her sweet, I suppose. She sold it all, as well as creaming money off the house-keeping allowance he gave her.'

She took a drink of her tea, then went on: 'I'd written a letter to Barbara in which I'd asked her to be careful. I asked her if she knew everything about this Liam, whether she was certain he could be trusted. She phoned me to give me a telling off.'

'You thought he was going to do a runner?'

She nodded. 'It just always seemed too good to be true.' She gave a rueful smile. 'You must think me terribly critical of my friends to not see them as attractive to younger people. But I'm afraid the same thing applies. He was only about twenty-eight, I believe. Handsome, fit, reasonably intelligent. And yet he falls in love with a fifty-eight-year-old housewife? I don't think so.'

Sam couldn't decide if Lorna was just a straightforward person who didn't believe in glossing over the issues, or if she was somehow slightly jealous of what Barbara had had. In either case, she looked defiant, as though challenging the officers to disagree.

'Mrs Fletcher-Norman was angry with you, when she phoned?'

Lorna softened a little. 'Not angry, exactly. She was just trying to persuade me that I was wrong about Liam. She was utterly convinced he was genuine. In fact, she said when they did make their escape, as she called it, she would bring him here for a visit so that I could see for myself.'

'What did you make of that?'

'I told her she'd be welcome.'

'So you parted on good terms?'

'Yes. Although I did post a letter to her on Wednesday morning to tell her not to rush into anything and obviously she hadn't got it by the time she rang me that night.'

Ron nodded. 'What time did she ring you on Wednesday?'

'It was about half past nine. I was just putting the dinner plates in the dishwasher. Andrew was watching some documentary on BBC Three. I had to take the phone upstairs because I couldn't hear what she was saying properly.'

'She was incoherent?'

'She was drunk.' She said it with an edge to her voice that suggested disapproval.

'When I eventually got her to make sense, it seemed that Liam had run off with all her money. She said she had given him access to her savings account so that he could get some money for a deposit on a flat. I don't know where. She'd gone to the bedsit he had in the village, an annexe off one of the bigger houses. The place was cleared out. She had been trying his mobile, but it was turned off.'

'What did you say?'

'Well, I certainly didn't say "I told you so", although perhaps I should have. I asked her where Brian was. She said he'd gone out with his fancy woman.'

'"His fancy woman?"' Ron repeated.

'I assume she meant Polly Leuchars. I suggested she should phone him and ask him to come home. She was beside herself. I was concerned for her state of mind, particularly given her set-back just over a month before. I thought she might try to harm herself.'

'And what did she say?'

'She calmed down a bit when I mentioned Brian. Seemed to bring her back to her senses. She said she was going to phone him. I promised I would call her in the morning to see how she was, and then we said goodbye. By that time she seemed to have cheered up a bit. I thought she was going to be all right.'

'How long had you been on the phone, roughly?'

'I'd say about twenty minutes or so. Afterwards I tried to phone Brian's mobile, but it was engaged. I assumed Barbara had got hold of him.'

'And the next thing you heard was the news?'

Lorna looked down at her lap. Her voice trembled slightly. 'Yes. I couldn't believe it.' She paused. 'Well, no, that's not true. Of course

250

I believed it, especially after our conversation on Wednesday. I just thought to myself, what a terrible business. I said as much to Andrew – what a terrible thing, to take one's own life.'

Sam stopped writing for a moment. 'I'm sorry, Mrs Newman.' Her voice was low, tender. 'It must have been awful for you, losing such a dear friend in such dreadful circumstances.'

Lorna gave her a weak smile. 'Thank you, my dear. Yes, it was awful. You're kind.'

Ron drank the last of his tea. He cleared his throat. 'You mentioned the letters, Mrs Newman?'

'Oh, of course. I'll get them.' She stood, bustled off down the corridor.

'Get all that, Sarge?' Ron asked Sam.

'Yep.'

They sat in silence until Lorna returned, carrying a thick brown A4 envelope. 'I think this is all of them.'

Ron took the package and looked inside. About twenty envelopes, opened. 'Thank you. I need to evidence these and give you a receipt.'

'Oh, are you taking them away?'

'I'm afraid I'll need to, Mrs Newman. They will become property of the coroner until after the inquest, as evidence into Mrs Fletcher-Norman's state of mind. Once the inquest is finished you can ask to have them returned to you.'

She looked a little crestfallen. 'I suppose that's all right.'

They bagged the package in a clear plastic evidence wallet and Ron wrote out a receipt and handed it to Mrs Newman.

'I need you to have a read of my notes, Mrs Newman, if that's all right,' Sam said gently. 'If you agree that everything I've written is accurate, I'll ask you to sign my notebook. If there's anything in

251

there you want me to amend, please say. Then I'll ask you to give me a written statement based on what you've told us. We need to have a bit in there to show that you've provided the letters as an exhibit for the coroner.'

They spent a few minutes in silence, broken only by the sound of the notebook pages turning. From time to time, Lorna nodded. Ron went to the bathroom, and was gone for an inordinate amount of time. Sam hoped he wasn't snooping. Or at least, not in an obvious way.

'You have very neat writing, my dear,' Lorna Newman said at last.

Sam laughed. 'It's a struggle, writing that fast, and trying to keep it legible.'

'I can imagine.'

Taking the statement took a little longer. Once it was done Lorna Newman offered them sandwiches to take with them for the journey, but they managed to refuse gracefully. Ron was desperate for a McDonald's.

'You were gone a long time,' Sam said, when they got back in the car.

'You thought I was having a poke round,' he accused.

'I did wonder.'

'I was having a dump. All right?'

'Well, I hope you opened a window.'

'Bastard dreadnought couldn't fit round the U bend. Had to beat it to death with the toilet brush, in the end.'

Lorna Newman was watching them from the doorway. Ron gave her a wave.

'Well, what did you think?' he asked, as they did up their seatbelts.

'I think we need to get the telephone records from Hayselden

Barn,' Sam said. 'So much of this case is going to come down to the phones. It's a good job we've got a good analyst.'

'Just as long as he doesn't get distracted by the boss,' Ron said with a smirk.

'What's that supposed to mean?'

'Oh come on. You must have noticed. He can't keep his eyes off her. Completely besotted.'

Sam considered it. 'He'll have to join the queue, then, won't he?'

'Judging by the rest of her options, I'd say he's in with more of a shout than the rest of us.'

'Give over. She's far too sensible. Especially . . . '

'Go on.'

'No. It's nothing.'

Ron was smiling at her now. It was his turn to drive, but even so he was glancing across at her, enjoying the way the conversation was heading. 'You were going to say "especially now she's learned her lesson", weren't you? Talking about Mr Hamilton?'

'It's gossip, Ron. Not very nice when it's about someone you get on well with. You driving, or dancing?'

He corrected the steering and brought the car back to the right side of the road, thankful it was clear ahead. 'Les's got a book running. Her and the DI is fifty to one, the analyst only gets eight to one.'

'And her abstaining for the duration of the case?'

'Two to one.'

There was a brief silence. Then something else occurred to Sam. 'What about me?'

This time Ron kept his eyes on the road ahead. 'What d'you mean, Sarge?'

'Come on, Ron. What're my odds?'

It took him a while to pluck up the courage. 'Last time I checked, twenty-five to one.'

That was a consolation, at least – her odds were better than Hamilton's. One very small victory to the girls.

13.52

Lou spent a moment checking her face in the mirror on the sun visor. Her hair was a bit tangled, so she ran a brush through it, squirted a bit of her handbag-sized bottle of deodorant under her top, ran her tongue over her teeth. She gave herself a stern look in the mirror.

There was no getting away from it. It was like an itch that wouldn't go away. Something in that kiss – the long, long kiss that had gone on for half an hour and had felt like thirty seconds. The way he'd touched her hair. Damn it. Would he turn out to be an utter shit like Hamilton?

With a deep breath in she put her hairbrush away and straightened her jacket. Time would tell.

Inside, a long bar ran along the back wall, with oak tables and benches interspersed with low sofas and coffee tables. Beside the roaring fire two high-backed fireside chairs stood as though guarding the warmth.

He was there already, at a small table, a pint of what looked like cola in front of him. He stood up when he saw her, and when she went over he kissed her cheek as though they were friends meeting up for lunch and they hadn't seen each other for ages. Which, perhaps, was a fair assessment of what they were actually doing.

'Hey,' he said. 'How are you?'

'I'm fine, thanks.'

'Have a seat,' he said. 'I'll get you a drink. What would you like?'

'Just an orange juice. I'll get it.'

'Go on,' he said. 'Pretend you're not my boss for a minute.'

'All right, then. Thanks.'

She watched him heading for the bar. Jeans, today, of course, and a blue hooded top with a stylised design on the back in white, formed out of two ice hockey players crossing sticks. Under it the words 'Briarstone Jaguars'. She turned her attention to the menu: typical pub fare, but a few unusual offerings as well.

It looked as though the Sunday lunch rush was coming to an end. Not many tables free, but a lot of empty plates and people sitting back in their seats.

Jason brought her drink. 'You decided?'

'I think the venison sausages,' she said. 'I'm intrigued.'

He went back to the bar to order the food.

The barmaid had dark hair, short, with red streaks. Lou wondered if that was Frances Kember.

'I missed you last night,' Jason said, sitting back down opposite her. 'I don't think I can wait until the case settles down.'

She felt her stomach do a little flip. She tried to smile, tried to make light of it. 'Hmm. It's very distracting.'

For a moment it was eye contact, nothing more, but the tension between them was electric. He smiled, a slow smile, stretched out a foot under the table and laid it against hers, just gentle pressure.

'I guess this isn't really the place, is it?'

'Not really.'

'Later? Tonight?'

She hesitated. 'I promised myself I wouldn't do this.'

'Why not?'

'Last time I did this with someone from work it all went horribly wrong.'

'Hamilton?'

She nodded, returned the pressure of the footsie game under the table.

'Sometimes you need a bit of time off, eh? What we're doing is important, but so is this.'

'Let's see what the rest of today brings, OK? My head's buzzing with it at the moment. That's why I thought it would be good to get out of the office for a bit.'

He looked up, past her head. She turned to see the barmaid bearing two platefuls of food. 'Here you go,' she said, putting the plates down on the table between them.

'Thanks,' Lou said. 'This looks great, thank you. Is Ivan around?'

'He was about to go to the cash and carry.'

'Would you ask him if he can spare us a minute? That would be great.' She handed over a business card.

'I'll send him out.'

'Thank you.'

When she had retreated into the back, Lou gave Jason a look. His foot was still pressed gently against her ankle. She liked it being there. Just having this contact with him made her feel good. Now, of course, she wondered what it would be like. Going to his house, late, straight from work – or would she go home first? Get changed? Or maybe he would come over to hers. She would have to tidy up a bit, change the sheets. The thought of what might follow was a delicious one.

'How was hockey?'

'Oh, good. We won.'

'Did you score?' she said, and then instantly regretted it.

'Not yet,' he said. And winked.

Christ.

'Sorry,' he said. 'I keep making you blush.'

She was about to answer but caught sight of a man approaching them.

Ivan Rollinson was slender, with dark hair, an aquiline nose, and clear, crystal clear, green eyes.

Lou introduced herself and Jason, they all shook hands, and Ivan sat down with them. 'I'm assuming you're the one in charge,' he said. 'I wondered if you'd come.'

Lou gave him a smile. 'Thank you for sparing us a minute.' She pulled her notebook out of her bag. 'I wanted to see if there might be anything else you might have recalled about Polly's visit on Halloween evening.'

He shrugged. 'I said everything to your officers who came here. She was waiting for someone. Then she left.'

'You said she was dressed up that night,' Lou said.

'Yes.'

'Did she often come in here dressed up?'

He gave a sort of smirk. 'Only when she was meeting women.'

Lou looked up from her notebook. 'She met people in here a lot, then? Women and men?'

He nodded. 'She was in here once, twice a week. Tuesday night was the first time she didn't meet somebody here.'

'Always different people?'

He shook his head. 'Same ones. Maybe – eight, ten different people.'

'Were these people you knew?'

'Some of them.'

'Would you tell me their names?'

He didn't reply.

'Mr Rollinson. It's vital that we make contact with all of Polly's friends. I'm quite sure nobody who was a friend to Polly would want to keep information from us. And I can assure you that none of them will know that the names came from you.'

He considered this for a moment. Then, 'Nigel – the man who owns the stables? She had a drink in here with him once or twice. They seemed to have a laugh, you know? As though they came from work. She was in her riding boots and jodhpurs. And Flora. She came in here a lot with Flora. At first she was in jeans. Then she was dressed up.'

'She dressed up for Flora?'

'Like I say, only for the women.'

'When was the last time she was in here with Flora?'

He shrugged. 'More than two, three months.'

'Anyone else?'

He gave a deep sigh, looked up again as though the answer might be printed on the ceiling. 'An older man, with grey hair. He lives in the village, comes in here with his wife sometimes.'

'You know his name?'

He shrugged again. 'No. The last time with him was two months ago, maybe longer.'

'Thank you. Mr Rollinson, do you know who the last person was you saw Polly with regularly?'

'There was a younger man, maybe three, four times. She was here with him last week and the week before. And a woman a few times.'

'Can you describe her?'

'Older – maybe forty, fifty? Fair hair. Very attractive, smart. Looked rich. But Polly always paid.'

'And you didn't recognise her – didn't catch a name?'

He shook his head. 'It was only twice, I think. In the last three weeks or so. I don't believe she lives in the village.'

'And you haven't seen her since?'

'No.'

'Or the younger man?'

He shook his head.

'Can you describe him?'

Rollinson was starting to look bored. 'Young. He wore jeans and jumpers, like he worked on the farm too. I thought he was another one from the stables.'

Lou noted this down in her book. 'Did you get the impression that any of these people were particularly special to Polly? As though one of them were a boyfriend, perhaps?'

'Or a girlfriend, you mean?' He smiled again. 'No. It was like they were *all* her best friend. She used to laugh a lot, always seemed to be having a good time, but she never drank alcohol. I asked her once what was her secret, and she said she was high on life.'

There was a pause. Rollinson seemed deep in thought, no doubt remembering Polly the way she'd been, all beauty and sparkle. 'The woman – the fair woman? The last time I saw them here, I think they had a disagreement.'

'When was this, can you remember?'

'Two weeks ago, more. Polly was in here and waited for her for about half an hour. She was chatting to Frances, the barmaid, and then to another one of the locals. They were playing darts and Polly was helping them keep score.'

'The woman came in, and Polly left what she was doing without a word, and went to sit next to her. The woman hardly spoke, acted as though Polly was not there most of the time. And Polly was smiling at her, trying to get her to look. They had a few drinks, and then the woman got up and left, and Polly followed, a few steps behind.'

'You thought they had had an argument?' Lou asked.

'Something like that. One minute Polly was happy and laughing and joking, the next she was looking at this woman as though begging her forgiveness for something.'

'And the last night you saw her. Halloween. What time did she leave?'

'I told the other one. It was late – half past eleven. Something like that.'

'On her own?'

'Yes.'

'Thank you, Ivan.'

He returned her smile, standing up. 'You're welcome. Come again.'

'We will,' Lou said.

She was still thinking through Polly's various assignations in the Lemon Tree as she followed Jason out into the car park. The light felt unbearably bright after the cosy shadows of the interior and she felt in her bag for her sunglasses. No sign of them – they must be in the car. 'Well, that was nice,' she said.

'Yeah,' he said, hands in his pockets.

'I'll see you tomorrow, then?'

'For sure.' There was something in the way he said it that made Lou alert.

Behind them, two couples exited the pub, the women laughing

about something. Lou moved closer to Jason, close enough to be able to whisper: 'What's wrong?'

He didn't answer, watching as the doors slammed on a Land Rover and a BMW.

'Get in.' Lou unlocked her car and went round to the driver's side. When he climbed in to the passenger side she turned in the seat so she was facing him. He was staring resolutely ahead at the hedge. She waited patiently.

'So,' he began, 'when you said we should meet for lunch – I was kind of hoping it would just be the two of us.'

'I don't understand – it *was* just the two of us.'

'Nah. That was you, me and the job.'

'I *am* on duty,' she said, making an effort to keep her voice even.

'Still,' he said. 'Is this what it would be like?'

'Yes,' she said. 'If we're lucky. On some jobs I might not get to see you for days on end. You should get your head round that right now or else there's no point carrying on.'

He looked at her then and for a moment she saw emotion in his eyes that she hadn't been expecting. Then it was gone. He shrugged, smiled, cupped her cheek and kissed her. *That's better*, she thought, breathed in, moved closer to him so that he could kiss her again, harder this time and now she didn't care if anyone was in the car park watching. Another minute and she didn't care about the job, either.

From her bag, Lou's phone bleeped.

She was so lost in his kiss she barely noticed, but Jason pulled back. He looked into her eyes, stroking his fingers down her cheek, over her chin, down her throat, lightly caressing her skin until he got to the neckline of her sweater.

'Can I see you tonight?' he asked. 'Please.'

'I'll try my best.' At least she was being honest – there was nothing Lou hated more than empty promises.

'You'd better get that,' he said. 'I'll see you later, Louisa.'

He kissed her again, quickly, fiercely, and then opened the door and got out.

She pulled the phone out of her bag and looked. There was a text from Sam. They were on their way back from Norfolk. And a voicemail from Paul Harper, the CSI who had been at the quarry yesterday.

It was time to head back to the real world.

5x5x5 Intelligence Report

Date: Sunday 4 November 2012

Officer: PC 9921 EVANS

Re: Op NETTLE – Liam O'TOOLE

ECHR Grading: B / 1 / 1

Database searches, employment records and Voters indicate the former tennis coach at the Morden Golf and Country Club was Mr Liam James O'TOOLE DOB 27/11/1981.

Andrew HART, General Manager at the club, confirms Mr O'TOOLE had been employed as a tennis coach at the club, from June until he left unexpectedly last week. He was expected to turn up for work on Thursday, but failed to put in an appearance. A letter of resignation was received on Friday morning, postmarked Briarstone. Letter has been seized for forensic examination, special property number CL/0004562/12.

Mr HART confirmed that both Mr and Mrs FLETCHER-

NORMAN were members of the club. Mr FLETCHER-NORMAN regularly played golf. Mrs FLETCHER-NORMAN had previously been an enthusiastic golf player, but in recent months had switched to playing tennis. She had been having tennis coaching sessions with Mr O'TOOLE (at a cost of £45 per hour) twice or three times per week. Mrs FLETCHER-NORMAN had a scheduled coaching session with Mr O'TOOLE in the afternoon of Wednesday, 31 October and this was the last appointment that day.

Mr HART would not discuss rumours relating to the relationship between Mrs FLETCHER-NORMAN and Mr O'TOOLE. He did, however, say that Mr O'TOOLE was particularly popular with female members of the club and he had received numerous complaints about his sudden and unexpected departure.

Email

From: PSE Paul HARPER, Crime Scene Investigation Team

To: DCI Louisa SMITH / Op NETTLE MIR

Subject: Ambleside Quarry scene

Date: 4 November 2012

Grading A / 1 / 1

Full forensic report to follow.

Re: Shot-put found at bottom of quarry, SP number CL/00003889/12

Forensic examination of scene suggests the shot-put was thrown into the quarry after the vehicle containing the deceased Mrs FLETCHER-NORMAN went over the edge. This is indicated by an indentation in the sandy base of the quarry followed by a second length of indentation. The first indentation occurs about 20m from the car park level, on a small ledge. Distance approx 2m out on a horizontal plane. Circular indentation in sandy soil, partially obscured by a plant growing to the left which has been squashed slightly. Smaller indentations around the area but NOT within the bowl-shape of the indentation suggest that the anomaly was caused after the period of heavy rain which took place on the night of 31 October. Bowl-shape of the indentation is consistent with the size and weight of the shot-put being thrown from the car park area above, and is likely to be the first place the shot-put came into contact with the quarry floor.

Second indentation occurs approximately 8m further down the slope and forms a track approximately 2m in length, through a patch of sand and light shingle, ending in a patch of scrub grass/weeds.

Approximately 2m further from this in the direction of travel indicated by the track is the patch of gorse bushes/dense grass in which the shot-put was found. This indentation is light and easily missed, indicating the force of travel of the object was much reduced and was effectively coming to rest.

Of interest is that the indentation CROSSES a larger indentation made by debris (namely the rear bumper) of Mrs FLETCHER-NORMAN's vehicle. This substantiates the premise that the shot-put was thrown from the car park AFTER the vehicle had gone over the edge. Due to the lack of heavy rain since 31 October, I would suggest this occurred after 0100hrs on 1 November and before 0915hrs which is when the scene was identified and effectively sealed. Will require Met Office confirmation as to exactly when the rain stopped in the area, but from personal recollection I believe it was dry when I was driving to work that morning.

Scene photographs have been taken and recorded, submitted to the incident room under separate cover.

5x5x5 Intelligence Report

From: PC David EMERSON, Tactical Ops

To: Op NETTLE incident room

Subject: Ambleside Quarry

Date: 4/11/12

Grading: A / 1 / 1

Searches continuing at Ambleside Quarry. A suitcase was located in undergrowth not far from the car park. Unclear how long it had been there. No identifying features but suitcase is full of clothes, including female underwear and a sponge bag containing toiletries. Suitcase looked to have been thrown into the undergrowth from the car park area.

CSI Paul HARPER in attendance, has removed same for forensic examination. SP number CL/0005682/12. PSE HARPER will submit further intel in due course.

5x5x5 Intelligence Report

From: Karen ASLETT – Source Co-ordinator

To: DCI Louisa SMITH

Subject: Nigel MAITLAND

Date: 04/11/12

Grading B / 2 / 4

Nigel MAITLAND has been organising regular shipments of illegal immigrants from Iraq/Kurdistan via Europe. On 31/10/12 a Lithuanian-registered lorry came through Dover.

14 illegals were concealed in a compartment between the cab and the main cargo area. These illegals were unloaded at MAITLAND's farm in Morden and transferred to a minibus.

MAITLAND prefers to conduct business off his regular premises but something went wrong with the shipment this time.

5x5x5 Intelligence Report

From: CE Paul HARPER, Crime Scene Investigation Team

To: DCI Louisa SMITH / Op NETTLE MIR

Subject: Ambleside Quarry scene

Date: 4/11/12

Grading A / 1 / 1

RE: SP number CL/0005682/12

Item received in labs. Good set of latent prints inside and outside case belonging to Mrs Barbara FLETCHER-NORMAN (found deceased Ambleside Quarry 01/12). Interior may well reveal DNA.

Contents of suitcase include clothes (mainly size 12), shoes (size 5), underwear, toiletries and make-up. No identification or anything else to indicate who it belongs to.

To confirm – handle of suitcase has NO prints, likely to have been wiped. Location of suitcase was well sheltered within thick undergrowth, despite recent rain the outside was still quite dry so unlikely that prints were washed off, particularly as latents found on outside of case (consistent with lid being pushed down to close the case).

16:12

Andy Hamilton let himself in to the MIR to find it empty, the only light from the dwindling day outside making the untidy space and the mismatched desks look forlorn. He had just come back from a fruitless trip to the Computer Crime Unit in the hope of finding out if there was anything of interest on Brian Fletcher-Norman's laptop computer. There was nobody there.

Nobody in the MIR either meant he didn't have to worry about accidentally giving something away, by smiling or looking like he'd got some action, or by looking over-tired. In years gone past he would have ended up telling someone about it, maybe Ron or more likely Les Finnegan, whose tastes ran to the distinctly perverse. He remembered one occasion – was it in the King Bill? – and everyone was pissed and having a laugh, right up to the moment when Les Finnegan started telling them about a warrant he'd been on where they'd found a fully equipped dungeon in the basement. They'd all been on warrants like that, Christ, these days it was unusual not to come across some sort of sex toy in the process of executing a search, but Les seemed to be particularly relishing the description of the room and what it had contained. Andy must have failed to express the right level of disinterest, because half an hour later he'd been calmly having a piss in the Gents, when Les had taken the urinal next to his and told him more than he ever wanted to know about what went on in the dungeons of the rich and famous.

Andy wasn't going to tell *anyone* about Suzanne.

He made his way to the desk he'd been using, turned on the workstation. He had reports to write up, statements and other things to catch up on, leave to authorise, emails to delete.

His head was still spinning with it all.

268

Communications with Karen had been tentatively resumed. She had never locked him out before, and for no apparent misdeed: he had been busy at work, and neglectful, which was bad but surely something that she should be used to by now? Locking him out was an extreme reaction and by rights he should now have moral supremacy – she owed him an apology. She had making up to do.

This morning it had crossed his mind that something else might have prompted her to lock him out. He considered that she might have found out something about one of his previous misdeeds, but then the first text came:

Hope u OK. Where did u sleep x

He replied when he pulled in to get petrol:

Went to Johns. U OK?

No 'x' to his reply. That would show that he was still offended, and hopefully lead to her trying a bit harder to make up. A few minutes later:

We need to talk. Try to get home on time tonite OK x

That was fair enough. And he needed something to stop him going back to Waterside Gardens. He felt like he'd had some kind of drug there, something that made him think about nothing else, want nothing else. He felt the pull of her like a physical bond.

He spent ten minutes deleting emails before he was distracted again. He looked at the clock on the computer – ten to five already. He could drive back to her place, spend an hour with her, and still get home to Karen and the kids at a reasonable time. After all, he didn't want it to look like he was dropping everything to get home to Karen because she'd told him to, did he? Especially after she'd locked him out. He needed to time it right – to prove to her that he was busy, that he was working on something really important, and

269

that no matter what tantrums she felt like throwing, he had other demands on his time. But he wasn't a quitter. He wasn't going to give up on his marriage, on principle if nothing else – she was stuck with him, for better or worse.

18:17

Lou had never been one to talk about breakthroughs, but this Sunday, this incredibly long Sunday, had that breakthrough feeling about it.

Paul Harper, the CSI at the quarry, had spoken to her briefly on the phone and referred her to the report he'd emailed over. Apparently he was on his way to church.

Reading the report was like throwing a bucket of cold water over the investigation, Lou thought. If the shot-put had gone over the edge of the quarry after the car, which is what Paul Harper seemed to be convinced of, then who the hell had thrown it? And why was Barbara's suitcase apparently hidden in some bushes at the top of the quarry and not in the boot of the car? Nothing was making sense.

And to top it all, just in case she'd thought about going to see Jason after all, he'd sent her a text:

Hey beautiful. Forgot my brother was coming to visit. Wd
still be great to see u wd love for u to meet him. X

Yeah. She had no desire to spend the evening listening to two Canadians talking about ice hockey.

In the end, desperation and the need to think things through led her to phone Hamilton's mobile.

'Hey, boss.' From the sounds of it, he was in the car.

'Are you on the way home?'

'Yeah. I spoke to the manager of the country club where

the tennis coach worked. Nothing too interesting, although it matches up what we got from O'Toole himself earlier. Did you see that?'

'I've been at the quarry.'

'It's on an intel report. How's it going at the quarry, then?'

'Big development – it looks like the shot-put went over the edge of the quarry after the car did.'

She let this information sink in.

'So she didn't have it in the car with her? Ah, bollocks. Looks like my theory's blown.'

'Someone wanted to use Barbara as a scapegoat for Polly's death, do you think?' Lou asked. 'To draw attention away from themselves?'

'So who would do that? Brian? Why would he want to kill Polly? It doesn't strike me that he'd be that bothered about being blackmailed or something like that. Most of the village seemed to know he shagged her.'

Another theory occurred to Lou right at that moment. 'Or maybe someone really wanted to kill Barbara, and Polly's death simply gave them the opportunity they were looking for?'

'That would suggest Brian again,' said Andy.

'Or the tennis coach, Liam O'Toole.'

'He'd already got her money; I don't think he needed to kill her too.'

'Did you get any more on him?'

'A fair bit, but most of it is still just more gossip. Half of the village thought he was God's gift, the rest of them seem to think he was a wanker. Benefit of hindsight, there, of course. But they all knew Barbara was carrying on with him. Which means Brian must have known, too.'

'Do we have any leads on where he might have gone?'

'His boss at the Golf and Country Club gave me some next-of-kin details for some woman in Ireland – they think it's his mother. Tried to call, no reply. I'll put it through the system in the morning. And I got his mobile number too, but it's disconnected.'

Lou sighed. 'This case is turning into one big tangled mess.'

'We've got plenty of evidence. I'm sure it will become clear. You know we always get there in the end.' His voice was soothing.

'What about Brian's computer?'

'I spoke to the guy who's on call. They expect to have some results tomorrow. He wouldn't give me anything else. He said we could hurry it along but we'd have to pay for it.'

That was no surprise. 'Oh, well, that's not bad; it usually takes weeks.'

'Anything else you need me to do?'

'No,' she said. 'Go home, I'll see you bright and early tomorrow.'

When she disconnected the call she put her head in her hands. There was nothing else she could do this evening and yet she didn't want to go home. She wanted to see Jason, despite how tired she was, despite the fact that his brother would be there. She could ask him to come round to hers – but that wouldn't work either. His brother would think she was rude. To put an end to the matter, she sent Jason a text:

Going home now. Enjoy your evening. See you tomorrow. x

Seconds later, her phone bleeped with a reply.

You OK? X

For crying out loud! It was late, and she was going to get chips on the way home. Every second was interrupting that process. One last text.

Yeah fine, tired now. See you tomorrow. X

When she got home, an hour later, a small bag of chips was nestling in her bag. She was starving. And the chips kept her from driving round to Jason's house. Food, a soak in the bath and an early night was all she could think about.

19:11

The studio was cold. Once the lights were on, Flora turned on the heating and put on the portable halogen heater to give the room an extra boost. She made a cup of instant coffee, and, with the blanket from the sofa around her shoulders, studied her unfinished canvases.

The big one of Polly needed more work, but her mind was on other things.

She looked through the various canvases stacked against the wall, some of them long abandoned, some of them experiments, some of them useless – and yet she had learned at art college the benefits of never getting rid of anything, no matter how disastrous. Like drafts of a document, her sketches and her failures plotted the path to whatever successes she enjoyed, which made them a part of the process.

There. Half-stuck to a smaller canvas was a portrait she had done of her father. It was from long before Polly had arrived at the farm, not long after she'd got the studio, which meant she was probably a year out of college at most.

Nigel's blue eyes stared at her out of a roughly worked face – bold lines, dark colours. His features were angular as they were in life, but this image, even more than the preparatory sketches and the other attempts, showed him as she knew him to be, with a vulnerability despite the coldness. Whatever it was that he did to earn

273

his money, he did it not out of greed but out of a desire to succeed – in this as in everything else he tackled. She admired him for that, despite everything.

Maybe this was all because she had let him down. She was supposed to be a farmer's daughter, wasn't she? And, since Felicity hadn't managed to produce a son and heir, she should have been learning the business, ready to take it over one day. But her heart had never been in it. When she told her parents that she had a place at art school, they had reacted much as she had expected them to: Nigel could barely speak to her for months afterwards. Felicity found things to worry about whilst trying to be supportive and encouraging in her own limited way. If it had only been the farm, Flora might have given up her place and done what had been expected of her. But it wasn't just the farm; it was the rest of it. The deals with those thugs he associated with. The drug imports that Felicity knew nothing about; the transportation of illegal workers from all over the world: people who'd travelled thousands of miles and ended up working in the shitholes of the UK, with no rights and very little money.

Months after she had told them about her college place, Nigel had taken her into his office one afternoon and told her all about it. He brought everything out into the open: who he was working for, how he started off organising the transport but then ended up taking over other parts of it, laundering some of the profits through the farm, handling cash and drugs and recruiting operatives because, at the end of the day, the rest of them were shit at it.

Flora told him she didn't want to know.

And in response he had offered her a deal: he would fund her college course, he would support her every step of the way, on the understanding that she would back him up when he needed it, and that one day she would be there to take things over. Manage the

274

farm, do whatever else needed to be done. If she didn't want to get her hands dirty, that was fair enough – he would allow her that – but she had to know, in order not to fuck things up for him. If she knew what was going on, she would know when to look away. And that way, Nigel could keep the money coming in.

And so they had continued in this uneasy dance, Flora the artist, Nigel the farmer. As unlikely a father–daughter relationship as you could ever encounter, more alike than they would ever admit. If her art had not been so successful, who knew? She might well have got more involved with the farm, might have even helped him practically with some of the financial day-to-day stuff. But she was a success, and she could afford the studio, and whilst she could take commissions when things got a bit tight, most of the time she was comfortable and working on whatever she wanted to.

Then Polly arrived, and upset everything.

Now Flora looked into the blue, blue eyes and saw in them something she had never seen before. She took the canvas over to the one she had been working on, Polly's canvas, and put them side by side; and whilst Polly's was more abstract, there was the same blue in the shirt that was supposed to represent Polly, and the way her eyes looked first thing in the morning when she had been sleeping in Flora's arms and had looked up at her – *that* moment. And it was the same colour. The *same*.

It meant nothing, of course. But Flora knew. And other things, things she had turned her mind away from: Nigel had told her he had been out late that night, had come home after midnight – but Felicity had said he had gone down to Yonder Cottage and Polly had made him cheese on toast. Flora had signed a statement at the police station declaring that she did not know the identity of any of Polly's other lovers. She had lied to them because he was her father and, even though she hated his guts right now, she still had that unswerving family loyalty that he didn't deserve.

But what if he had killed her? What if Nigel had been the one who had killed Polly?

Day Five – Monday 5 November 2012

06:45

From her desk, Lou saw Jason arrive. He was laughing and joking with Barry Holloway and Mandy before he'd even got his coat off. And then he looked over towards her office, and met her eyes, and smiled.

Already in his email inbox was a load more phone data, and the download of Brian's phone had finally come through from the CCU, and been sent to the analyst directly. Lou had received a copy of the email but the attachment wouldn't open. She was dying to know what it contained.

It definitely felt as though a turning point had been reached in the investigation. Beyond the interviews, the weeding out of the useful witnesses from those who claimed to have seen nothing, heard nothing, from those who claimed to have seen everything but clearly hadn't, there was a point in every investigation when a piece of information came in that felt different.

And this morning, there were several.

Right, she needed coffee before the briefing. Time to get going with it.

07:18

Jason had been sitting at his desk when the call came in. Barry Holloway took it, and even across three desks and half the room, Jason could see him sit up a little straighter.

'Right you are. Yes, all right then. Ready now, is it?'

When he'd finished the call, he addressed the room. 'We've got some CCTV of Polly from the town centre. Who wants to go get it?'

There was only Les Finnegan, Jason and Mandy in the room. Les stood and looked across to Jason. 'Fancy coming along? Get some fresh air?'

The TV Unit was across the car park in a temporary building, pending their move to the refurbished custody suite along with Computer Crime. The cabin they were in was ridiculously unsuitable, freezing cold in winter and dangerously hot in summer. It was temporary, and yet they'd been in there nearly three years and all the other police stations had to rely on this unit for any downloads, leading to a huge backlog. Of course, being on site and being able to turn up and wait was a distinct advantage.

Inside, the unit hummed with servers, printers and various recording devices. The council CCTV had sent over four disks with all the recordings from the town centre CCTV cameras for 31 October and some poor sod in the TV Unit had spent the last two days viewing everything between the hours of half past twelve and four, the times that Felicity Maitland had given for Polly's trip into town.

Josh Trent, the technical analyst, took them over to a desk in the far corner. 'Grab a chair,' he said.

The computer screen was frozen on a scene from the High Street, shoppers stopped in their tracks in the pedestrian precinct. The time display showed 13.04, the date 31/10/2012.

'Ready?' said Josh, fingers poised over the keyboard. Jason and Les were both glued to the screen. With CCTV it was often a case of 'blink and you miss it'.

For a moment there was nothing, just people walking slowly up and down the High Street, shopping bags bulging. From the right, a young female crossed and sat on a bench. Blonde hair in a pony-tail. Black coat. A few shopping bags, and a small tan-coloured bag worn with the strap across her body.

'That's her?' Jason said, quietly.

Les nodded. 'Hair's pretty recognisable. Is that it?'

Josh gave a self-satisfied look. 'Keep watching.'

The girl on the screen checked her watch. The time reference on the screen had clicked round to 13.06. After a moment she fished inside one of the carrier bags and brought out a bottle, dark coloured, a flash of a red label – Coke? She unscrewed it and swigged from the bottle, replaced the lid and put it back inside the bag. She sat back, one leg crossed over the other.

13.07. 'She's waiting for someone,' Les said.

Polly stood up, stretched, leaving the bags behind her on the seat. She turned to face up the High Street, her back to the camera. She had her hands on her hips. Checked her watch again. Turned, hair swinging over one shoulder.

'Watch this bit.' Josh indicated the top left of the screen.

From there a young man appeared with a young woman, who was walking slightly in front. He was carrying half a dozen shopping bags. As they passed Polly, the man kept watching, turn-ing his head to stare at her until with a smack he walked into a lamp-post.

They all laughed, despite themselves.

13.09. Polly checked her watch again. Then she snatched up her bags and walked swiftly up the hill in the direction of the bus sta-tion and the arcade. They watched until she disappeared out of sight.

Les and Jason both looked at Josh. 'That it?' Les said, obviously wondering why he'd bothered to leave his nice warm office for five minutes of watching a blonde bird being stood up.

Josh looked smug again. 'No, of course that's not it. Patience, lads, please.'

Les started to look pissed off and Jason stifled a smile – Les was so easy to wind up.

A few keyboard strokes and a few mouse clicks, and a new file had loaded. This one was from inside the shopping centre. Much busier here. Mums with buggies, elderly people dragging shopping trolleys behind them. At the top of the screen was the entrance to Marks & Spencer. The exit to the High Street was just visible off to the right. The time stamp at the top read, disconcertingly, 14.22.

'The time's wrong on this one. The council CCTV unit confirmed they'd not got around to putting the clock back. Other than the hour it's right, though. So about one twenty. And here she comes.' He stuck a finger, nail bitten to the quick, in the top left corner of the screen, and clicked the mouse.

From the top left, Polly appeared, half running. Her right hand was held up to her face. Same jacket, jeans, shopping bags in her left hand. She was heading to the High Street entrance.

'She's on the phone,' Les said.

'Right,' Josh agreed. 'Now she's going back out to the High Street.' After only a few seconds Polly had disappeared out of the right of the screen, her blonde ponytail swinging behind her.

The screen froze again and they all breathed out, leaned back and relaxed.

'She's going back to the bench?'

Josh nodded, his eyes shining. 'This is so cool. How often do we get any useable CCTV? We're so bloody lucky all the cameras were pointing in the right direction. Although I'm afraid the next shot's a bit iffy. Can't have everything.'

He loaded the third file, and once again the High Street appeared. The sun had come out, the icy street was shining, and there was a disconcerting glare at the top of the screen because the camera was pointing almost directly into the sun. The starburst effect covered the top half of the screen, the bench where Polly had been waiting only just visible in the bottom corner.

'Ready?'

The camera clock imprint showed 13.26. A mouse click, and the dark shapes walking up and down the street started into life. Polly came down the street, running, facing the camera this time. It was not possible to make out her face, but somehow it seemed as though she would have been smiling. The phone was gone, the shopping bags still in her left hand, swinging against her leg. She dropped them on the bench, turned around a full three hundred and sixty degrees, then sat down on the bench.

'Here we go,' Josh said quietly.

Polly jumped back up and ran to the left, throwing her arms around a figure that had appeared. They all leaned closer.

'I think it's a woman,' said Jason. 'She's not that much taller than Polly, look.'

'Nah, that's a proper waxed jacket. Look at the shoulders. Got to be a male,' said Les.

For a moment all that was visible was a bulk where Polly had folded her whole body around the figure. The blonde head moved slightly.

'They're kissing,' Josh said.

Les leaned closer. 'What – like a snog?'

'It's a bloody long kiss, anyway,' said Josh.

13.27. As they moved towards the bench the figure emerged from the flare of the sunshine. A dark jacket, red gloves, black shoes, black trousers underneath. That was about all you could see. The other figure pulled away abruptly, gripping Polly by the upper arms. Red gloves against the black of Polly's coat. Polly seemed to shake herself free.

Polly went to sit down on the bench, but the figure took her hand and pulled her up. Back to the camera.

'Whoever that is knows the camera's there,' Jason said quietly.

Les looked up at him scornfully.

'I thought that, too,' said Josh.

The figure took Polly's left hand and pulled her away from the bench. Polly looked like she was struggling to keep up. The shopping was left on the bench. Right before they went out of the view of the screen, they saw a last swing of Polly's blonde ponytail as she looked back towards her shopping bags – one arm extended out towards the bench. Then she was gone.

The footage kept running.

13.28. 'She's left her bloody shopping behind,' Les said.

People walked in and out of shot, some of them pausing to look at the shopping bags. The sun seemed to go behind a cloud, and the footage went momentarily dark while the camera adjusted, and then came back to normal. A better view this time, with the flare missing.

'I take it there's more?' Les grumbled, fidgeting in his seat.

'A bit. Hold on. Nearly there,' Josh said.

13.29. Polly reappeared, standing near the bench, looking back over her shoulder in the direction from which she'd come. She raised a hand, once, and waved. Presumably to the person she'd been with, the person who seemed to be avoiding the CCTV.

Polly's hand went to her lips, and then back to a wave, blowing a kiss goodbye. She stood for a moment, watching. Then picked up her shopping bags and turned her back to the camera, heading up the High Street once again.

They continued watching as the camera clock flashed to 13.30, then the screen went blank. For a moment they just sat there.

'That's it?' asked Les.

Josh nodded.

'That's fantastic,' Jason said. There must have been a huge amount of work to get those three sections of footage. 'The DCI is going to be thrilled, Josh. Good stuff.'

Les shot him a look which said 'arse licker' and went back to Josh. 'Nothing else of the person she was with?'

'Nothing. The camera by the river is out of action,' Josh was saying. 'Camera one outside the Co-op was pointing in the other direction and the one at the other entrance to the centre is fixed on the doorway of Carphone Warehouse following those burglaries. All the other ones that were working have been checked.'

'What about the shopping bags? Any chance of identifying them?' Jason asked.

Josh shrugged. 'There's one that looks silver, might be a Debenhams one. We checked there. Their CCTV operator is on holiday and he's the only one who knows how to work the system.'

Les interjected. 'We put out a message via Storenet last week, asking all town centre shops to check their CCTV. I bet you none of them bothered.'

Jason sighed. It was rare to get anything truly useful from CCTV,

283

but to be fair to Josh, this was still a pretty good result. 'Can we have the footage?'

Josh handed Les two disks in paper envelopes. 'I made you two copies. Let me know if you need any more, but don't go overboard. Those things cost money.'

Jason shook his hand. 'Thanks, Josh. That's great.'

Walking back across the car park, Les Finnegan puffing away on a cigarette, trying to walk slowly so he could have a precious few more moments' inhalation time, Jason considered the figure and mentally ticked off the list of people in the case.

'I'll be in in a minute,' Les called after him, as he swiped his pass and dragged the door open. Jason didn't hear.

REPORT

To: Op Nettle

From: PSE Jason MERCER

Date: Monday 5 November 2012

Subject: Op Nettle CCTV /ANPR

Following the CCTV footage produced by the TV Unit showing a female who may be Polly LEUCHARS meeting up with an unidentified nominal in Briarstone town centre, ANPR cameras searched for the relevant timeframe on 31/10/12 with the following result:

Briarstone Station NCP car park:

36 NRM – cherish plate registered to Nigel MAITLAND. Accessed car park at 1245hrs, exit marked up as 1402. Accompanying image shows male driver, vehicle Land Rover.

All others negative result for the indexes of vehicles known to the enquiry.

OP NETTLE BRIEFING – AGENDA

Monday 5 November 2012 08:00hrs

Summary DCI Smith

Analytical charts – PSE Mercer

CCTV – DC Finnegan

Nominals & Intel – DC Holloway

AOB and taskings

07:52

Andy Hamilton had made an effort to come in early. He knew he was skating on thin ice all round; with Karen, with Lou, with everyone on the team. He was starting to be a liability.

He'd managed to reach some sort of a truce with Karen last night. A whole night without him had softened her temper; that, and the fact that he was home in time to help feed the kids, do bath time and get them ready for bed. After that he'd run her a bath, put in lots of bubbles, lit a candle. While she soaked, he ordered them a takeaway, which was about as close as he ever came to the kitchen. She emerged, dressed in her towelling bathrobe, as the Chinese arrived at the front door.

After that, of course, she wasn't angry at all any more. She told him they would have to have a 'serious chat' about what his expectations of her were (more like *her* expectations of *him*, he thought, biting his tongue) and how long this could carry on before their marriage would fall apart. She didn't want to be another statistic, she said, another policeman's wife who'd had enough of coming second to whatever investigation it was that was the current big thing. They had the kids to consider.

He'd been contrite. Reached for her hand. He'd even teared up and perhaps that had been the clincher. She had snuggled into his lap and he'd slipped his hand inside her robe. She told him he stank and should go and have a shower. It was good-natured and she was right. He'd had a shower that morning at Suzanne's flat, but of course she had no male deodorant.

'Couldn't John have loaned you some deodorant?' she called up the stairs.

'He'd run out,' he called back.

By the time he'd had his shower she was in bed, fast asleep. When he reached for her, she nudged him away, sleepily. He left her in peace. Bridges had been built; he could cross them another time.

'Right, everyone ready?'

Lou was at the front, ready to start the briefing. She looked good, as usual, dark blue trousers today, red suede high heels, a snug jacket that nipped in her waist over a plain white top, hair loose over her shoulders.

He was sitting near the front, freshly scrubbed and with an ironed white shirt, top button undone because his neck had grown and he couldn't actually do it up any more, tie done up around it to conceal it.

She gave him a smile. Well, thank fuck he'd met with her approval today. He was sick of being in her bad books.

The briefing room was busier than yesterday; Ali Whitmore was

286

back, Jane Phelps, Barry Holloway and Ron Mitchell all in attendance. Lou had managed to rustle up a few uniformed PCs as well, which suggested something was kicking off.

'OK, let's get on with it,' Lou said. 'Can we have some hush?'

The analyst looked nervous, Hamilton thought. Not for the first time he caught the glance he gave Lou and wondered if there was anything going on there. In his dreams, maybe. Lou didn't go for that geek type – she liked men with a bit more about them.

'We've had several crucial pieces of intel in the last twenty-four hours. It's all incorporated on the charts, which Jason's going to go through in a second, but first I've got a summary of the recent developments.

'Number one: Brian Fletcher-Norman recalls having an argument with his wife on the night of the murder of Polly Leuchars. He believes she went out some time after midnight and returned in a state of hysteria. He didn't realise why, believed she was drunk, left her and went to bed.

'Number two: We have some recent source intel on Nigel Maitland, suggesting that his latest venture is a people-smuggling operation which he is conducting with the McDonnell brothers. There is a 5x5x5 to indicate that a shipment was received at the farm on the night of thirty-first October. As we all know, Nigel prefers to keep his legitimate business well away from anything dodgy, so there must have been a special reason for this to take place at the farm, if the report is accurate.

'Number three: A friend of Mrs Fletcher-Norman, Lorna Newman, confirms that Barbara was depressed before the murder. Mrs Newman states she had a telephone conversation with Barbara at around nine-thirty on thirty-first October. Barbara had just been badly let down by a man she had been conducting an affair with –

more about that in a minute. When Mrs Newman spoke to Barbara she described her as drunk and hysterical.

'Number four: Tac Team has recovered a suitcase from bushes near the car park area of the quarry, which has Barbara Fletcher-Norman's fingerprints on it. It seems likely she had a suitcase packed ready to run away with O'Toole. The suitcase had been thrown into the undergrowth, and fingerprints wiped from the handle.

'Number five: CSI suggests that the shot-put, which we believe is the murder weapon for Polly Leuchars, was thrown over the edge of the quarry after the vehicle went over. Likely timeframe for this is early Thursday morning. This means it's pretty much impossible that the shot-put was in the car, and also that Barbara could not have thrown it into the quarry herself.

'Number six: According to Mrs Newman, Mrs Fletcher-Norman had been saving money in preparation for leaving her husband. The man she had been seeing seems to have absconded with this money on the day of Polly's murder, leaving Mrs Fletcher-Norman particularly distressed. The man, Liam O'Toole, has not been seen since. Mrs Newman estimates that the money amounts to several thousand pounds. We've been trying to trace O'Toole but no luck so far.'

She paused for breath. There were whispers of conversation in the room, but most of them were giving her their direct attention. 'Any questions so far? Right then, Jason – can you take us through the charts?'

'For sure,' he said. 'Let's start with the timeline.' A new image clicked on, a series of interconnected lines. One for Barbara now, one for Brian, and one for Polly.

'There are a few significant changes on here now that we've had

288

more information from Brian and from Lorna Newman. Brian indicates that he heard Barbara making a phone call. We might assume this is the call she made to Lorna, but we will need phone records to check. The billing has come back, but only this morning and I haven't had a chance to work through it yet.'

He indicated a highlighted area from ten until midnight. 'Here's where we have a problem. Brian says he came home from working late between eight and nine in the evening and didn't go out again. He had a drink, read the paper, argued with his wife. Then he went and had a bath, fell asleep for a while and then came downstairs to lock up. He says he bumped into Barbara who had come in via the back door. Then he went back upstairs to bed.'

He pressed a key on the laptop and Lorna Newman's information overlaid Brian's and Barbara's timelines.

'Mrs Newman states that during her phone call with Barbara, which took place at about nine-thirty, Barbara said that Brian was "out somewhere with his fancy woman". According to Brian's statement, he was sitting downstairs reading the paper at the time.'

'Hold on,' Alastair Whitmore interrupted. 'Maybe she simply didn't hear him come in?'

'I've been in the Barn,' came a voice from the back. Jane Phelps. 'You have to really bang that front door to make it shut. If he'd come in, she would have heard him. Definitely.'

'He said he shouted up the stairs when he got home and she didn't answer,' Lou interjected.

'Why would he lie about that?' said Andy.

'Because he was out with Polly?'

'She was at the Lemon Tree, remember. She was stood up.'

'What time was she there until? Anyone know?'

Jason pointed at the timeline. 'She left between eleven-thirty and eleven-forty-five, according to Ivan Rollinson.'

A pause, then Lou said: 'We've got a medical disclosure form in place now; waiting for the results on that. We're looking to give Brian a slightly more robust interview once the medics have given the go-ahead. I think there were some significant gaps in what he told me yesterday. Right. Thanks, Jason. What's next?'

'The second major issue we need to clear up is right over here . . . ' He scrolled over to the far right of the timeline, indicated the early hours of Thursday morning. 'The vehicle went over the cliff some time after the rain started, which was about nine on Wednesday thirty-first. The PM on Barbara Fletcher-Norman concurs with Brian's statement that she must have gone out again some time after midnight. The car was discovered by the witness at about seven-thirty on Thursday morning. The scene was secured at about nine-fifteen.'

'Surely that means Barbara Fletcher-Norman couldn't have been Polly's killer?' Ali Whitmore said. 'Surely that must rule her out?'

'It doesn't rule her out of the murder,' Jane said. 'It just rules her out of throwing the shot-put over the edge, that's all.'

'Why would someone else throw it over? Where the hell did she leave it?'

Jane shrugged. 'She might have still done the killing. Maybe she had an accomplice.'

'Or she left the shot-put somewhere where it would implicate someone else?'

'Such as . . . ?'

'I don't know. Brian, maybe?'

Lou raised her hands: 'Right, everyone. Let's try and keep this ordered, Jason needs to finish up. Then we can talk about it till the cows come home. Jane?' This last directed to Jane Phelps, who was muttering something to Ali Whitmore at the back.

'Sorry, ma'am,' she said, and Lou gave Jason the nod to continue.

'Thanks,' he said. 'I'm almost done.' He moved the timeline forward to the discovery of the suitcase thought to belong to Barbara Fletcher-Norman. 'So – this suitcase. We need to get a positive identification that it belonged to Barbara, but the only person that can realistically do that is Brian. You might want to wait for that. If we assume for now that it is Barbara's, then we need to consider when it was packed, and where it came from. It's possible that she'd packed it that afternoon to go away with Liam O'Toole, and forgot it was there until she got to the quarry. Then, for whatever reason, she took it out of the boot and threw it into the bushes before she went over the edge—'

'Wiping her prints off the handle first,' Jane interjected. 'Sorry, ma'am.'

'No,' Jason said, 'it's a valid point.'

'There were gloves on the passenger seat,' Lou said. 'Red leather ladies' gloves. Maybe she was wearing them when she got to the quarry. Maybe her hands were cold. Maybe she used them when she threw the suitcase into the bushes, and then took them off before she went over the edge.'

'That's a lot of maybes,' someone said from the back.

'Of course, the biggest unanswered question is why she would take the suitcase out of the boot at all,' Jason said. 'But if she had gloves on, it's possible that any prints on the handle could have been obscured. So we still don't know whether she threw the case away. Let's not forget she was pretty intoxicated. She was also in

291

a state of distress. Irrational behaviour is pretty much a given, right before she committed suicide.'

'I don't think she did,' Jane said quietly. 'I know she was depressed, having been let down so badly by Liam O'Toole. But I'm really not comfortable with the logistics of her driving all the way to the quarry, through the pouring rain, when she was that drunk. And then, for some reason, throwing the suitcase away before going over the edge. And then someone else getting rid of the shot-put.'

'You're saying it was an accident?' This from Barry Holloway.

'I'm saying someone pushed the car over.'

'Is that possible?'

The debate was interrupted by Hamilton's mobile phone bringing the *Exorcist* theme loud and clear into the equation. 'Sorry,' he muttered, and headed for the door at the back. 'DI Hamilton? Yes, hold on.'

Meanwhile the room erupted with people interjecting on similar cases they'd experienced in the past, cases with automatic cars and manual cars, the degree of the incline, the lack of a barrier or a fence between the car park and the edge of the quarry.

Lou raised her voice above the noise. 'People, can we simply review the evidence for a moment? The *evidence*, not speculation. We know from forensics that Barbara Fletcher-Norman was inside Yonder Cottage when Polly was dead or dying from her wounds. We don't have any other identifiers for any other person around the time of death. So Barbara was definitely there. And the murder weapon ended up in the same place she did.'

'Yes,' said Jason, 'but *after* she was dead.'

'Then we're looking for an accomplice?' Jane Phelps said.

'Hold on, Jane – we have evidence she was there, not evidence that she did it.'

'Same thing,' Jane muttered.

There was a pause.

'Right,' Jason said, 'I'm done.'

'Thank you, Jason,' Lou said. 'Barry, can we look at nominals next? Les, we'll come on to the CCTV in a minute.'

Mutters from the room.

'Right then,' Barry Holloway began. 'I'm expecting a bit of discussion around these, along the lines of things we were talking about. Just to be clear, these are nominals we're interested in for the murder of Polly Leuchars. We're not talking about Barbara going over the edge of the quarry.' He gave a nod to Jason, who obligingly clicked over to a new slide.

NOMINALS

Barbara Fletcher-Norman

Nigel Maitland

Brian Fletcher-Norman

Flora Maitland

Unknown Female (A) – 'Suzanne'

Unknown Nominal (B) – CCTV image

'We have circumstantial evidence linking all of these people to the victim and the crime. Barbara, obviously, we have the forensic evidence linking her to the scene, and the murder weapon linked to the location of her death, even if it definitely wasn't her that threw it over the edge of the quarry. In addition, we have a pretty strong motive in that Barbara was convinced that Polly was having an affair with her husband. Despite her own marital infidelity, it seems from Lorna Newman's statement that she was more upset by this affair than by previous ones because of Polly's proximity to their home address.

'Secondly, Nigel Maitland. We have had intelligence that he had had an affair with Polly. We have forensic evidence that he had been upstairs in Yonder Cottage, but since he is the owner of the property and technically her landlord, we cannot assume anything from this. We have intel to suggest that Nigel's activities have moved closer to home recently, and in particular that he took delivery of some illegal immigrants at the farm on the night of thirty-first October. It's possible that Polly became mixed up in this, either as a witness or as a participant, and that she became dangerous to the criminal operation as a result. We know from an ANPR capture that Nigel Maitland was in town at the same time as Polly during that day, and we have CCTV footage showing Polly meeting someone – more on that in a minute. Seems possible this could be Nigel.

'Thirdly, Brian Fletcher-Norman. His daughter has confirmed that he told her he had had an affair with Polly, but he has denied this to us on two occasions. We have forensics linking him to the downstairs at Yonder Cottage, but again he may have had legitimate cause to visit the cottage as he took riding lessons with Polly. There is nothing to indicate the forensics there are recent. We have a witness statement suggesting that a woman matching Polly's description was in a small blue vehicle in a lay-by or driveway on Cemetery Lane at about eleven-thirty on the evening of thirty-first October. Having examined the layout of the lane, it seems that, realistically, this can only be the driveway of Hayselden Barn, as the witness describes it being near to a bend. It's possible that Polly had given Brian a lift home from somewhere, and it was he that she was arguing with.

Polly's car was a dark blue Nissan Micra, which would fit the description of the vehicle seen by the witness. If it was Brian, then there is an indication that they knew each other rather better than he has described to us, and also that on the evening Polly was killed they had some sort of disagreement or argument.'

'It could have been Nigel in the car,' Ali said. 'Don't forget we had his fingerprints in there.'

'Yes,' Jane said. 'It could have been either of them – or someone else entirely.'

'Hold on a sec,' Lou said. 'Ivan Rollinson at the Lemon Tree said Polly left the pub no earlier than eleven-thirty.'

There was an almost audible groan from the group. 'She's right,' said Whitmore.

'We need to chase that up. Either one of them has the time wrong, or it's not Polly in the car. She can't be in two places at the same time. Sorry, Barry – carry on.'

'Right. Well, that's about it for Brian. The only other thing to consider is the heart attack – it came on when the officers were telling him about his wife's body being found, but he said in the interview with the DCI that he was feeling bad when he woke up. It's worth considering whether he had had more of a stressful night than he led us to believe.

'Next – Flora Maitland. Another one who had a relationship with Polly. By all accounts she's been pretty distraught following Polly's death, but who knows how she really felt? She doesn't have any alibi for the relevant time; she could well have gone back to Yonder Cottage to confront Polly and ended up being a bit too physical with her.'

'Where's the DI gone?' Lou asked suddenly. Hamilton hadn't returned since taking the call on his mobile. There was a general shaking of heads and she tutted with annoyance. 'Anyone else want to comment on Flora?'

Jane Phelps cleared her throat. 'I don't think it's her, ma'am. I think she's in bits over Polly's death. When Sam was taking her prints at the farm she said Flora was barely holding it together.'

'That brings us to the woman Brian is supposed to be seeing, according to his daughter. She claims he told her he was having an affair with someone called Suzanne, who Polly had introduced him to. Suzanne had also had a relationship with Polly. Mrs Lewis says she was asked by her father to contact this Suzanne and tell her that he was in the hospital, which she did. She knows nothing else about her.'

'The number appears on Brian's phone as "Manchester Office",' Jason said. 'Has anyone checked to see whether she's someone he works with?'

'I did,' Ron Mitchell said. 'The company Brian works for is a global shipping company. They don't have an office in Manchester. Someone was going to contact their clients, subsidiaries, to check – I haven't chased them yet. I also checked that Brian was in work that day, as he said he was. The woman I spoke to agreed he left the London office at around six-thirty on Wednesday; allowing for traffic he would have been home around eight.'

'Was Brian asked about this Suzanne when you saw him, ma'am?' Jane asked. She was taking notes.

Lou shook her head. 'Didn't get around to that one. Didn't want to antagonise him, he's got a real downer on his daughter. Every time you mention her he goes on about what a liar she is.'

'He's a charmer, isn't he?' Jane said.

'Yes, he is rather. Still, rest assured it's on the list of things we need to know once we get the medical thumbs-up.'

Hamilton opened the door and tried to get back to his seat quietly. The room was full and he had to climb over several pairs of knees to get there, muttering 'Sorry' every time.

'Can we carry on now the DI's back?' Lou said.

'That's my bit done,' Barry said. 'Les has got the CCTV.'

'Les?'

Les Finnegan turned his attention to the laptop. 'Can someone kill the lights for me please?'

The room was duly plunged into semi-dark. 'Right, we've got three different files here so it's going to take a good few minutes if you want to see the lot, but I think it's important that you do.'

The first file loaded and the image of the High Street, the bench in the bottom right, filled the screen. Some of the detail was lost by projecting it to that size, but it was reasonably good quality.

There was complete silence as the first file ran. At the end of it, someone said:

'Poor old Polly. She got stood up a lot that last day, didn't she?'

There was a ripple of laughter.

'Right,' Les said, loading the second file, 'watch closely, this one's really quick.'

There was an audible leaning forward in chairs at the footage of Polly running through the shopping centre, mobile phone clamped to her ear.

'That it?' said Hamilton.

'Nearly done. One more to see,' Les said, loading the third file. This time the silence only lasted a few seconds into the footage.

'Shame about that bloody glare.'

'Can't see fuck all. Sorry, boss.'

'She's waiting for someone,' came a voice from the back.

'Well, duh, of course she is.'

'Wait for it,' Les said.

The dark-clad figure appeared from the left and Polly rushed into that embrace. When they realised they were witnessing a kiss, there was a little uncomfortable shuffling and a low wolf-whistle from the back of the room.

'Who *is* that?' Jane said.

'Not Felicity?'

'No, you muppet, that's a bloke. Look at the shoulders.'

'It's Barbara. She had a jacket like that.'

'Barbara's snogging Polly? I don't think so.'

'It looks like Nigel Maitland to me,' Ali Whitmore said. 'Besides, I'd bet money he knows where all the CCTV cameras are in town.'

'That's all,' Finnegan said. 'Shall we put the lights back up?'

The lights were turned on and everyone settled in their seats, blinking.

'I've got stills of the figure in the last file,' Les said, 'if you want to pass them round.'

He handed a pile of prints to Hamilton, who sat for a moment perfectly still, holding them, looking at the picture.

'Recognise someone?' Lou said. 'Andy?'

'Sorry, boss,' he said with a start. 'Lost in thought for a minute there.' He took the top sheet and passed the rest behind him to Ali.

'I've got the still on the Op Nettle briefing slide, so all the patrols can see it.' Les said. 'Someone is bound to recognise who it is sooner or later.'

'OK, everyone, settle down please. We've still got the intel requirement to get through. Barry?'

Barry Holloway cleared his throat. He was starting to sound

hoarse. 'Intel requirement – firstly Brian Fletcher-Norman. We need to clarify his account. Suggest to him that he was out for at least part of the evening, see what comes back from that. Also need to challenge his denial of having an affair with Polly. We need to find additional intelligence to corroborate Mrs Lewis's statement. I suggest that house-to-house is also completed for the entire route between Hayselden Barn and the quarry – not just for sightings of Barbara's car, I know that was completed.

'Secondly, and I know this is a tough one – we need to get more intel out of Nigel Maitland. We need to know what he was doing in town on the thirty-first – did he see Polly while he was out? He might have seen her and recognised the woman she was with. You never know your luck.'

'We'll need to get his solicitor on board,' Lou said, 'what's his name? That infernal little man with the aftershave ...'

'Lorenzo,' Hamilton obliged.

'That's it. Well, we'll give it a go.'

'Thirdly, we need to press on with the identification of the person in the CCTV. Find out who it is and why Polly was meeting them.'

He paused for a moment. Lou looked up. 'Anything else?'

'I think someone needs to interview Taryn Lewis again,' he went on. He was definitely losing his voice.

Lou gave him a warm smile. 'Thank you, Barry. I know you worked really hard to get this all finished for this morning. I appreciate it.'

She stood and faced the room again, left hand on her hip tucked under her jacket pocket. 'Sam's on Late Turn today, so let's sort out some work for you lot to do, shall we?'

*

09:25

Hamilton left the briefing room, trying to catch Lou's attention. 'Boss, can I have a word?' he asked, as she marched past behind Jason.

'I've got to go to a meeting with the Superintendent – can it wait, Andy? About an hour or so I think?'

He hesitated, then gave her a smile. 'Sure. I'll catch up with you later.' She breezed past.

He had been assigned to supervise the second round of house-to-house for the route from Hayselden Barn to the quarry. He had a team, including a whole bunch of probationers who were champing at the bit to get out there and do some 'real' police work, so realistically it shouldn't take long if they could find anyone at home. He could think of more exciting things to do, he thought, heading out. Today had started off so well, waking up late to the noise of the children and the smell of cooking breakfast. And whatever the rest of the day brought, he couldn't be late home tonight. He'd promised Karen he'd take her and the kids to the firework display at the local fire station.

But on the passenger seat of the car, slightly out of his line of vision, was the grainy still shot taken from the CCTV. *Was* it her? It was something about the shape, the physique, that reminded him of her. And then there were those red gloves.

He shook his head, telling himself to not be ridiculous. It was because he couldn't get her out of his head, that was all. It was far more likely to be Nigel Maitland, or someone else entirely.

09:45

Stuart Ward had taken on rather a desolate air for Brian. The bed directly across from him stood empty, its occupant having died yesterday. At least that one had gone quietly. Last night the man in the bed next door had also chosen to depart, but in a rather more spectacular fashion. Some heart monitor had alerted the nurses who came at full pelt with their equipment. That, no doubt, was why they called it a crash trolley, since it had collided with Brian's bed on the way past, waking him up and giving him the fright of his life.

A lot of shouting, rushing people, consultants being summoned, together with the cloud-patterned curtains being hastily pulled and re-pulled around the bed, lest Brian should be in the least bit concerned about what might be happening behind them.

Whatever had caused his demise, the man was beyond recovery, and after a long, long while and, by the sounds of it, a great deal of effort, all the various doctors and nurses went their separate ways. The dead man was left there until the porters came to take him away in the early hours. When Brian woke the next morning, the bed opposite was clean and covered in freshly laundered sheets. The one next door was naked, down to its rubber mattress.

Get me the fuck out of here, Brian thought to himself, not for the first time deeply regretting not having spent a few extra pounds for the company healthcare insurance that would have placed him comfortably in a private hospital, away from all this degradation, despair, and death.

To add to it all, the weekend had been dreadful. Normal ward rounds didn't take place and the food was even worse than it was in the week. His only consolation had been a visit from the registrar, who had looked at his notes, listened to his heart, and declared that in all likelihood he could be sent home on Tuesday or Wednesday.

'Really? That's great.'

'Assuming, of course, you have sufficient care at home.'

301

Brian was silent for a moment.

'Do you have someone at home who can look after you?'

'Yes,' he said at last. 'There's someone.'

As soon as the registrar had gone, Brian had donned his dressing gown and taken himself off to the day room. It was an effort getting there; even walking just a few steps was physically exhausting. How could he cope at home on his own? He couldn't. He would need help. How handy, then, that he knew someone who happened to be an experienced private nurse?

In the day room he had managed to put in a quick call to Suzanne. As always, on the phone, she was brisk. There was no point indulging in idle talk. He told her about the registrar and listened to her response. It wasn't quite the solution he'd had in mind, but it would do for now. Agency nursing was going to cost a fair amount of money; but if it meant he could get out of this hell-hole, then he would have to swallow the cost.

Suzanne would make arrangements for someone to take care of Brian as soon as he was discharged. Meanwhile she would maintain a discreet distance, despite his protestations that he needed her. She would have none of it.

Suzanne ended the call abruptly and Brian made his way back to bed.

For a fleeting moment, Brian thought about Barbara. Had it hurt, he wondered? Or had she been almost anaesthetised by the alcohol she had drunk?

He remembered her cold features, the mouth set in a hard line. 'It's no use, Brian. I'm leaving you. I've found a man who can truly love me.' Her words were slurred, her diction indistinct.

'Good Lord,' Brian had said. 'This must be some character. Well-off, is he?'

She had shaken her head so fiercely that she had almost lost her balance. 'We'll make do.' Then she had laughed.

And now she was gone. She wasn't his problem any more. She wasn't going to spend a penny more of the money he'd earned; it was all there for him to do with as he pleased.

10:02

Hamilton returned to his car, parked in the same lay-by that their Crimestoppers witness must have found himself parked in, the night that the blue car was spotted. Realistically, Hamilton had thought when he parked there, it must have been the driveway of Hayselden Barn that the vehicle had been sitting in; there was the lay-by, fifty yards further on. There wasn't another driveway within a mile in either direction that could have accommodated a parked car. Most of them had gates bang up to the road, or were not the sort of drive-way you would just stop in. Here the gate was about ten yards from the road, leaving an entrance-way suitable for a car to pull into temporarily.

It had to have been Polly in the car. But who was with her? Brian? Nigel?

The weather was definitely colder again, the wind biting his cheeks. He would have preferred to have been inside the office rather than playing Plod out here on the house-to-house.

The probationers were keen, though, he'd give them that. And, to be fair, there weren't a huge number of houses between here and the quarry. It was mainly country roads, plenty of bends, a few open fields. The houses that were here were mainly large, set back from the road. If anyone had seen anything it would be a fucking miracle.

Inside the car, he shut the door, keeping the wind outside. From

303

where he sat, he could see half into a drainage ditch that ran along the edge of the field bordering the garden of the Barn. A traffic cone, green with algae, was sticking out of it. A crisp packet fluttered, caught on something that looked like the wheel of a bike, then it was lifted by the breeze and was gone. He leaned forward in his seat and then he got out of the car again and went round the front of it to the edge of the ditch.

It was a gent's road bike, half-submerged in the metre or so of water in the bottom of the ditch. Vegetation mostly concealed it, but Andy could tell it hadn't been there long. The bike wheel had mud and grass caught in the spokes, clumps of green that were wilting to a khaki colour. He looked across to the Barn, and back at the bike. The seeds of an idea were forming. Across from the lay-by a rough mud track led off along the other side of the ditch, forming a natural boundary edge to the field. A green sign, half lost in tangled foliage, proclaimed this to be a footpath. He wondered where it went.

He hunted in his glove box for the map book he carried with him and located the page that contained Cemetery Lane and half of Morden village. There was the track – a dotted line heading off into green space. He traced the line with his finger through a further field. At the edge it split off in two directions, one heading to the east and meeting up eventually with the Briarstone Road. The second track headed due west before splitting in various directions, finally running along the top of a dark-coloured structure on the map marked up in small letters as 'Quarry'.

He looked up the track. What would that be like in the dark, on one of the windiest, rainiest nights of the year? And on a road bike?

He looked down at his shoes. 'Fuck it,' he muttered under his breath, and pulled his mobile from his jacket pocket.

'John. It's DI Hamilton. Can you take over for a bit? I need to go for a walk. Right. Yeah, I'll take the phone.'

Back out into the cold air. He went through the boot of his car and found a raincoat; it was thin but it might keep some of the wind out. He pulled it on over his head, locked the car and set off up the track.

Away from the road, all noise was deadened and for the moment even the wind seemed to have dropped. He looked over the fence to his right, the structure of Hayselden Barn rising beyond it. By far the biggest thing other than the Barn for seemingly miles in any direction was a great horse chestnut tree, its branches bare, all the leaves blown away. The wind made it sway and dance like a living creature.

The path was muddy as he'd expected, but it was cold enough for the ground to be hard underfoot and it was easy going to start with. At the end of the field he came to a stile and another green FOOTPATH sign indicated the right of way continued into the field beyond.

He spotted the cows, a few dozen Friesians, across the other side of the field. Hamilton wasn't fond of cows, in the same way he wasn't fond of large dogs or any other unpredictable animals. But these seemed to be content to get on with their grazing, and he could see the path across the field would take him away from them.

Nevertheless he crossed the field quickly, keeping an eye on the cows and not looking where he was going, until he sank almost up to his ankle in a fresh cow-pat.

'Ah, fucking hell,' he said loudly, wiping as much of the shit off on the grass as he could. He continued, this time keeping his eye on both the cows and the grass under his feet.

At the other side of the field the path disappeared into a

hedgerow. He paused and looked back the way he had come. He had completely lost sight of the road now, but the roof of the Barn was within sight over the top of the hedge, in the distance. He estimated he had walked about half a mile. The clouds overhead were darkening and it looked like it might rain. He shivered. He hated this time of year.

Heading towards the hedgerow, he could make out a gap leading to a field beyond. He cursed his clothing, wishing he'd decided not to try and impress Lou with how smart he could look in a navy wool suit and had gone for jeans and heavy-duty boots instead. He could really do with something warm, like a fleece. And a woollen hat.

Never mind. At least the rainproof jacket he was wearing would keep the worst of the brambles away from his suit jacket. He squeezed through the gap in the hedge, fending off prickles and branches, and to his horror his clean shoe sank deep into a water-filled ditch. Now both shoes were ruined, both socks wet through.

At last he burst through the hedge and found himself at the bottom of a steep, grassy slope. He scrambled up it and found himself on a dyke, which seemed to go for miles in either direction. On the top of the dyke a well-worn path looked like a good place for walking dogs and bike riding.

That was a thought. He looked back down to the gap in the hedge. He doubted whether a bicycle could be squeezed through that gap, but then not everyone was his size. Could you do it all in the dark, though? It was hellishly dark around here at night. And with the rainy weather there would have been no moon either.

He looked left and right, the dyke and the path stretching as far as the eye could see in either direction. He looked at his watch. He felt spots of rain. He remembered from the map book that the distance to the feature marked 'Quarry' was at least three times the distance from the road to the junction where the path split in an easterly/westerly direction – presumably the place where he now stood.

He debated his options, then scrambled back down the bank and fought his way back through the hedge.

To his alarm, however, the other side of the hedge revealed a sudden gathering of enormous, curious-looking Friesians, seemingly waiting for the large odd man to return through the hole in the hedge.

Another change of plan, then. He fought his way through the hedge a third time and decided he would just have to go for a long walk.

He pulled his mobile out once again, hoping for a signal. 'John? Hello? Yeah. It's DI Hamilton again . . . Can you hear me? . . . How about now? Ah, right. Listen, have you still got a car at the quarry? . . . OK. Can you get them to stay there? I'm walking to the quarry now and I need a lift back. OK?'

The signal finally died. He hoped it wasn't about to start pissing it down; that really would be the final straw.

10:19

Flora had had a productive day yesterday. For some reason, her mother's visit had sparked in her a new level of creativity. She had moved the large canvas of Polly to one side, and had started a new one, a portrait, but less abstract. It was Polly, of course. It was corn silk and blue, mainly. And some red, the colour of her heart.

She had fallen asleep in the studio, about three in the morning. All those hours she had worked, not eaten, barely drunk anything.

By the time she felt the exhaustion hit her she had a headache and was covered in paint. She curled up on the old sofa, pulled the blanket over her and fell asleep.

She'd woken this morning feeling nauseous with hunger. Without bothering to change or wash she headed out to find something to eat. There was a greasy spoon on the corner – the owner was called Bob. He never batted an eyelid when Flora came in covered in paint.

'Good night, was it?' he asked when Flora opened the door.

Inside it was warm and smelled of good coffee. She shrugged. 'It was good in some ways, Bob. That's as much as I can hope for.'

He gave her a lopsided grin. 'What you having today, then?'

'Gutbuster. Coffee. OK?'

'Five forty-five then.' When she had handed over a five pound note and a fifty-pence piece, he nodded towards the table by the window. 'I'll bring it over.'

Outside on the pavement people rushed to and fro.

She was avoiding him. Recognition of the fact slid into her consciousness now as easily as the denial which had preceded it. She would have to go and see him, talk to him, even if it was the last thing she wanted to do. There was no point waiting for the police to do it. They would carry on dragging their heels, leaving him to it, waiting for their evidence package or whatever it was they were doing. But something had happened that had changed her father. It wasn't just Polly's death, there was more to it. As though he knew something. As though he was guilty ...

And what, then, could she do about it? She couldn't tell the police. They couldn't be trusted. And besides, all she had so far were her suspicions, the awareness that there had been some kind of shift in her father's demeanour. And who was better placed to find the truth than her? Nobody else could get as close to Nigel as she could. Somewhere there would be some kind of evidence.

Thinking about her father made her headache worse. The coffee arrived first, and she had nearly finished it by the time the vast oval plate arrived. Bacon, sausage, fried egg, fried bread, beans, black pudding, mushrooms, grilled tomato and sautéed potatoes with two slices of buttered toast clinging precariously to the side.

She ate.

11:04

Lou had been providing Mr Buchanan with his daily update, but now she was back in the incident room, complete with a tray of coffees and muffins from the canteen. Everyone was on the phone; everyone, except for Jason who was waiting in the doorway to her office looking serious.

'What?'

'Phone stuff,' he said. 'I'm not done, but yeah, it's – interesting.'

'Have a seat.'

She had brought two of the coffees and two muffins in with her, and while he talked she pulled chunks off the side of hers and ate.

'So, Brian's mobile phone download to start with. One of the other analysts said this to me when I started doing phone work: ninety per cent of text messages sent over the network are porn. I didn't believe it at the time, but hey.'

Lou laughed. 'Really? He's a right one, that Brian, isn't he?'

'This is serious stuff, Lou. Bondage and shit like that. There are about thirty images on there of him with a woman.'

She stopped chewing. 'Anyone we know?'

Jason shook his head. 'She's quite particular about not showing her face, funnily enough. And there's more. Brian's billing. There are a whole lot of calls to a number ending 987, in and outgoing. Long calls and texts. This is the same number that was in contact with Polly's phone up to the night she died. This is the number she called when the cellsite shows the phone was in Forsyth Road. It's saved in Brian's phone as "Manchester Office".'

'Suzanne?'

'Yeah. It's got to be her.'

'What about Brian's cellsite?' Lou said. They needed to find Suzanne, find her quickly.

'That's where it gets even more interesting. Assuming Brian was using his phone and hadn't given it to someone else, it cell-sites all around Briarstone and Morden from the evening of the thirty-first into the early hours of the first. Most of the calls were back and forth between his number and the one we have for "Manchester Office".'

'Briarstone?'

'I'm going to plot all the calls on a map, so we can see where he was at what time. There's one call near the quarry at . . . ' he looked at the paper in his hand, 'two-thirty in the morning. Then the next one is at three, back in Morden. That's a long one, nearly twenty minutes, and it's the last contact.'

Lou was staring at him, rapt. Brian's phone had been near the quarry, in the early hours. 'Can you get all this in a brief report for me? I'll get everyone back here for four this afternoon for a brief-ing, OK?'

'Sure.' He smiled at her. 'So, you want to see some filthy pics now?'

'Of Brian? I think I'll pass. If you can get a still of the woman showing her face rather than anything else, that would be great.'

310

13:11

Andy Hamilton was back in his car, heading towards Briarstone. He'd been home and had a shower, got changed and gone straight back out again.

Bastard cows, bastard mud. His shoes were ruined and his suit had a bloody great rip in the seat. He'd rarely been this pissed off and now, to cap it all off, there was a voicemail and a text from Lou telling him to get his arse back to the office for a briefing at four.

At least the house had been empty when he'd got back. Karen was out, shopping probably, or at her sister's. It was a blessed relief, a rare moment of perfect peace.

His mobile rang and he pulled over into a side street to answer it. 'Andy Hamilton.'

'Yeah, this is Stacey from the CCU. You asked us to take a look at a laptop for Operation Nettle. Want the ref number?'

'No, I know the one you mean. Has it been analysed?'

'We've still got some more to do on it, but I got a message to give you an update.'

'Anything useful so far?'

'Lots of porn. Fetish stuff.'

'What sort of fetish?'

'S&M mainly. Lots of amateur shots. I would think it's the machine's owner since most of the pictures feature this one man. Looks quite old, grey hair. Are you in the office? You can come and have a look if you're really desperate.'

'I'm out at the moment. When I get back in later I'll come over.'

'As long as it's before half two, I'm on earlies today and there's nobody else here.'

Fucking typical. He rang off, promising to visit as soon as he

MG11 WITNESS STATEMENT

Section 1 – Witness details

NAME:	Samantha Jane BOWLES		
DOB (if under 18; if over 18 state 'Over 18'):	Over 18		
ADDRESS:	Seaview Cottage Cemetery Lane Morden Briarstone	OCCUPATION:	Smallholder

Section 2 – Investigating Officer

DATE:	Monday 5 November
OIC:	PC 11625 BRIGHOUSE

Section 3 – Text of Statement

My house is situated close to Hermitage Farm, approximately a hundred yards further along Cemetery Lane and on the opposite side of the road. From my kitchen window I can see both entrances to the farm clearly.

On the evening of Wednesday 31 October 2012 I was in my kitchen. At about eleven o'clock at night I saw a lorry in the driveway that leads to Yonder Cottage. I see lorries going in to the farm occasionally but they always use the other drive as it is much wider. It looked to me as though the lorry was stuck as it was parked with the rear of it still in the lane. I thought it was odd that the lorry was there at that time of night.

When I went back into the kitchen approximately twenty minutes later to turn off the lights, I noticed that the lorry had gone.

We went away the following day for a long weekend and I was unaware of the events at the farm until today.

Section 4 – Signatures

....

WITNESS: (Samantha BOWLES)

....

OIC: (M Brighouse PC 11625)

could. Not that he was particularly interested in looking at pictures of Brian Fletcher-Norman getting jiggy.

There was something more urgent he needed to do. It had been playing on his mind all day, and he could not go back to the office until he'd sorted it out one way or another. The news that Brian was into S&M made a difference to it all, too.

She was unlikely to be there, he reasoned, after all it was the middle of the day, a Monday. She would be at work, whatever that was. But it was worth a try. At the shopping centre he turned right, towards Waterside Gardens.

14:29

'You want tea?' Ron Mitchell asked.

'Yes, please,' Jason replied.

'Yes, please,' Sam piped up.

'Fancy a pint later?' Ali asked. 'You too, Sarge,' he said in Sam's direction.

'Depends,' Sam replied. She'd come in early to catch up on things.

Ali and Jason exchanged glances. 'Depends on who's going?' Jason asked.

'Something like that.'

Whitmore grinned. 'How about we don't mention we're going out?'

Sam looked up at last from her keyboard and treated them to a warm smile. When she smiled like that, her whole face lit up and she was suddenly beautiful. 'You're on,' she said.

Whitmore made them all a cup of tea and they went back to their respective desks for half an hour. Then Whitmore's phone made a chirping noise and he started chuckling.

'You're all right, Sam,' he said. 'Definitely up for that pint, then?'

'Why's that?' she asked, looking up again.

'The DI's managed to take himself off for a big adventure in the great outdoors. John Langton says he's trod in cow shit, fallen in a puddle and literally gone through a hedge backwards – then he had an argument with some cows and turned up at the quarry because he needed a ride back to his car.'

Sam laughed louder and harder than Jason had ever heard her. Into this scene of merriment Lou walked, looking tired and harassed after her second meeting of the day with the Superintendent.

'What's the joke?' she asked.

Whitmore handed her the phone with the text that John Langton had sent him. She read it and a slow smile spread across her face, which turned into a laugh when she read the bit about the cows. Then she tried to look stern and failed. She met Jason's eyes.

'We're going out for a drink later. You coming?' he asked.

'Just us?'

'Just us.'

'If we can get away,' she said with a smile, 'I think the first round is on me.'

14:30

He kept the engine running for the heat, but even so he could see his breath in the cold, stale air of the car. It smelled of beer, cow shit and rain. He watched the minutes tick past on the clock.

He wasn't sure what he was going to say to her, how he could justify intruding on her once again. She was addictive, intoxicating, that was all there was to it. It wasn't that she was even beautiful, not in the same way Lou was, or Karen, for that matter. He was trying not to think too hard about what they'd done, about how it was so far beyond kinky as to be actually dangerous. And yet, the thrill of

314

it was not only that of trying something new. It had been an unbelievable high. He wanted, *needed,* more.

That was it. He got out of the car, glancing casually up and down
the road. Not a soul to be seen. He crossed the gravel and rang the
doorbell for Flat 1.

He was half expecting her not to answer, even though the sleek
black Merc was parked on the gravel. But moments later the door
opened and there she was.

She smiled when she saw him, looked up at him from under her
lashes with an expression that someone who didn't know her might
mistake as demure.

'Back so soon, Inspector?'

'I need to ask you something,' he said. He'd intended to be
firmer with her, use the voice of authority, use his size – something.
But instead he found his resolve slipping.

She stood aside to let him in.

14:35

She called at the farmhouse first. The front door was unlocked but
nobody was home. So much for security, Flora thought. She rang
her mother's mobile.

'Yes, what is it? Flora?'

Flora could hear the wind, the intermittent noise of traffic.
'Where are you, Mum?'

'Hacking with Marjorie. Is everything all right? Where are you?'

Flora realised that her mother had no idea she had been at the
police station giving them a statement and decided it was not worth
enlightening her. 'I'm at the farm. The front door's unlocked; I
thought you were being more careful.'

'There hardly seems any point locking it when the bloody police have been crawling all over everything. Honestly, I feel quite violated by it.'

Flora tried a change of subject. 'Do you know where Dad is?'

'Gone out somewhere, I think. I don't know, he never tells me bloody anything ... '

There was no sign of Nigel's Land Rover in the yard, and heading up to the barn she could see all the other cars were in their spaces. He must be out with Connor, Flora thought. The pick-up truck Connor seemed to have adopted for his own use was missing.

The barn door had been locked but Flora knew where the spare key was. She also knew that the CCTV he had set up to record everyone who entered the barn was motion-sensitive, and sent an alarm text to his mobile unless you deactivated it as soon as you entered the doorway. She had memorised the code for it, but she had never had to use it before so entering the number was nerve-wracking. Why was she even doing this? What was she thinking?

She closed the door behind her and made for the office. It was empty, of course, but there was a presence there, nonetheless. The room was warm, the smell of alcohol, leather, the wax on her father's Barbour jacket, oil, mud. Wherever it was they'd gone, they had been in here quite recently.

She had a quick look at Nigel's desk, but she could tell immediately that the paperwork was for show. Not that he didn't have a legitimate farming business to run, but most of the paperwork was stored in the main office, the Portakabin beside the other barn. This was simply a carefully arranged display of farming crap that would fool anyone who might have managed to bypass all of Nigel's security.

The ladder to the roof space was raised, but she lowered it, careful not to make any noise, even though there was no one to hear.

It was dark up here. She found the switch, and the roof space was illuminated brightly by a single bulb hanging from the ceiling. Not taking any chances, she raised the ladder again but already she could see there was a problem: the door of the safe was hanging open, and it was completely empty. And then she realised that the police must have been here. So had they removed everything? Or had Nigel managed to get it all out and hidden somewhere else?

Then she heard something, and quickly turned off the light. Sitting in silence, the dark loft space and the office barely lit below, listening, knowing that something was wrong but not able to determine what. Was it a car, from the lane?

Then, another noise, outside somewhere. Voices. Looking down through the rungs of the raised ladder, she could see into the office. She heard the main door of the barn open and the bleep made by Nigel entering the disable code for the alarm.

'I still think he fucked up big time, you can't get away with shit like that and he knows it.'

That was her father's voice.

'You know I ain't sayin' that. You know I agree with you. It's one fuck-up after another with him, right? But it's nothing we can't put right.'

Then the two men – no, three – entered the office and she saw the tops of their heads. Nigel was the first, followed by a man she didn't recognise. Overweight, with a full head of curly greying hair. A dark-coloured jumper, smelling from all the way up here of beer and tobacco. Behind him, Connor Petrie.

'Want me to sort 'im out?' That was Petrie.

'You've done enough sorting out, haven't you?' Nigel said sharply. 'Go home. I seem to remember giving you a job to do, remember?'

Suitably chastised, Petrie crossed his arms and left the office.

317

The second man lowered his voice. 'You think it was him?'

Nigel didn't reply at first, then Flora heard a deep sigh. 'You're not talking about the shipping, are you?'

'No. I'm talking about what happened on Wednesday night.'

'Not here. All right?'

'Why not? Nobody here but us, right?'

'Still don't want to talk about it. What's done is done. There's nothing we can do about it now except minimise the risk.'

'I'm not calling it off, if that's what you mean. Got too much invested in this, Nige. Too much at stake.'

'I'm saying they can wait.'

'You're not that worried. If you was worried we wouldn't be having this conversation here, would we?'

Nigel laughed. 'Bizarre as it sounds, this is still the safest place. At least I know the police aren't listening in. Can't trust anywhere else, right?'

'So what you want to do?'

'I think we should postpone for a week, maybe two.'

'Fuck that! You serious?'

'It's too risky.'

'It's fucking risky letting him down! The man's a complete psycho. You want to postpone, you can fucking be the one to break the news, all right?'

'He'll be fine. He can wait another couple of weeks. Besides, it'll be worth his while, won't it?'

There was a pause, then. Flora was starting to get cramp in her leg. She heard the sound of the drawer opening, the chink as the bottle of whisky was brought out, the twist of the bottle top.

'What about Petrie?'

'I don't know.'

'You can't just leave him here. He's another liability. That kid's fucking not right in the head, if you get my drift.'

'Nor would you be, if you'd seen what he's seen.'

'Did he *see* it, though? Or did he *do* it?'

'Seriously. We are not talking about this. All right?'

There was a long pause, and then, finally, in a low voice, Nigel's companion said: 'Whatever. I've got to go, anyway. I'll ring you about Friday, right?'

'I'll see you out.'

Flora breathed out, a deep breath, as the two men went to the main part of the barn. There was a chance they'd both leave and not come back, but even so she stayed as still as she possibly could, listening to the door of the barn opening and closing, and, a few moments later, a car door banging and a diesel engine starting.

She moved her leg, stretched it out in front of her.

And nearly died when a voice from down below said: 'Flora. I know you're up there.'

14:40

'I thought you'd be at work,' was the first, inane thing Andy had thought to say.

'I'm catching up on paperwork,' she said. 'And I am actually busy, so unless there's a good reason for you being here, I'd rather you called another time.'

She was speaking to him as though Saturday night had never happened. As though he was here to try and sell her double glazing, or persuade her to change her gas supplier.

'I need to ask you some questions,' he said.

'In an official capacity?' She had an amused smile on her face, unconcerned about his unexpected arrival. She took him into the

319

living room and motioned for him to sit, then sat on the other end of the white leather sofa, tucking her feet underneath her.

'Not at this stage. Although I probably should ... shit, I don't know.'

'Not a good sign, is it?'

He looked at her longingly, her presence affecting him. And it was pathetic, rotten that he felt so lost, so *scared*, in her company, as though she could hurt him, as though she could control him somehow, despite the fact that he was six foot three and seventeen stone of muscle and flab and he could probably have lifted her with one arm.

'You want to ask me about Brian, don't you?'

She looked so relaxed it was disarming.

'Yes. I want to ask you about Brian.'

'How did you know about us?'

Well, you just told me, he wanted to say. But of course he couldn't. 'Brian told us. In a roundabout kind of way.'

She scoffed at this. 'I doubt that very much, Inspector Hamilton. Brian knows better than that. It was probably that daughter of his, wasn't it?'

Andy didn't answer. If she told him something important it would be completely inadmissible. He should never have come back. The moment he realised she might be involved, he should have gone straight to Lou and told her everything and bloody hoped for the best. The longer he stayed, the more he put everything at risk. Not only his marriage or his role on this enquiry – he was risking the investigation, he was risking his whole career, he was risking the reputation of the Force.

'Are you all right, Inspector?' she asked, her tone kind. 'You've gone pale.'

'I should go,' he said.

'Are you worried about all this? You needn't be. Everything we say to each other, everything we do here, it's between *us*. You know that, don't you? We trust each other.'

'We've only just met,' he said weakly.

'Even so, you don't need to have any concern over my discretion. I expect the same thing from you. Whatever happens with your enquiry, our time here is between us alone.'

He rested his head in both his hands, elbows supported on his knees, needing to get this right, needing to decide. He never bloody trusted anyone; it wasn't worth it. Rely on hard work and evidence.

'And besides,' she added, leaning forward and resting her hand lightly on his thigh, 'I can help you.'

'Help me? What do you mean?'

'I can steer you in the right direction. In terms of gathering evidence.'

'Please don't say anything that means I've got to arrest you. If you're involved somehow, I don't want to know. Right?'

'Oh, don't worry. I'm not involved. But I can put you straight on a few things. I can be your – what do you call it? – grass. Your informant.'

He raised his head then, feeling the beginnings of a sense of relief. She had given him a way out of the mess, an excuse. If anyone asked, she'd had information for him relating to the enquiry. And he had to protect his source at all costs, meaning he didn't have to tell anyone. There were procedures in place for dealing with things like this, of course. There was a whole unit dedicated to managing sources and protecting them. But this, a one-off information exchange in relation to a specific enquiry, he could manage it himself.

'I can't pay you,' he said.

Suzanne laughed, threw back her head, exposing her throat. 'I don't want payment! Is that what you thought?'

That was what sources were usually after, is what he'd wanted to say. 'What *do* you want?'

Her answer, when it came, was simple. He hadn't understood what she meant but hadn't asked her to clarify. She clearly had her own agenda and he would go along with it because now he had no choice. There was no other option for him but to agree.

'Compliance,' she said.

REPORT

Re: Liam O'TOOLE DOB 27/11/1981 of No fixed abode

Monday 5 November 1545hrs

From: DC 8745 Alastair WHITMORE

To: Op NETTLE

On Monday 5 November at approximately 1545hrs I took a call from a male claiming to be Liam O'TOOLE, formerly employed as a tennis coach at the Morden Golf and Country Club.

O'TOOLE claimed he was employed until Wednesday, 31 October 2012, when he handed in his resignation, stated this was due to issues with the management of the club, specifically their response to complaints he had made previously about harassment by some female clients which O'TOOLE felt had not been appropriately addressed.

O'TOOLE went on to say that Barbara FLETCHER-NORMAN was one of his regular clients at the club. She had been having private tennis lessons for some months. O'TOOLE stated that he made efforts to keep the relationship strictly professional, however she made it clear she wanted to pursue a sexual relationship. He states he told her on several occasions he was not interested. He also heard rumours from other clients that he and Mrs FLETCHER-NORMAN were having an affair and he believed this rumour had originated from her.

As a result of this rumour, O'TOOLE was subject to a disciplinary meeting on 29 October, with the manager at the club, Mr Andrew HART. Despite his claims that nothing was going on other than harassment towards him, O'TOOLE felt he was not believed and therefore decided to resign and leave the club immediately.

On 31 October a lesson had been scheduled with Mrs FLETCHER-NORMAN, after which O'TOOLE told her he had handed in his resignation and he was planning to leave the area. O'TOOLE stated she became very upset and even offered him money not to go, which he states he declined.

O'TOOLE claims he left the club at approximately 1500hrs on 31 October and travelled directly to his sister's house in Dublin, Republic of Ireland, arriving there in the late evening. On Monday 5 November O'TOOLE accessed his personal emails for the first time since arriving in Ireland, and he received an email from Gary STEVENS, a former colleague who works as a fitness instructor at the Morden Golf and Country Club. STEVENS informed O'TOOLE that the police had been looking for him in relation to the death of Mrs FLETCHER-NORMAN, hence the reason for his call.

A Whitmore

There was no sign of Hamilton. Lou knew he'd wanted to go home early today, but a job like this one was unpredictable, they all knew that. When something major broke, you wanted to be there. She'd called his mobile, sent texts, even, as a last resort, phoned his home number just in case something had happened to his phone. There was no reply there, either. At that point, Lou was really pissed off.

'Does anyone know where the DI was going?' she shouted across the briefing room. They were already late starting, and the atmosphere which had already been buzzing was rising to excited anticipation at the prospect of an arrest.

'Ma'am, I think he went home to get changed,' Ali said. 'John Langton said he was soaked.'

'Well, I think we're going to have to start without him. Someone can update him later.'

She was only half listening as Jason began to run through the phone work he'd done, the cellsite analysis showing that it was likely that Brian Fletcher-Norman had provided a completely fabricated list of events for the night of Polly's death.

They would have to prove that he'd been using the phone that night. But realistically, who else would have been using it? He'd not reported it lost or stolen. He'd told Taryn Lewis where to find the phone in his home office and she had handed it over to the search team who had turned up at the Barn. Was that going to be enough? Of course not. But Brian didn't need to know that, not yet anyway.

At least there had been some good news. Ali Whitmore had called in: he had been back to the Lemon Tree, and whilst waiting for his pint of cola, had noticed that the clock on the wall was an hour out. When Ivan brought him his change, he'd asked him about it. They hadn't got around to putting the clock back, he'd said. It was a good week since the end of British Summer Time – but, more to the point, when Ali asked him to confirm whether he could now be sure of the time Polly had left the pub on the night of the thirty-first, he became confused. Something about knowing what time to call last orders, and it had been 'not too long' before that. But the crucial thing was that he wasn't sure. Which meant that the woman arguing with the man in the car could have been Polly after all.

'So, priorities,' Barry Holloway was saying. 'We're still waiting for a subscriber check for the number identified by Jason as attributed to Suzanne. With a bit of luck, it won't be too long. The computer problems at the service provider are fixed and they're now working their way through a backlog, apparently. In the meantime we're looking at the voters' register for Briarstone, concentrating on the areas around the cellsite locations. We need to go back and ask all of Brian's associates who she might be, starting with his place of work. We need to find her,' Lou said. 'And as soon as Brian's discharged, we're going to nick him and take him to Briarstone custody suite, assuming they've got space. We need to make sure he doesn't get a chance to speak to his lady friend first.'

16:52

It was dark outside. Felicity had sent a text to Nigel to tell him that she was going to the cinema with Elsa and Marjorie, and he could find himself some dinner.

He'd smiled at this as though it was funny. 'Looks like we got let off the ordeal of your mother's cooking, Flora-Dora.'

'Don't call me that,' she said.

He was still smiling, which infuriated her even more. 'So,' he said. 'To what do I owe the pleasure?'

For a moment she couldn't think of a suitable excuse for being in his private office.

'And, perhaps more importantly, what happened at the police station?'

'How did you know about that?'

He chose to reply to her question with another: 'So what happened?'

'Nothing. They asked me lots of questions, I answered them, they let me go.'

'What were they asking about?'

Flora looked away. 'Polly, of course. I think they were looking for her phone. They kept asking me where it was.'

'Did they arrest you?'

'No.'

Nigel let out an audible breath. 'Well, that's something.'

Flora asked, 'Who was that man with you?'

'Nobody you need to worry about, Flora. Unless you're suddenly going to start taking an interest in my business affairs, that is.'

Then she thought of something else: 'What happened on Wednesday night?'

'I don't know what you're talking about.'

'That man that was here. He was talking about something that happened on Wednesday night. Was he talking about Polly?'

There was a momentary hesitation, as though he was thinking carefully about his response. 'This has nothing to do with Polly, I can assure you.'

She didn't believe him. 'Why did you tell me you were out until

326

midnight, when you actually came back at eight? Mum said you came home and went down to the cottage to see Polly. She said Polly made you cheese on toast.'

He laughed, then, a proper belly laugh. 'She said that? How bloody typical of her.'

'Are you saying she got it wrong?'

'Not at all. I had cheese on toast at the cottage. Then I came home. Your mother went to bed. I went out. I came back at midnight, as I said to you. Now, Flora, what's all this about?'

She didn't answer, her mind working over everything he'd said. Infuriatingly, he was right: the two differing stories she and her mother had been told did not actually contradict each other.

'You think I had something to do with Polly's death?'

'Did you?'

His face reddened, and the smile that had been playing on his lips disappeared in a moment. 'Of course I didn't. How dare you even ask me that!'

'I don't know what to think,' she said quietly. She wanted to remain angry with him but her fury lost some of its energy in the face of his anger.

'You *don't* think, Flora, that's the problem. You get these ideas in your head and you don't think them through properly. Did you say anything about me to the police?'

He stood up, suddenly, and towered over her and she pulled back in her seat, alarmed. 'Of course not!'

'You only need to give them an idea, a hint, and they will fucking have me over. *You* know that, *they* know that. They will pin you down and fucking question you until you give them what they're looking for.'

'I won't tell them anything!'

327

'You'd better fucking not!' He took a step back, ran his hand across his forehead and through his hair, and Flora took that opportunity to get out of his way.

She stood up, pushed past him and ran out of the office. Behind her, she heard him shouting: 'Get back here!'

Out in the fresh air, her heart racing, she ran to her car, fumbled with the key, turned it in the ignition and sped away, the tyres kicking up a spray of gravel and skidding alarmingly until they found their grip. She braked, briefly, at the bottom of the driveway, praying he wasn't running after her and risking a quick glance into her rear-view mirror to check. It was getting dark, but even so she could see the side of the barn and no sign of him. A car was coming up Cemetery Lane from her right and she waited for it to pass.

'Come on, come on!'

It dawdled past and in the moment that the road became clear there was a bang on her car roof and, as she screamed in fright, the dark shape at the driver's side window moved and the car door opened, letting in a sudden gust of cold air. She had time to hear him shout, 'Flora!' through the door before hitting the accelerator hard and lurching forward into the road. The car door swung outwards as she turned, then slammed shut again as the car straightened.

She was whimpering, looking back in the rear-view mirror into the darkness. He would get the Land Rover. He would follow her.

Moments later she had to brake as she caught up with the dawdling car that she'd had to wait for. There was no room to overtake. Her heart still thudding, she realised that there was no car behind her. He would be there by now, if he was going to follow her.

Then her phone buzzed in her pocket with a text message. She pulled it out and glanced at the display. It was from him:

We will discuss this tomorrow. Think about what I said.

OK, then. He was leaving her to think about things: this was good. She had some time. But not to think. She had thought enough, no matter what his opinion was. It was time for action. And she knew exactly what it was she needed to do.

17:42

She got up as soon as she was finished, leaving Hamilton lying there, splayed across the bed like a star, arms and legs numb and his head full of her, her scent, her taste, the sound of her voice.

He was exhausted, and at the same time more alive than he'd ever felt in his life before. The decision made, the moment for action passed, there was nothing else to do but allow his flesh to melt, to give in to it, to forget about the fear and simply accept that what was done was done, it was too late to go back. Too late to undo what had taken place. There was no point even thinking about it any more.

'I can't believe we just did that,' he said to the empty room.

He heard the noise of the shower in the bathroom, for a brief moment thought about getting up and joining her in there, but he doubted he had the strength to lift his head, let alone attempt a Round Two.

He lay still, dozing, until he heard the sound of his mobile phone bleeping from his trouser pocket. Where had he taken them off? He couldn't remember.

A few minutes later she was back, wearing a robe, silky. She sat on the edge of the bed and slipped it off her shoulders, lifting her hands to tease her hair back into some sort of a style. Her back was tanned, smooth, muscles beneath the skin. She kept herself very fit, that much was clear. How old was she? He had no clue, only that she must surely be older than him. Forty-five? Fifty? Suddenly he was dying to know, but even he knew such a question was unspeakably rude. He stretched out a hand and touched her back, his fingertips trailing across from her right shoulder to her left hip.

She half-turned, treating him to an indulgent smile.

'You need to go,' she said.

'Not yet.'

'Your phone hasn't stopped bleeping. They're probably thinking you've had an accident, or been kidnapped, or something.'

'What time is it?'

'Nearly six.'

He sat up, then, in a hurry. 'You're kidding me?'

'Not at all. As I said, you need to go.'

The thought of having to explain to Karen why he was late to take them to the fireworks was enough to get him upright. His clothes were scattered everywhere, his trousers in the bathroom, his jacket hanging over the chair, shirt and socks in the living room.

There were missed calls and a series of texts from Lou. The last one, brief and to the point:

Where r u? Call in. Urgent.

He sighed deeply, looking at it. Whatever she had done to him, this woman, it was complete. He knew he should have called Lou straight back, damn it he knew he should have responded when he'd heard the phone bleeping. He took his job seriously. He loved being a police officer, for all the shitty hours and the lack of resources and the being sworn at and assaulted. He loved every second of it. Of making a difference. And in the space of two hours

330

he'd gone from being a proud upholder of Her Majesty's Peace to being deeply ashamed of himself.

And there was no turning back. Not this time.

18:02

'Gotcha,' said Barry Holloway. 'Ma'am!'

Lou looked up.

'You want the good news or the bad news?' he said, his eyes twinkling.

'Bad news?'

'The subscriber check on the number called by the landline – it's a pay as you go, no subscriber registered.'

'Well, that's no great shock. What's the good news?'

'It's that "Manchester Office" number. She's registered it!' Barry said. 'She's only bloody registered it!'

And there it was – subscriber shown as Ms Suzanne Martin, Flat 1, 14 Waterside Gardens. Jason was already opening the mapping software, looking for an aerial image of Waterside Gardens and plotting its location in comparison to the other scenes, overlaying the cellsite data from Brian's phone billing.

'That's weird,' he said.

'What is?'

'I thought the address was familiar. It's where Flora lives.'

'Flora lives with this woman?'

There was a pause. 'No, Flora has Flat 2. This is Flat 1. But bizarre, don't you think?'

'Can't be a coincidence,' Barry muttered. 'At least it explains that cellsite. It must have been this Suzanne that Polly was visiting that night, not Flora.'

The plan for an arrest phase was well underway. Sam Hollands had

331

been put in charge of preparing the arrest packages for Brian Fletcher-Norman, in hopeful anticipation of having enough evidence to take before a magistrate and get a warrant. Jason had been busy summarising, printing off charts, timelines and spreadsheets in support of the package.

What they had so far wasn't enough, though, and Lou knew it.

'Trouble is,' Lou said to Sam, 'we don't want to risk Brian's health. And we definitely don't have enough evidence to arrest Suzanne with what we've got. If we arrest Brian there's a risk that Suzanne will do a runner.'

And Hamilton was missing. He still hadn't returned Lou's calls, and this time when she'd dialled his home number, a woman answered. She sounded pissed off, even more so when Lou told her who she was and what she wanted.

'No he bloody isn't here! He should be, though, and it's bloody typical of him to be late again. If you find him first let me know!'

Two things hit Lou with a sudden, dramatic force, when she disconnected the call to Karen Hamilton. The first was that this was the woman that Lou had unwittingly wronged. When she had found out that he was married, the pain she felt had been as much for the woman she'd never met, didn't know, as for herself and the end of the relationship before it had even really begun. Lou didn't know anything about her, didn't want to know because she felt bad enough as it was, and yet she had still formed a mental picture of this woman, the strength of her, bringing up Andy's children while he was away working ridiculous shifts and putting himself in danger in the line of duty. She would be strong and yet resilient; long-suffering. Patient. The Karen on the phone sounded less patient, more livid.

The second thing, with as much certainty as it was possible to have, was that something bad had happened to Hamilton and that, wherever he was, he was in deep shit.

'Barry,' she said. 'We need to put a trace on the DI's phone. I think he's in trouble. Do it now.'

18:07

Back in his car, dressed, trying to calm down enough to decide what to do, Andy Hamilton stared at his phone and then looked up through the windscreen to the gravel driveway and the front door of Flat 1, 14 Waterside Gardens.

To start with, he sent a text to Karen's mobile, preferring that approach to calling her directly. Firstly she wouldn't stop shouting at him and he had other things to do. Secondly, he was afraid to.

Sorry, delayed at work. On way now. x

Message sent, he dialled Lou's mobile number. It connected almost immediately.

'Andy? Where the hell are you?'

'Sorry, ma'am,' he said, with a note of forced cheerfulness. 'Been in traffic, no mobile signal. What's up?'

In the background he heard her shouting something to Barry Holloway, and then she was back with him.

'You had no signal? It's been *hours*. Where were you?'

He was thinking on his feet, which at first was scary but then pretty quickly it became exhilarating. Maybe this was why the offenders spent so much of their time lying, often when they didn't even have to. It was almost fun. A rush.

'I was out near the quarry, took a wrong turn and came up against a tractor that had broken down. Been bloody directing traffic for the last God knows how long. Sorry. What have I missed?'

'As long as you're all right. I was getting worried.'

'Were you?' he was surprised at the note of concern that had replaced the fury. 'Really?'

She ignored his question. 'So where are you now?'

'Outside the town centre. Not far. Do I need to come in? Only I'm late taking the kids out to the fireworks?'

'Your call, Andy. I don't think there's much you can do here, to be honest. We're putting an arrest package together for Brian Fletcher-Norman and preparing one for his girlfriend. Jason got the cellsite back and it looks like Brian was flitting backwards and forwards between Briarstone and Morden on the night Polly was killed. In between long conversations with that woman Polly met up with at the shopping centre.'

'You've ID'd her, then?' he said, his heart sinking.

'Subscriber check goes down to Suzanne Martin, and get this – she lives in the flat downstairs from Flora.'

Shit! Shit on a brick.

'Andy?'

'Yeah,' he said, finding his voice. 'So – where are you up to on the arrest packages?'

'We've got about enough to bring Brian in, assuming the hospital will let us. They're looking at discharging him tomorrow morning, so we're leaving him where he is tonight and we'll pick him up first thing. Sam's going to get the warrant. With a bit of luck he'll give us enough to arrest Suzanne. Anyway, you've got a rest day tomorrow so I'll see you on Wednesday. Enjoy the fireworks, OK?'

He was being let off – he couldn't believe it!

'Thanks, Lou.'

'Besides,' she said, and he could hear the smile in her voice all the way across the slightly dodgy mobile line, 'by the sounds of it you've probably had quite enough of farms for one day . . . '

5x5x5 Intelligence Report

Date: Sunday 4 November 2012

Officer: PSE Kelly FRANKS, Financial Investigation Officer, Fraud Unit

Re: Op NETTLE – Liam O'TOOLE and Barbara FLETCHER-NORMAN

ECHR Grading: B / 1 / 1

Barbara FLETCHER-NORMAN, DOB 14/06/1953

Several bank accounts, including ISAs and stocks. One bank account of note is with the Eden Building Society and is in subject's maiden name of Barbara CROFT. This account received payments of various amounts, once or twice a month from the account opening in August 2009 until Friday 31 October when the account contained £22,941. At 11 on 31 October Mrs FLETCHER-NORMAN attended the Briarstone branch of the Eden Building Society and withdrew £20,000 in cash. She required the manager's authorisation to do so and as this is a large amount a SAR was raised (this needs to be followed up).

Liam O'TOOLE, DOB 1/5/1980

One current account into which regular wages payments from Morden Country Club Leisure Ltd were made. Overdraft facility of £800, which was used regularly. Occasional payments in of £100 and £200 over the course of the past 12 months.

No further accounts on record, although it should be considered that this subject is of Irish nationality and further authorisation will be required for further enquiries into overseas bank accounts.

18:22

Flora had thought it might be difficult to find the house, but in the end it was so easy it was almost funny. She drove through the town centre and into Tithe Wood, once Briarstone's largest social housing estate, the houses now mostly privately owned. From the light of the orange street lights overhead Flora could see the confusing juxtaposition of front gardens containing neat lawns and borders, potted bay trees and brick-paved driveways, alongside knee-high weeds, cars on bricks and ancient sofas rotting in the rain.

A few moments after turning into Kensington Avenue, she saw it. Parked at an angle, two wheels on the mud that might once have been a grass verge, was the Mitsubishi L200 pick-up that Connor Petrie was using.

Flora pulled in to the kerb behind it. She got out of the car and looked at the houses. It wasn't hard to guess which one might be the Petrie residence. Various cars were parked haphazardly along the kerb in front of the Mitsubishi, and the long, overgrown driveway was populated with a selection of other vehicles in various states of repair. On the scrubby patch of grass and mud in front of the house was a child's swingset that looked lethal, an empty pram on its side, a set of goalposts with no net and a mattress.

A boy and a girl, teenagers, were coming out of the house as she approached. The door slammed behind them and a dog started barking.

'Hello,' she said to them.

'Wotcher,' said the boy, eyeing her suspiciously. 'All right?'

'Is Connor in?' Worth the risk, she thought. Even though she was now convinced she was right, because the family resemblance was a remarkable one.

'Dunno.'

They carried on past her. It was the confirmation she needed. She knocked on the frosted glass panel of the front door, which rattled in its frame, no doubt loosened by the repeated slamming. The dog barking continued, and then she saw a figure approach. The door was opened by a woman wearing a vest top and a pair of tracksuit bottoms.

'Is Connor in?' Flora said again.

'Who's asking?'

'Flora Maitland,' she said. 'It's urgent.'

The door shut in her face. She heard the woman shout: 'Connor! Someone at the door for you.'

Flora waited, glancing at the road behind her, expecting at any moment to see her father's car pulling up.

The door opened abruptly and there he was, in all his ferretty glory. 'What you want?' He clearly hadn't forgiven her for pushing him into the dung heap on Thursday.

'Dad sent me,' she said, dropping her voice into an urgent whisper. 'He's been arrested. He told me to come and get the stuff he gave you to look after.'

It was the moment of greatest risk. She half-expected him to ask her what the fuck she was talking about; after all, would her father really have trusted this halfwit with the contents of the safe? But there had been so little time to dispose of it all, and there had been the moment in the space above the office when Nigel had told Connor to go home; reminded him that he had been given something to do.

It was nothing more than an educated guess. And her suspicions were confirmed when the expression on Connor's face changed from a scowl to a gawp. He was buying it. 'You're joking,' he said. 'Fuck!'

337

'Yeah,' Flora said. 'He wants me to move it again, he thinks they might get a warrant to search your—' she broke off, trying to find the suitable word, settled on: '—house.'

'Wait,' Connor said. 'I should ring him, to check—'

'You can't do that,' she said quickly. 'The police have got his phone.'

'Right, right. Course. Fuck! Wait. How do I know he sent you?'

'For crying out loud. He told me your address, right? How would I find you otherwise?'

He seemed reassured by this, then he frowned again. 'Fuck. Nigel's been nicked, I can't believe it! What are we gonna do?'

'Look, they could be here in a minute. We need to get the stuff into my car.'

'Where are you going to take it?'

'Safer for you if you don't know.'

He hesitated. Flora could almost see the cogs whirring inside his skull as he tried to work out what else he should be doing. Then he seemed to reach a decision. 'Wait here, yeah?'

The door slammed shut.

Flora breathed out. So far, so good. But she was in deep shit now. Nigel might phone Connor at any moment.

A few moments later, the door opened again, and Connor pushed a cardboard box towards her with his trainer. 'You take that one. I've got the other one.'

She picked up the box. It was heavy, the top flaps interleaved shut. Without hesitation she made her way back down the driveway. Back at the car, she put the box down on the pavement and unlocked the boot. Connor was behind her, looking up and down the road anxiously as though the police might appear at any moment. In Kensington Avenue they probably often did.

'Glad to be rid of it, to be honest,' he said, sniffing. 'Not the sort of stuff I like having under me bed. You know what's in there, right?'

'I don't want to know,' Flora said, 'so don't tell me. I'm just bloody doing as I'm told.'

'Yeah. When's he gonna be out, do you know?'

'No idea. He said he'd contact you as soon as he can. He seems to think it's going to be OK as long as I can take care of this stuff.'

He nodded excitedly. 'Yeah, yeah. They ain't got nothing on him, other than what's in there. You bloody take care of it, right?'

'Don't worry,' she said, taking the second box from him. This one was much lighter. She slammed the boot lid down and went to get in the driver's door.

'Wait a sec,' he said.

'What?'

'Did he say anything about the phone?'

Shit. What did he mean? 'The phone?' She had one hand on the open door, looked back over her shoulder at the road as a pair of headlights suddenly illuminated them both. She pulled the door in closer as the car passed.

'Does he want me to drop it, or what?'

For a moment Flora's mind was a terrifying blank. Then, 'He didn't say anything, but then he only had a second and I guess this was his priority. Did you have an agreement, then? To do something with the phone if he was arrested?'

'Yeah,' Connor said. 'He told me that if he got nicked I was to drop the phone and get another one.'

Flora felt relief wash through her. 'Yes, that's probably a good idea. Drop your phone. He'll come and find you when he's out. Just keep your head down for a bit.'

'You won't want me over at the stables then?'

'No. Don't worry about the stables. I'll sort that out.'

'Fucking excellent!'

She got in the car and started it, tried to pull away smoothly, but the tension caused by her own mad behaviour was making her jumpy. When she got to the end of Kensington Avenue and turned left, back towards the main road, she started to laugh. Her hands were gripping the steering wheel as though it was about to fly off. *What have I done? What the hell am I doing?*

19:25

'Your phone's been ringing,' Chris said when Taryn came back down the stairs, bathrobe on over her pyjamas, hair in a towel.

'Well, you could've answered it,' she replied, rooting through her bag for the phone. She had had several glasses of wine in the bath, trying to relax, worrying about Flora. Her first thought was that something had happened, that Flora had been arrested again, but the missed calls – three of them – were all from an unknown mobile number.

There were no voicemail messages. Irritated, she redialled. It was answered straight away – and the voice on the other end, imperious, impatient, was a familiar one.

'Taryn,' said her father. 'They're going to discharge me tomorrow. Can you come first thing? I don't want to have to wait for those awful patient transport volunteer people.'

Her father must have borrowed a mobile phone from someone. She considered it for a moment, thinking about where Brian was planning to go. Would the police just let him back into the Barn? She didn't even have his key. Surely he wasn't imagining that he could come and stay with them? And she had to be at work by half past eight.

'Does it have to be first thing?' she asked. 'I might be able to take an extended lunch break.'

There was a pause on the other end of the line. Chris, on the sofa with his feet on the coffee table, was watching her face, mouthing 'don't let him give you any shit'. Brian didn't do compromise. It felt likely that he was working himself up into a rage and she contemplated what Reg might say if she phoned in to ask for the morning off, just as the answer came:

'That would be really kind of you, Taryn. Thank you.'

Well, that was unexpected. She raised her eyebrows for Chris's benefit. 'OK, then,' she said. 'I'll give you a call in the morning, shall I?'

'Thank you,' he said again.

She couldn't resist the little dig. 'Isn't your lovely lady friend available to come and pick you up?'

Another pause. 'She has – other priorities,' he said.

'Is she married?' Taryn asked.

'No, she's not married. That's not what I meant. It's . . . it's just not possible to ask her.'

The wine she'd drunk was igniting her curiosity and giving voice to it: 'Are you going to marry her, Dad? Now that Barbara's out of the picture?'

'No,' he said after a moment, and there was an audible sigh. 'No, I rather think not.' His voice sounded so strange, so unlike his normal brusque tone that Taryn had to sit on the arm of the sofa.

'Have you had a falling out?'

He chuckled slightly. 'No, not that. I don't think I should get married again, you know. Wives are more trouble than they're worth. Don't you think so?'

'I'll have to ask Chris about that,' she said, and winked at her husband who had glanced up on hearing his name mentioned.

'I think ... I rather think Barbara was very unkind to you, Taryn,' Brian said.

Taryn didn't reply, shocked to hear him say this.

'And I think I was, too. I'm very sorry for it.'

'Dad—?'

'It takes something like this to make you realise, you know.'

'Nearly dying, you mean?' she said and then instantly thought how tactless that sounded.

'Oh, I've nearly died before,' he said, his tone light. 'It's not as bad as you'd imagine.'

'What do you mean?'

'A dicky ticker,' he said, 'and a woman that likes to kill people. Makes you put everything into perspective.'

The wine she'd drunk was making the turn the conversation was taking seem more than surreal. She was about to ask him what he meant, but before she had the chance, he brought things to an abrupt end.

'Anyway, if you can get here tomorrow I'd really appreciate it. Very kind of you. You know my number now, in any case. See you tomorrow I hope.'

'All right, Dad. I'll ring you first thing.'

'Good night, then.'

'Bye, Dad.'

Taryn sat for a moment staring at the handset before reaching across to replace it.

'What was that all about?' Chris asked.

'He said she liked to kill people,' Taryn said quietly.

'Who? Barbara? Doesn't surprise me in the slightest. We're all bloody better off without her.'

342

Jason had barely paused for breath all day, and now Sam was back with the warrant for Brian's arrest, barely five minutes passed before the officers who'd stayed behind had their coats on, ready to go out to the King Bill.

Sam, the only one still on duty, was staying in the office to prepare the briefing for the arrest and interview team for the morning. Lou spent a moment debating what to do, stay or go. But then she saw Sam's face and realised that actually she preferred to get on with things on her own. Besides, Jason had already left with Ali and Jane.

'Don't stay past your hours, Sam,' she said. 'You've done enough.'

'Ma'am. I was hoping I could swap shifts and do an early turn tomorrow?'

Lou looked at her. Sam already knew what the answer would be; she was just trying her luck. 'I really appreciate what you've done, Sam. You've been brilliant. But you'll have to wait until your shift, all right? You need your rest the same as everyone else. And you never know, we might be able to bring Suzanne in, and I'll need you for that.'

By the time Lou got to the King Bill, she had promised herself she was only going to buy a round, maybe two, and then make sure everyone buggered off home. They weren't celebrating, not yet, anyway. This was all about putting a barrier between the case and going home. It was a transitional phase, involving beer.

And at the bar, the crush of people from the team along with every other random punter, most of whom were Job themselves, she found herself standing next to Jason who was pressing against her like some frotteur on a crowded underground train. As she necked the bottle of beer someone had lined up ready for her, alongside Ali

343

and Jane and Les Finnegan who smelt as though he'd snuck in a couple of whisky chasers already, she felt Jason's hand on her waist. She looked round at him, his green eyes so close to hers, closer than they'd been since the night she'd spent tangled round him on his sofa.

'How *did* you get that black eye?' she asked with a smile.

'What?'

It was loud in here, music from some local band coming from the function room upstairs – and they sounded good, too – so she repeated her question, a little louder, a little closer to his ear.

'I got a stick in the face, of course.'

'Don't you wear some sort of mask thing?'

'Yeah, on the ice. This was in the changing rooms.'

Lou laughed because it was quite funny after half a beer and an improbably long working day, and he laughed too. 'What, on purpose?'

'Maybe. Who knows.'

'Someone from the other team?'

'Does it even matter?'

'I'm just interested.'

But he didn't answer, distracted by Les Finnegan talking about the pornographic pictures of Brian and his lovely lady friend on the phone and what he could sell them for, if he had half a mind to get started in the granny porn market.

Lou felt for Jason's hand, gave it a squeeze, intending to let go. He held it.

21:53

Flora was sitting on the floor of the kitchen, a small windowless room at the back of the studio where she made cups of coffee and washed out her brushes. The main studio, a large room with big windows overlooking the car park at the front of the building, was in darkness. Her car had been moved round the back, behind the second warehouse, and was partly concealed by two large dumpsters full of cardboard for recycling. To the casual passer-by, nobody was home.

She had shut the kitchen door before turning on any lights, boiled the kettle, turned on the radio with the sound low so that the thought of being here all on her own was not quite so scary.

Now, with her third mugful of black coffee in hand, she had almost reached the bottom of the first box.

The contents had been by turns eye-opening, confusing and, frankly, terrifying.

Large brown envelopes containing bundles of cash, fifties in great wads, bound with elastic bands. There were files, too, in three thick lever arch folders. One marked 'Leeds', one marked 'Liverpool'. The other with nothing on the spine at all. Inside the files were plastic sleeves, each one containing personal details, photocopies of passports, birth certificates, phone numbers, addresses from all over Eastern Europe, North Africa, Asia. One plastic sleeve in the unmarked folder contained nothing but credit cards, new-looking, all in different names.

Then there was a large carrier bag containing passports, lots of them, different sizes, different colours. Flora pulled one out at random. The picture was of a young girl, dark-haired, aged about twelve. The date of birth on the passport would have put her at seventeen. The name on it – in a Cyrillic script and in roman letters too – Ekaterina Ioratova.

Flora pushed the passport back inside the bag.

Underneath the bag she'd seen something else. Something black, solid: a handgun, and next to it a cardboard box with ammunition.

She had been removing everything and laying it out on the floor, but when she got to the gun, she stopped. This had suddenly got crazier.

She got to her feet and turned her back on the boxes. This was no good. She had to think.

Whatever her father was doing – and she knew it had to be bad – unless it had something to do with Polly, she wasn't interested. And he had lied to her. Despite his clever explanation of the way he'd spent that Halloween evening, something about it didn't ring true.

They weren't seeing each other any more, were they? So why would Nigel go and spend two hours with Polly in the cottage on the night she died?

The second box was still unopened. She sat down on the floor again, opened the box. Inside was a file which she recognised as relating to the farm business. Everything in it was a copy of a legitimate document that was filed in the stables office. So why had he given this to Connor to look after?

She lifted the file and underneath it was another carrier bag. A sudden chill ran through her as she understood. The file was Nigel's final line of defence. Whatever was in the bag, he'd used the file to disguise it, as though someone raking through the contents would somehow hesitate over the file and decide that this box was unimportant.

Flora lifted the bag clear of the box. It was surprisingly light. She looked inside, at the same moment as her phone started buzzing on the work surface above her head. She reached up for it. Taryn.

Where are you? Everything OK? Just checking up on you. T.
xx

She sent a swift reply:

All fine. Will ring you later. Xx

She opened the bag and looked inside, and then tipped the contents out into her lap. And here was what she had been looking for. Another wad of cash, bound up with elastic bands, and a small, black mobile phone.

23:45

Karen was asleep, the kids were asleep and he'd gone out to his car in his socked feet, not wanting to make a sound. Driving away as quietly as he could. Back to Waterside Gardens.

Back to her.

She opened the door to him after what felt like an age. It had crossed his mind, waiting on her doorstep and hoping that once again Flora or anyone else for that matter wouldn't see him here and wonder what he was doing, that she might have someone else in her flat. She might have any number of people who called on her, not just guys; family, friends maybe.

But she was alone. 'It's very late,' she said.

She didn't look especially pleased to see him and he was nervous about her reaction when he came inside.

'We need to talk,' he said.

'That sounds ominous, Inspector,' she said. She followed him into the living room, got a second glass out of the cabinet and poured him some wine from the bottle she'd been drinking.

'My name's Andy,' he said.

'I like calling you inspector,' she said with a smile. 'I find it a turn-on, fucking a policeman. Especially one with a rank.'

'Please,' he said. 'Don't tempt me, not now. This is important.'

'I'm sorry,' she said, making an apologetic moue. 'Go on.'

'You said you had information for me. Something that would help.'

'I thought you'd forgotten all about that. I certainly managed to take your mind off it this afternoon, didn't I?'

She handed him the glass of wine and sat on the sofa, crossing her feet neatly at the ankle. 'You might as well sit down,' she said.

Andy started to get his phone ready to record what she had to say, but she picked it up off the table and turned it off.

'Can I at least take notes?' he asked.

'No.'

He gave up, then. He had a feeling that it was all shit anyway. She was still playing with him, teasing him. Anything she told him would be on her terms and would likely be fabrication. 'How about we start with you telling me how you met Brian,' he said.

Suzanne gave him a slow smile. Her eye contact was direct. 'We met through mutual friends, earlier this year.'

'Mutual friends? Who?'

She drank some of her wine, watching him over the rim of her glass. When she had finished, she put the glass down on the table in front of her. 'That's not relevant to our discussion.'

'You and Brian – what was the nature of your relationship?'

'Very similar to the one I'm having with you.'

'You were lovers?'

'He is my sub. Do you understand what that means?'

Andy took a big gulp of wine to try and help him swallow the facts she was offering him – or rather, the comparison of their brief association with what she had done with Brian Fletcher-Norman.

'You did that – that thing you did with me?' he asked. 'You suffocated him?'

'The term for it is breathplay. Yes, that's one of the things we enjoy.'

'So you're – forgive me, this is all new to me – you're in control of him? You tell him what to do?'

The smile faded from her lips. She smoothed her skirt, reached forward for her glass of wine. As she did so her blouse gaped and he saw the curve of her breasts, smooth, white. 'You have to understand the nature of control. Brian is a very strong man, a very controlling man. In his career and at home he is completely dominant, focused, authoritative. In order to relax he likes to relinquish that need for decision-making. But that doesn't mean I am taking control.'

'What *does* it mean?'

'You remember I told you to indicate if you'd had enough by raising your hand?'

Andy remembered. The thought of it, even now, made him inexplicably aroused. 'Yes.'

'You were in control, then, weren't you? All you had to do was signal that you wanted to stop. So effectively you were telling me what to do.'

Something she'd said had made him feel uneasy, but he couldn't think what it was. Her turning the conversation round to the things they'd done, the way she was sitting there, curled around herself, was distracting him from Brian. Then he had it.

'You said Brian was dominant at home as well as at work,' he said. 'What do you mean?'

The smile was back. 'Exactly that. He's confident, arrogant and utterly selfish. Why do you think his wife was planning to leave him? Why do you think his daughter hadn't spoken to him for months? He's ruthless and doesn't care for anyone but himself.'

'His wife was planning to leave?' He knew this already, of course. But he wanted to hear her take on it; if she was telling the truth about this, it would be easier for him to assess if she was telling the truth about the rest of it.

'She was going to run off with her tennis coach, according to Brian. He wouldn't have stood for that, of course. Brian never tolerated anything that didn't happen under his terms.'

'What do you mean?' he asked again.

She tipped the last of the wine into her mouth and swallowed, her eyes on him. 'You want me to spell it out for you?'

'Yes,' he said.

'Barbara was going to leave. Brian wasn't going to let her get away with it, with stealing his money and humiliating him, but he couldn't do anything to harm her, of course, could he? Because then he would have got the blame. He couldn't just do away with her. And he couldn't force her to stay, nor did he want her to. He loathed her by that stage.'

Andy was feeling cold, all of a sudden. The chill of it was travelling through his body like an anaesthetic, paralysing him with horror, as he saw the facts of the case being revealed as though she was a conjuror dramatically pulling away a silk cloth.

'What did he do?' Andy asked, trying to keep his voice light.

'What do you think? He set her up. He made it look as though she had committed a violent murder because she was jealous of his relationship with the girl next door – which of course never happened – and then he pushed her car over the edge of the quarry as if she had been suddenly overcome with remorse. He's very clever, you know. He's been thinking this through for a long, long time. The only thing he didn't bank on was his own dicky ticker, the fact that his heart couldn't take all that running around in the middle of the night.'

'Why are you telling me all this?' he asked, his mouth dry. The wine was all gone.

Suzanne smiled at him again, got to her feet. He looked up at her as she placed a hand on his shoulder. 'Because I don't want anything more to do with him. If he can do that to his wife, control or not, I'd rather not be anywhere near him, Inspector.'

He stood, towering over her, looking into her eyes. He wanted to kiss her but he was starting to understand that she had to make the first move. He didn't want to frighten her, especially given everything she'd told him. It had to be true. The most logical explanation of all – and sooner or later, now he knew where to look, there would be forensic evidence that would substantiate what she'd said.

'How do you know that's what happened?'

'He came here that night and told me what he was planning to do. I tried to talk him out of it but he had his mind set on it. He wanted her out of the way so he could be with me, and that poor girl was going to be the one who would pay the price for Barbara's mistake. I was afraid. It went beyond the boundaries of our association and I told him that. But he went ahead and did it anyway. He knew I would never be brave enough to tell anyone.'

'You just told me,' Andy said, touching her cheek.

'I told you in confidence,' she said. 'And because I know you can do the right thing with this information, which will get a murderer locked up and therefore mean I am safe. Do you understand what I mean?'

'I can only use the information to look for evidence, Suzanne,' he said. 'Unless you're willing to make a statement and support a prosecution.'

She looked away, clearly thinking about this. She took hold of his hand and squeezed it, like a little girl seeking comfort. 'If you arrest him,' she said, 'and I know he's definitely not going to be let out, I'll consider making a statement. Is that good enough?'

Hell, yes, Andy thought. This had gone from his worst nightmare to a dream ending to a case that had been heading down the toilet along with his marriage, his career and his life. He could say he'd come here looking for Flora, which was true, that Suzanne had given him the intelligence in confidence and he'd been trying to persuade her to trust him, make a statement. He'd not wanted to share the information with the team because of the risk to her life if Brian found out she'd talked. Suzanne had all but told Andy that she was terrified of him. It could work. It could actually work.

Suzanne led him out of the living room into the bedroom, as though she had said everything that she needed to say and that now the time for talking was over; he would be able to comfort her, provide her with reassurance that Brian was gone and that she had no need to fear him any more.

'I need to go,' he said, without enthusiasm. 'It's really late.'

'Stay,' she said, pulling him closer. 'For a little while.'

Moments after that he felt a swell of satisfaction that this clever, gorgeous and sexually insatiable woman was now, with Brian out of the way, all his.

23:52

It was a mobile phone, just a mobile phone. It lay black and inert on her knee, until she picked it up and pressed the button to turn it on. It was a cheap handset with a keypad and a small display. For a moment she had thought it was Polly's phone, that this was what the police had been searching for, that Nigel had it and that must mean that he had killed her. But a glance told her it wasn't Polly's expensive smartphone at all. So whose phone was it?

352

She worked her way through the menus to find the list of contacts, hoping that would give her a clue as to who it might belong to, but that proved to be even more confusing. They were mainly initials: B, F, R, C.R, J and a few brief names and nicknames: Dev, Kel, Ken P, Dozer, Legs, Ian, Psych. She looked for 'Polly' but the name wasn't there, not even a 'P'. Then she had a thought, started to type in Polly's number, and before she had got too far the predictive text suggested she might like to dial 'Y'. Polly's number, definitely, stored under a single letter Y.

She tried the same thing with her own number, and her mother's but both drew a blank.

Flora left the contacts list alone and turned to the stored text messages. There weren't many; whoever owned this phone either didn't like texting, or believed that deleting as you went along was a sensible policy.

There were no text messages sent to or received from 'Y'.

There was one text, received on Thursday from 'Dev', with a mobile number and nothing else. Two texts on Friday from 'J' and one just said '*ring me*'. The second was another mobile phone number. The third, and final text message, sent at 08:56 on Saturday morning, was from 'F':

Coming to collect, be ready 20 mins

Nothing made sense, nothing! Flora could feel the frustration and anger rising inside her. All of this effort, all her subterfuge, and it was for nothing! Whoever had this phone had Polly's number, but that was no help at all.

She ran through the call history to see if that made any sense. On Wednesday there had been intermittent calls back and forth between 'J' and 'Dev' and 'Psych', and then in the evening the contacts increased until the phone was in almost constant use. Flora scrolled

353

through it, wondering why Wednesday, what was so special about it? Polly was still alive then, doing whatever it was she had been busy doing on Wednesday – and then she saw it.

One missed call, on Wednesday night, from a landline number she recognised – the number for Yonder Cottage.

Flora stared at the handset, thinking hard. Polly had called this phone on Wednesday night at twenty-three forty-three. The next contact logged on the call history was to voicemail, ten minutes later. Flora selected 'voicemail' and dialled.

A second later it connected. 'Welcome to voicemail. You have no new messages. To listen to older messages, press one. To listen to—'

Flora interrupted the voice and pressed one on the keypad.

She held her breath and listened.

'Nigel? Don't you EVER do anything like that again, you hear me? I am fucking livid right now. What the hell were you thinking? I've told you I want nothing to do with any of this! How dare you put me in that situation? I can't believe it, you total fucking idiot. I'm this close to calling the bloody police on you, you complete TWAT.'

23:54

I shouldn't be doing this, Lou thought.

He held the door open for her, held out his hand – as though she needed help! – and in any case, she'd only let go of his hand briefly in order to open the door of the taxi.

He didn't bother to put lights on, didn't take her into the living room this time, didn't offer her food or put music on or even kiss her. He waited for her to kick off her shoes in the hallway and then he led her by the hand up the stairs to his bedroom at the front of the house. There was light coming in from outside, through the blinds; street light, enough for her to see him undoing the top buttons of his shirt, tugging it out of his trousers and then pulling it over the top of his head, ruffling his hair the wrong way. His face was shadow. She couldn't see the expression on it or his black eye, for that matter, the injury she knew for a fact hadn't been caused by a hockey stick or else why would he be so evasive? There was more to it than that.

But she didn't care about that right now. *I need sleep*, her subconscious protested feebly, thinking about the arrests tomorrow and how she would need to be focused, ready to do a press conference if necessary, certainly ready to brief Buchanan and probably the Assistant Chief Constable too . . .

'Stop that,' he said, quietly, running his fingers over the frown creasing her forehead.

'I shouldn't be here,' she said.

'Shh.'

Then the chink of his belt as he undid it, and as though that was some kind of signal she realised that she was standing there like a complete lemon, mouth open, probably stopping just short of a drool. So she reached out a hand and found the bare skin of his chest. It was hot to the touch, the muscles under the skin solid, tense. He caught hold of her hand and brought it up to his mouth to kiss. Pulled her closer.

'Louisa,' he said, and kissed her.

Oh, God, it felt so good to give in to it. She could no more have gone downstairs, called a cab on her mobile, than she could have walked over broken glass. It wasn't only sexual attraction, it was like this – this – *longing* to be with him.

She let him undress her. He did it almost reverently; and while his clothes had been discarded where they fell, he took each item of hers and folded it, leaving it on the chair at the end of the bed.

And, thinking that she needed to be sensible here, needed to take charge of the situation and point out that maybe they had half an hour, an hour at most and then she would have to go home so she could get some sleep, he took control of things and her body responded to him as though it was separate from her, with no intention of behaving sensibly at all . . .

In the early hours of the morning, as her breathing slowed again for what felt like the fourth or fifth time, he was stroking her arm with his eyes closed, as though he was sleeping, even though she knew he was wide awake because of the smile on his lips. She whispered to him:

'Someone whacked you one, didn't they?'

'Hmm? What are you talking about?'

'Your eye. You got punched.'

'Louisa, it doesn't matter. It really doesn't. You can sleep now, you know . . . unless you want more?'

'Why won't you tell me?'

'Because it doesn't matter. It's done with.'

'Was it over a woman?'

He let her go abruptly, sat up in bed and turned on the bedside light. She blinked at the sudden brightness, pulled at the sheet in order to cover herself.

'Hey,' he said, tugging the sheet out of her grasp. 'Don't do that. Let me see.'

'Why did you turn the light on?'

'To get this over with. It's no big deal. I was in the locker room and one of the guys on the team was smack talking another of the guys on the team. His wife has cancer. I got mad. I picked a fight with him. He clipped me in the face with a stick. And that is it, the full story. Are you happy now?'

'What the hell's smack talking?'

'You know. Mouthing off.'

He was absolutely telling the truth. 'Why couldn't you tell me that before?'

'Because it's no big deal. We're buddies again now. They all think it's funny that I got a black eye from it. The only problem with it now is your personal insecurity.'

'Not my insecurity. My professional curiosity.'

He laughed, nodded. 'Right. I believe you. Totally.'

She found herself smiling.

'I really like you,' he said. 'I know it's only been a few days, but you don't need to feel insecure.'

She leaned over and kissed him, and then got up from the bed and started to get dressed.

'Where are you going? Hey, come back to bed.'

'I'm glad we've established that you like me,' she teased. 'I can go home now and get some sleep with what's left of the night.'

Day Six – Tuesday 6 November 2012

08:47

Lou was in the canteen on the top floor at Briarstone police station with Jason, Ali Whitmore and Jane Phelps. She'd ordered a full English breakfast for them all and they were keeping a close eye on the kitchen to make sure that there were no dangerous hygiene violations taking place. Unlike the canteen up the road at Police Headquarters, the Briarstone nick canteen was known to be a bit hit and miss. The kitchen was open plan, enabling the customers to watch their food being prepared from start to finish. This should have been reassuring, but unfortunately it wasn't.

Lou felt strangely relieved that Andy Hamilton was on a rest day. He was one less headache for her to deal with. Under normal circumstances she would have been grateful for every warm body she could get her hands on for the arrest phase of the operation, but keeping an eye on him was proving such hard work it was much better for everyone if he was out of the picture, for today at least.

It had all gone smoothly and, for a change, everyone seemed relaxed. Relieved.

Brian had been arrested as soon as he had been discharged. He had looked shocked, but had reserved his right to remain silent. He had spoken to his solicitor, who was waiting for him when he was brought into custody.

Brian's doctors had confirmed that, for now, he was fit to be interviewed. The Force Medical Examiner had been briefed and the forensic nurse practitioner on duty in Briarstone nick had been asked to stay close at hand while the interviews took place.

Lou felt exhausted, not least because she'd only had four hours' sleep. Bits of the time she'd spent with Jason kept coming back to her and distracting her from the sudden flood of information that was pouring in to the MIR via Barry Holloway.

Later, she thought. *Tonight I'm going to ask him to stay at my house. And even if all we do is sleep, I want it to be with him there . . .*

'Ma'am?'

There was something about the tone of the voice from behind her shoulder, and the way Jane Phelps' smile had died on her face looking at the expression on Ron Mitchell's face as he approached Lou, that made her realise that this was not going to be good news.

'What is it, Ron?'

'Flora Maitland is downstairs. She's insisting she wants to talk to you.'

08:52

Flora had been waiting for nearly an hour. The front office of the police station opened at eight and she had been here since the doors had been unlocked. She had asked to speak to whoever was in charge of the investigation into the murder of Polly Leuchars.

The front office was an interesting place to sit. A man came in to report a stolen car. The woman on the counter ran through a series of questions, made notes, but the story kept changing: he'd last seen it on Sunday evening, then he corrected himself and admitted driving it to work yesterday. He'd left it parked outside his house, then he said it had been stolen from the car park where he worked. Flora could feel the woman's frustration building, and then she realised that the man was drunk. This early in the morning?

Eventually, the man went.

Flora asked, 'How long will it take? Do you know?'

The woman had responded: 'Sorry, love. No idea.'

A woman came in to ask about some lost property, then another woman with a buggy and a toddler, asking whether her boyfriend was in custody again because he hadn't come home last night. A sign on the wall offered people the chance to discuss their query in a private room, but nobody seemed bothered by Flora's presence. She felt as though she were fading, becoming transparent. If she sat perfectly still, nobody would even be able to see her any more.

At eight forty-five a man in a suit turned up. He was there for a meeting with someone from Crime Prevention. They made him sit and wait. He sat opposite Flora and stared at her in a way that made her feel uncomfortable. He was probably wondering what she was there for, and then she realised she probably didn't look too good.

'Will it be much longer, do you think?'

'I've rung them, they know you're here. I expect they're all busy at the moment.'

She had barely slept, just dozed in the kitchen at the studio with the blanket around her shoulders. When it got light and nothing had happened, no phone calls, no texts, she tried to decide what to do. She wanted to phone her father, demand to know what he was doing, what Polly had meant by her frantic voicemail.

The last few days had been such a nightmare. First Polly's death, and then her father acting strangely. How could she not suspect him? And having listened to Polly's voice, tearful, furious and terrified on that message, she was jumpy and afraid. She was imagining all sorts of things, her mind flitting from one possibility to the next. Why hadn't he used the gun, if he was going to kill her? Because he hadn't had it with him, of course. He had got her voicemail and had gone down to the cottage to confront her about it, whatever it was and of course she hadn't made him cheese on toast, how ridiculous! – he had gone there to talk to her, and they'd had another row, and he'd hit her too hard and she had died. And after that he'd been covering his tracks, establishing an alibi with friends, or whatever it was he'd done. But no, that wasn't right either, was it? He'd been at the farm. He had told them he was at home, with Mum. And he was relying on Felicity to cover up for him, relying on her being vague and confused as she always was but nevertheless unflinching in her support of him.

Think, Flora, think. Her eyes kept moving from the front desk to the clock on the wall. Why were they taking so long? The longer they left it the more her resolve started to slip. This morning she had been certain of what she needed to do: go to the police and tell them she was ready to talk, as long as they were prepared to offer her some protection.

She had left the studio as it began to get properly light, looking around in case someone was waiting for her outside. Nobody there. She hurried to her car, checked it carefully. It seemed all right. Started OK. Before she did anything else, she had a very important task to complete: she drove to the farm, in through the driveway beside Yonder Cottage so that nobody in the farmhouse would know she was there. She left the car outside Polly's house and walked up to the stables, keeping an eye out all the way. Nobody was around, of course. Felicity would still be fast asleep.

The horses were surprised to see her but seemed quite happy to have an early breakfast. After they'd been fed she led them one by one to the paddock and turned them loose. They stood around looking dazed. That was fine. She wouldn't bother mucking out. Felicity probably wouldn't even check; she would see them out in the field and think – what? That Petrie had suddenly decided to do his job properly? Actually, knowing her mother, she probably wouldn't even care. Either way, by the time the horses needed to be brought in again, the day would have taken its course and nothing would be the same again anyway.

After the stables, there had been nothing else for it but to go to the police station. There was no point in going to her flat – that was a dangerous place now. Her father would be looking for her soon enough, and the flat would be the first place he would check. She couldn't risk going to Taryn's, either. It would be wrong of her to involve her friend now that the stakes had become so much higher.

'Do you think you could ring them again? I've been here ages,' she asked.

'They're based over at HQ, could be a while yet. Sorry, love. Try to sit tight, I'm sure someone will be here before too long.'

The longer she waited, the more uncertain she became. Every few minutes she checked her phone, even though it would vibrate for any incoming calls or texts. Since last night's text, Nigel had remained silent. This could mean one of two things: either he was carrying on with his daily business, blissfully unaware of her activities, or he had spoken to Connor Petrie, in which case she was in deep shit.

Yes, the police station was the only safe place at the moment, and as much as she didn't particularly like or trust the police, especially after they had brought her in for questioning, searched the flat and accused her of murdering the only person she'd ever loved, they were definitely a better prospect than confronting her father.

And then her mobile phone vibrated in her pocket. She pulled it out and looked at the display: Taryn. And just at that moment the door to the side of the reception opened.

'Flora?'

Flora looked up. The woman who had called her name was holding open a door next to the reception desk. 'Would you like to come this way?'

Flora pressed the button to reject Taryn's call and sprang to her feet, wiping her hands down the front of her grubby, paint-stained jeans. 'Thanks, yes.' Her heart was bouncing around in her chest.

Focus. Think.

Above the swirling, panicky thoughts, Flora was acutely aware that what she was about to do amounted to a further act of betrayal and that from this point on there was no turning back.

The woman was young, slightly built, wearing a smart suit that made her look older than she probably was. Her long, dark, glossy hair must have taken a lot of effort to straighten every morning. Flora could never see the point of all that stuff.

She was led into a small, artificially lit room with a table and two chairs, a metal filing cabinet upon which sat a pile of dog-eared magazines, a box of tissues, and a plant that was so green it had to be made of plastic.

'Have a seat,' the woman said.

Flora sat. The woman pulled the chair out from the desk and sat in the open space beside the table.

'My name is Detective Chief Inspector Louisa Smith. I'm leading the investigation into Polly's murder and I understand you wanted to see me?'

'You're in charge?' Flora asked, surprised. She had a momentary vision of the brash, intimidating Detective Inspector Andy Hamilton and wondered how he could possibly be subordinate to this smiling, softly spoken woman.

'Yes, I am. How can I help?'

'Well, it's about my father,' Flora began. This was the moment, she thought. After this, her choices would diminish. She hesitated, feeling panic and confusion and, in all of that, still this terrible aching in her heart because of Polly. And she was tired now, so tired. Despite the emotions, all she wanted to do was lie down on the floor of the room and sleep. And how could any of this possibly make sense?

'Your father – Nigel Maitland?'

Flora swallowed. She didn't want to cry in front of this woman but it looked like it might happen anyway. 'I'm so scared,' she said, her voice a whisper.

'Why are you scared, Flora?'

There was a long moment, a long, painful moment when she debated with herself about what to say next. And then, in a small voice, she said: 'I'm scared of getting things wrong.'

'You don't need to worry about that. If you have information for us, it's up to us to make sure we know what it means. So you see, you can't get things wrong, Flora.'

Flora took a deep breath in. 'He's been acting strangely since Polly's death. I think something happened that night, but I don't know what. I just know he's been odd. And he was having an – an affair with her. I supposed that's what it was.'

'With whom? With Polly?'

'Yes. He said it ended months ago, but I don't know if that was true.'

'In what way is he behaving strangely?'

Flora thought about this, and the confusion and the doubt seemed to lift a little. She couldn't tell them about the phone, or about

365

Polly's voicemail message, because to do so would be to admit to the boxes and their contents. She had hidden them under the kitchen sink at the studio which wasn't the best hiding place, but at least they were out of sight. How could she tell them what she knew? How to start something like this? And, once started, how to stop?

There was a knock at the door behind Flora. She looked round as Lou Smith looked up. A man wearing police uniform opened the door. 'Ma'am. Sorry to interrupt.'

'What is it, Noel?'

'Need a quick word, sorry.'

Lou stood up. 'Excuse me for one moment,' she said, and left the room.

Flora felt cold, chilled, and after all the panic, all the nervous tension, strangely calm.

Then the door opened and Lou came back in and sat down. 'I think what we should do, Flora, is talk about this properly in an interview suite. I don't want you to worry; you're quite safe here with us. We just need to do things in a particular way to make sure we don't miss anything. Would you mind waiting for a while, until we can sort out a proper interview room?'

Flora shrugged. 'I guess so.'

'Can I get a cup of tea or coffee sorted out for you?'

'Coffee would be good. Thank you.'

'I'll be back as soon as I can,' she said, and then the door shut behind her and Flora was on her own again. She put her head onto her folded arms.

09:14

Bloody typical, to be called away right at that moment. Outside the interview room, she took Noel Brewster to one side. 'Can you make

366

sure Flora Maitland doesn't leave before I've had a chance to speak to her again? If she starts to look like she wants to go, will you come and find me?'

'Yes, ma'am,' Noel replied.

'Promise?'

'Absolutely.'

'And can you get her a coffee? Thanks.'

Lou ran up the stairs to the office at the back of Briarstone police station that the team had been allocated while the interview was in progress. The MIR at Headquarters was only fifteen minutes' drive away, but even so, having everybody together, here, able to view the interview as it happened by video link was essential.

Only Jason had been left behind, to complete as many charts and reports as he could in the time they had left to interview Brian.

'Sam and Ron are in already, ma'am,' Les said. 'The solicitor didn't take long.'

'Who is it?' Lou asked.

'Simon McGrath.'

Could be worse, Lou thought. He wasn't a complete pain in the arse, but the chances were he was still going to have advised his client to answer 'no comment' to every question put to him.

They all grouped as best they could around the monitor that provided a direct link to the interview room. They could see Brian sitting at a desk, a middle-aged man in a dark suit sitting next to him, the ceiling lights reflecting off the top of his bald head. A smaller, pop-up window in the bottom of the screen was feeding the image from the camera in the opposite corner of the room – Sam and Ron, getting themselves settled.

Sam went through the initial proceedings of the interview, setting

367

up the recording, introducing everyone present, reminding Brian that he had been arrested and cautioned, and asking him if he understood everything.

The first few questions were straightforward, going over subjects that he had already quite happily discussed with them on previous occasions in the hospital.

'Can you tell us when you first met Polly Leuchars?'

To his credit, Simon McGrath was allowing Brian some freedom to answer the questions he felt comfortable with. The story was trotted out again: golf with Nigel Maitland, riding lessons.

The questions gradually moved around to Barbara. The answers, again, nothing they had not already heard. She was a jealous woman, prone to drinking too much and being aggressive.

And then, out of the blue: 'She was having an affair with her tennis coach. His name was Liam O'Toole.'

Neither Sam nor Ron showed any surprise at this, which was excellent. They had prepared well, they knew exactly what he had told them previously and this was the moment that they were venturing on to new territory.

'How did you know about this?' Sam asked.

'She told me,' Brian said. His voice was low, sorrowful, as though the memory was painful, although his body language looked relaxed enough. 'I'd had my suspicions, of course. She was spending a fortune on tennis lessons, and where she had been so bloody miserable before, she seemed to have perked up in the last few months.'

'When did she tell you, Brian?'

'That last night. It was one of the vicious things she threw at me before she buggered off out.'

Sam took her time, writing some notes. 'Can you take us through

368

the events of that evening again, Brian? Let's start with you getting home from work.'

'I got home from work, and she started a row with me—'

'What time was it?'

'Between eight and nine.'

He was sticking to the events as he had outlined them to Lou before, in the hospital. Sam knew this too. Lou found herself listening to the repeated story and tuning out; she kept thinking about Flora, in the interview room downstairs. She had looked exhausted and yet fidgety, as though she was on the verge of losing the plot. Loui wondered what on earth Flora was doing here, what she was so afraid of. As soon as she had the opportunity, Lou was going to go down and check up on her, make sure she was all right.

Once Brian had told the story all the way up to the police knocking on his door the next morning, Sam tried a change of subject.

'Are you a keen cyclist, Brian?'

'I cycle occasionally to keep fit. I prefer golf.'

'Where do you keep your bike?'

'Usually in the garage at home.'

'And when did you last go for a cycle ride?'

'I don't know. Weeks ago. The weather has been bad.'

'Is this your bike, Brian?'

The video screen showed Ron passing something across the table. Both Brian and Simon McGrath studied it closely.

'Looks like it. Hard to say.'

'Why is it hard to say? It's quite a distinctive bike, isn't it?' Sam said. 'An expensive one, too. Have another look.'

There was a long pause, which included glances and a few private words being exchanged between Brian and his solicitor.

'I can't be sure,' he said at last.

Sam looked as though she was going to ask again, but then Simon McGrath spoke: 'My client has answered the question. I'd appreciate it if we could move on, and I'd like to remind you that we need to take regular breaks. Mr Fletcher-Norman is still recovering from a serious illness.'

They were clearly reaching the periphery of Brian's comfort zone. He was happy with his original story, that much was clear; now, every question they asked him would be thought about, discussed, and then quite possibly not answered. And they hadn't even mentioned his phone yet. It was going to be a long day.

09:25

'How are you feeling, Brian?' Sam asked.

'Tired,' he had replied.

'We will try and keep things to the point, then, shall we?' said Ron.

'Let's talk about your phone, Brian,' Sam began. 'Can you take me through the calls you made on the night of thirty-first October?'

'I don't remember,' he said.

'Can you confirm that this is your phone?'

Ron passed the evidence bag across the desk towards Brian and Simon McGrath.

Simon McGrath leaned across to his client and made some comment.

'It's a common type of phone,' Brian said.

'Very well,' said Sam. 'It was given to us by your daughter, Mrs Taryn Lewis. She said she found this phone in your office at Hayselden Barn, your home address. It has your fingerprints on it. The numbers saved in the address book generally have been identified as people known to be your associates, including a number saved as "Office" which, according to your company's website, is the main switchboard number for your workplace. There's also a number saved as "B MOB" which, according to a subscriber check, is registered to your wife, Barbara. Do I need to go on?'

Simon McGrath looked annoyed. 'Was that an actual question, Sergeant Hollands?'

'All right,' Brian said. 'It's my phone.'

Sam retained her calm, interested expression. 'Very well. Can you confirm that you had this phone in your possession on the night of thirty-first October?'

Another consultation between Brian and his solicitor, this one longer. There seemed to be a disagreement between them. Sam was watching them closely.

'I don't remember,' Brian answered at last.

'Your daughter said it was in your office. Is that where you left it?'

'Yes, it must have been.'

'Did you make any calls on the night of the thirty-first?'

'I don't remember,' Brian said again.

'Well, then, let me remind you. This phone made several calls during the evening, specifically to a number which is saved in the contacts as "Manchester Office". Do you remember making those calls?'

'My client has already said he doesn't recall making the calls,' McGrath said.

'I am just trying to help him out,' Sam said. 'Do you remember making any of those calls, Brian?'

'I don't know.'

Sam flipped through the paper file in front of her, and brought out four photocopied sheets. 'This is the statement you provided to PC Yvonne Sanders on Sunday fourth November. Can you confirm that this is your signature?'

'Looks like it,' Brian said.

'You remember making the statement?'

'She brought it with her for me to sign. Sunday evening, I think.'

Simon McGrath leaned towards his client and whispered something in Brian's ear which Sam did not quite catch.

Sam brought out more sheets of paper – the photocopies of Yvonne Sanders' handwritten notes. 'This is your signature too, Brian. You signed the notes contemporaneously to say that you agreed that it was an accurate record of your discussion.'

'Do you have a question for my client?' said McGrath, without looking up from his own notepad.

'My colleagues took you through the events of the evening of thirty-first October, from your arrival home to you going to bed. You did not mention once making any phone calls.'

'I told you, I don't remember making any calls,' Brian said.

'Can you tell me who "Manchester Office" is?' Sam asked.

'It's a work number. A client. I don't really know. I don't know why I rang them. I was feeling unwell.'

'We've identified this number as belonging to a woman called Suzanne Martin, who lives in Briarstone. Does that help? Maybe you remember speaking to her on Wednesday night?'

Brian's face was colouring and he was looking increasingly uncomfortable. 'Look, I keep telling you I don't remember.'

Sam leaned back in her chair and took a deep breath. 'Very well,' she said. 'Let's move on. We have evidence from the phone's service provider about the calls made by this phone on the night of the thirty-first, Brian. It's called cellsite data and it tells us where this phone handset was when it was in use. Do you understand what that means?'

Brian nodded.

'Could you answer yes or no, please,' Ron said. 'For the tape.'

'Yes,' Brian said. His voice was raised an octave. He cleared his throat. 'Yes, I understand.'

'The phone that you have identified as yours, and in your possession on the night of the thirty-first October to first November, made several calls to the number registered to Suzanne Martin. One of those calls, made at . . . ' Sam checked her notes, ' . . . made at half past two in the morning, was in the vicinity of Ambleside Quarry. Can you confirm that you made that call, Brian?'

Brian's voice had gone.

'Could you speak up, please?' said Ron.

'I don't – I don't remember.'

'I suggest that my client needs a break, Sergeant,' said McGrath.

'We've only just had a break, I'm sure he can manage another few minutes. Can't you, Brian?'

'I'd rather get this over with,' he said.

'It would be very easy to wrap this all up if you could think carefully and remember what you were really up to that night, Brian. After the call made at the quarry, there's another call made to the same number at three in the morning. A long call, nineteen minutes and twenty-three seconds in duration. That call was made from Morden again. What about that one? Nearly twenty minutes, Brian. Do you remember making that call?'

There was a pause. Brian was staring at Sam across the desk. As she watched, a tear fell from his eye onto his sweater, absorbing into the navy cotton and spreading into a neat, dark circle.

'Brian? What was it you were discussing with Suzanne Martin?'

Still no response.

Sam, calm as ever, tried a different tactic. 'I'd like to point out, Brian, that this morning you've claimed that you don't remember anything about the phone calls made that night, but I believe you're not telling the truth. You told us when you were interviewed before that your memory of the night had come back, that you remembered having an argument with your wife and then you went to have a bath and went to bed. And now you're claiming that you don't remember making phone calls in the early hours of the morning all around the county. That's going to look very bad. Do you understand?'

At last he cleared his throat and leaned forward in his chair. 'All right,' he said, 'all right.'

Simon McGrath started to speak but Brian raised his hand to wave him away. 'There's no point, is there? It's all going to come out sooner or later, isn't it?'

Brian looked up again, right into Sam's eyes. She was struck with how afraid he appeared, his eyes desperate for help.

'I can't help you, Brian,' she said, quietly, 'unless you tell me the truth. Let's start from the beginning again, shall we?'

'I killed her,' he said.

Sam's heart skipped a beat. She took a slow, deep breath in, not allowing the mask of calm to slip. 'Who?'

'Barbara. My wife. I pushed her over the edge of the quarry. So what is it you want me to tell you?'

10:27

Flora was taking too long. It wasn't the traffic. It just felt as though time itself had slowed and she was fighting against it. Fighting against everything, now.

374

Going to the police station had been a mistake. What did she expect them to do? What could she prove? Nothing. They wanted evidence. And what evidence could she give them? All the stuff in the boxes, there was no point in giving them that. Apart from the voicemail message she had left on that phone, none of it had anything to do with Polly. And the message, by itself, proved nothing. They would take it and keep it on file and nothing would happen.

They were all scared of Nigel and Joe Lorenzo, the police. He was too difficult for them to touch. It made them reluctant to do anything, and as a result he kept getting away with it. He had been getting away with it for years.

Flora took a detour past the studio, to check that everything was as she had left it. Her intention had only been to check the car park, to look for the Land Rover or the Mitsubishi pick-up, but once she was there and saw the car park was completely empty, she pulled in and turned off the engine.

Upstairs, the air was freezing cold. She glanced around the main studio, but nothing had been disturbed. The kitchen, too, was as she had left it this morning: her blanket in a pile on the floor, unwashed mugs in the sink, the radio on the counter. She pulled open the cupboard door, and inside were the two boxes.

She could take it with her.

She had thought this before. In fact, over the past few hours the thought had been there, persistently at the front of her mind, nagging, pestering. She could take the gun, threaten him with it. See if that did the trick.

A few minutes later, back out in the car, Flora was heading towards Morden again.

When Taryn had arrived at the police station she had been tense and tearful. Sam Hollands had phoned her at home, and when she heard the words 'I'm calling about your father', her immediate thought had been that he had suffered another heart attack and died. She barely registered what Sam said next, because her reaction to the thought of him dying had taken her completely by surprise. Despite how she'd felt, especially recently, being forced into being nice and kind and all the things she thought she was anyway, she had never thought for one moment she would feel this dramatic wrench of sorrow.

And then Taryn realised that Sam wasn't calling to tell her he was dead, after all, and she had to ask Sam to repeat what she had said.

Arrested.

Immediately she had so many questions: Where? When? What do I need to do? And all she could think was how Barbara had somehow engineered this, must have somehow set him up to take the blame. She had come straight away, phoning Flora on the way, fretting and panicking and working herself up into a state because Flora wasn't answering, and everything was made worse because she couldn't find a parking space.

'Mrs Lewis?'

Taryn looked to her right, and saw a smartly dressed young woman holding open the door that led back towards the front counter.

'My name is Detective Chief Inspector Lou Smith,' said the woman, offering her hand. Taryn shook it, confused. 'Can I call you Taryn? I wonder if we could have a quick word? Let's go in here, shall we?'

They were in a small interview room, nothing in it but a desk and two chairs either side of it.

'Have a seat. I was hoping to talk to Flora. She was here earlier but she left. I don't suppose you know where she is?'

Taryn reached into her bag for her phone, checked it. No missed calls, no texts. 'I didn't know she was here. I tried to ring her, but she didn't answer. Is she all right?'

'I don't know. I have to say I'm quite concerned about her.'

'Are you?' Taryn said.

'Before you arrived, she asked to see me. She seemed quite agitated. And yet when we had a few minutes to talk, she seemed uncertain and confused.'

'I don't think she's been sleeping. She's been so upset, you know. About Polly.'

'Understandable,' Lou Smith said. 'I believe she and Polly were in a relationship for a time.'

'Yes. She was devastated by what happened. I'm worried she's not coping.'

'Taryn, I have some news about your father. We've just charged him with murder.'

Taryn didn't answer for a moment. Unlike Flora, unlike her father, she had never felt any distrust of the police. In fact, she had rather liked that tall, chunky one who had met up with them in the café. Sam Hollands had been so kind to her, and now this woman, who seemed so genuine too. She couldn't think of anything to say.

'He'll be taken before the magistrate in the morning. We'll continue to interview him until then, but we will make sure he gets plenty of rest and the custody nurse will be keeping a close eye on him, so you don't need to worry.'

Taryn cleared her throat. 'Can I see him?'

'Maybe later. It's all a bit hectic right now. I'll make sure we keep you updated.'

'Thank you,' Taryn said, as though Lou had offered her sympathies. She hadn't. Then another thing occurred to her: 'Does he need anything?'

'I'll make sure someone asks him. He might like a suit to wear in the morning.'

'Of course.'

Lou smiled. 'We're doing everything we can to minimise the stress of the situation, so try not to worry. But I'm afraid we're running an investigation into a very serious offence. We need to establish exactly what happened as quickly as possible.'

'And you think my dad killed Polly?'

Lou's eyes flicked up to meet Taryn's. 'What makes you say that?'

'I don't know what he was arrested for. Nobody's told me.'

'He's been charged with the murder of Barbara Fletcher-Norman.'

Taryn was confused again. 'But I thought she killed herself? She drove herself over the edge of the quarry, didn't she?'

'There are still a lot of questions we're trying to answer.'

Taryn said: 'He said something really strange to me, on the phone. He called last night to tell me he was being discharged from the hospital today, he asked me to come and pick him up . . . and we were talking about Barbara, and he said "she liked to kill people". I didn't know what he meant. I mean, I assumed he meant Polly, but even so . . . it was such a strange thing.'

'You're sure he was talking about Barbara?'

'I thought he was, but now . . . I don't know. I'm sorry, I really don't know. He sounded quite casual about it, I don't think I took what he said seriously.'

Lou Smith leaned forward in her chair. 'Taryn. I think it's really,

really important that I find Flora. Do you have any idea where she might have gone?'

11:14

It was only when she parked outside Yonder Cottage that Flora noticed her hands were shaking. She gripped the steering wheel tighter to see if that would help. Deep breaths. She needed to chill out. She needed to think.

But there was no time to think any more.

She got out of the car and slammed the door behind her, setting off up the driveway. A moment later she was passing the stables. Behind them, in the paddock, Elki stood by the gate chewing, watching her. The other horses were all out in the field with her, where she had left them this morning.

She carried on round the bend at the top of the driveway. Of course, she could have driven all the way up and parked outside the barn, but she needed a few moments – cold air on her face, the smell of the farm, a chance to get her bearings.

The door to the barn was open, the Land Rover parked outside. She walked in without hesitation, over to the office. Nigel was sitting inside, watching her approach through the glass panel in the door. He had a glass in his hand, whisky already even though it wasn't lunchtime. His face was florid.

Flora did not knock, just opened the door and went in.

'You might as well sit down,' he said, after a moment.

She sat.

'You look worse than I thought you would,' he said. 'Where did you sleep?'

She shrugged. 'I didn't sleep.'

'Figures.'

379

He offered her the bottle of whisky and she took it, gulping it back in the hope that it would help, somehow give her the courage that she desperately needed.

'So,' he said. 'What is it you want, Flora? I'm guessing you're here because you want something.'

'I want to know what happened,' she said.

'It's not what you think,' he said.

'Don't tell me what I think!' Her anger was swift, out of nowhere. She tried to calm it again with a big gulp of whisky, fire going down her throat. 'Just – just tell me the truth, if you can.'

He took a deep breath in, his bright blue eyes studying her. 'Here's the deal, then. I will tell you everything that happened that night. You will then go and get the items you removed from Petrie's house last night, and bring them back here. After that, we will decide how we can move on from this. Agreed?'

So he knew. Despite the pulse pounding in her head, the fear that this was all some sort of trick, Flora nodded. 'Agreed.'

'There was a delivery that night. Something went wrong and it turned up here at the farm instead of the place where the driver should have gone.'

He didn't continue for a moment, looking across Flora's shoulder as though he was remembering it.

'A delivery of what? People?'

He didn't answer the question, but carried on as though he hadn't heard. 'It was late, it was dark, I had them on my phone telling me to sort it out and I was getting angry because all of this should have been straightforward.'

'Who's "them"?'

'Friends of mine. Believe me, that's something you don't want to know.'

He drank from his glass as though it was water. Flora passed him the bottle so he could refill his glass, and then accepted it back from him and drank some more, pretending she wasn't trying to match him gulp for gulp. If he wanted an anaesthetic against this awful discussion, so did she.

'What's that got to do with Polly?'

'Polly had been out somewhere. The lorry was blocking the drive so she couldn't get in and she drove round the other way, to the farmhouse, and walked back down through the yard. She saw me and came over, asked me what was going on. I told her it was a feed delivery that had come in the wrong way.'

He stopped and his eyes went up to the ceiling. Flora realised he was actually showing some emotion now. She knew how that felt: recalling Polly, remembering her alive. Every thought of her, walking, talking, breathing, smiling – it hurt like a weapon.

'She didn't believe a word of it,' he said.

'I'm not surprised.'

'I told her to go back to the cottage and stay there, told her to go to bed. But she was, I don't know, weird. She'd been crying and she was unsteady on her feet, as though she was drunk. And she was all dressed up. She looked . . . she looked . . . '

He put the glass down carefully, deliberately, on top of the papers on the desk and ran his hand across his face, through his hair.

'Then what happened?'

'She kept demanding to know what was going on. And I got the impression she didn't even really give a shit, she just wanted someone to shout at. She wanted an argument. And the driver, the driver of the lorry, he'd been making phone calls, I'd been making phone calls. And then the Petrie boy turned up with some others. I'd sent him off to get some help, meaning he should find somewhere else for the lorry to park up overnight and do the handover, and instead of doing that the stupid little fucker had gone and got half of his crazy family. And everyone was standing around arguing, and Polly was there, arguing too, even though it had nothing at all to do with her. I kept thinking the neighbours were going to hear, that Brian or that mad wife of his would hear and call the police.'

A tear slid down Nigel's cheek, and the sight of it was somehow more alarming than anything she'd seen or heard today.

'I could have done something,' he said. 'I had no idea it would end up the way it did.'

He rubbed the tear away, sniffed. 'Anyway, in the end she'd had enough and she went back to the cottage. We managed to reverse the lorry out, went ahead with the rendezvous in a different location. It took hours, during which she phoned and left a message on my voicemail to have a go at me all over again. I tried to call back, but there was no answer so I assumed she must have gone to bed. I went back to the farmhouse. I hadn't realised Polly's car was still parked outside. The keys were inside, so I drove it round to the cottage. All the lights were off and I walked back round and went in the house.'

He fell silent again.

The whisky was making Flora's lips feel numb, and asking questions felt like a chore, like an effort.

'That's it?'

'Yes. Flora, I don't know for sure what happened to Polly.'

'But you think it was one of the men who were here? One of your friends?'

'It's possible, although I don't know why. They're fucked in the head, half of them off their brains on gear of one sort or another. I don't think it was Petrie, unless one of his uncles told him to do it.

He may be weird, but I don't think he could cope with that level of violence without giving himself away afterwards.'

Flora thought about it. She thought about Petrie, the weaselly little shit, with his hands on Polly. Her brain was working better now. The alcohol, maybe. Gradually things were starting to make sense.

'You said ... you said to that man, who was in here yesterday. You said that he'd seen something. You were talking about Petrie. You said, "You'd be mental too, if you'd seen what he'd seen." What was that all about?'

Nigel didn't answer. He was swilling whisky round his mouth as if it was mouthwash before swallowing it in big gulps. His glass, once again, was empty. He reached for the bottle, refilled his glass and put it back on the table between them.

'Dad? What did you mean?'

'Petrie was acting up the next day. Excitable. I thought it was just because he'd had a late night. Then, when all the police were here in the afternoon, he told me he'd seen all the blood.'

'*What?*'

'I asked him what he meant. He said he'd been in to see Polly, early. He used to call for her on the way to the stables sometimes, did you know that? He said he'd gone in the back door and seen the blood. He said he'd been scared and had gone home for a few hours.'

'Dad, why didn't you tell the police?'

'Oh, have a word with yourself, Flora. The kid knows way too much about the business. Think he'd just stick to what he's told to say?'

'So what did you do?'

'What do you think? I told him he'd imagined it and sent him home.'

383

'He *imagined it*? Are you serious?'

Nigel laughed briefly. 'I know. But it seemed to work. Then on Saturday I went round and had a long conversation with him and his dad, made our position clear. He's been all right since then.'

There was another question she needed to ask, something that had been plaguing her for days.

'You know Mum thinks you're Polly's—'

'I know what your mother thinks. She's got this idea in her head that I had an affair with Cassandra Leuchars and Polly was the result. Right?'

Flora nodded.

'I don't know, is the honest answer. Cassandra told us all that Polly was conceived after she came back to the UK, that she went and got herself pregnant thanks to some donor centre, or whatever they call it. We didn't see her again for nearly three years because they went off to the States and I didn't think any more of it. Look, does it even matter?'

Her mouth dropped open. 'Of course it fucking matters! Are you *mad*?'

'Flora,' he said. 'Don't raise your voice.'

'You were screwing her, Dad, and I was in love with her. She could have been your daughter! She could have been my sister!'

He sighed, so calm, so matter-of-fact. 'It's incredibly unlikely. I only slept with her mother once or twice, and believe me Cass Leuchars was sleeping with absolutely bloody everyone. And it's not as if I wasn't careful. Do you have any more questions, Flora, because this subject is now closed.'

Flora gritted her teeth. He'd taken advantage of Polly, hadn't he? He might have told her that their relationship had only been sexual

384

in the last few months, but why should she believe him? He might have been abusing her for years. They'd all taken advantage of her, hadn't they? All the people she'd got involved with. They'd all been prepared to take whatever Polly gave, because she was generous and kind and loving and she had so much love it was spilling out of her, love and pleasure and desire. And none of them had been there when Polly needed them. None of them.

Not even Flora.

'We had a deal, Flora.' Nigel's voice was perfectly calm. 'Now I expect you to go and get me those items. Come straight back here and there will be no more said about it. Understand?'

She stood up, unsteadily. She was clearly in no fit state to drive, but he let her go. The air outside the barn was colder, the breeze bringing her back to life again. It wasn't far to the studio. The chances were, she might only pass one or two cars on the way.

11:49

It was a relief, in the end.

They took Brian back to his cell and shut the door, locked it. It wasn't silent, it wasn't even quiet, he could hear shouting from somewhere further down the corridor, the officers laughing and joking at the desk, but it was good to be alone for a moment.

He hadn't cried in years. He hadn't cried when Barbara died, he hadn't felt much need to cry with pain or self-pity when he'd been in the hospital, even though he'd felt plenty of both. But he cried in his cell. Shoulders shaking, tears squeezing from between tightly closed eyelids, face in his hands.

Just a few moments, that was enough. He pulled himself together quickly. *Can't be doing with it, no point.*

The cell door opened again and they brought him food, pasta with some sort of sauce, a bread roll, a yoghurt and a paper cup of water.

'All right, Brian?' the custody officer asked him. 'Want any magazines, anything like that?'

He shook his head, accepting the tray onto the plastic mattress next to him.

'Can I see my daughter?'

'I'll see if I can sort something out. But you're feeling all right? You don't need the nurse?'

The nurse, oh God, the nurse. He'd be perfectly happy if he never saw the woman again, heart attack or no heart attack.

The officer went away again. They'd already explained all the rules to him, what he could expect from them. He had been charged with the murder of his wife and he was to be taken to the Magistrate's Court tomorrow morning. There was no likelihood of bail. Seeing the magistrate was going to be amusing, Brian thought. He knew most of them; some of them he counted amongst his close friends.

The food remained untouched next to him. It smelled odd, synthetic. Even the water, when he got close to it, had a metallic odour that put him off.

In the end, he had decided it would be better all round if he told the truth about what he'd done. He was so tired, in any case, so fed up with the whole thing. He could not even blame it on a momentary lapse of judgement because there had been so many of them over the years, starting with the first time he was unfaithful to his first wife, to Jean, Taryn's mother. Because once you'd done it once there was no point not doing it, was there? If he'd remained faithful, he would never have misbehaved with Polly, he would never have met

386

Suzanne, and if he'd argued with his wife and she had fallen, he would not have allowed himself to be persuaded that killing her instead of calling an ambulance was the best course of action.

Once the admission had been made, Simon McGrath, who had been almost jumping out of his seat, changed his stance towards damage limitation, told him exactly what he might expect and how he could still get off with a lighter sentence, particularly if there was evidence that he had been coerced into this course of action by his partner.

Tired of it, so tired. He listened to McGrath and nodded, and then went ahead and answered their questions anyway.

The woman who was doing most of the questioning, with the hint of a Brummie accent, did not give anything away. The man beside her straightened in his chair, flushed, and began to fidget as Brian explained what had happened, bit by bit. Every time they asked him a question in relation to Suzanne, that would have implicated her in any of it, he answered with a 'no comment'.

No comment, nothing to say about that. No comment . . .

He owed her nothing, but he felt safer to leave her out of it. Taking the blame for Barbara at least meant he didn't have to see Suzanne again, didn't have to confront her, feel the force of her disapproval.

It ended with more questions about Polly.

'I don't know anything about that,' he'd said.

'Did you see Polly that night?'

'I don't remember.'

'Brian,' Sam Hollands had said. 'Let's not start that again.'

He waited for the question, looking at them both.

'We have fingerprints in Polly's car – on the steering wheel, the handbrake and the gearstick, among other places – which have been identified as yours. So the evidence suggests that at some point recently you drove Polly's car. What can you tell us about that?'

He had had to provide his fingerprints, along with a cheek swab, a search and the loss of the last vestiges of his dignity when he'd been brought in. He hadn't even thought about it.

He took his time answering, considered making up some story about helping her to park the car earlier in the week, but there was no point. He wanted to get it all over with. The trick of it was thinking about what to say without going into detail.

'I saw Polly in town. She was upset because she had arranged to meet a friend who had not turned up and I offered to drive her home, because I thought she might have been drinking. So I drove her home.'

'Which friend?'

'She didn't say.'

'Come on, Brian. You drove her some distance and she was upset, but she didn't say who had upset her?'

'I don't remember.'

'Where did you meet her?'

'In town, somewhere. I don't remember.'

Sam Hollands had paused then, checked her notes, taken her time with the next question. He took the opportunity to fill the pause, hoping that this would deflect her attention away from Suzanne.

'When we got back to Morden there was a lorry blocking the drive to Yonder Cottage, so I pulled in to the drive of the Barn, across the road, and got out of the car to see what was going on. Polly climbed into the driver's seat and drove up the road to go in the other drive, the one that leads to the farmhouse. That was the last I saw of her.'

'What time was this, Brian?'

'I don't know. Late. Half past eleven, maybe twelve.'

'And what did you do then?'

'I went home and had a bath, as I said.'

There were more questions about Polly. They explained to him about the shot-put, suggesting he had taken it to the quarry and thrown it over. He had not. They explained that they believed it was possible he had killed Polly in order to frame Barbara for murder. He had done nothing of the kind.

Time passed. They were still having regular breaks, but now they took him back to his cell, leaving the nurse outside, for which he was grateful. She kept checking his blood pressure and that was about it.

When they charged him with Barbara's murder, it was a relief. Now he would get some peace, he would be able to rest.

He picked up the tray of food, which had long since grown cold, and moved it over to the floor beside the cell door. He moved like an old man because sitting in one position had made him stiff and his shoulder twinged when he bent down with the tray. Then he went back to the bed and lay down on his side. Everything was uncomfortable, but he was going to have to start learning to put up with it.

Soon he would get to see Taryn again, at least. The thought of that made him smile. The only thing he had left now was her.

12:14

Hamilton had had a queasy, off feeling all morning. This wasn't like him. Yes, he was a player, yes, he liked flirting and misbehaving when the opportunity presented itself – but this was a whole new ballgame. The situation, which had started with her telling him about Brian's calculated plan to get rid of his wife, which back then

389

had seemed almost straightforward, was now beginning to feel uncomfortable. He was used to working as part of a team. This new policy of going it alone – which admittedly was brought about by his failure to behave himself – was not sitting well.

Karen and the kids had gone round to visit her sister, and although he had promised to stay home and put some things in the loft, he found himself pacing the living room, trying to find the way to get himself out of the mess.

In the end, he dialled Lou's number, half-expecting to get her voicemail. But she answered.

'Andy?'

'Sorry to bother you, boss,' he said, keeping his tone light. 'Just wondering how it went this morning.'

He could hear the sound of her heels on a linoleum floor. That meant she was in a custody suite, probably Briarstone nick.

'All fine so far.'

'Has he said anything?'

'We've just charged him. He's admitted to killing his wife – accidentally. Nothing about Polly.'

'What about that woman he was seeing?'

'No comment to that. He's having a rest now while we get everything ready for the magistrate tomorrow morning.'

This was the moment he should have told her what was going on. Not ideal to do it over the phone, but equally the longer he went on like this, the worse it would be once the suits at Professional Standards got hold of him.

'Is everything OK with you?' Lou asked. The faint echo had gone; she must have got herself into an office.

'Yeah, yeah. I think – I don't know – I might have a few answers.'

'About what?'

'A – a few loose ends. It can wait until tomorrow morning.' Brian would get charged no matter what. Nothing Andy told them now would affect the visit to the magistrate tomorrow anyway. Better to think everything through, plan how to tackle it. Make sure he had all the facts.

'Andy, I don't like being kept in the dark. You know that. If you want to talk to me about it—'

'No, no. Honestly, it's fine. I'll be in tomorrow, we can talk then.'

And after he'd rung off, there had been nothing left to do but get into his car and drive across town. He parked outside 14 Waterside Gardens. And before he could talk himself out of it, he was knocking on her door.

Suzanne opened the door promptly, as if she'd been expecting him, and let him inside. She was dressed in smart black jeans, a beige cashmere sweater, simple gold earrings. As always, she looked immaculate, and calm.

'No uniform today?' he said, trying to sound jovial.

'It's my day off,' she said. 'I was half expecting to see you, Inspector. I wanted to make sure I was appropriately dressed.'

'I came to tell you Brian's been charged. He's admitted to dumping Barbara Fletcher-Norman in the quarry.'

Suzanne looked up at him sharply. 'Really? Good heavens.'

'Don't worry. He refused to answer any questions about you.'

That made her smile. 'Good for him.'

'There wasn't enough evidence to charge him with Polly's murder, though.'

She seemed perfectly at ease with this idea. 'Would you like a coffee?' she asked brightly. 'It's a bit early for wine, I think.'

'Coffee would be nice.'

'Are you here for sex, Inspector Hamilton? Or are we just going to talk today?'

She was clearly amused by his expression. He should know her well enough by now to realise that she took delight in wrong-footing him.

'Well. I – er – I don't think I would turn it down. If it's on offer.'

Suzanne laughed, ran her fingers through her hair. 'Very well, then. Let's have coffee first, shall we?'

He followed her into the kitchen, leaned against the kitchen table and watched her as she busied herself with an expensive-looking coffee machine, retrieved two plain white cups from the cupboard, added tablet sweetener to one of them. Just a couple of days ago she had felt him up in here, left him shocked and breathless. It felt like years ago.

He moved up behind her and placed a hand in the small of her back. She flinched slightly. Behind her, then, sliding his hands around her waist and holding her against him while the coffee machine made a loud churning noise and dribbled dark liquid into the two cups.

'Not yet,' she said, removing his hands firmly and stepping to the side, turning to face him.

'Sorry,' he said, unsure of what he was apologising for. 'I thought—'

'You may touch me only when given permission. That's one of the first things you're going to have to learn, if we are going to enjoy this regularly. Do you understand?'

'I'm not sure,' he said. 'I mean, don't get me wrong, I really enjoy the way you do things, but I've never tried this – whatever it is – before.'

'Then I shall have to teach you. That's all part of the pleasure of it, learning what you enjoy. And the same goes for me. I have particularly enjoyed making you wait for it, seeing your face when you think I'm going to reject you. And then seeing your expression change when you realise what's coming. You give a lot away, did you know that?'

'It's all a game to you, isn't it?'

'Not at all. I am deadly serious about it.'

Andy gave a short, ironic laugh. 'Deadly. That's an interesting choice of word.'

She smiled at him. 'You're right. But this is all part of why I became a nurse. I've always enjoyed breathplay, but only within the boundaries of safety. I know what a high it gives you if you're being fucked just at the moment of losing consciousness. There is no orgasm on earth as powerful, unless you're using drugs, and that's something else entirely. But there is a risk – and at least with me you know you're safe. You're always in control, you can stop at any moment. And if you choose not to stop, and you lose consciousness, then you know I can resuscitate you if need be.'

'That's very reassuring. Where is it you work?'

She stared at him, crossing her legs at the knee. The coffee machine had stopped whirring. 'Milk and sugar?'

'Yes, please.'

She pushed one of the cups and a sugar bowl towards him, getting a spoon out of the drawer. 'Help yourself.'

While he stirred in some sugar – two spoons, he had a feeling he was going to need the energy – she got a carton of milk out of the fridge and passed it over to him.

'I'm doing agency nursing at the moment,' she said. 'I was working overseas until two months ago.'

'Whereabouts?'

393

'Oh, all over the world. I was in Dubai for most of this year.'

'Sounds great. Why did you come back?'

Suzanne laughed. 'Even sunshine gets boring after a while. Shall we go and sit down?'

She carried both cups into the living room, put them on the low table, and eased herself onto the sofa.

'I can't believe how calm you are,' he said.

'I'm a good actress, Inspector Hamilton. You'll get to appreciate that when we have more time to play together.'

Play? Such an odd word to use. There wasn't anything casual or recreational about it. What she did was focused, determined, meticulous.

'I wish you'd call me Andy.'

'If I do that it will change the dynamic of the relationship,' she said. 'I like things the way they are.'

He picked up the coffee and tasted it. One of those fancy ones, flavoured with something – hazelnuts? Caramel? It wasn't bad, anyway. Maybe needed another sugar. He was aware of her eyes watching his movements closely, unblinking, and for a moment, despite how relaxed she appeared, he had the impression of being stalked by a big cat, relaxed, purring, waiting to pounce.

'How did your colleagues take the news about Brian?'

'I'm on a rest day today. So I haven't told them. It might be that I don't need to.'

'That would be good for both of us, wouldn't it?'

'I need to ask you some more questions,' he said. 'There are still some things that don't make sense.'

'Such as?'

Andy took a deep breath in. 'Polly Leuchars. Her phone called your number the night she died.'

'She was just phoning to see how I was. We were friends, of course.'

'But she came over to see you. The cellsite showed the phone was in this area.'

'She called me. If they ever ask me about it officially, I will tell them she was probably visiting Flora and that they should ask her, not me. Poor Flora. I would imagine she's taken it very badly.'

'But she wasn't visiting Flora, was she?'

Suzanne smiled. 'I'm so tired of all this, you know. I wish life could hurry up and get back to normal. It's wonderfully exciting, but really rather tiresome.'

'What happened, Suzanne? You met Polly in town earlier that day, didn't you?'

She drank her coffee. 'She wouldn't seem to get the message that things were over between us. I was with Brian and I couldn't deal with her, too. I'm quite monogamous, you know, Inspector. I only have enough attention for one sub at a time. And besides, Polly was such hard work. She liked bondage in particular, you know, she liked to be restrained, and I find rope play an unnecessary chore. To do it properly, safely, takes a long time. Brian was turning out to be much more fun. So I told her quite plainly that she should move aside but she kept on and on, phoning me, asking to meet, pretending it was to be simply as friends. So I met her in town and asked her to stop calling. She said she would if I would come for one last drink with her, in the Lemon Tree. I agreed, to get rid of her.'

'But you didn't turn up?'

'Brian came over. We were busy.' As if that explained everything.

'So she drove over to Briarstone to find you?'

'Walked in through the back door. It was unlocked. Honestly, Brian's face. I asked if she wanted to join in, but she simply stood there over the bed, sobbing as if she was unhinged. She was absolutely distraught. Brian and I didn't know what to do with her. In the end, I told Brian to put his bike in Polly's car and drive her home.'

'He did that. They had an argument when they got to the Barn.'

'Yes, he phoned to tell me. The first of his many calls that evening. Polly was trying to persuade him to leave me, so that I would go back to her.'

'Then what happened?'

'You know the rest. Polly drove her car back across the road to the farm. Brian went home, but Barbara had seen him pull up in Polly's car and had assumed he'd been out shagging her. They had a lengthy argument about it, lots of shouting and yelling and long miserable silences. Quite funny, really, when you think about it. Then eventually she got all mad and went over to confront her.'

'And Brian followed her? He killed Polly while Barbara was there?'

She didn't reply, finished off her coffee instead.

Hamilton could feel the pressure building behind his eyes, the beginnings of a sore throat. He was probably run down, coming down with the flu. He felt overwhelmingly tired by the nightmarish situation that he had managed to get himself tangled up in and the knowledge that it would get worse, much worse, unless he stopped it now, called a halt to it.

'I can't see you, Suzanne, you know. I have to steer clear.'

She laughed, quite casually. 'Oh, I don't think so.'

'It's for your own security more than mine. They'll realise

396

there's something going on. The more time I spend here the more risky it is.'

'There's no risk. Not if you do as you're told. I said the same thing to Brian.'

He didn't answer straight away, let his head rest heavily back on the sofa cushions. He almost missed it, that last comment, thrown in so casually. And yet there it was, and as exhausting as it was he would have to ask: 'What do you mean, you said the same thing to Brian?'

'You're as bad as he was, Inspector Hamilton. When things start to get a little fragile in your personal lives you go to pieces. He rang me to ask me what he should do. And he would have been fine, except he just forgot the shot-put. If it hadn't been for the shot-put I wouldn't have even left the house that night.'

Andy Hamilton felt the blood draining from his face and hands.

He dreamed of moments like this, of suspects who were intelligent and lucid and not actually psychotic on drugs or methylated spirits telling him exactly, truthfully, what had happened when someone had been murdered. He dreamed of it happening in an incident room, the action being neatly recorded on DVD for generations of trainee detectives and maybe a true-life TV show. He dreamed of a confession coming in response to a particularly pertinent, insightful observation, or a question he'd placed before the suspect that was so perfect they could not help but raise their hands a little in mock surrender, before uttering whatever the non-clichéd equivalent of 'it's a fair cop, guv' was these days.

But this particular confession made everything much, much worse.

What he should do, of course, was arrest her right now. She'd made a confession to him. He should cuff her and take her down and book her in, because that was what he was trained to do and to do anything else was to take him even further down the path that led away from his police pension and now, probably, towards some sort of serious misconduct charge and possibly even imprisonment himself. And yet he was so shattered, so tired, he doubted he could even manage to restrain her if he had to.

'Don't you want to hear about it?'

Not really, no, was what he wanted to say. *No, what I want to do is run away and hide from my wreck of a life.* What he actually said was: 'Go on then.'

She took a deep breath in, looked at the ceiling for inspiration. 'Where to start? Well, Brian phoned me in a panic on Wednesday night. Barbara had gone over to Yonder Cottage to confront Polly, and when she came back she was hysterical and covered in blood. Brian was trying to calm her down, trying to get her to make sense, when she slipped over on something – I guess she was drunk, that's how she was most of the time – and she hit her head on the side of the kitchen worktop and passed out. That was when he phoned me.'

'You said – last night – you told me that Brian had planned it all. He was setting her up.'

'I think you misunderstood. He saw the opportunity to pass the blame on to Barbara.'

'So if that's the case, why did he ring you? What was it he thought you could do?'

Suzanne smiled at him. 'I'm surprised you even have to ask. What is it you all want, Inspector? All of you men who think you are brave and strong and manly, but in fact are completely clueless and helpless the moment you're confronted with a problem? He wanted me to sort it out for him.'

'Why didn't he just call an ambulance?'

'Why indeed. I wondered that myself.'

'Why didn't you tell him to call an ambulance, then?'

She didn't answer for a moment.

'Because I saw the opportunity it presented. For Brian, and for myself.'

'The opportunity?'

'He had said himself. It was his idea. He was going to kill her somehow and make it look as though she committed suicide. Then she'd be out of the way and he'd be free to be with me.'

'Is that what you wanted?'

Suzanne laughed out loud, tilting her head back. 'Good grief. Of course not,' she said. 'I never thought for one minute he'd actually do it. He had no idea who had actually killed Polly, even though Barbara was raving about death and murder and blood everywhere. Brian thought she'd been in a fight, something like that. And now she'd hit her head it made it all rather awkward. Brian knew she'd try to implicate him, try to get him to take the blame for it. It was so much easier to reverse the situation, to make her take responsibility for being permanently drunk, and a nasty bitch as well.'

'You spoke to him when it happened,' Andy said. His stomach was churning in a way that made him wish the bathroom wasn't so far away, even though it was just across the hall from where he sat.

'He kept phoning me for advice. Honestly, it's like he couldn't manage to make a single decision on his own. He put Barbara in her car and then he put his pushbike in the boot. He wanted me to meet him at the quarry and give him a lift home – as if I'd do that! I wanted to be nowhere near him, or her, or any of it. In the end I had to give him a bloody list of instructions of things to do, things not to forget. Put her seatbelt on. Make sure you don't adjust her driving position in the car, even if it's difficult to drive it like that. Check the boot of the car before you push it over the edge. Take clean clothes with you to change into and get rid of the clothes you were wearing when you did it. Have a bath when you get home. Don't clean Polly's blood out of the kitchen. It was quite simple, really. Assume Barbara had done something horrible to poor Polly, let her take responsibility for it.'

'And he rang you when he was done?'

'He told me he'd found the suitcase with her clothes in it in the boot of the car.'

'Why couldn't Brian simply have phoned the police instead of killing her? She would have ended up getting the blame anyway.'

Suzanne looked at him as if he was dense. 'She had a head wound. He'd pushed her against the side of the worktop and she was unconscious. I believe he also told me that she'd wet herself, which was a detail more than I really needed, but it served to tell me that she was quite badly hurt. We couldn't risk Brian being charged with her murder, or GBH, or whatever it would have been.'

'I guess not.' It was hard to focus. All this information – the thought of all this running around in the middle of the night, Brian cycling from Briarstone to Morden – no wonder they hadn't found his car on the ANPR when they'd looked. And the small nugget of consolation – he'd been right about that bike. The one in the ditch, covered in mud and tufts of grass. Brian had cycled back from the quarry.

'It was all fine until Brian was on the way home. He phoned me, all out of breath because he was cycling through a field, and he said we should have got something more concrete to link Barbara to Polly, to be on the safe side.'

'Why couldn't Brian sort that out when he got home?'

She sighed. 'Because there was a limit to what I could trust Brian not to fuck up, Inspector. Pushing Barbara off a cliff edge was one thing, going into Polly's house when he didn't need to was something else entirely.'

'So you did it yourself?'

'I did it myself.'

'Polly was – dead?'

'Very much so.'

'Weren't you worried about leaving forensic evidence?'

'Of course. I was quite careful, but you would have needed a reason to link me to the scene, and there wasn't much chance of that. Besides, I believed that once your lot had found Barbara covered in blood, then you'd stop looking for anyone else.'

She smiled at him, completely calm. It dawned on him that she was mentally unstable, might actually be a complete psychopath, and she was telling him all of this because she knew he wasn't going to survive to share the story further.

A second later and he had dismissed the thought. He was a good judge of character, always had been; and he had a nose for trouble. He was always the first to spot the fight that was about to kick off, the disagreement that was going to escalate to the use of a weapon. He was famous for it. And she was telling him all this, the whole story, because she trusted him. She was afraid of Brian, wasn't she? *Brian* was the one who'd killed his wife. Suzanne had been terrified, had turned to Andy for protection, for advice. He couldn't go back on it now. There was no path back the way he had come, there was only the path ahead. His head span, his stomach growled and churned.

'So you took the shot-put?'

'I took a bag with me. It was quite obvious that it had been the weapon. It was lying right next to her head, covered in blood. I'm assuming they found it, by the way?'

He nodded, deliberately choosing not to add that they'd worked out quite quickly that it had been thrown from the top of the quarry after the car had gone over.

'So, you see, I don't really see that there's cause to worry. What can they prove? That Brian phoned me several times over the course of the evening.'

'Is that what you're going to say in interview? Your solicitor will probably advise you to go no comment. Just so you know.'

She considered this. 'I'll worry about it when it happens. I'm good at thinking on my feet, you know.'

Really? he thought, *I'd never have guessed.*

'What would happen if they knew what I've told you? And that you didn't share that information?'

'I'd get the sack. Lose my pension. Probably face criminal charges.'

'Criminal charges, really? Goodness, how dramatic.' She laughed again and her voice was light when she spoke. 'It puts you in a very tight situation, doesn't it?'

'We trust each other. You've trusted me, and I trust you,' he said. His voice sounded as if it came from a long way away, as though he was under water.

'And it's working fine so far, isn't it? So let's just carry on as we are.'

That was clearly the end of the discussion. Andy was worried for a moment that he had made her angry, somehow, but there didn't seem to be much he could do about it.

She said to him, her voice low, 'Aren't you going to finish your coffee? Or do you want me to make you another?'

12:15

The MIR was empty. A few minutes later Lou found Jason in the canteen, halfway through a sandwich. He waved at her, waited while she queued up to get a coffee and a Cornish pasty.

'Good to see you eating properly,' he commented, when she sat down opposite him.

'I'll have a vegan stir fry later, all right?'

'How's it going up the road?'

She lowered her voice, but there was nobody within earshot of them. 'We charged Brian. He admitted pushing Barbara's car over the edge of the quarry. He came out with this long explanation of how she fell over and hit her head, and he thought he'd end up getting into trouble for it so he went to the effort of trying to make it look like she'd killed herself.'

Jason nodded. 'It's crazy enough to be true.'

'Les contacted Adele Francis who did the PM – she said that the open skull fracture could well have masked an earlier head injury. She's going to take another look. We should hear back by tomorrow.'

'What about Polly?'

'He still claims Barbara must have done it, but he's wavering. In all honesty I don't think he knows what happened to her.'

'And Suzanne Martin?' Jason asked.

'Interesting, but frustrating. He went "no comment" every time her name came up.'

'You think he's protecting her?'

'Quite possibly. I'm going to go over his interview now and see if there's anything in there we can use, but for now I think we should bring her in for questioning and see what she has to say for herself.'

She bit the end off the pasty and blew the steam out of the interior of it.

'You're gonna enjoy that,' he said.

'Absolutely.'

'What kind of meat is it?'

'No idea. Could be anything.'

He shook his head slowly. 'It's not like there aren't some healthy choices up there.'

She put the pasty down slowly and decided to change the subject before she got seriously pissed off with him. 'I'm also worried about Flora.'

'How come?'

'She was at the nick when it opened this morning, asking to see whoever was in charge. I went down, but she didn't seem that keen to talk. Then we had to start things off with Brian, and when I got back to the interview room Flora had gone.'

'That could have been about anything,' Jason said.

'You didn't see her – she looked like she was falling apart.'

Jason considered this while Lou chewed.

'She seems to have taken Polly's death particularly hard,' Jason said. 'I don't think there's anything weird about that. Love does that to people.'

He had finished his sandwich and was watching her eat with an intense interest that Lou found disconcerting. Eventually she put the pasty down, wiped her hands and mouth on the paper napkin. 'Why are you so obsessed with what I'm eating?'

Jason had the grace to look a little embarrassed. 'Well, you know. Your arteries. You kinda need them?'

She had finished, anyway. The rest of it didn't look nearly as appetising.

'What are your plans for the rest of the day?' he asked.

Lou drank half of her coffee in one big gulp. 'I need to go and see Mr Buchanan. Get that out of the way as quick as I can. Then I'm going to take someone and go and look for Flora Maitland.'

'Isn't Andy Hamilton supposed to be watching out for her?'

'It's his day off. Isn't that typical?'

12:25

'What if I told you it was me?'

Andy Hamilton was lying stretched out on Suzanne's bed, fully dressed, although she had undone his jeans, taken off his shoes. He was feeling queasy. Definitely coming down with something. And he felt so tired – exhausted. His eyes were closed and it felt like an overwhelming effort to open them.

He hadn't fully heard what she said, but registered it as somehow important. 'What? What did you say?'

'I said, what if I told you it was me?'

'You said you'd always tell the truth, Suzanne,' he said, his tone measured.

'And so I do,' she said. 'So I'll tell you. I killed her.'

'We're talking about Polly?'

'Of course.'

There was silence for a moment. He stared at her, trying to focus. So many things he needed to ask, and how to handle this? How to deal with it? And he could have been cleverer with his questions, but all he could manage to ask was: 'What happened?'

'She was such a nuisance. I was fed up with it. After she turned up at the flat uninvited I was just so angry with her. I went in to the cottage, up to her bedroom. We talked for a little while. She wanted me to tie her up, I refused. She wanted me to choke her. I did that

405

for a bit but then she got upset again, so I stopped. She was getting to be so difficult, so tiresome – she didn't know what she wanted. If I left things as they were I had no idea what she might do. I tried to leave, and she began screaming and flinging herself at me. We got down the stairs and she was holding on to me. I reached for something to get her to let go, and in the end I hit her with that shot-put just to get her to shut up.'

Hamilton felt sick. So casual. She was so fucking casual about it, it was terrifying.

'You must have been covered in blood,' was all he could think to say.

'Yes, it was a little messy. I took a pair of Polly's jeans and one of her sweaters from the laundry basket in the kitchen. When I was getting changed I heard Barbara coming in. She was swaying and I could see she was going to get the fright of her life, but it was really rather funny to watch. She didn't even see me because I'd gone into the downstairs cloakroom. She ran out again a few moments after that.'

'What did you do with your clothes?'

'I put them in a big brown paper bag and hid it in the middle of the pile of bonfire pallets they set alight in the park yesterday,' she said. 'I'd be surprised if there's anything left. Big effigy of the Prime Minister on top of it, I believe.'

She had drugged him, somehow. The thought came to his aware-ness teasingly, hovering out of reach and then, when he grasped at it, the realisation made his heart beat faster, made him start to panic. There had been something in that coffee. Was it all part of her game, her fetish?

He tried to focus, tried to put all his efforts into sitting up, get-ting the hell out of here.

'It's all right,' she said, soothingly. Her hand was on his chest, pushing him gently back. 'You don't need to move. You don't need to worry about a thing. I need to go out in a minute, and I want to make sure you're safe while I'm gone.'

'Where're you going?' he said. His voice was slurred, like he was beyond drunk.

'It doesn't matter. I just have some errands to run. But I need you to stay here and sleep, and then, when I get home, we can continue your training if you like. I have so many delicious things to teach you.'

'I need to go ... to work. They'll come looking for me ... '

She laughed. 'No, it's your day off, remember? Your "rest day". So you can rest here.'

The tiredness was like a heavy blanket, covering his whole body. Something over his face, too, something soft, the breath of something brushing his cheek. Somehow it was too much effort to open his eyes.

He could feel something pulling, moving him about, his body inert. There were noises, too, someone else breathing. He fought through the glue in his brain, trying to think, trying to concentrate. Her. It was her.

'I'd like to say I'm sorry,' he heard her say. 'I should be sorry, shouldn't I?'

He tried to move a hand, lift the hand as she had told him to, if he wanted it to stop. He wanted her to stop whatever she was doing, let him rest, let him sleep.

'I'm running out of options,' she said. 'This is the only way left ... '

He murmured.

'It's all right,' she said, soothingly, her voice close to his ear. 'I'll take good care of you, Inspector Hamilton.'

407

It would be so easy to sleep.

For a moment he drifted, warm and quiet and left alone, and everything was fine.

Minutes passed.

Something happened that made him aware again. The warmth had gone and there was a chill, a breeze moving over the skin of his body. His face was hot, a sheen of sweat on his forehead. The air around his face was warm, damp. He could not move his limbs. Something about his breathing sounded odd, enclosed. He forced his eyes open and saw only a pale light, diffused, foggy, in an odd oval shape with darkness at the edges. Like looking down a tunnel. They said death was like this, wasn't it? He needed to head towards the light if there was a tunnel and the thought of it made him want to laugh. He tried experimentally to move but nothing worked.

His chest so heavy that even breathing was hard work, so much hard work. Easier to sleep. Easier to just let go.

12:25

The visit to Buchanan's office had been mercifully brief: the Superintendent had gone for an emergency dental appointment. Lou left a message with the assistants that she would brief him whenever he was free, then raced back to the MIR, phoning Sam as she did so.

Of all the people to take with her, Sam Hollands was probably the one she should not have chosen. She was busy going over this morning's interview, checking things, preparing for the trip to the Magistrate's Court in the morning. But Sam was the one Lou trusted the most. And she was probably in desperate need of some fresh air.

A few minutes later, Sam was behind the wheel of a Ford Focus belonging to Area CID. All the Major Crime job cars seemed to be in use. Despite the rules about keeping cars clean inside and out – you were supposed to run a vehicle check before you got in one, for heaven's sake – this one looked like the inside of a High Street litter bin on a Saturday morning. Crisp packets, takeaway bags, newspapers – all shoved into the back seat.

Lou opened a window slightly to get rid of the scent of burger and testosterone.

They went to the farm, first, and nobody seemed to be home. The farmhouse was locked up, the offices all closed and empty. No sign of any cars. For a few minutes Lou looked down the drive back towards Yonder Cottage, the stables on her left.

'Where is everybody? Place is like a ghost town,' Sam said.

'Do you know where Flora's studio is?'

'Not offhand.'

Lou turned and headed back towards the car. 'I'll look it up while you drive,' she said. 'It can't be far.'

In the end, they never made it to the studio. They were heading through Briarstone when Les Finnegan phoned Lou's mobile.

'Ma'am. Where are you?'

'London Road, stuck in traffic. What's up?'

'I'm just ahead of you at an RTA. Cause of your traffic jam. Can you get here quick? It's Flora Maitland. You won't believe what she's got in her car.'

Deploying the blue lights and siren scared the crap out of the young lad in the stationary car immediately in front of them, but to give him his due, he moved neatly onto the pavement and gradually a path through the traffic opened up ahead of them like parting waves.

It wasn't far. About half a mile further up the road Flora's car was embracing a lamp-post. An ambulance was already on the scene, as was Eden Fire and Rescue Service, who were in the process of preparing to cut the roof of the car away to get to the driver.

Sam pulled to the side of the road, as far out of the way as she could. Two patrols were already on the scene, one of them managing traffic, the other collaring as many witnesses as they could get their hands on. And on the pavement, grinding a cigarette with the toe of his brown leather slip-on, was Les Finnegan.

'Is she conscious, Les?' Lou said, as they got close to him.

'In and out,' he said. 'Hard to say how injured. She stinks of booze, though. I reckon she's paralytic.'

Lou looked across to the remains of the car, but there were so many fluorescent jackets grouped around the driver's window she couldn't see who was inside.

'What were you saying about the car?'

'All over the back seat: files, passports, credit cards – and this.' He held up a brown envelope and opened it enough so that Lou and Sam could see the contents.

'Jesus Christ!'

A black handgun, inside one of Les's handy clear plastic evidence bags.

'What the fuck are you doing with that?' Sam said. 'Sorry, ma'am.'

'Couldn't bloody leave it in there, could I? Not with that lot all over the car. Anyway, don't worry. I've put in a call to Firearms, they're coming to collect it.'

'I need to talk to her,' Lou said.

'They won't let you near,' said Les.

410

But she was already crossing the road, opening her warrant card and holding it up for the Fire and Rescue team leader in his white helmet on the way past.

'Not a good idea to get close,' he said. 'Can you stand back?'

'I just need a minute,' she said. 'Less than that. Please – it's really important.'

'We need to get her out. You'll have all the time you need after that.'

Lou changed the tone of her voice from one of friendly camaraderie to one that permitted no further argument. 'This is a police scene. We're just waiting for Firearms support, and I need to speak to the witness. I won't take long.'

'Put this on, then,' he said, offering her a spare helmet and a dust mask. 'You don't want to be inhaling any glass shards. And try not to get in the way.'

It was way too big and must have looked comical, but at least it gave her the authority to get in close to the smashed driver's window, next to a green-suited ambulance technician. Given the state of the car, Flora looked in reasonable shape. At some point she had vomited and the inside of the car smelled appalling; an oxygen mask was over her face, blood already drying on her cheek from a cut above her eye. A quick glance on to the back seat confirmed what Les had told her.

The medics were trying to keep Flora awake, chatting about inane things while the rescue teams prepared the cutting gear.

'Flora, can you hear me?' Lou said. She lifted the dust mask from her face briefly so that Flora could see who it was.

She couldn't move her head or turn it because they'd already managed to get a neck brace around her. 'It's you,' she said, her voice muffled slightly through the plastic mask.

411

'Yes, it's me. Lou Smith. From earlier. I'm sorry we didn't get longer to talk.'

'My dad. I have to get back.'

'Flora, earlier today you wanted to tell me something. Do you remember?'

'No ... it wasn't that. I was wrong after all.'

'You can tell me now,' Lou said. The medic who was right next to her shot her a look.

'Your – what's his name? – the big one ...'

Lou had to think for a minute. 'You mean Andy Hamilton?'

'That's it,' she said. 'Hamilton. I wish he'd leave me alone.'

Lou smiled at her. 'Shall I ask Sam to keep an eye on you instead?'

'Yeah, Sam. She's nice. I don't like the other one. He's downstairs all the time.'

'You need to move away now.' The Fire and Rescue officer had a hand on her upper arm, pulling her away.

'Downstairs? You mean waiting outside for you?'

'No,' Flora said, her voice becoming indistinct. 'The other flat.'

'I'll come and see you as soon as you're in the hospital,' Lou called. 'Try not to worry.'

Then she was taken back across the road, picking her way over bits of plastic from the smashed bollard and broken glass to where Sam was waiting. Les was sitting in the back of an unmarked van that had just arrived. Firearms, clearly, come to take charge of the weapon. Les would be briefing them ready to take over control of the scene.

'What did she say?' Sam asked. 'Is she all right?'

'I think she'll make it. I hope so, anyway. Can you do me a favour? Make sure Les stays with the car and doesn't let that evidence out of his sight, whatever Firearms say. We'll need to start bagging it as soon as the roof comes off. Don't let Traffic take over or do anything until that's done, OK? Get one of the patrols to stay with Flora, especially if she's not too badly hurt after all. I can't risk losing her again.'

'We're going to arrest her?' Sam asked.

'Soon as we can, yes, I'm afraid so.'

'And Nigel Maitland?'

'I'll see if I can get the surveillance team on him until we've been through the stuff and got enough to arrest him. Christ knows we'll need plenty of time on the clock to argue the toss with that solicitor of his.'

'Right.'

As soon as Sam had gone out of earshot, Lou pulled her mobile phone from her jacket pocket and dialled Andy Hamilton's mobile number. 'Come on,' she said. 'Answer, you piece of crap.'

There was no reply. Lou swore gently, disconnected the call and redialled the number she had called yesterday. This time, the call was answered.

'Hello?'

'Hi! Karen, it's Lou Smith. '

'He's not here. No idea where he is.'

'Oh.'

'Went out this morning, hasn't come back. If you find him, tell him to get his arse back here, would you?'

When she had promised to do just that, Lou hung up and looked around for Sam. She was with Les Finnegan, standing by the back of the Firearms van.

'Sam!' she called, already heading back to the car. This time, she was going to drive.

413

Taryn Lewis had told her – she had actually fucking *told* her everything she needed to know. Her father had said, '*She likes to kill people.*' Lou had thought Brian had been talking about Flora Maitland – but he wasn't talking about Flora at all, or Barbara for that matter. He was talking about *her.* Suzanne.

She likes to kill people . . .

12:40

'What do you think?' Lou said.

They were parked on Waterside Gardens, across the road from number 14. A single car, a black Mercedes, was parked on the gravel driveway, and further down the road, clearly in their line of sight, was Andy Hamilton's people carrier.

'I don't know. He could be . . . I mean, it's his day off, right?'

Lou frowned. 'She's a suspect, Sam. A bloody suspect. You really think he'd . . . ?'

Sam looked like she didn't want to say it, but went ahead anyway. 'You know him better than me. What do you think?'

Lou sighed heavily. 'I don't want to do this, I really don't. Everything about this feels bad.'

'What do you want to do?'

There was no official procedure, no guidelines for a situation like this one. This wasn't something they could train you for, as a Senior Investigating Officer, but then no situation was like any other, was it? They trained you to think on your feet, make decisions and hope to God they were the right ones. And if you made the wrong decision, heaven help you. You weighed up the pros and cons and you did your best. The only thing you could do.

'Try his number again,' Lou said.

'I just did. Still nothing.'

414

'OK. We need to get Tac Team down here but we're going to go in, whatever happens. Let's hope to fuck he's in there interviewing her or something sensible like that.'

Sam called it in and Lou kept her eyes on the house, the two doors side by side at the front, the one on the right would lead to Flora's first-floor flat, the other one to the ground-floor flat where Suzanne Martin lived.

'They're on their way,' Sam said.

A moment later, the door on the left opened and Sam and Lou both sat up straight. The woman who came out – who looked a lot like the figure on the CCTV footage – was in a hurry. She slammed the door and hurried over to the Merc, opening it and getting inside.

'Sam,' Lou began, as the Merc's wheels sprayed gravel in an arc, turning fast in the driveway. 'You follow her. Call back-up.'

As the Mercedes flew past, Lou got out of the car and ran across the road while Sam climbed across to the driver's seat, started the car, and moved off in pursuit.

Lou's heels crunched on the gravel as she hurried across to the house. Her mind raced through the possibilities of all the things that might confront her in this woman's flat. Not least the body of Andy Hamilton. The last thing she should do was go in there by herself.

The door had slammed fast, and would not open. She rang the doorbell, knocked on the door hard. Looked in through the letter-box. Nothing. The empty hallway stretched away towards the back of the house. A smell drifted to her. Coffee, she thought. And something else, something she could not identify.

'Andy?' she called through the letterbox.

Nothing. Not a sound. Halfway up the hallway was a door to the left, and on the floor by the door was a pile of clothes, crumpled into a heap. On top of the pile, a mobile phone. Lou reached for her own phone and speed-dialled Andy Hamilton's number – and the phone inside began to ring.

That was enough. Technically she needed a warrant to enter the premises. For her own safety, she should wait for back-up, for the proper equipment. But under these circumstances she could argue that there was a risk to life.

She went around the side of the building, looking for a back door. There was a wrought-iron gate at the side, which opened easily. And there, a second door, glass panels top and bottom. She tried it. Locked! Fuck it.

Lou went into the garden and, holding a piece of roof tile over a drain, was a brick. That would do it. She went back to the door. 'Andy!' she shouted. 'I'm coming through the back door, stand back.'

Then, one arm up shielding her eyes, she hammered the brick at the glass.

It took two blows before the glass smashed on the tiled floor of the kitchen and over the step outside. The hole was big enough to put her arm through, and to her immense relief the key was in the door on the other side. She turned it, and opened the door.

'Police!' she called. 'Anyone in here?'

Nothing. From a long way off, she could hear a siren. Was it Sam's back-up? She must have stopped the Merc . . . that was good.

She crossed the kitchen to the door at the far end. The hallway stretched up towards the front door. To her left, a door opened into the sitting room – empty. To her right, the pile of men's clothes and a closed door. *Deep breath and open.*

It took a second to register what she was seeing.

The man was stretched out on the bed, naked apart from leather straps around his ankles and wrists, which were attached to cords

416

leading to the corners of the metal bed frame. But his head – the most bizarre thing of all – was encased in a wooden box, his neck disappearing into a padded hole at its base. On the top of the box was an oval shaped hole, which should have revealed his face.

The whole box was wrapped in cling film.

A second later, she realised that he wasn't breathing.

'Andy!' She took hold of a wrist, felt for a pulse. His hand was swollen, bluish already. Kneeling on the bed she could make out his face through the cling film. He was blue. His eyes open, staring, unseeing.

'Andy! Can you hear me?' She tried to pull the cling film away, tried to tear at it with her fingers, poke holes into it, but it was layer upon layer, wrapped and wound tight, and her fingers were ineffectual.

Back to the kitchen, pulling out drawers looking for a knife, a screwdriver – something! Shit, shit – nothing. And then, the last drawer she came to, a set of stainless steel cutlery. Back to the bedroom, to the box, using a blunt dinner knife to snag at the plastic. Then there was a hole she could pull at it, make larger, and at last she could see him properly.

'*Andy!*'

Her hand inside the box, touching the skin of his face; he felt clammy. He needed air, he needed mouth-to-mouth – and there was no way she could get close enough to his mouth with the box in the way.

Yelling with frustration, back to the kitchen – scissors, there had to be a pair of scissors in here – all the time wondering about how long he'd been like this, if it was already too late to make a difference. *He was dead, he was dead. Too late.*

No. Lou pulled at the door of the dishwasher. Inside, clean and shiny, a basket full of cutlery and amongst it a black-handled sharp kitchen knife. *Yes*.

In the bedroom Lou knelt on the bed, sawing at the cling film at the side of the box, tearing the loose bits away, pulling at strands that just became stronger until she cut them free. Once she was down to the bare wood she pulled the cling film away, exposing the box. His face was grey-blue.

The knife was slipping out of her hand, and she saw there was blood everywhere. Where was it coming from? Had she cut Andy's neck somehow? She couldn't see a wound.

At last the lid could be lifted and she took hold of a handful of Andy's damp, dark hair, lifting his head out of the box and pulling the box away, throwing it off the bed.

'Breathe, damn it! Andy!'

As soon as she was certain he could get air, she started chest compressions but his body bounced on the mattress, flailing underneath her clasped fingers. She had to get him off the bed. She took hold of the knife again, hacking at the black cord that secured his wrists to the bed. It snapped quickly and she moved to the other arm. By the time she was sawing at the cord, taut between his ankles and the bottom of the bed, the knife was blunt. The cord frayed, then gave way. The last one took the longest and in the end she gave up, abandoned the knife and pulled at his arm to drag him off the bed with one leg still tied.

He was so heavy and inert that at first she thought she would not be able to move him. Finally she dragged the corner of the bedspread and he came with it, slithered to the floor like a dead fish.

Now she could do it. His chest was slathered in blood, and it was only when she started the compressions with all her weight behind it that she realised it was her hand the blood was coming from. 'Andy!' she shouted, as much to reassure herself that he was still there.

Was she imagining it, or was his skin a more normal colour? And now she could hear steps on the gravel outside. 'Get in here!' she roared. 'I need help! Get in here now!'

The sound of boots on the broken glass in the kitchen. 'In here!'

She didn't look round but she knew they were there, both from the sound and from the muttered 'Jesus!'

She didn't want to stop, not for a second, until she knew Andy's heart was beating strongly and wasn't going to stop; didn't want to see their expressions as they took in the naked officer, the cords tied tightly around his wrists and ankles, one still attached to the corner of the bedstead.

And it was only when one of them said to her, 'Stop, guv, let me take over now,' and his colleague, who had been radioing for an ambulance, pulled her gently to one side, taking her hand and raising it, pressing tightly against her palm, that she saw through the tears that the cut to her hand was deep.

13:02

'I'm sorry about your hand,' Andy Hamilton said.

He was sitting upright on a trolley in the back of the ambulance, wrapped in blankets that were barely enough to cover him. Two hairy shins faced in Lou's direction. She was on the jump seat the technicians used, her hand bound up in a great wad of bandage, holding it still as she'd been instructed.

'It's OK,' she said.

The paramedics were about to cart them both off to hospital to be checked over, but Hamilton was recovering by the minute.

419

'How are you feeling?' she asked him.

He gave her a look. Stupid question, of course. She'd never seen him brought so low.

'What was it?' Lou asked.

'She must have drugged me. I think it was the sweetener tablet – I thought she'd put it in her cup.'

'I didn't mean that. I meant, what was that bloody box for?'

'Oh, that. I read about them. It's called a smother box.'

'Sounds charming. You into all of that sort of thing, then?'

'Not any more.'

Lou's phone was ringing. It was Sam.

'Ma'am. The nominal has stopped at an office block on the London Road, just past the hospital. Lots of businesses in there, according to the sign. You want me to go in? I would have intercepted her outside but—'

'Don't worry, Sam. I don't want you to tackle her without back-up. What's the building called?'

'Constantine House. It's the second turning left after the hospital. Opposite the entrance to Sainsbury's.'

'Wait for me there. Don't move unless she does, right?'

The back doors of the ambulance opened and the paramedic came back in. 'Let's get you both strapped in, then, shall we? Time to go to hospital.'

But Lou was already clambering out.

'Lou,' Andy called.

His use of her first name was what made her stop.

'Be careful,' he said. 'She – I think this is all just like fun and games to her. She doesn't give a shit.'

Lou responded with a smile he probably didn't deserve. 'I'll bear that in mind. Can I borrow your car?'

Hamilton's car was surprisingly clean and tidy. She'd had to pull the seat forward about three feet in order to reach the pedals and it wasn't easy with a bandaged hand, but thankfully it was an automatic – gear changing would have been a challenge too far. Lou sped off in the direction of the one-way system through the town centre, praying that the traffic would have cleared.

She had got as far as the one-way system when the sirens started. Two marked cars overtook her at the lights and a third turned into the main road from East Park Road, all of them going at top whack and heading in the direction of the hospital. If she'd been in a job car she could have turned on the lights and followed them, but Andy's people carrier was designed for safety and not for speed.

Swearing at the cars in front of her, she went as fast as she dared until finally she could see the hospital buildings on the left, the supermarket ahead. There were blue lights everywhere and police cars parked haphazardly on the road, another inside a small car park by a squat, square office building. She pulled in to the car park.

Black uniformed officers were gathered in a crowd in one corner of the car park, but they all looked relaxed and they were starting to disperse, heading back to their abandoned patrol cars.

Lou got out of the car and went over to them. Sam Hollands was holding open the door to one of the patrol cars as an officer built like a tank helped a blonde woman into the back seat. She was handcuffed, and clearly still trying to put up a bit of a fight.

'You sure you don't want to wait for the van?' the officer was saying to Sam.

'Not if it's in Newhall, Steve, it'll take too long.'

'Get your hands off me!' the woman was yelling.

The gentle helping hand became a shove. 'Keep that up and you'll end up on the floor again, and we don't want that, do we?'

'Ma'am,' Sam said, seeing Lou approach. She had a graze on her cheek and dabbed a tissue at it. When she raised her hand, Lou could see a nasty-looking bite mark on it.

'Jesus, Sam, what the hell happened?'

Sam indicated the door of the office building. 'It's a nursing agency,' Sam said. 'Turns out she was here to collect her payslip but there had been some mix-up with it. She came out just as I finished talking to you, and she was in a bit of a grumpy mood.'

From the back seat of the car, a high-pitched shout. 'You have no idea, *no idea* how much fucking trouble you lot are in! How dare you!'

'Fortunately I had my radio to hand,' Sam carried on, as calm as she would be a year or so later, reciting from her contemporaneous notes in the witness box, 'as whilst attempting to arrest her she resisted and bit me, so during the assault I was able to call for emergency assistance. PC Steve Johnson here has been particularly helpful.'

PC Johnson was still standing beside the car in case the occupant decided to kick off again.

'Good job we're handy for the hospital,' Lou said. 'As soon as we're done here you're going to get that wound cleaned up. You might need jabs.'

'I'm assuming she hasn't got rabies,' Sam said. She hadn't lost her sense of humour. 'I'm up to date with my tetanus and Hep C.'

'You bit yourself, you crazy bitch!'

'That's enough,' Johnson said. 'You need to calm down now.'

'Shut the fuck up!'

Lou looked down at the woman through the car window. Her face was red and contorted with rage, her blonde hair messed.

'Would you stay there a moment?' Lou asked Steve Johnson. 'I'd like to have a quiet word with our suspect.'

'Ma'am? You sure?'

Lou opened the front passenger door and climbed in, shutting it behind her. She turned in the seat and faced the woman whose hands were cuffed awkwardly behind her. She looked like she was calming down, her skin returning to a more normal colour. She was breathing hard, her eyes a cold, pale blue.

'You're Suzanne Martin?' Lou asked.

'Who the fuck are you?' she responded.

'My name is Detective Chief Inspector Louisa Smith, and before you get carted off to the nick and we start the long and arduous process of making sure you're safe and comfortable while we interview you, I wanted to tell you something.'

'I know who you are,' Suzanne said. 'You're his boss, aren't you? Well, no wonder he has a problem with following simple instructions.'

'I'm usually a very fair person,' Lou said, her voice even. 'But let me tell you that in this case what I'd really, really like to do is drive this car somewhere isolated with you inside it, and rip you apart with my bare hands for what you've done to my officers. I will do everything that's in my power to make sure we get you convicted and put in prison for a long, long time and when that happens I will crack open a bottle of something and look forward to you getting everything you deserve while you're in there. Do you understand?'

Suzanne's lips were a thin, tight line.

Lou had expected some sort of a response but when none came, she opened the car door and climbed out, shutting the door behind her. Sam was chatting with Steve Johnson and the other patrol officer who'd arrived in the car, a young woman who obviously knew Sam by the way they were laughing together.

'Are you two able to book her into custody?' Lou asked.

'I'll go with them,' Sam said. 'I made the arrest.'

'Only if you go to the hospital straight afterwards,' Lou said.

'I will, I promise. How's Andy?'

'He's going to be OK,' Lou said. It would only be a matter of time before details of Andy's rescue would filter out – no doubt distorted into a far more amusing and humiliating version of the truth – but she would not be the one to start that particular ball rolling.

She watched as the car pulled out and turned back to Andy's family wagon, noticing for the first time the child seats in the back, the grubby-looking pink fluffy rabbit in the footwell. She picked it up and nestled it into the smaller of the two car seats, debating whether to strap it in and realising that she wouldn't have the first clue how to do it.

EPILOGUE – Thursday 8 November 2012

09:56

Lou had been sitting outside DCI Neal Farrar's office for twenty-five minutes and it wasn't as though she didn't have other stuff to do. She looked at her watch – again – and was considering maybe coming back later when the door opened and he beckoned her in.

'Neal,' she said, shaking his hand. 'I appreciate this. Thank you.'

'How's the hand?' he asked.

'Twelve stitches. Pinches a bit, otherwise fine. Thanks for asking.'

'I don't think there's much I can tell you, Lou, you know that.'

'I still don't understand. He's my DI. He was completely pivotal to the investigation.'

'The suspect's been charged, I understand?'

'Yes, she's been charged. The search team went back in there yesterday and found Polly's DNA. Not much of it. Flakes of blood on the hallway carpet. And they found what was left of Polly's phone in the dustbin. Smashed to pieces, even the SIM. And there's plenty on her laptop about her particular kink.'

'Suffocating people?'

'Breathplay. Every possible way to almost kill someone by cutting off their air supply. Of course, she thought she could always bring them round again, thanks to her medical knowledge. Taryn Lewis told us that her father said Polly seemed to think Suzanne had killed people before, overseas. That might be why she felt the need to come back to the UK. We think she met Polly while she was

425

travelling, and came here to find her. We're looking into the time she spent travelling, now. She was working as a private nurse in Dubai just before she came back to the UK – in a bit of a hurry. I'm hoping I might get a trip in the sunshine out of it at least.'

'Well, you know where to come if you need back-up.'

'Funny, you're about the fifteenth person who's said that.'

'What about Fletcher-Norman?'

'He's still saying nothing to us about Suzanne. Maybe now she's in custody, he will feel more comfortable talking about her.'

'Interesting case, isn't it? Have you ever come across someone like that before?' Farrar leaned back in his chair, swivelling gently from side to side.

'Never. Neal, she's unbelievable. She hasn't shown any sign of remorse, at all. She seems to find the whole thing slightly amusing. Scares the shit out of me, if I'm honest. Andy was lucky to get out of there alive.'

'You do realise that Andy Hamilton's behaviour all through this investigation was a major cause for concern, Lou? It needs to be looked at thoroughly, and while that happens he has to be suspended.'

'It will have a positive outcome, though, won't it? Please tell me he's not going to lose his job over this. He's a good officer, even though he might come across like a right fuckwit sometimes.'

He managed a smile. 'I know. But there are plenty of officers out there who are good at their jobs without compromising matters with witnesses. It was unnecessary, wasn't it?'

Lou felt like telling him about it all, about the affair she'd had with him herself. How he'd lied to her. How when he'd turned up on the first day of Op Nettle, her heart had sunk because she didn't want to be anywhere near him. And so she didn't trust him – her own DI – didn't listen to him, didn't give him anything decent to work on. Therefore anything that had happened to him, his decision to take risks, go it alone – surely that had been her fault as much as his? And if he was suspended for a lapse of judgement, then surely she should be, too?

She stood up, then, and said her goodbyes. 'You'll call me if there's anything you need? A statement, anything?'

'We'll get round to that soon enough, don't you worry.'

Lou found an empty office and used it to call Hamilton's mobile. 'Hello?'

'Andy, it's me. How are you?'

There was a long pause. 'All right, I guess. How are you?'

'I'm not supposed to call you. I've just been to see Neal Farrar in Professional Standards.'

'Ah. Was that a good idea?'

'I'm trying to help, you big twat.'

'Thanks. Appreciate it.'

'Don't know what good it will do, though.'

'Look, Lou. Everything works out for the best, right? It's going to be a pain in the backside but you know what? I'm at home spending time with Karen and the kids. She's not stupid, she knows full well that my job's on the line.'

'Have you told her what happened?'

'Some of it. It wasn't easy, put it that way. But for the time being, strange as it sounds, we're getting on all right. It's like I – oh, I don't know – like I forgot that I like being with them. No, I *love* being with them.'

'That's good, Andy, that's good to hear.'

'You take care of yourself, Lou?'

'I will. I'll see you soon. Need you on the team.'

He laughed then. 'No you don't. I'm your worst nightmare, remember?'

'You're everyone's worst nightmare.'

She disconnected the call and looked out of the window at the former custody block across the other side of the car park. The decorators had moved in, which meant it was only a matter of time before Computer Crime moved in. Brian had been remanded; his lover was still in the custody suite at Briarstone nick, trying to talk her way out of a murder charge and yet running out of things to say now that they had some hard evidence against her.

Lou looked at her watch. She was going to fit in a visit to see Flora in the hospital, take Sam with her. Somehow she felt there was a whole lot that Flora had left unsaid, and now Lou was more than ready to listen.

Acknowledgements

I want to thank the brilliant team at Sphere, particularly Catherine Burke for her patience, and for having faith in me when I didn't believe in myself. Lucy Icke and Thalia Proctor have also made this book so much better thanks to their genius ideas and creative input – thank you all so much! Thank you too to my agents, Annette Green and David Smith, who have helped me develop as a writer, and for calming me down and keeping me sane when the excitement got a bit much.

The first draft of *Under a Silent Moon* was written during November 2006 as part of the annual National Novel Writing Month (www.nanowrimo.org) challenge, and thanks are due to the wonderful people behind the website without whom this book undoubtedly would not exist at all.

To my fellow NaNoWriMo participants, and Jacqueline Bateman in particular, who kept me going with write-ins both real and virtual, thank you. I assure you, it's your turn next. Lillian George helped me greatly with one particular scene, and provided support when I began to doubt whether this book could ever be completed – I'm very grateful, Lillian.

Thank you to Dave Forster, Karen Aslett, Samantha Bowles and

Suze Dando for allowing me to use their names and for not minding how they were used. As well as lending me her name, and tirelessly listening to me wittering on about my plot, Sam had a tremendous influence on how this story developed and many of the twists and turns are entirely thanks to her. I hope she approves of how it turned out.

Special thanks to the people who shared their expertise on various matters – and please be assured that any mistakes are mine, not theirs. To Lisa Cutts, Gina Haynes, Janice Maciver, Katie Totterdell, Alan Bennett and Hugo Benziger who advised on various aspects of police procedure; Nicola Samson who put me straight on equestrianism; Floss Wilks, for help with Fire and Rescue; Jess Adair, who helped me with Taryn's job; and Andy Kelly and Caroline Luxford-Noyes, for help with medical matters, thank you all so very much.

Sarah M'Grady, Lisa Cutts and Mitch Humphrys all helped me enormously by reading through complete drafts of this book and making sure that I kept some degree of accuracy. Thank you!

Tricia Brassington, Jeannine Taylor, Shelagh Murry (who introduced me to NaNoWriMo in 2005 and therefore got me here in the first place), Heather Mitchell, Judy Gascho-Jutzi and Cat Hummel all helped me to try and get Jason to speak and behave like a true Canadian. The decision to make him Canadian in the first place was all thanks to Cat – I really hope I did a good job with him.

During the editing process I decided to change the name of one of my main characters, and I turned to Facebook to help me; so I'd like to thank Chris Gage, Johanna Malin, Barb Stricsek, Lindsay Healy, Natalie Tamplin, Kate Matrunola, Sharon M. Godfrey, Jody Conklin, Jo Bober and Becky Allatt, who all suggested that 'Barbara' would be the best name for her.

I want to express my gratitude to the staff at i2 (IBM) in Cambridge, who generously gave up their time to help me produce fictional Analyst's Notebook charts for this book. John Gresty, Ron Fitch, Mark Fleet and Steve Dalzell looked after me and made sure I knew what I was doing with the software; Julian Midwinter, Patrick Miller and Stephanie Juergens-Joerger worked hard to help me get the permission I needed to use the charts in the book. Most of all, I want to thank Christian McQuillan, who was the one who answered the phone to me that day and must surely have regretted it. Without doubt this book would have been a very different one without him, and I am enormously grateful for his tenacity, patience and warmth.

As always, I'm very thankful for the support and love of my wonderful family, and especially my boys David and Alex, who put up with me. I love you lots.

Author Note – Appendix

When people hear that my previous job was as a police intelligence analyst, I'm often met with a blank look, and this may be partly due to the absence of analysts in police dramas in film and in crime fiction. And yet the role is a really important one which can have a significant impact on the success of an investigation.

After seven years working for Kent Police, I am still painfully aware of the limits of my expertise. Here's the thing – the police force operates on a 'need to know' basis. If you don't need to know something, then you won't hear about it. Even working on a particular case, you will only have access to the intelligence that directly applies to your job role, even if the investigation isn't particularly sensitive. This has nothing to do with parochialism – the data is secured by legislation, including the Data Protection Act, which means that nosing around and showing an interest in something that doesn't concern you is not only frowned upon, it is actually illegal. My knowledge of the way things work is based on my experience, and what other people are able to share with me.

An easy way to describe the analyst's role is that it seeks to answer the big question, 'what if ... ?' Intelligence analysts work within various different departments in the police (and other organisations, but that's another story). Some analysts work in neighbourhood policing teams, looking for patterns in what they call 'volume' crime (car thefts, burglaries, criminal damage, for example). This will include geographical analysis, for example 'hotspot' mapping, and temporal analysis – showing where and when crimes are statistically most likely to occur. A smaller number of analysts work in more specialised fields, particularly in serious crime. There are analysts working within Fraud and Financial Investigation Departments; analysts who deal specifically with organised crime; analysts who work in Public Protection, providing profiles of sex offenders, and seek to minimise the risk to the most vulnerable people in our society. There are analysts working in Professional Standards who provide support to corruption cases, too.

The analytical role which always seemed to be the most interesting to me was that of the Major Crime analyst. The principles are the same – looking for patterns and details that someone else might have missed, providing an easy-to-read, at-a-glance guide to whatever it is that the police need to know – but the investigation is often developing at speed, with an urgent need to get to the truth before further crimes are committed.

Phone analysis – or, to give it a more recent and more accurate title, Communications Data analysis (these days our contact with others takes many different forms) – is often a crucial part of the investigation: data is supplied, under strict protocols, by service providers, and is often simply a spreadsheet of numbers. Historically, police officers received little to no training in interpreting this data, despite the fact the evidence it can yield may prove vital to an investigation. With Major Crime incidents such as murder, rape and armed robbery, the early hours and days of an investigation are the most important and so the quicker the data can be interpreted, the quicker an arrest might be made.

As well as communications data, the analyst has at his or her disposal various specialised software programs to create a visual interpretation of events and relationships between nominals involved in the investigation. This may include a timeline of events, which is useful to keep track of what happened when (and to prove when a witness statement can't possibly be accurate), and various network or association charts, to highlight the links between people, places and events. There are examples of both timelines and association charts for Op Nettle included in the appendix that follows.

Often charts will expand over the course of the investigation, with the analyst printing out wall-sized copies (we sometimes have access to big plotter/printers, otherwise we spend ages sticking sheets of A4 together) so that investigators can catch up on recent developments in the case as well as spotting potential new leads or opportunities.

If the phone analysis reveals something particularly interesting – for example, to demonstrate links between phones – this can also be displayed visually and interpreted further by the software. This is often used to show which phones are in use by criminal associates, weeding out less relevant numbers – takeaway food shops, girlfriends, family members and chatlines. Another way charts might be used is in relation to cellsite data – and one such chart is included here.

When I first started to write crime fiction it was important to me to try and get as much procedural accuracy as possible into my stories – a very difficult balancing act, trying to find that tipping point between the excitement of an unfolding plot and the tedium of paperwork and legal bureaucracy. Usually crime fiction tends to tip the scales in favour of drama and suspense, not only because even the most assiduous research cannot compare to years of experience in the unique working environment of law enforcement, but also because reading about 'real life' police work would mostly be quite dull.

It's difficult to explain how it's possible to get excited by a spreadsheet, but believe me it is. Spotting the beauty of a pattern in pages of numbers, or noticing that one particular contact between two phones that really shouldn't have any connection, yet they do – that's something I hope the charts that follow will convey.

It's exciting to me, anyway. The ability to assist an investigation, believing that you might hold the crucial bit of information that will unravel a case and bring a serious offender to justice, is intensely rewarding. I hope *Under a Silent Moon* will give you an insight into the role of an intelligence analyst. I have tried to keep the events surrounding the investigation into Polly's murder as accurate as I can. The world of policing in the UK is constantly changing, and at a faster pace more recently with even more pressure on resources and staff. Aspects of police procedure have changed even in the time it's taken to edit this story, and will likely have changed further by the time you read it. Keeping things accurate isn't easy. In the interests of plot and suspense, I have also taken some small liberties. I hope you will forgive me for that.

Elizabeth Haynes
June 2013

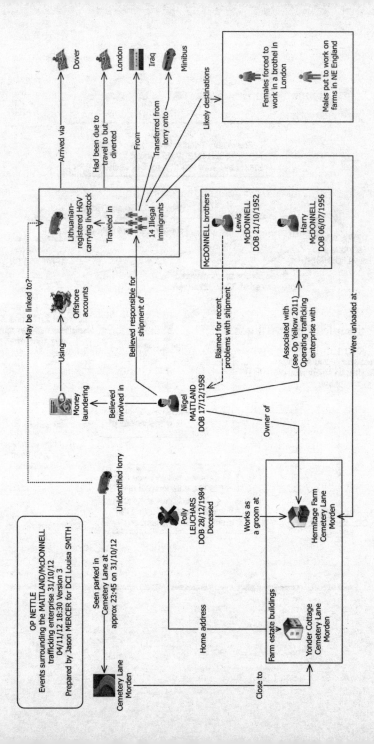

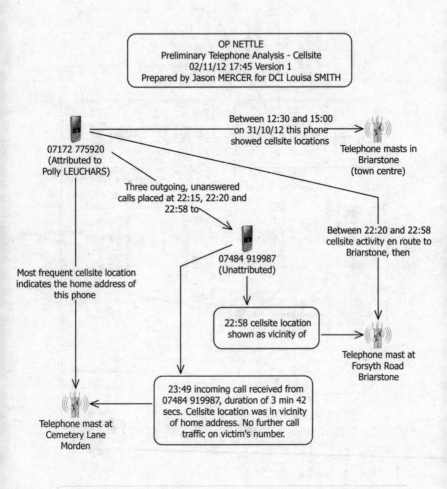

OP NETTLE
Preliminary Telephone Analysis - Cellsite
02/11/12 17:45 Version 1
Prepared by Jason MERCER for DCI Louisa SMITH

07172 775920
(Attributed to
Polly LEUCHARS)

Between 12:30 and 15:00
on 31/10/12 this phone
showed cellsite locations

Telephone masts in
Briarstone
(town centre)

Three outgoing, unanswered
calls placed at 22:15, 22:20 and
22:58 to

Between 22:20 and 22:58
cellsite activity en route to
Briarstone, then

07484 919987
(Unattributed)

Most frequent cellsite location
indicates the home address of
this phone

22:58 cellsite location
shown as vicinity of

Telephone mast at
Forsyth Road
Briarstone

23:49 incoming call received from
07484 919987, duration of 3 min 42
secs. Cellsite location was in vicinity
of home address. No further call
traffic on victim's number.

Telephone mast at
Cemetery Lane
Morden

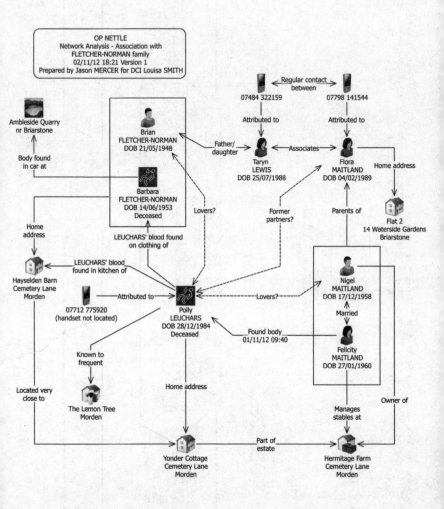

OP NETTLE
Network Analysis - Association with
FLETCHER-NORMAN family
02/11/12 18:21 Version 1
Prepared by Jason MERCER for DCI Louisa SMITH

Ambleside Quarry
nr Briarstone

Body found
in car at

Brian
FLETCHER-NORMAN
DOB 21/05/1948

Barbara
FLETCHER-NORMAN
DOB 14/06/1953
Deceased

Regular contact
between
07484 322159 ←→ 07798 141544

Attributed to   Attributed to

Father/
daughter   Taryn
LEWIS
DOB 25/07/1988   Associates   Flora
MAITLAND
DOB 04/02/1989   Home address

Flat 2
14 Waterside Gardens
Briarstone

Lovers?   Former
partners?   Parents of

Home
address   LEUCHARS' blood found
on clothing of

LEUCHARS' blood
found in kitchen of

Hayselden Barn
Cemetery Lane
Morden   Attributed to   Polly
LEUCHARS
DOB 28/12/1984
Deceased   Lovers?   Nigel
MAITLAND
DOB 17/12/1958

07712 775920
(handset not located)   Married

Known to
frequent   Found body
01/11/12 09:40   Felicity
MAITLAND
DOB 27/01/1960

The Lemon Tree
Morden

Located very
close to   Home address   Manages
stables at   Owner of

Yonder Cottage
Cemetery Lane
Morden   Part of
estate   Hermitage Farm
Cemetery Lane
Morden

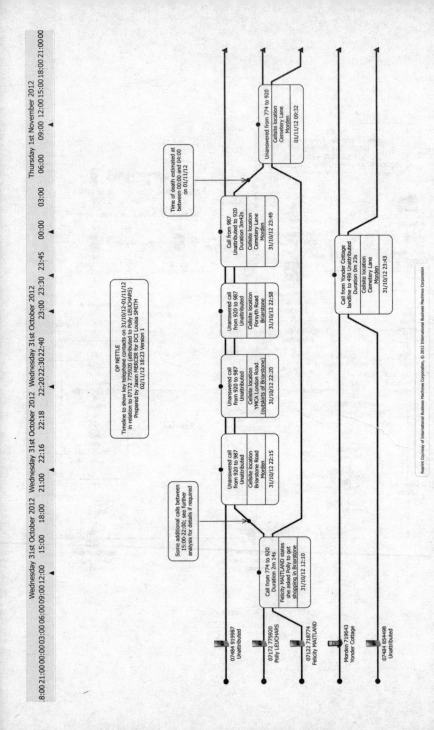

Wednesday 31st October 2012 Wednesday 31st October 2012 Wednesday 31st October 2012 Thursday 1st November 2012

18:00 21:00 00:00 03:00 06:00 09:00 12:00 15:00 18:00 21:00 22:00 22:30 22:40 23:00 23:30 23:45 00:00 03:00 06:00 09:00 12:00 15:00 18:00 21:00 00:00

22:16 22:18

OP NETTLE
Timeline to show key telephone contacts on 31/10/12–01/11/12
in relation to 07172 775920 (attributed to Polly LEUCHARS)
Prepared by Jason MERCER for DCI Louisa SMITH
02/11/12 18:23 Version 1

Some additional calls between
15:00–22:00; see further
analysis for details if required

Time of death estimated at
between 00:00 and 04:00
on 01/11/12

Call from 774 to 920
Duration 2m 14s

Felicity MAITLAND states
she asked Polly to get
shopping in Briarstone

31/10/12 12:10

**Unanswered call
from 920 to 987**
Unattributed

Cellsite location
Briarstone Road
Morden

31/10/12 22:15

**Unanswered call
from 920 to 987**
Unattributed

Cellsite location
YMCA London Road
(outskirts of Briarstone)

31/10/12 22:20

**Unanswered call
from 920 to 987**
Unattributed

Cellsite location
Forsyth Road
Briarstone

31/10/12 22:58

Call from 987
Unattributed to 920
Duration 3m42s

Cellsite location
Cemetery Lane
Morden

31/10/12 23:49

Unanswered from 774 to 920

Cellsite location
Cemetery Lane
Morden

01/11/12 09:32

**Call from Yonder Cottage
landline to 498 Unattributed**
Duration 0m 23s

Cellsite location
Cemetery Lane
Morden

31/10/12 23:43

07484 919967
Unattributed

07122 775920
Polly LEUCHARS

07122 718774
Felicity MAITLAND

Morden 719643
Yonder Cottage

07464 854498
Unattributed